William Irving Paulding, James Kirke Paulding

The Bulls and the Jonathans

comprising John Bull and Brother Jonathan, and John Bull in America

William Irving Paulding, James Kirke Paulding

The Bulls and the Jonathans
comprising John Bull and Brother Jonathan, and John Bull in America

ISBN/EAN: 9783337391256

Printed in Europe, USA, Canada, Australia, Japan

Cover: Foto ©Andreas Hilbeck / pixelio.de

More available books at **www.hansebooks.com**

THE BULLS

AND

THE JONATHANS;

COMPRISING

JOHN BULL AND BROTHER JONATHAN

AND

JOHN BULL IN AMERICA.

JAMES K. PAULDING.

EDITED BY WILLIAM I. PAULDING.

IN ONE VOLUME.

NEW YORK:

CHARLES SCRIBNER AND COMPANY.

1867.

CAMBRIDGE:

STEREOTYPED AND PRINTED BY JOHN WILSON AND SON.

CONTENTS.

INTRODUCTION

JOHN BULL AND BROTHER JONATHAN.

THIS work owes its existence to the uneasy relations between Great Britain and the United States in the beginning of the present century. After a great deal of ill-feeling on both sides, Congress declared war, on the 18th of June, 1812. The book was already published on the 5th of September in the same year, as appears by a letter of the author. Probably it had then been "out" some little time.

The satire is so transparent that there is scarcely need of elucidation; but I have nevertheless added a few notes. For information and suggestions in regard to some obscure personal and political allusions I am indebted to the kindness of an early friend and literary associate of Mr. Paulding, Gulian C. Verplanck.

The present reprint is from Harper & Brothers' edition of 1835, the only one of which I have been able to procure a copy. To this there were a few notes by the author, which I have distinguished by the date. Those now subjoined have none. It will be perceived that some matter must have been introduced after the publication of the first edition. Not having a copy of this for collation, I am unable to discriminate it exactly; but think that the allusions to "Major Jack Downing" and to the travellers subsequent to "Lawyer Janson" comprise about all.

It now seems a pity that Mr. Paulding should have singled out tourists for caricature. But he wrote in an atmosphere of acerbity, about matters then really of almost national concern, though at the present day they can scarcely be made to appear in that light. He looked upon the whole detracting tribe as mercenary calumniators of an entire people, with no claim to either courtesy or grace; and pitched upon the individual subjects of attack, rather as types of the different styles of British objector, than from any personal feeling or knowledge of the parties.

I extract from the Appendix to the two-volume edition of Webster's Dictionary, page 1552, the following account of the two national nicknames.

BULL, JOHN. A well-known collective name of the English nation, first used in Arbuthnot's satire, "The History of John Bull", usually published in Swift's works. In this satire, the French are designated as Lewis Baboon, the Dutch as Nicholas Frog, &c. The "History of John Bull" was designed to ridicule the Duke of Marlborough.

BROTHER JONATHAN. A sportive collective name for the people of the United States.

When General Washington, after being appointed commander of the army of the Revolutionary war, went to Massachusetts to organize it, and make preparations for the defence of the country, he found a great want of ammunition and other means necessary to meet the powerful foe he had to contend with, and great difficulty in obtaining them. If attacked in such condition, the cause at once might be hopeless. On one occasion, at that anxious period, a consultation of the officers and others was had, when it seemed no way could be devised to make such preparation as was necessary. His Excellency Jonathan Trumbull, the elder, was then governor of Connecticut, and, as Washington placed the greatest reliance on his judgment and aid, he remarked, " We must consult Brother Jonathan on the subject." He did so, and the governor was successful in supplying many of the wants of the army. When difficulties afterward arose, and the army was spread over the country, it became a by-word — " *We must consult Brother Jonathan.*" The origin of the expression being soon lost sight of, the name *Brother Jonathan* came to be regarded as the national sobriquet.

Of course a work of this character loses much of interest and point by the mere lapse of time. The most laborious annotation, the fullest historical knowledge of the period, would fail to put the reader in the place of a cotemporary to whom the subject had been for years a matter of daily thought feeling and discussion. Many of the hardest hits therefore have lost their force for us of to-day; or, at all events, we no longer see distinctly where or to what extent they took effect. At the same time the merits of the production are far from being altogether ephemeral. Apart from the fun of the book and the shrewd exhibit of national peculiarities, it is a specimen of simple, straightforward, idiomatic, English, such as it is not easy to match.

W. I. P.

DIVERTING HISTORY

OF

JOHN BULL AND BROTHER JONATHAN.

CHAPTER I.

How Squire Bull quarrelled with his youngest Son, Brother Jonathan, and forced him out in the woods; and how the Squire, when Jonathan had cleared away the woods, grew to be very fond of him, and undertook to pick his pockets, but got handsomely rib-roasted for his pains.

JOHN BULL was a choleric old fellow, who held a good manor in the middle of a great mill-pond. This manor, by reason of its being quite surrounded by water, was generally called *Bullock Island.* Bull was an ingenious man, an exceeding good blacksmith, a dexterous cutler, and a notable weaver and pot-baker besides. He also brewed capital porter, ale, and small-beer, and was, in fact, a sort of jack-of-all-trades, and good at each. In addition, he was a hearty fellow, an excellent bottle-companion, and passably honest as times go.

But what tarnished all these qualities was a devilish quarrelsome, overbearing disposition, which was always getting him into some scrape or other. The truth is, he never heard of a quarrel going on among his neighbours, but his fingers itched to be in the thick-.

est of them; so that he was hardly ever seen without a broken head, a black eye, or a bloody nose. Such was Squire Bull, as he was commonly called by the country people his neighbours — one of those odd, testy, grumbling, boasting old codgers, that never get credit for what they are, because they are always pretending to be what they are not.

The squire was as tight a hand to deal with in doors as out; sometimes treating his family as if they were not the same flesh and blood, when they happened to differ with him in certain matters. One day he got into a dispute with his youngest son Jonathan, who was familiarly called BROTHER JONATHAN, about whether churches ought to be called churches or meeting-houses; and whether steeples were not an abomination. The squire, either having the worst of the argument, or being naturally impatient of contradiction, (I can't tell which), fell into a great passion, and swore he would physic such notions out of the boy's noddle. So he went to some of his *doctors*, and got them to draw up a prescription, made up of *thirty-nine different articles*, many of them bitter enough to some palates. This he tried to make Jonathan swallow; and finding he made villanous wry faces, and would not do it, fell upon him and beat him like fury. After this, he made the house so disagreeable to him, that Jonathan, though as hard as a pine knot and as tough as leather, could bear it no longer. Taking his gun and his axe, he put himself in a boat, and paddled over the millpond to some new lands to which the squire pretended some sort of claim, intending to settle them, and build a meeting-house without a steeple as soon as he grew rich enough.

When he got over, Jonathan found that the land was quite in a state of nature, covered with wood, and inhabited only by wild beasts. But being a lad of mettle, he took his axe on one shoulder and his gun on the other, marched into the thickest of the wood, and clearing a place, built a log-hut. Pursuing his labours, and handling his axe like a notable wood-man, he in a few years cleared the land, which he laid out into *thirteen good farms:* and building him-self a fine frame-house about half finished, began to be quite snug and comfortable.

But Squire Bull, who was getting old and stingy, and, besides, was in great want of money on account of his having lately been made to pay swingeing damages for assaulting his neighbours and breaking their heads — the squire, I say, finding Jonathan was getting well to do in the world, began to be very much troubled about his welfare: so he demanded that Jonathan should pay him a good rent for the land which he had cleared and made good for something. He trumped up I know not what claim against him, and under different pretences managed to pocket all Jonathan's honest gains. In fact, the poor lad had not a shilling left for holiday occasions; and had it not been for the filial respect he felt for the old man, he would certainly have refused to submit to such impositions.

But for all this, in a little time, Jonathan grew up to be very large of his age, and became a tall, stout, double-jointed, broad-footed cub of a fellow, awkward in his gait, and simple in his appearance; but show-ing a lively, shrewd look, and having the promise of great strength when he should get his full growth.

He was rather an odd-looking chap, in truth, and had many queer ways; but everybody that had seen John Bull saw a great likeness between them, and swore he was John's own boy, and a true chip of the old block. Like the old squire, he was apt to be blustering and saucy, but in the main was a peaceable sort of careless fellow, that would quarrel with nobody if you only let him alone. He used to dress in homespun trousers with a huge bagging seat, which seemed to have nothing in it. This caused people to say he had no *bottom;* but whoever said so lied, as they found to their cost whenever they put Jonathan in a passion. He always wore a linsey-woolsey coat, that did not above half cover his breech, and the sleeves of which were so short that his hand and wrist came out beyond them, looking like a shoulder of mutton. All which was in consequence of his growing so fast that he outgrew his clothes.

While Jonathan was outgrowing his strength in this way, Bull kept on picking his pockets of every penny he could scrape together; till at last, one day when the squire was even more than usually pressing in his demands, which he accompanied with threats, Jonathan started up in a furious passion, and threw the TEA-KETTLE* at the old man's head. The choleric Bull was hereupon exceedingly enraged; and after calling the poor lad an undutiful, ungrateful, rebellious rascal, seized him by the collar, and forthwith a furious scuffle ensued. This lasted a long time; for the squire, though in years, was a capital boxer, and of most excellent bottom. At last, however, Jonathan

---

* The destruction of tea in Boston harbor, followed by the revolutionary war and the acknowledgment of independence.

got him under, and, before he would let him up, made him sign a paper giving up all claim to the farms, and acknowledging the fee-simple to be in Jonathan for ever.

CHAPTER II.

How Jonathan made good the old saying, that a man don't know when he is well off, and got married.

As soon as Jonathan had thus, as it were, disinherited his father, and set up for himself, he, like other young fellows just out of leading-strings, thought it high time to get a wife.* So he got himself an excellent one from among the tenants, by whose aid he prospered exceedingly. But when old Mrs. Bull,† Squire Bull's wife, of whom I shall speak more anon, heard that Jonathan had taken to himself a helpmate, and begun house-keeping on his own account without asking her consent, she flew into a great passion and scolded roundly. This madam, though Jonathan's own mother, never much liked the poor fellow, and it was all along of her advice that Squire Bull kept the lad so short of money; for Mrs. Bull used to insist upon it that young boys should never be allowed any pocket-money: it only led them into mischief and bad company.

As soon as she found out Jonathan's marriage, she

* The old Congress.   † Parliament.

went to Squire Bull, and talked away just as old women are used to do to their husbands. She told Bull the poor stripling would be ruined by his wife, who was a low-bred, impertinent minx, that nobody knew. "I tell thee, John," quoth madam, "that this poor silly fellow is no more fit to marry than the child unborn, and will come to naught as sure as you are alive, if you don't take means to get him out of the hands of this little upstart, ill-bred, illegitimate minx." All this while the squire would be walking about, with his hands in his waistcoat pockets, and his head drooping on one side, whistling as people do when they don't know what to say.

Then the old lady would put on her hat and cloak, sally forth among the gossips of the neighbourhood, and complain of this daughter-in-law. She would turn up her nose at her, and declare she would never acknowledge her, not she — a good-for-nothing, impudent hussy, to thrust herself into so respectable a family as Squire Bull's. "For my part," exclaimed she, "I sha'n't take the least notice of her, not I — as they have brewed so they must bake; as they make the bed so they must lie in it;" together with a number of other equally wise sayings. Then she tried to persuade the neighbours not to visit Mrs. Jonathan, and absolutely quarrelled with several of them for acknowledging her as Jonathan's wife.

As to Mrs. Jonathan, she was not much behind-hand with old Mrs. Bull; and, when she heard of the old lady's giving herself such high flights, would put her arms a-kimbo and exclaim, "Marry come up! I wonder, forsooth, who Mrs. Bull is — a mighty great madam, to be sure, to give herself such airs. Why, it is but the other day that old Oliver What-d'ye-callum kicked her *rump* for her, and turned her out of Squire Bull's house in a jiffy. In good truth, madam, my lady mother had better look at home and mind her own affairs, I can tell her that."

But what provoked old Mrs. Bull more than any thing else was, that her daughter-in-law used to dress just like the old lady, and imitate her on all occasions, insomuch that people would say that Mrs. Jonathan was very much like her mother-in-law, and, considering her education, behaved herself quite like a lady.

These family disturbances used to annoy Jonathan not a little; nevertheless, he found great reason to be satisfied with his wife, who turned out to be a very notable woman and right thrifty housekeeper, so that, when she died, she left behind her among the tenants an excellent name, though old Mrs. Bull could never bear to hear her mentioned. By her advice and assistance, Jonathan prospered in all his affairs; his farms grew more valuable every year; the number of his tenants increased rapidly; and so successful was he in all his speculations, that the neighbours prophesied, if he lived to be an old man, he would be one of the richest of his day.

In a little time the tenants began to build a great many boats, to carry their grain to different parts of the great mill-pond, insomuch that you could hardly go into any part of it without meeting them. This made Squire Bull not a little jealous, for he was the greatest boatman that ever was known, and could not bear to see Brother Jonathan, whom in his cups he called a rebellious rascal, prosper so handsomely in his affairs.

But young Jonathan went on steadily, without troubling himself about his neighbours' business; and by dint of regular living, plain diet, and wholesome exercise, daily acquired strength, until at last he grew so stout, that, though he did not know much about boxing or cudgel-playing, he was able to wrestle a fall with any lad of his age in all the neighbourhood. Still, you could see he had not come to half his strength as yet; and that when his sinews were a little hardened, and his joints stronger-knit, woe be to the blockhead that should wantonly provoke him to raise his fist, for it would come down like unto a sledge-hammer!

CHAPTER III.

How Squire John got a flea in his ear, and how his fingers itched to get the whole mill-pond under his thumb.

AFTER this great quarrel, John Bull and Brother Jonathan continued on speaking terms, and seemed quite reconciled; but it was all grimace on the squire's part, for he could never forgive poor Jonathan for making him give up the farms in the way he did. Now Jonathan, though in the scuffle with Bull he had got some scratches, the scars of which remained a long time, I verily believe felt many yearnings of affection for his old dad, and if he had been treated with any sort of fatherly kindness, would have loved him with all his heart. But the old fellow never missed a chance of doing Jonathan an ill turn, and wherever they met would be biting his thumb, and snapping his fingers, at him. All which Jonathan put up with on account of the respect he still could not help feeling for the father that begat him. In his heart he made all sorts of excuses for him, considering he was old, infirm, and almost in his dotage.

The squire, by reason of his living on an island, kept a huge parcel of boats to ply to and again to different parts of the great millpond, which was a good many leagues about, and where he sent vast quantities of his blacksmith's work, and excellent porter. By this means his tenants grew to be exceeding expert boatmen, and would venture out at all times, let the wind blow ever so hard.

John, instead of being satisfied with this, was every now and then ripping up an old claim, which, (even if his ancestors had ever made it good), had been given up long before. The foundation of the claim was this:— It seems some of the Bull family, being great boasters in their cups, used now and then to pretend that, because they had the greatest number of boats, they ought to be lords of the mill-pond, which they swore was part of the manor of Bullock.

This notion took highly among their tenants, but their neighbours only laughed at it, till one of these doughty fellows went out upon the mill-pond, and undertook to make them all pull off their hats as a sort of compliment for his great good-nature in letting them sail their boats there. Then they thought the joke was going too far, and great disputes were carried on for many years. At last this big fellow got his bitters; for chancing one day to meet an old neigh-

bour of his, one Mynheer Van Tromp, a great fish-
erman, catching herrings, he swore he should pull
off his hat, or else push off and not fish any more.
Mynheer Van Tromp smoked on, without taking any
notice, upon which John Bull's ancestor undertook to
lay hold of his hat to pull it off; but Van Tromp,
without taking his pipe out of his mouth, gave him
such a pat on the head with his paddle, that he was
glad enough to let mynheer's broad brim alone after
that.   But for all this, the Bulls would now and then,
whenever they could do it safely, revive these pretensions, which they never could be brought to give up
until they were fairly cudgelled out of them by the
neighbours.   Whenever this happened, they always
took care to reserve the right, as they called it, though
they gave up the exercise of it; and if the least pretence offered, would be at their old capers again.

John Bull, the subject of our history, by reason of
his being troubled with a lack of understanding, was
obliged to trust his business altogether to a parcel
of hireling servants; who, as is always the case, managed to cheat him out of the profits of his manor,
until at last he grew quite poor, and lived pretty
much by borrowing and other shifts.   The squire was
not a little nettled at this, and forthwith ordered them
to make out their accounts, to see how matters stood.
These cunning varlets were not a little frightened at
being brought to a reckoning, but they soon devised a
scheme to hum John a little.   This was no other than
persuading the poor noddy that the great amount of
his debts was a proof of his vast riches.   This was a
little too deep for Bull's sounding-line; but when a
man does not know his own business, it is absolutely

necessary that he should believe in somebody; and so the squire shrugged up his shoulders, and said, " I suppose it must be so, and all that sort of thing — but hang me if I can make it out."

But these false rogues, knowing that the truth must come out at last, because John was even obliged to borrow money of his tenants in order to pay them their own interest, and that he must fail unless his means increased greatly, did put it into his head to get all the business of the mill-pond into his own hands, under the old pretence that the whole of it belonged to him, and that he had all along permitted the neighbours to use it out of his own good will.

This was tickling John just where he liked it; but he had somehow or other, I don't know how, managed to get, among his tenants, the character of a mighty honest fellow; and he knew if he lost this, by being too barefaced in his injustice toward his neighbours, the tenants would not lend him any more money. It was therefore proper, in order to keep up his good name, to find out some cunning pretext by which he might satisfy the tenants and quiet his own conscience. The squire belonged to that class of honesty which scruples much less at doing wrong than in being found out. To such folks a poor excuse is better than none; and luckily, while they were casting about in great perplexity, John's great enemy and rival, Beau Napperty,* helped him to one of the neatest in the world. It is proper to say a few words of this Beau, who will act no small part in this renowned history.

* Napoleon I.

CHAPTER IV.

Of Beau Napperty; and what sort of a chap he was.

IT is not worth while to tell how old Lewis Baboon,* an honest fellow enough, was killed by his tenants in a drunken frolic; and how his neighbour, Squire Bull, with one Fred Brandenberger,† and the old President of the College,‡ first made believe they wanted to get back his estate for his heirs, and then began to carve it out among themselves. Fred and the old President did not care two coppers for the Baboons, but took sides with John, because he supplied them with spending money, paid their scores wherever they went, and tickled their vanity by patting them on the back, and calling them the deliverers of the neighbourhood. This was the way with John, who always paid the piper, let who would dance.

It is well known that these three fellows, in trying each to get a slice of the manor of Frogmore, as that of the Baboons was called, got their fingers burnt to a blister, and were glad enough to get home as well as they could, especially when little Beau Napperty took up the cudgel.

Beau Napperty, as I have heard say, was called Beau because he was no beau at all; but, though the greatest soldier of his day, wore a little three-cornered cocked-hat without any feather, and would have cut no figure among our militia officers on training-days.

* Louis XVI.   † King of Prussia, Elector of Brandenburgh. 1835.
‡ Emperor of Austria, head of the Electoral College. 1835.

Some great generals, who shall be nameless, seem to think the finer soldiers are dressed the better they will fight; but it was not so with little Beau Napperty, who, with a parcel of ragamuffins without breeches, did not care a fig for the best man in all the neighbourhood. It must be confessed, however, that he wore a most monstrous sword, which he could hardly drag along after him; and those who could see a great way into a millstone, prophesied he would soon wear himself out by trailing this huge toasting-iron. He was withal one of the most active little fellows in the world; it seemed that he could be in two places at a time; and I can tell you that whoever got to windward of him must sail right in the wind's eye, and get up before daylight. He carried a great pinch-beck box in his breeches pocket, out of which he took snuff every half minute. He was, moreover, a lad of great mettle, and would not turn his back on the best man that ever stepped.

Beau Napperty was born in a little scrubby island, not far from the manor of Frogmore; and there being no school-masters thereabouts, was sent to an academy in the latter place, where he studied club-law with all his might, and, it is said, practised it on the pates of his school-fellows. He was all the time playing soldier, and strutting about in a paper cocked-hat, with a wooden sword, and marching ahead of the boys with as much gravity as if he had been a general. They say he was as proud as Lucifer, and did not much mind robbing an orchard or steal-ing water-melons; though he never betrayed his ac-complices, but stuck to them like a hearty fellow. Many other stories were told about him, little to his credit, but I don't vouch for their truth; because, when he got to be a great man, he fell out with John Bull, who is one of those old fellows that fight and scold at the same time, and, if they can't beat you, are pretty sure to take away your good name.

Beau Napperty was quite a lad when old Lewis Baboon was killed by his tenants in a drunken frolic. In the confusion that followed he took part with the tenants; who, after squabbling and fighting with each other about who should be lord of the manor, setting up one and putting down another, and running riot at an awful rate like so many Indians, at last quietly suffered Beau Napperty to put the bit into their mouths, and ride over them rough-shod, as the saying is. They wanted a master, and they got one, with a heart and a hand stout enough to hold in a team of wild horses.

After this he was always in hot water with his neighbours, especially Squire Bull, with whom he had many a bout at cudgel-playing. He almost always beat John on land, and John always beat him on the water; so that each had one of the elements to brag on; and as one scuffle balanced the other, neither of them was likely to give out. Some people said this everlasting bickering was the fault of Beau Napperty, and some laid it all to Squire Bull. For my part, I could never make head or tail of it; and finally came to the conclusion, that these quarrels, like most others I have seen in my day, were brought about by faults on both sides. It takes two people to make a fight, as it does a flint and a steel to strike fire. Be this as it may, betwixt Beau Napperty

and John Bull and his friends, the whole neighbourhood was kept in a turmoil, from the time I was
a little boy until I grew up to be a man and
became a justice of the peace on one of Jonathan's
farms.

But whoever began the quarrel, Squire Bull certainly struck the first blow; for I happened to be
looking on at the time, as I shall relate in the next
chapter.

CHAPTER V.

How Squire Bull took a violent liking to Lewis Baboon (after he was dead),
and in company with one Fred Brandenberger, and the old President of
the College, set about getting the Manor of Frogmore for his heirs, as
they said.

Now, after the death of Lewis Baboon, John Bull,
who bitterly hated him and his whole generation when
alive, began to speak well of them, and to talk that it
was a shame for this upstart fellow, Beau Napperty,
to be suffered to hold the manor of Frogmore. In
short, he worked himself up into a violent fit of compassion and generosity; insomuch that he determined
to set about recovering this inheritance for his particular friends the Baboons, as he said. He forthwith
went to work, and sent over whole boat-loads of his
tenants, to join the tenants of Fred Brandenberger
and the old president, both of whom agreed, from
pure love of the Baboons and of Bull's guineas, to
help along the good old cause, as it was called.

Before they set out, however, these three wise
fellows clubbed their brains together, and put up a
public notice in divers places, calling upon Baboon's
ancient tenants to rise up and kick Beau Napperty
out of the manor. They also set forth their long
friendship and intimacy with old Lewis Baboon, who,
they swore, was one of the best landlords that ever
broke bread; and finally professed the greatest regard,
not only for the rights and welfare of the good tenants
of Frogmore, but likewise of the whole neighbourhood.

Now this was a good one; for everybody knew
that Fred Brandenberger and the old President of the
College cared no more for their own tenants, much
less those of other people, than if they were so many
beasts. True it is these tenants were for the most
part a set of mean-spirited rascals, who suffered their
overseers to kick and cuff them about like dirt; and,
by dint of having their rents raised every quarter-day,
their fields laid waste, and their sons taken off by re-
cruiting parties, had become so miserably poor, that
they were on the very verge of starving. It must,
however, be confessed, that Bull's tenants were better
off, though their rents were so high that they hardly
knew which way to turn themselves to raise the
money. In order to pay these rents, the greater part
of them were forced to live upon bread and cheese
and small-beer. Yet, for all this, they sung songs
about *roast beef;* so that, though their bellies were
filled with bread and cheese and windy small-beer,
their fancy teemed with sirloins of beef, which was
equal to having the best meal in the world. They
were also allowed the privilege of grumbling, provided

they grumbled in reason; of which John's attorney, one Vicary Gibbs,* was to be the sole judge.

However, Brandenberger and the old president, who knew their tenants were obliged to believe just what they were pleased to tell them, went and pasted up, on the gallows and whipping-posts that abound in their manors, an advertisement, calling upon them to come forth and defend their rights, properties, and the good old customs of the manor, against that quarrelsome fellow Beau Napperty, the enemy of right, the friend of wrong, the oppressor of his tenants, and the general disturber of the whole neighbourhood. Then, in order to convince the tenants of their happy condition, they sent round overseers and bailiffs, to take from them what little they had left, that they might be better able to defend the remainder, and, if they demurred, to cudgel them into a proper estimation of their rights and liberties.

The honest tenants wondered, as usual, where these mighty blessings they were thus called upon to defend were hid; and puzzled their heads to little purpose to comprehend how the peace of the neighbourhood was to be preserved by setting it together by the ears; but they soon had their wits quickened by a proper application of chains and cudgels, and at the same time Bull's sturdy fellows were handsomely cheated into the matter by Mrs. Bull, who was a great talker, and could almost make black appear the white of your eye.

* Sir Vicary Gibbs, attorney-general of England, as such was very bitter politically; and in his prosecutions so much so, as to excite popular indignation. He was appointed in 1813 a puisne judge of the common pleas, and in 1814 chief-justice of the same court; and died in 1820, leaving a high reputation for ability and integrity.

As many battles and cudgelling-bouts will take place in the course of this history, it may be just as well to explain how it happened that Bull and the rest of them did not now and then get clapped up for these breaches of the peace. The truth of the matter is, that John and the rest of the old landlords, though they always put the laws in force against the tenants, paid special little attention to any statute but that of club-law, and never abided by the opinion of any justice, unless it was in their favour. They had, to be sure, a sort of a system of laws among them; but nobody could ever tell what it was exactly, for they never could agree about it themselves. Whenever there was any dispute, it was mostly settled by a bruising-match, in which all the tenants took part; and the party that got beat was held to be in the wrong. The constables and justices, being generally under the thumbs of the landlords, kept out of the way when there was going to be a battle; and so it came to pass that all their disputes were finally settled by the great statute of club-law.

CHAPTER VI.

Of Mrs. Bull; and how she made good the old saying, that the gray mare
is the better horse.

It was an old practice in the Bull family, that the heir, immediately on succeeding to the estate, should choose a wife. This custom, I have heard, originated in a few pranks of the ancient Bulls, some of whom are known to have been very mischievous fellows, insomuch that they were continually poaching about and tampering with the tenants' wives, some of whom got their virtue not a little singed.

The manner of choosing John's helpmate is this :— The tenants are apprized that on such a day they are to assemble, to select the squire a wife to take care of the interior of his house, and keep his back warm; and also to watch over the welfare of his tenants, as well as to give her husband good advice. The tenants accordingly come together, and the first thing they do is to get drunk as pipers, in order to be the better able to see clear. When this ceremony is over, they give their voices, some for one and some for another; and she who has the most voices in her favour is immediately put into a great chair, and carried about by the tenants with much rejoicing. After this, those who have had time to grow sober get drunk again, and then go home mightily tickled with their day's work. And this is always the way in which the wives of the Bull family are chosen.

John Bull in his day had several wives, some of them no better than they should be, and one in particular that fairly drove him out of his house, as may be seen by consulting the records of the manor. His present wife, though not such a termagant as some that he had, was yet one of the most extravagant hussies in the world, and spent John's money faster than he could earn it, a great deal. And then her character was not a little fly-blown, for people did not scruple to say that Bull's overseers took great liberties when his back was turned, and in fact did pretty much what they pleased with her.

Be this as it may, one of the first things this lady did was to set about raising some money to pay the expense of turning out Beau Napperty and restoring the Baboons to the manor of Frogmore; for as to Squire Bull, he could not get money to buy a pot of beer without asking his wife for it.

In order to induce the tenants to come out handsomely and consent to the raising of their rents, madam began to cry out rape and murder as hard as she could; and told them that Beau Napperty had a design to come over with a great parcel of boats, to burn their houses and barns, turn them all out of their farms, and pick their pockets handsomely besides. Now Bull's tenants have always been noted for swallowing whales, and accordingly they were horribly affrighted when they heard what was coming to pass. They told madam to take away every thing they had in the world, and moreover got together, armed with cudgels, broom-staffs, pitchforks, and what not, determined to defend their empty pockets to the last extremity, and pommel the Beau to his heart's content if he offered to meddle with Madam Bull. It was truly a laughable sight to see them parading backwards and forwards along the beach, beating the water into a foam with their staffs, and insulting women and children most manfully, just like veteran soldiers.

When John saw himself so strongly backed, he snapped his fingers, kissed his wife, who he swore was an honest wench, and considered the business as good as done. He had not the least doubt that in a little time his *dear friends*, the Baboons, would hold up their heads as high as he, Squire Bull, chose to let them.

CHAPTER VII.

How Squire Bull sent over a party of his tenants to kill frogs in the great *Bog-Meadow*, and how they caught a Tartar instead of a Bull-frog.

BULL about this time had a tall, lank-sided, sharp-nosed *Overseer*,* who always had his hair tied up in a long queue, and wore a pair of breeches that reached about to the middle of his knee-pan. He was thought by those who knew him best to be an honest fellow, and a good friend to John; but a quarrelsome dog, that loved a bout at cudgel-playing above all things, and hated Beau Napperty worse than Satan himself. To gratify this hatred, he did not care how much money he wasted; and as long as he could get at the tenants' coffers by means of John's wife, who kept the keys, he did not care whether the squire had money to pay his score or not. In the course of a few years he ran poor John in debt up to the ears, insomuch that it was and is still supposed that he will never be able to pay a quarter of it, if he were to live fifty years longer.

This thunder-bolt of a fellow, finding John one day in a humour to do a silly thing, put it into his wise head to play Beau Napperty a trick by sending some of his tenants across the mill-pond, to break down the fences, fill up the ditches, and burn the hay-stacks, in a large bog-meadow called *Bellygium*, from the portly bellies of the honest ditchers that had burrowed in

---

* William Pitt, noted for his lank figure and short breeches. Gilray called him "the bottomless Pitt", and represented him so in his caricature.

the mud there. This place Beau Napperty had somehow got into his possession, and by reason of its
being low and subject to overflowings, it abounded
with fine large frogs, of which the Beau and his tenants were exceedingly fond. Now the cunning overseer did persuade Squire Bull, that if he could only
once get possession of this bog-meadow, the tenants
of Frogmore would labour under such a scarcity of
frogs, that as sure as a gun they would get into a passion, and turn Beau Napperty neck and heels out
of the manor.

John thought this the very wisest plan he had ever
heard of in the whole course of his life. He forthwith swallowed a huge flagon of small-beer, a liquor
exceedingly potent in sharpening a man's wits; rubbed
his hands with great glee; put his forefinger to his
nose, with a most knowing bend of his head towards the right, and then ordered his son *Fred* to be
called.

Fred * was a stout, brawny young fellow, originally
intended for a *parson*, though I cannot learn that he
ever preached, except over his liquor. Not liking a
parson's life much, he enlisted in the army; and, by
dint of mounting guard a few times, wearing a great
cocked-hat and a red coat, swearing stoutly, and
drinking deeply, acquired great experience, and rose
to be a jolly royster of a corporal. When John saw
Fred come strutting into the parlour, looking like a
most invincible bully-rock, he was wellnigh tickled
to death with his gallant deportment, and swore that

---

* Frederick, Duke of York, and Bishop of Osnaburg. 1835. — Bishop
of Osnaburg was a German lay title, derived from the secularized bishopric
of O., and appropriated to younger sons of the King of Hanover.

none but Corporal Fred should go with the party to kill frogs in the great meadow. Then did Bull gather together a great many boats and catamarans; he put many of his most expert tenantry aboard, and fairly pushed them off, with orders not to spare a single soul among all the frogs.*

Now when the fractious little Beau Napperty heard that Bull had sent over his tenantry to commit trespass upon his marshes, he fell into one of the greatest passions ever known, and swore that Parson Fred should rue the hour he came over into his pastures. Then did he gather a great body of his tenants from all parts of the manor of Frogmore; then did he make a speech of one minute and a half, the longest he ever made, in which he exhorted them to defend right valiantly their beloved frogs; assuring them at the same time, that if any of them got a black eye or broken head in the scuffle, they should every mother's son of them be made corporals. He then threw his cocked-hat into the air, and bawled out liberty and equality as if the old boy had been in him. Upon this the light-heeled Frogmoreans cut a caper full two yards high, and scampered off, fully resolved to carbonado Parson Fred pretty handsomely.

Everybody knows the upshot of this business, so there is no occasion for me to tell it over again. Suffice it to say, that Parson Fred played his old pranks. Instead of keeping his party together, and looking out for the Frogmoreans and the frogs, he was always carousing it lustily; inquiring me out where the best taverns were, and where he could find store of goodly, plump, round, rosy-faced wenches, of which

* The expedition to Dunkirk, in 1793.

last he was mightily fond, insomuch that he would almost give up his liquor for them.

While he was thus wasting his time, the Frogmoreans came, a singing songs, cutting capers like grasshoppers, and flourishing their broom-staffs, with full intention of giving Bull's tenants a how-d'ye-do that they would not forget as long as they lived. John's fellows, as they always do, stood to it manfully; and if Corporal Fred had kept himself sober, they would most likely have played the mischief with the frogs, and laid a great many of them on their backs. But honest *Fred*, instead of minding his eye, was, as usual, busily employed carousing it away, so that in a little time it was found necessary to *fall back* — a cant phrase of John Bull, who is famous for cant and slang — and which means running away as fast as legs can carry you. This *falling back* continued till they found themselves near the shores of the mill-pond; when, not being able to fall back any farther unless they fell into the water, they were obliged to promise the Frogmoreans, that, if they would let them go about their business, they would never come there again.

The Frogmoreans consented with great pleasure, being heartily glad to get rid of such a set of sturdy dogs, who every one took as much thrashing as a good sheaf of wheat. As for the honest Belgians, or Bellygians, they would actually have rejoiced too at the departure of the roystering parson and his buxom crew, had their phlegmatic dispositions admitted of such a great exertion.

Squire Bull was inclined to grumble at the ill success of this frog-party, more especially when he came to look over Fred's tavern-bill; he made wry faces, and had a great mind to bastinado the corporal, until his slim overseer with the short breeches told him it was one of the most *brilliant affairs* that ever happened; and that though there was not much profit got by it, there was a vast deal of honour. He likewise assured him that though Corporal Fred was a little too fond of the bottle, yet when he was sober he was quite a match for the pope, the d—l, and Beau Napperty, together. Bull, who was as much afraid of the pope as a child is of a bugaboo, and with about the same reason, was tickled to the heart to hear he had such a bully in his family, and forthwith began to assume the airs of a gigantic champion and invincible boxer.

Instead of minding his business as he used to do, weaving his cloth, and keeping his forge going, he did nothing but flourish his cudgel, swearing at the same time that one of his tenants would thrash two Frogmoreans, and that he would soon do Beau Napperty's business for him, that's what he would.

CHAPTER VIII.

How Squire Bull incontinently turned knight-errant, and went about righting the wrongs of all his neighbours, in such a manner that they all wished in their hearts he would mind his own affairs, and let them alone.

IT was about this time, I think, that Bull took it into his wise head, that, being such a valiant boxer and expert cudgel-player, and able besides to go

through the horse-exercise with the broadsword, it
was his business not only to take care of his own
tenants, but also of all his neighbours.   Accordingly,
when any of the neighbours complained of Beau Napperty, John took their part without making the least
inquiry into who was right or who was wrong.   He
was always ready to help them along, though in general they were the most beggarly tatterdemalions in
the world, and heartily deserved what they got, for suffering their own landlords to impose upon them as
they did.

I will give an instance of Bull's humorous and
laughable knight-errantry, as a specimen of his mode
of righting his neighbours' wrongs.   Adjoining the
manor of Frogmore, at no great distance from Bullock
Island, there is a long POINT* puts out far into the mill-
pond, which belonged to an old fellow who boasted of
his great family, and used to tell everybody that his
manor was so extensive that the sun never set upon
it.   Puffed up with his vast landed property, he took
great state upon himself, and passed his time like a
perfect gentleman, without doing any thing but play
the fiddle and ride a hunting.   In fact, he thought
himself such a high fellow, though a most ignomi-
nious poltroon and notorious cuckold, that he lorded
it over his tenants as if they were so many beasts of
burden.   What with raising of rents, paying the parsons, of whom our stout lord himself stood in great
awe, and the consequent idleness of the tenants, who
had no spirit to work for the d—l and find themselves, as they said, the manor, though excellent land,
had got to be quite barren for want of cultivation.

* Spain.

The tenants also, though once a lively, industrious set of fellows, were now little better than a pack of ignorant, superstitious knaves, so that every one that saw them thought it was high time that the old codger of a landlord was turned out, and somebody else put in his place.

Now Beau Napperty, who was a stanch admirer of the rights of men, and liked to keep them all to himself, having a great parcel of poor relations to provide for, thought to himself that he would take away the manor, and give it to his brother *Joe.** So what does my gentleman do but invite Don Carlos,† as he was nicknamed, and his family, to come and take pot-luck with him. They accepted his invitation, bringing with them all the children; and Beau Napperty took good care they should not find their way home again.. Then he sent his brother Joe to take possession of the manor, by the grace of God, as he was pleased to term it.   The first thing Joey's people did was to rob a church, by which he got a good swarm of priests about his ears. They forthwith called Joey all sorts of names; and exhorted the tenants to rise up in defence of the invaluable privilege of being plundered by Don Carlos.

The tenants found this but reasonable; and, coming from all quarters, began to rain such a shower of dry blows on Joey, that he was fain to make a precipitate retreat from his farm-house of Mad-ride, which is so called because the women are all madcaps, and the tenants ride as if they were out of their wits,— that is, on jackasses instead of horses.

When the great righter of wrongs, Squire Bull,.

* Joseph Bonaparte.   † Charles IV. of Spain.

heard that Beau Napperty had seized the old don's manor, he, as usual, began to swear till he was blue. He called the don his particular friend and bottle-companion, though they had never given each other a good word in the whole course of their lives, and were always snarling and fighting about nothing. And finally, Bull urged, as a particular reason for taking the part of the old don, that he belonged to the ancient family of the Baboons, for whom, ever since he had nothing to fear from them, he professed the most invincible friendship.

Resolved to put this matter right in favour of his *old friends*, he set himself to work, and gathering a huge parcel of boats, he put his tenants on board, and sent them over to the *Point*, to help along in resisting Beau Napperty and his brother Joey. The old don's tenants, who did not want anybody to meddle in their affairs, looked askance at these unwelcome intruders, whom their parsons styled a set of wicked rascals, because they did not hold that a piece of bread was a shoulder of mutton. So they told Squire Bull's tenants they might go to some other market with their mutton, and, as they came over without an invitation, they might get back as they could. Now the poor misled fellows turned themselves to get home again; but, before they were able to reach their boats, they were heartily drubbed by some of Beau Napperty's tenants, and lost all their clothes and provisions.

But Squire Bull was as obstinate as a mule, especially when he happened to be in the wrong; and stuck to it manfully, until he at last succeeded in redressing the injuries of old Don Carlos, by putting his son Don Ferdinand* in possession of the *Point.* And Don Ferdinand showed his gratitude by doing John all the ill-turns in his power.

While Squire Bull was thus disinterestedly fighting for the liberties of the neighbourhood in one quarter, Beau Napperty was not behind-hand in upholding the rights of man in another. This John called defending the church, and Beau Napperty protecting the rights of man, — one and indivisible. Betwixt the two, the whole neighbourhood, far and near, by land and by water, was kept in a state to which plague, pestilence, and starvation, are no more than "a huckleberry to a persimmon," as they say in some of brother Jonathan's farms down South. They put me in mind of a fable I made out of my own head one day, which I will write down here, as I think it too good to be lost.

The porcupine was once seized with an unaccountable fit of universal benevolence, so that he could never see any of the weaker sort of animals but he must pity them, and either carry them on his back, or cover them with his body, for fear the sky might fall on them, as he said. The consequence was, most of the poor little devils got so pricked and worried by the quills of their troublesome protector, that in a short time they had scarcely a drop of blood left in their bodies, and were reduced to skin and bone. Upon this the wretched survivors came to him in a body, and with great humility requested, that in future, when his majesty saw them in any difficulty, he would graciously suffer them to get out of it as well as they could, without his " non-intervention."

* Ferdinand VII. of Spain.

In this way John wasted his substance and played his pranks, until he got all the neighbours about his ears except Brother Jonathan, whom however he soon after mortally offended by some of his foolish new-fangled pretensions.

————◆————

CHAPTER IX.

How Beau Napperty cunningly manages to humbug Squire Bull into several absurd capers.

BEAU NAPPERTY, the lord of the manor of Frogmore, which is just over against Bullock Island, was a knowing fellow as any you will see, and had studied Squire Bull's character until he could read him backwards. He knew him to be an obstinate old fellow, who, when he once got any thing into his head, stuck to it as a fowl does to a crumb. He also knew by experience, that whenever he did any thing, good or bad, Squire Bull would set his face against it, merely to show his independent spirit. Accordingly, whenever he wanted to bring any thing to pass that was out of his own power to do, he made John do it for him, by pretending to be at something quite the contrary.

Now Squire Bull and Beau Napperty, as everybody knows, by reason of their continually disputing and railing at each other like village shrews, and of a thousand offices of bad neighbourhood, had at last arrived at such a pitch of hatred, that they would not have hesitated one moment to ruin their tenants to a man by their rascally quarrels, rather than frankly shake hands, and forgive and forget like good fellows. If either of them could do the other an ill-turn, he did not care how much his tenants or the innocent neighbours suffered by it, for they were set upon ruining each other, whatever might be the consequence. Every day they were denouncing each other as rogues and I know not what. One day, Bull would publish Beau Napperty for the greatest thief in all the neighbourhood; the next, Beau Napperty would advertise Bull as the most notorious pirate in the world; until at last the better sort of people began to think they were neither of them any better than they should be; and I believe they were not much out in their reckoning.

Among the various plans invented by Beau Napperty to get John into difficulties, was one which succeeded to a miracle, as it afforded Squire Bull a pretext to revive his claim to the exclusive property of the mill-pond. This was all John wanted, as I said before; and he snapped at it as if it had been the most delicious morsel in the world.

Now Beau Napperty's plan was this. He knew that as long as Squire Bull continued to carry on the brisk traffic with his neighbours which his great number of boats and the excellent quality of his wares enabled him to do, he would be able, in spite of all his mad capers, to keep himself out of jail. He therefore set to work to knock this business on the head; and went about boasting that he would take care in future that none of the neighbours should carry on any business with Bull, or receive any of his wares; for if he found it out he would burn every stitch of them.   He then put on his little cocked-hat, buckled on his enormous toasting-iron, and blustering roundly among the neighbours, soon bullied most of them into shutting their landings to Bull's boats.*

Brother Jonathan, however, who was the very best customer Bull ever had, paid no attention to this flourish of Beau Napperty, but went on doing business with the squire as usual. Yet did that foolish old fellow just manage to do for Beau Napperty what he could not have done for himself.

Bull, as is too often the case with warm old codgers who have more money than wit, was generally surrounded by plenty of poor rogues; who, by humouring his whims, and patting his foibles on the back, managed to live at his expense, and generally got something handsome settled upon them in the end.

These rogues, though they could not for the life of them help laughing at Bull's claims to the mill-pond, yet, on hearing of Beau Napperty's grand Frogmore flourish which I just mentioned, told the squire that now was the time to drive all the neighbours clear from the pond, which he might do without losing his character, under pretence of being even with them for shutting him from their landings. They swore he was sole proprietor not only of this mill-pond, but of all the mill-ponds in the universe; and then they would tip each other the wink, as much as to say, What a rum-jockey Johnny is.

What made John the more eagerly bite at this, was a notion that he had now a fine opportunity of

* The Berlin decree.

paying off some of the old score he owed Brother Jonathan, whom he hated not a little, and of whose prosperity he had a long time been jealous. But this was a secret which he had sense enough to keep to himself; he therefore pretended to take all these rogues said for gospel— and it would have made you split your sides to see him pull up his old leather breeches with one hand, and with the other pelt Jonathan's boats as far as he could see them. This, in the cant of the day, he called maintaining the freedom of the mill-pond, encouraging boat-sailing, and other rare names, that signified directly the reverse of what the squire did.

John's prime excuse for this new method of maintaining the freedom of the mill-pond was, that it was done to retaliate upon Beau Napperty; for he maintained that since the neighbours were not allowed to trade with him, it was but right that they should be prevented from carrying on any business with Beau Napperty. This was what he called impartial justice; and the squire swore roundly, that whoever grumbled at such a fair retaliation, was not a bit better than a hanger-on of Beau Napperty. He used to boast, too, that by this rare system he should in a little time reduce Beau Napperty and his tenants to skin and bone; though at the very moment he was slily supplying them with whatever they wanted.

CHAPTER X.

How Squire Bull was mortal mad at Jonathan for giving shelter to his poor
tenants, who came over because they could not got enough to eat at
home.

THE great sufferer by these pranks of Squire Bull
was Brother Jonathan, who had never taken any
part in these vile quarrels, but continued to carry on
his business with whomsoever gave the best price for
his grain, without minding much either the Beau or
the squire. He cared not a rush for Beau Napperty's
threat against the neighbours who did business with
Bull, and, so far from submitting, went openly to
Bullock with his grain, just as he used to do before.

Formerly the pope and the d—l were the prime
objects of John Bull's hatred, and it was a moot
point to which of them he bore the greatest antipathy. Afterward he came to dislike Brother Jonathan exccedingly; but, in the end, Beau Napperty
came in for a principal share of his abomination.
He never, however, missed a fair opportunity of
giving a fatherly benediction to Jonathan, who had,
since his first quarrel with the squire, given him
divers causes of offence. By keeping aloof from the
disputes of the neighbours, and by a sober, discreet
behaviour, Jonathan had, without any intention of
injuring the old squire, got a great deal of his business from him. Now the squire, who had suffered
greatly in the trial between him and Beau Napperty
who should do each other the most harm, could not
bear to see Jonathan enjoying the fruits of his peaceable disposition.

Another great eyesore to Squire Bull was this: Jonathan had such a great quantity of land to spare, and his farms held out so many temptations to Bull's tenants, that, whenever they had an opportunity, they would leave Bullock Island and come over to settle. They were always received with kindness, and assisted with many little neighbourly offices. This the squire swore was undermining his interests, and acting the part of a secret enemy; because it was Jonathan's duty, as a good neighbour, to drive them home again. "Zounds!" would the squire exclaim, in a furious passion, "no man born in my manor shall ever get out of it, if I can prevent him. It is the happiest, the most pious, moral, plentiful, and all that sort of thing, manor in the world; and those who can't live in it may starve, for aught I care." This he said when in many parts of his manor one sixth of the tenants were on the parish, and another sixth living on a short allowance of oatmeal and potatoes.

The fact of there being more people in Bullock manor than it could support, without a more equal division of the land, was so notorious, that a fusty *old bachelor* wrote a book against breeding up children to starve. He was answered by another, and a controversy arose, which lasted till nobody would read a word more on the subject.* In the meantime, the women, who won't listen to reason, went on in their old way, and the evil increased.

For all this, the squire's maxim was, once a tenant always a tenant; and such was his wrath against Brother Jonathan for giving his poor runaways a

* A reference to the controversy about Malthus's book.

meal of victuals sometimes, that in revenge he used to chase Jonathan's boats, and when he overtook them would kidnap his rowers, under pretence of their being his runaway tenants. It must be noted, that though Bull held that no tenant could leave Bullock manor, yet he made no scruple whatever of sheltering the tenants of the neighbouring farms whenever they came over, which indeed was but seldom, for they were pretty sure of getting insulted by the squire's tenants, who cock up their tails and cackle like fowls in a barn-yard whenever a strange bird comes among them.

Now Brother Jonathan, though a pretty hard talker and a considerable dealer in words, was in the main a good-natured young fellow, who did not lightly get into a quarrel, but loved gain, and hated fighting if he could avoid it. He therefore pocketed these affronts of Bull with a few wry faces, and continued to treat him with respect, though, in addition to all these ill-turns, John used every now and then to fling it into Jonathan's teeth that he had a sneaking kindness for Beau Napperty, which I believe was a piece of the squire's own invention.

Affairs were in this way when Bull, as I before said, put forth his pretensions to the property of the mill-pond, and ordered his boats, which swarmed all over, to take any of Jonathan's they found looking towards Frogmore, unless they had stopped at one of his *landings* to pay for his permission.* Then it was that most of John Bull's sensible tenants began to perceive that the squire had a soft place in his skull. They could see with half an eye that Beau Napperty

* British orders in council, &c.

neither had prevented nor could prevent Jonathan
from carrying on his business with Bullock Island,
and, that if matters were left to their natural course,
all Jonathan's trade would come into Bull's hands.
Besides all this, they foresaw that John's conduct
would at length overcome Jonathan's patience, and in
a little time deprive him of the only real friend he had
in the world. They felt, despite all that was said by
John's secret friends dispersed over Jonathan's farms,
about his great liking for Beau Napperty, that the
young man, who ate, drank, spoke, thought, and did
every thing like his father, was willing, nay anxious,
to be on good terms with him, if he was only treated
with common politeness. He had beat Bull like a
man, and forgiven him like a good fellow.

CHAPTER XI.

How Jonathan consulted his wife about these matters aforesaid, and got
plenty of talk, but no cider.

ALL the former pranks of Bull had been borne by
Jonathan with most exemplary patience. True it is,
he sometimes complained, and his wife scolded; but
this generally blew over in a little time, and all was
calm again. But when at last the squire began to
meddle with his *pockets*, and to rob his boats under
pretence that they were going over to Frogmore, Jonathan began to be angry, as well he might.

He straightway called unto him his wife,* laid the

* Congress.

case before her, and asked her what was best to be done. This new wife of Jonathan's was a plaguy hard hand to deal with, and had just as much to say in the house as Mrs. Bull. Indeed, Jonathan could do nothing without her having a finger in the pie. She was an honest woman enough, as times go; but when you've said that you've said every thing — for she did nothing but talk, talk, all day, and sometimes all night, so that poor Jonathan could hardly sleep for her.

The honest truth of the matter is, that she was one of the most whimsical, cross-grained, contradictory, and bedevilled termagants, that ever fell to the lot of mortal man. With but one body, she had as many minds as she could hold, and was almost always of at least *seventeen** different opinions. Her face had all the appearance of one of your patchwork coverlets, and the different parts seemed to be collected from all quarters of the globe. She had an eastern squint of the eye, a northern aspect, and a southern complexion. Then her language resembled the confusion of Babel; at one time she talked like a Frogmorean, at another like Bull's wife herself; sometimes she talked half-French half-English, and very rarely she talked like Brother Jonathan's wife.

This capricious lady had undergone various changes since she became the poor man's helpmate. One time she was bedizened out like one of Bull's cast-off mistresses, and then would my lady insist that Jonathan should hug Bull in his arms, for he was an honest old

* The number of the States remained at this figure for between nine and ten years, Ohio, the Seventeenth, having been admitted on the 29th of November, 1802, and Louisiana, the Eighteenth, on the 8th of April, 1812.

fellow as any in the world. But the very next minute, perhaps, she would come out dressed in all the tawdry finery of one of Beau Napperty's ladies, with her face painted as red as fire, and her neck and shoulders all bare: and then she would insist upon it that Jonathan should have no friend but Beau Napperty, who was the most sincere, good-natured, agreeable, and entertaining little caitiff that ever escaped hanging. In some of her sober fits, which however occurred very seldom, she would appear in the decent homespun dress that became the wife of a plain yeoman like Jonathan, and then she would talk in a manner exceedingly sensible and rational. In short, to sum up the character of this whimsical lady, there were hardly as many humours among the multifarious wives and concubines of Solomon, as were concentrated and gathered together in this singular composition of notions, called Brother Jonathan's wife.

—◆—

CHAPTER XII.

How Jonathan began to bristle up when he found his boatmen did not pay as they used to.

JONATHAN seldom or never consulted this wife of his, without having abundance of reason to rail at the respectable institution of matrimony. Heaven preserve us!, how she would scold whenever any thing went wrong in the affairs of Jonathan's farms; and how she would lecture the poor man about any thing that came into her head, until Jonathan, finding she would have her say, thought to let her say what she pleased first, in hopes she would let him do as he liked afterwards.

Now when Jonathan got the account of Squire Bull's order to seize all his boats on their way to the manor of Frogmore, he consulted his wife about the method of proceeding; but that talkative lady, as usual, before he had half got through with his story, fell into a furious passion and began to abuse Squire Bull. I wish you had heard the pretty names she fastened upon his back. She called him prating gabbler, liquorish glutton, lubberly lout, ruffian rogue, paltry customer, scoffing braggart, cod's-head booby, noddipeak simpleton, ninnyhammer gnat-snapper, and various other names that nobody could tell where she picked up.

Every morning of her life, regularly, as soon as breakfast was over, for at least six months, did she ring the changes, over and over again, on the subject of Squire Bull's order, with this single difference, that when she was tired of rating Bull, she would turn about and give Beau Napperty and Brother Jonathan a most fearful broadside. Jonathan turned up the whites of his eyes, shrugged his shoulders, abused his stars, and groaned in spirit, to hear his dame talk at such a furious rate; and, finding there was nothing but incoherences and abuse to be got from her, advised her, as the warm weather was coming on, to make a tour round the farms till the dog-days were over.

Madam accordingly took herself off, and Jonathan for some time enjoyed a little comfort, and smoked his pipe in peace. But this calm lasted not long; the winter approached, the lady returned to the HALL, and as, during her recess, Bull had been at his old tricks, her disposition to scold was stronger than ever.

The patience of honest Jonathan, too, was now worn quite threadbare; and he began to think it was high time to toe the mark, and try to put an end to the squire's troublesome pretensions. He was not a little spurred on to this by the grumbling of his boatmen, who began to complain that they could not go out into the mill-pond on the most trifling occasions, without being insulted, or having some of their rowers taken away by John's boats. They further told Jonathan, that if matters did not soon mend, they should be obliged to haul in their horns, and walk afoot on Sundays, instead of riding to church in fine painted wagons.

The tradesmen of Jonathan's farms, who under their good easy landlord had grown rich, assured him, that only a few years before, they could afford their wives and daughters silk stockings, fine muslins, pearl breast-pins, and pianos, and such like luxuries; but now, such was the unparalleled distress of his estate, these poor creatures were obliged to put up with shabby Canton crapes and old-fashioned silks, and, instead of playing the piano or reading novels, were brought to the degrading necessity of making up their own linen, and even mending their own clothes.

I believe I have observed before that Brother Jonathan was a lad who would not fight without good reason, and was not easily put in a passion. He was not a man always on the look-out for a quarrel, like Bull, and, indeed, often put up with ill treatment rather than disturb the neighbourhood. It was this which encouraged the squire to treat him as he did; for his toad-eaters always assured him that he might fillip Jonathan o' the nose as often as he pleased, without making him do any thing more than bluster a little. But they didn't know Jonathan, as we shall see anon. I must say that he held what your great folks call honour, dog-cheap; likening it to a great bone, which, being thrown out into the highway, sets all the dogs of the neighbourhood by the ears. He used to say, for he often talked more sensibly than people expected from such a raw country-fellow, that this same honour was in general nothing but ambition, revenge, envy, self-interest, or some other scoundrel passion, the victim of which, knowing that if he came out with it in its naked deformity he would be scouted at, did dress it up in the likeness of something respectable, and palm it upon the world.

Among other singular notions, Jonathan held that a man ought to try all possible means of redress before he undertook to right himself by force; which opinion was exactly opposite to that of his neighbours, with whom it was generally a word and a blow, the latter of which commonly came first.

But though our shrewd Jonathan cared little for that kind of fighting which turns upon what fine folks call the point of honour, he had spirit to resent injuries. Fighting honour he likened to a great bully, who generally appears with a broken head or a black eye. But there was another kind of honour on which he prided himself — the honour of being a father to his tenants, and making them comfortable in this world.

When, therefore, he found that Bull's foolish pretensions began to undermine the prosperity of his people, he seriously set to work to bring John to reason, if possible. He first took away all his business from Bull, and refused to have any thing to do with his tenants in the way of barter.* It is supposed pretty generally, that if Jonathan had held on obstinately to this, it would in the end have prevented the terrible hubbub which afterwards took place. But here his own tenants did the business for him. They raised such a clatter about his ears, that in a little time he was obliged to permit the boatmen, who said Jonathan was a poltroon and ought to fight Bull at once, to go out and get pommelled and robbed to their hearts' content.

Being driven from this plan of bringing the squire to reason, he determined, before trying the strength of his arm against Bull, to see what the law would do for him.

———◆———

CHAPTER XIII.

How Jonathan brought his action of damages against Squire Bull, but was cast under the old statute of club-law.

JONATHAN therefore filed his declaration against Bull, of piracy on the high seas, trover and conversion, trespass on the case, covenant, debt, detinue, ejectment, waste, and *quare clausum fregit*. He also sued him upon the statute; upon action popular; action

* The embargo act of December, 1807, and other similar measures of less extensive application.

civil; action personal; action mixed; action real; and
action temporary and perpetual. He thought the
deuse would be in it if he did not catch Bull in some
of these snares, and lay him by the heels. This, declaration I think they called it, took up about four
quires of paper; had one hundred and ninety-seven
counts, and contained the usual amount of repetitions
and words that signify nothing.

After the customary delays, the suit came on before one JUSTICE SCOUT;* and Jonathan's lawyer, who
was selected, like a race-horse, for his wind, made a
speech, in which he said the same things over and
over again so often, that, had not the honest justice
fallen fast asleep, he must have been more than
mortal. Bull's lawyer answered him in a speech
which all the people in court said was twice as good,
because it was twice as long. Mr. Justice Scout,
being refreshed by his nap, listened to him with great
attention, and took several notes, which made folks
think the speech was a very deep one.

These speeches being made, and everybody being
quite tired, the court adjourned. The next day, at
it they went again; and Jonathan's lawyer proved
clearly enough, that, by the old customs of the neighbourhood, all the neighbours had an equal privilege to
use the mill-pond, except just as far as the water-lots
extended in front of the different manors and farms.
In reply, the squire's lawyer cited some old parchments, which nobody could ever find; talked of the
ancient rights of the Bull family, which nobody ever
acknowledged; and of old customs of the manor,
which no soul could remember. But what he partic-

* Sir William Scott. 1835.

ularly dwelt on was the statute of CLUB-LAW, which, though not in any books that he knew of, was older than the common-law; had always been acted upon by the Bull family, and had this singular excellence, that it applied equally to every side of every question, and justified every action, good or bad.

The proofs being got through, Mr. Justice Scout, like a most worshipful and upright fellow, sent to Squire Bull to know how the law stood that day, as one asks which way the wind blows, knowing that it is always changing. Bull told the justice that the law of the day was that Jonathan must lose his boats, and pay handsome costs into the bargain, to sicken him of going to law. When Justice Scout got his cue, he pretended, in order to make people believe that he followed his own judgment, that, this being a very knotty cause, he must have time to make up his mind. Then he dismissed the court till next day, went home, swallowed a good supper, and slept all night, without once thinking of Jonathan or his cause.

———◆———

CHAPTER XIV.

How Justice Scout proved that changing one's mind is a proof that one grows wiser, and that a real wise man is like a goose, and casts his opinions as often as she does her feathers.

THE next day Justice Scout gave his opinion thus :—

" GENTLEMEN,

" It was a maxim of former times, that if a man would be uniformly wise, he must change his mind every day. Now, as I alter my opinions whenever the wind changes, I must be a wise man. 'Tis true, I said the other day that the law was the same at all times and to all persons; but having since that grown a wonderful deal wiser, I have wisely altered my opinion. It would be a fine thing, truly, if a stranger had the same rights in Bullock Island as the lord of the manor himself. No, no; let us have none of these new-fangled principles of liberty and equality foisted over the old and *unchangeable* customs of the manor. Law, in fact, is one thing one day, and another thing another day; which is entirely agreeable to the oldest and greatest law in the world, the law of nature, which on the very face of it declares that all things are subject to change. Really, gentlemen, it seems nonsense to insist on these obvious points. Would you fly in the face of nature? Certainly not; and therefore, I take it for granted, you will all see the propriety of changing the law of boats every day or two.

" The law, as it stands to-day, is —" Here Justice Scout sent his tipstaff to Squire Bull, to know if the law had not changed since yesterday, and, being satisfied on this point, went on —

" The law, gentlemen, as it stands to-day, is, that Mr. Jonathan having broken the venerable statute of club-law, and infringed upon the rights of Squire Bull, to wit, the right of the strongest, by sailing boats on the mill-pond without the squire's leave, has forfeited all claim to common justice, and must therefore pocket his losses, pay costs, and keep out of Bull's way at his peril."

Hereupon the tenants, who were tickled to the very

marrow with this permission to plunder Jonathan, threw up their hats, gave three cheers, and turning out one and all, saved his worship's horses the trouble of dragging him home.

———◆———

CHAPTER XV.

*Jonathan writes a letter to Squire Bull, which puts him in a mighty passion, and costs " Master Canynge " * a great pull of the ear.*

JONATHAN, when he heard how his lawsuit had turned out, as is common in such cases, fell foul of the law, and forgetting that it was only the abuse of a good thing that he had to complain of, did belabour with hard words the whole system. Then he called the lawyers a pack of drivelling chatterboxes, who one half of the time did not know what they were saying, and the other half said nothing to the purpose. But the cream of his blessing fell upon Justice Scout, who, instead of asking what the law was, only inquired about Squire Bull's opinion of it, and who, he swore, was just fit to be chief-justice of the manor of Beëlzebub.

Having thus burned his fingers with the law, Jonathan thought he would try what reason would do. Having often heard say that there is reason in all things, he did not know but he might find a little in Squire Bull's pate, so he wrote him the following letter :—

* George Canning, the celebrated wit and statesman, from 1807 to 1809 British Secretary of State for Foreign Affairs.

" *To John Bull, Esquire, of Bullock, greeting.*

"HONOURED FATHER,

" Though I am your son, I have always got more kicks than coppers from you; and now I am grown up to be of age, I don't choose to put up with any more of your plaguy nonsense. I have a right to sail boats on the mill-pond for all your silly claims, which have got you many a broken head, and will get you many more before you die, if you don't mind your hits, old gentleman. Moreover, I have a right to do business with whom I please, as long as I don't go against the old customs of the neighbourhood; and to visit where I think fit, without Mr. Bull's leave, and be hanged to him. So please take notice, that I shall carry on my business as I have always done, and visit Beau Napperty when it suits me.

" S'life, daddy, do you think that though I was brought up in the woods, I am to be scared by an owl? Don't think to bully me, daddy; for, though you tell such famous stories about our ancestors, everybody knows that the Bulls have been going down hill till they have got nearly to the bottom; and, between ourselves, people say they all look up to me to support the family honour in future. Though they do make such a fuss about their great riches, and all that, it's all in my eye Betty Martin; and I don't believe they are any better than their neighbours, for all they hold up their heads so high. Everybody knows, daddy, that you owe a great deal more than you are able to pay, and that you can't meet the interest of your debts without borrowing money, raising your rents, and robbing the neighbours' boats. For my part, I am heartily glad you disinherited me, for now I shall not be liable for any of your extravagances.

"Was it the part of a good neighbour or an honest man, daddy, to steal my boats, and, after that, order your pitiful, weathercock justice of the peace to twist the law so as to make me pay the costs of claiming my own property? I know you want money bad enough, and for that matter I would not mind lending you some to keep you out of jail — but I don't choose to have my pockets picked, not I; and as for your famous *club-law*, mayhap two of us can play at it, if you come to that.

"So look ye, daddy, if you don't let me alone when I am going about my lawful business, and quit taking my boats and tenants, like a highway robber as you are, you may expect an otherguess sort of a pommelling than you got from me when I was only a boy. Beware of my wife too, who has done nothing but scold for several years past, and who threatens to clapperclaw you whenever you come in her way. Take a friend's advice, and look sharp, for she has a two-edged tongue, and the nails of a catamount.

"I expect, if you are an honest man, as you say you are, though I find people in general don't give you credit for being one, that you will pay me for the property you have cheated me out of by means of Justice Scout; and, moreover, promise me faithfully never to serve me so again. Another thing that I had like to forget until just now is, that you are to quit coming on board of my boats and taking out my people under pretence of getting back your tenants, who come over to settle on my farms. It is a sin and a shame, daddy, to keep the poor fellows from giving up their leases, when you are every year raising their rents, so that now they can hardly keep themselves from starving. You say your tenants are the best off of any in the neighbourhood, and if they are such fools as to quit your manor, the sooner you get rid of them the better. For my part, I scorn to act in this manner, but allow my tenants to go where they please.

" The long and the short of the matter is, that if I am satisfied in your answer, I am ready to drink a glass with you and be friends. If not, you and I will be two, I guess, daddy ; and, to show you that I am in right good earnest, I hereby let you know that I shall not wait more than five or six years for your final answer, being in a great passion, and somewhat in haste.

" Your dutiful son, as you behave,
" JONATHAN."

This letter Jonathan sent over by his lawyer, who had directions to back it with the longest speech he could possibly make.

—◆—

CHAPTER XVI.

How Squire Bull took upon himself to be hugely insulted at Jonathan's friendly letter, and sent him a pretty sort of an answer.

WHEN the sturdy high-handed Bull got this letter, he examined the direction with great attention, not knowing the writing. Then he thrust his hand into his red waistcoat-pocket, from which he pulled a great pair of iron-rimmed spectacles made by a neighbouring blacksmith, an excellent workman, which, after wiping off the dust with his bandanna handkerchief, he placed with great deliberation across his nose. Then, drawing his great chair to the light, he carefully broke the seal, and, scratching his head to assist his comprehension, began to spell out the contents.

It was worth a hundred pounds of any man's money to see the wry faces he made as he began to enter into the spirit of Jonathan's epistle. Before he got a quarter through, he laid down his pipe with such emphasis that it broke into a thousand pieces. As he proceeded, he struck the table with such force that the pot of beer, which was his most trusty counsellor and companion, danced about like a pea on a tobacco-pipe, and finally overset on the floor, while the old fellow's visage gradually puckered up like a cabbage-leaf before the fire. When he had fairly got through, he very leisurely tore the letter into a million of little pieces, walked with the most stately and grim solemnity to the window, and very deliberately threw them to the d—l, to whom he always consigned any thing that gave him great offence.

Then taking a turn or two to consider what was proper for his dignity, he called for one " Master Canynge," a sort of jester and buffoon, whom John employed to write his letters and make him laugh when he was melancholy. They used to dub him John's secretary, inasmuch as he generally answered the squire's letters that came from abroad, because he was thought to spell better than any of Bull's servants. As for the squire himself, he did not often venture to write his own billets, and when he did they were in such a villanous cramp hand, so full of incoherences, and so interlarded with bad spelling, that it was more trouble to read them than they were worth.

Bull told Master Canynge of Jonathan's letter, and directed him to answer it forthwith; but the jocular secretary told him, with great submission, that in order to answer a letter properly it was necessary to know its contents. The squire, who was famous for sometimes listening to reason, hereupon immediately began to fumble in his pockets; then he turned them all inside out, ransacked every hole and corner of the room, pish'd and pshaw'd like fury, and at last recollected having torn and thrown it out of the window. Canynge relished this joke hugely, swore it was the best thing he had seen in a long time, and began to laugh like a whole swarm of flies at the squire's forgetfulness. His mirth was however arrested by John's laying hold of his ear, and giving it a hearty lug in order to make him serious, telling him at the same time he was an impudent rascal to laugh at his betters.

" Master Canynge " hereupon sat down, and, being not a little confused with the tingling of his ear, as well as somewhat ruffled at the squire's application, wrote the following singular and impertinent answer to Jonathan's letter. Bull, who hated reading as much as he did writing, signed it, as was his usual custom, without knowing what were its contents. It was immediately despatched, and ran thus : —

"*To Mr. Jonathan, greeting.*

"You lubberly Yankey!

"Don't think I'll give up my rights, privileges, and prerogatives, to such a hop-o-my-thumb, mint-sling, rum-jockey as thou art. Why, thou unnatural cub, answer me one thing — did I not beget thee, villain! — and could I not have begotten thee or not, just as I pleased? Body o' me! what an undutiful rascal thou art, to be pestering with impertinent letters the father that begat thee, and who, by refusing to do so, might have made a nobody of you.

"Thou art, moreover, a great blockhead, as well as an ungrateful dog, son Jonathan, to be in the least angry at my conduct towards thy boats, seeing I don't mean to do you the least injury, all my plans being to plague that little caitiff Beau Napperty, to be revenged on whom I would send you and all your rascally generation to the d—l. Body o' me! I say again, Squire Sapskull, did not I beget thee? And am I not one of the most honest fellows in the whole neighbourhood? I say it myself, I have said it a thousand times, and therefore it must be true.

"I have twelve hundred boats on the mill-pond, and if you doubt my assertions, I will demonstrate them with the aforesaid boats in the twinkling of an eye. Plague take the fellow! — dost not see, thou animal with half an eye, that if I plunder your boats, it is all for your own good, because it enables me to annoy the more effectually that little villanous Frogmorean, who, if I did not keep him within bounds, would come over and upset your whole household, you booby? Here am I now, cutting and slashing in all directions at the disturber of the neighbourhood, Beau Napperty: and though it must be confessed most of the blows fall upon you, and others upon my own pate, yet in the eye of sober reason I do you no harm, because I intend none, upon my honour; all I mean is to annoy the *common enemy* of all, and prevent his doing you manifest injury.

"Besides, thou unreasonable, pestilent rogue, am not I an *honest fellow*, and is not Beau Napperty a *knave?* And is it not reasonable that an honest man should have the same privilege as a knave? Things are come to a pretty pass in the world, if honesty can't rob and plunder as well as knavery; and therefore I maintain, and prove by my twelve hundred boats, that I have as good a right to rob as Beau Napperty, nay, a better than he, because I am such a fine, honest fellow, and make such good use of what I get. And did I not beget thee, villain? Answer me that, I say again.

"You can't wait for my answer, you say. You ungrateful villain, to talk in this way to the kindest father that ever turned his son out of doors! You can't, hey!—well, here is my answer. I'll plunder your fir-built boats, with a bit of striped bunting stuck on a corn-stalk for a flag—I'll snap my fingers and bite my thumb at you as often as I please—I'll disown, disinherit, and unbeget you, and swear you are the son of a French barber and a Dutch fishwoman. I am a religious man, an affectionate father, and I don't care who knows it.

"Therefore, look ye, friend Jonathan, my son—I hold that the right of doing wrong is inherent in all honest fellows that have twelve hundred boats like myself. It is moreover *necessary*, because I can't get the better of Beau Napperty, whom I am pleased to hate beyond all other men, without it; and it is moreover proper, because it is much better that honest fellows like me should flourish by evil means, than that knavery, which is Beau Napperty, should flourish at all. So don't pester me with any more of your complaints, or tell me any more of your wife's threats. I am an honest fellow, dam'me! I begot thee, and have a right to do what I please with my own children; and, what's more, I will.

" Thy abused father,
" JOHN BULL."

When " Master Canynge " had finished this letter, he went and lounged about the squire's parlour, cracked his jokes as usual, wrote lampoons and songs, and quizzed the kitchen wenches till they swore he was the drollest dog in the whole manor. After this he went to the CHAPEL* and tickled Bull's wife till she squeaked, entertained John's overseer with some good stories, and, after swallowing a couple of mugs of strong ale, went to bed and dreamed he was made high-bailiff of the manor of Bullock.

* St. Stephen's chapel in the old Westminster Hall building, then used for the sessions of the House of Commons.

CHAPTER XVII.

Squire Bull talks so foolishly, and acts so unseemly to Brother Jonathan,
that the poor fellow don't know whether to laugh or cry.

IN due time Jonathan received this curious letter,
which proved pretty clearly that Bull thought him
a fool or a coward. He put it into his wife's hand,
and that talkative lady, who generally took it out in
scolding, was in such a quandary, that she hardly
knew whether she stood on her heels or her head.
She uttered so many queer notions on the subject, one
treading in the steps of the other, that Jonathan could
not, for the soul of him, tell what she would be at.
The truth is, she did not exactly know herself; but, as
he asked her opinion, she thought she must say something. So she went on for a whole six months at
least, dinning it away like a parcel of bells playing
at random — each a different tune. Sometimes she
talked like a farmer; sometimes like a tobacco-
planter; sometimes like a boatman: but most generally like a woman.

In the meantime Bull and Jonathan wrote letters to
each other every day. Bull sometimes would profess
a great fatherly kindness for Jonathan, and then, in
the very next letter, twit him with being a friend of
Beau Napperty; treating him at the same time as if
he were a mere nobody, and insisting on the right
which he had under the famous statute of club-law.
It was not a little curious to see the fetches the squire
made use of to bolster up his new law. In one of
his letters, he insisted upon it that there was no good
rule to decide who was in the right, except to find out

who was the strongest. "Doth not," said John, "the strong animal prey upon the weak? It is a law of nature, friend Jonathan; and therefore it's nonsense for such a slack-breeched fellow as thou art to talk against it. S'life, what is the use of being strong if one can't play the d—l, and all that sort of thing, now and then a little?"

Then John had another curious argument, which he probably picked up in some last dying speech and confession, and which he called the necessity of the case. This he swore was a good excuse for robbing on the highway or on the high seas. "A fellow," quoth John, "robs on the highway from the necessity of the case: that is, because he wants money to buy horses, fine clothes, and all that sort of thing. True, he is hanged for it if caught; but if he is knowing enough to evade, or strong enough to bully, the laws, or rich enough to bribe the judges, he is held to be an honest man in the eyes of all men of sound sense, and comes off with flying colours, and all that sort of thing." Bull was insufferably vain of this rare system of reasoning, and boasted that he had twisted a rope strong enough to hang a dozen such simple fellows as Jonathan.

Jonathan half cried and half laughed at the squire's nonsense, for he could not help seeing, and feeling too, that though necessity might be a very notable justification for a pick-pocket, it was not the most satisfactory to him who had his pockets picked. But the tenants, who sometimes had these letters read to them, were, many of them at least, imposed upon by Bull's arguments, and actually came to think, or pretended to think, that the squire was on the right side of the ditch.

The tenants of Brother Jonathan were, in truth, a rare set of fellows, collected helter-skelter from all parts of the neighbourhood, and presenting such an odd medley of faces, that it might be said they looked like everybody, and everybody looked like them. Their minds were as varied as their faces, and, as they prided themselves upon thinking for themselves and speaking their notions freely, hardly any two thought or spoke alike, for fear they might be suspected of wanting an independent spirit. In fact, the tenants of no two farms ever pulled the same way; and though, at the time of Jonathan's marriage, they had all agreed to stick together and support one another on all occasions, yet from the moment of that union they seem never to have agreed in any one thing whatever.

Maybe you have seen before now two dogs, who, while they had their own will and could do as they pleased, were the best friends in the world; but being chained together, from that moment began to snarl and show their teeth, and never drew the same way afterward. Or, to give you a more rational example — perhaps you have seen a young couple in the first rudiments of an everlasting affection, toying, casting sheep's-eyes, and slyly squeezing each other's hand under the table. Peradventure you have come back that way, and seen this same couple wedded, disputing their road through the world inch by inch, and administering comfort to each other by mutual recrimination, sturdy opposition, and grumbling compliance.

If you ever saw any thing of this sort, you have some notion of the notable connexion subsisting among Jonathan's tenants. There was continually something or other turning up somewhere or other that went against the grain of some one or other of these wiseacres, who, sagely concluding that it was the duty of the landlord to take care of him in preference to anybody else, would begin to speak his mind, as he called it: that is, to abuse Jonathan and everybody that took his part. I have known the barking of an exceeding small, insignificant puppy, to set all the dogs of a neighbourhood howling like fury; and so it generally happened in the farms, where the scolding of one tenant caused a great outcry in the end. But, as this subject is a little curious, it may be worth while to trace these matters more distinctly.

CHAPTER XVIII.

Touching the farms called Southlands, and what roystering blades the tenants were. Also, of those honest, hearty fellows, the boys of the Middlelands.

BROTHER JONATHAN, as I said before, had a great estate in lands, which, that he might be able to tell one farm from another, came to be called by several names, such as the Southlands, the Middlelands, Down East, and Far West. This division, in time, proved a great source of heart-burnings and contentions among the tenants occupying these different farms, who, because they had different names, began, like a parcel of blockheads as they are, to fancy themselves separate peoples with separate interests, and to squabble among themselves about nothing or next to nothing. In process of time, these sectional feelings grew into fruitful sources of trouble to Brother Jonathan, who had much ado to keep them from falling together by the ears at town-meetings and elections. Many people thought they hated each other worse than they did Squire Bull's tenants, and I believe they were half right.

The tenants of the farms commonly called Southlands, having plenty of negroes to work for them, and nothing to do but amuse themselves, did, as will often happen with country blades, amuse themselves pretty considerably with horse-racing, cock-fighting, barbecues, and the like. They were also wonderful boys for what they called anti-fogmatics, being certain mint-juleps, which, to say the truth, are exceeding toothsome of a foggy morning, and mighty potent in keeping away chills and agues. They are supposed to make a man somewhat belligerent, an opinion to which I incline, seeing I remember I once felt their effects myself at a training, in the which I charged quite through a numerous phalanx of naughty boys, in despite of old shoes and unseemly maledictions.

But for all this, the Southlanders were a set of frank, jolly, hospitable, high-spirited fellows, with hearts always open and above-board. A man might live among them free of expense till the cows came home, if they did not kill him with good living and mint-juleps. For my part, I always did and always shall like them, and I don't care who knows it.

These sturdy roystering blades disliked the tenants Down East, of whom I shall speak anon, because they came among them with little one-horse carts, laden with wooden bowls, tin-ware, and the like, and made divers good bargains out of them in the way of trade. It would do your heart good to hear some of the stories, true or false, told about these travelling pedlers, who wore high steeple-crowned hats, and were about the 'cutest fellows you ever saw. As there is no error more common than to condemn a whole community for the fault of one, the South-landers, judging from a few bad samples, came at last to consider the Down-Easters no better than they should be. Now the first thing a Southlander thinks of, when he catches himself in a passion, is fighting; so whenever he was taken in in a bargain for a wooden clock, or some such thing, he was pretty sure to pommel the tin-trader, who not unfrequently had scruples of conscience about fighting. When the trader got home, of course he told terrible stories of gouging and the like; so that in time these came to be thought little better than bullies, and those down-right rogues, though people who were best acquainted with them knew better.

Those who tenant the flourishing farms of the Mid-dlelands are for the most part steady, sober-minded farmers, expert boatmen belonging to the great land-ings, and comfortable tradesmen well-to-do in the world. They agree mighty well together, as also with the tenants of the other farms; or if they chance to quarrel about nothing, the one class balances the other, and the farms don't get into a sweat as they do in other parts of Brother Jonathan's estates.

It will be found by those who take the trouble to inquire, that in all Brother Jonathan's farms where this mixture does not prevail, the tenants are very ignorant and headstrong in their opinions and prejudices. Having but one exclusive road to prosperity, they conclude there is no other way but this in the world, that what is their interest must be everybody's interest, and that whenever that is affected the whole world must be turned upsidedown. But on the contrary, where, as in the farms I am treating of, the different orders of men are mingled together, the perpetual collision of interests in time wears away their different asperities, and introduces a reasonable regard for each other's welfare.

And now I am in for it, I will make another sage remark, which will be found equally true with the last. It is this: that those farms which form the extremities of Brother Jonathan's property have always been more easily agitated and set in motion than the others; and in this they exhibit a striking analogy to the parts of the human frame. The tickling of the soles of the feet will set one kicking at a furious rate; and the touch of a feather at the nose causes the proboscis to be violently agitated, while the rest of the body remains quiescent. So, if you meddle with the farms of Southlands, which form, as it were, the legs, or with the farms Down East, which constitute the snout, or proboscis, of Brother Jonathan's domain, you will always find a mighty deal of agitation and grimace in them, while the more noble parts that lie in the vicinity, as it were, of the *heart*, remain undisturbed.

CHAPTER XIX.

*Of the 'cute boys of Down East, and how they got the name (among them-
selves) of being wiser and better than their neighbours.*

THE farms belonging to Brother Jonathan, Down
East, it is said, were originally taken on long leases,
by a set of conscientious fellows who left Bullock
Island a great while ago, because Squire Bull, who
was a very religious man, and head of the church by
custom of the manor, made a law " abolishing diver-
sities of opinion in religious matters," dreaming, like
a great blockhead as he was, that he could make all
people think alike, which in my opinion is about as
easy as to make them all look alike. These good
people went through terrible hardships, which they
bore like men, till they cleared their lands; and, having
suffered so much for opinion, it is no wonder if they
should be a little obstinate sometimes.

Some of these were of the sect of the witches, and,
I am credibly informed, came over the mill-pond on
broomsticks. The tenants, however, soon found out
these diabolical sinners, and got rid of them, as we
extirpate caterpillars, by smoking them out. Many
ignorant people have their fling at the tenants Down
East for being so much afraid of witches, and Squire
Bull often cracked his jokes on them about it; but
they had all better hold their tongues, for, if the truth
were known, the whole neighbourhood was pretty
much in the same box at that time, and most especially Squire Bull's tenants. Be this as it may, the
Down Easters took such good care to get rid of the
witches and wizards, that for many years past they

have been entirely extinct, unless, as some suppose, there is a cross of their blood in Major Jack
Downing.*

These Down-Easters are excellent good boatmen, as
well as great takers of codfish, alewives, and a certain
fish called dumbfish, for some reason I wot not of, seeing all fish, so far as I know, are dumb. Be this as it
may, they are very much addicted to dumbfish, particularly on Saturdays, and such is the salutary effect of
this regimen, that the greatest scolds in the capital
town of the Down-Easters say nothing but their prayers all that day. It is moreover observed, that neither
the courts nor the meeting-houses (except that of the
Quakers) are open on Saturday, for that both parsons
and lawyers are incapable of speechifying. These
things are so curious, that I thought them worth re-
cording in this diverting and true history.

Squire Bull, who abuses everybody, has trumped
up from time to time divers tough stories about these
good people, to whose discredit I know nothing, except that they stopped me once travelling on a Sunday when I was going to be married, and a pestilent
rogue from somewhere Down East took me in with a
wooden clock which would not strike, because, I suppose, it had been brought up upon dumbfish. In fact,
they are shrewd hands at a bargain, as the following
true story will exemplify.

An Oatlander, a tenant of Squire Bull, as sharp as
a razor, once rode away Down East on the back of a
horse that had wall eyes, a switch tail, shambling

* Charles Augustus Davis published in Philadelphia, in 1834, " The Life
of Andrew Jackson, President of the United States. Illustrated with numerous cuts. By Major Jack Downing of the Downingville Militia."

gait, and marvellous spindle-shanks. There was hair enough in his fetlocks to stuff a sofa, and you might have counted his ribs at the distance of half a league had they not been well covered with a coat of matted hair that entirely prevented this disgrace. Our adventurer went on at a miserable pace till he came in sight of a neat looking tavern, when he clapped spurs to his steed, who, with a most desperate effort, trotted up to the place in a truly gallant manner.

At the gate of the stable-yard stood a raw-boned, long-sided, rosy-cheeked, light-haired lad, who seemed gaping about as if he had just thrust his nose into the world. He wore a light-blue linsey-woolsey coatee, no waistcoat, and a pair of tow-linen trousers, that, by reason of his having outgrown them, reached just below the calf of his leg; but what they wanted in length they made up in breadth, being of that individual sort called by sailors cannon-mouthed. But what most particularly fixed the stranger's attention was a white hat, which, on account of its having been often caught in the rain, had lost its original outline, and marvellously resembled a hay-stack in shape and colour.

This figure was leaning over a gate, with one hand scratching his head, and supporting his chin with the other, in the true style of listlessness and simplicity. Our adventurer marked him for his prey, and, after some conversation, finding he had a horse, offered to *swap* with him. The youth, after the fashion of Down East, first asked him what was his name, what countryman he was, where he came from, and where he was going; together with other questions equally necessary.

Having received satisfaction in these points, they fell to work, and our Oatlander never had a tougher job in his life. At last, however, a bargain was struck, and he went on his way, chuckling at having taken in the clodhopper. All at once, however, his horse insisted on lying down, and his mirth came to the ground with him. While he was standing over his steed, endeavouring, by the vigorous application of kicks and cuffs, to persuade him to rise, who should come jogging along but the lad with the hay-stack hat, who assured him that his horse would infallibly get up when he was tired of lying down; that he did not care to rest himself in this manner above eight or ten times a day, and was in other respects so good a beast, that if he would give him twenty dollars to boot he would *swap* back again. Our luckless traveller was fain to agree; so, mounting his former resurrection of dry bones, he made the best of his way out of the neighbourhood, and not one of his countrymen has, ever since, ventured to settle in those parts, or drive a bargain with a Down Easter.

By reason of the women being exceedingly fruitful, the farms every year are obliged to swarm, after the fashion of beehives; the young ones leaving the old hive to find room elsewhere, which they do easy enough, having a singular faculty in getting on in the world which smacks a little of witchcraft. It is observed, that like locusts, wherever they light, they soon clear all before them, and drive away the old settlers.

This has especially been the case in those parts of Brother Jonathan's farms that were tenanted by those who came of the stock of some honest Bellygians, who paddled over from the great bog-meadow I spoke of in the first part of this history. These were a parcel of industrious, sober, steady, slow-motioned, deliberative, pursy, thick-legged, four-square boys, with faces much wider at the bottom than the top, like to the angels that are cut on the old-fashioned head-stones. They were great smokers of tobacco, and walked, worked, deliberated, and sometimes slept, with a pipe in their mouth. Such was their love of this practice, that it is reported the clerk of a certain parish, not being able to get any tobacco, did incontinently cut up the bell-rope, which he smoked, to the great scandal of the church.

Mercy preserve us! what work the Down-Easters made among these slow-motioned fellows. In a little time they would evaporate and disappear, as it were, in their own smoke, nobody knew where; like the Indians, when the white people get among them and civilize them with brandy.

Between the tenants of Down East and those of Southlands there did exist a deal of ill-will: this was partly owing to the cause I mentioned before, partly to difference of manners and customs, for the former abhorred horse-races, cock-fights, and mint-slings, preferring thereto apple-brandy, tea, cucumbers, pumpkin-pies, thanksgivings, general trainings, and other harmless luxuries. There were also certain interests which seemed to clash between these two — I mean certain petty, every-day interests, such as lead little fellows by the nose in opposition to their lasting happiness.

But the most growing portion of Brother Jonathan's estates was an immense tract of new lands he had purchased since he came of age, away beyond the mountains, which came to be known by the name of the Far West. He bought it a great bargain of Beau Napperty, who was no great hand at clearing new lands, or handling any sharp-edged tool except his great toasting-iron. These new farms are among the best lands Jonathan had; and you may depend upon it, the Down Easters, and the tenants of the other farms, who had worn out the soil, were not backward in settling them, for Jonathan wisely let them have the land cheap and gave a long credit. All the bold, enterprising fellows, who wanted elbow-room at home, or had more little curly-pated rogues of children than they knew what to do with, pulled up stakes, and went forth to seek the promised land of the Far West. In process of time they multiplied into ever so many thousands, and the children grew so fast that some thought they would never be done growing.

Being used from childhood to lay out in the woods under the canopy of heaven, which they called a sky-blanket, to hunt the bears and other wild animals that were at first as plenty as tame ones Down East, they grew up a hardy, independent race, that feared nothing, cared for nobody, and justly thought themselves equal to any folks in the world. They sometimes bearded Brother Jonathan himself, and told him to his face that if he did not mind his P's and Q's they would pay no more rent, and put it into him before he could prime his rifle.

They were the greatest shots — I don't mean with the long bow, though some of them were pretty good at that, but with the rifle — that ever were seen.

They could kill a squirrel on the top of the highest tree that ever grew in all out of doors, without stirring a hair of his skin; and not a man among them but would have thought himself a cowardly varmint, who would not stand at a hundred yards' distance, and let them shoot at a pint-pot on the top of his head, without winking.

I have heard say, for I never was there, that they are the most hospitable people in the whole neighbourhood, insomuch that they sometimes lick a fellow for refusing to come in and take pot-luck. This I know, for I had it from his own mouth, that a man got taken up, and was very nigh being *regulated*, only for passing five or six houses without stopping and taking something. They mistrusted him for a horse-stealer.

Altogether, they are about as fine a set of fellows as I would ever wish to see; and it shall go hard if, when I have finished this stupendous history, I don't pay them a visit, luxuriate in barbecues with my old friend Justice Wildgoose, and hunt bears with Davy Crockett. Like the Southlanders however, they had a mortal prejudice against the Down-Easters, which I am in good hopes will die away in time, when all the old wooden clocks are worn out. For my part, I believe in my heart you can always find something good among all sorts of sinners; and I have always thought it was a great piece of nonsense for people living in the same tub to be continually trying to kick out the bottom.

The upshot of all this was, that let Jonathan do what he would, he was sure to get into a scrape, and was all his life between hawk and buzzard, as they say. If he pleased one he was sure to displease the other, and never poor fellow's ear burned so often; for I verily believe there was not a minute in the twenty-four hours that he was not abused by somebody or other.

CHAPTER XX.

How Squire Bull, seeing Jonathan's farms at sixes and sevens, takes advantage thereof.

Now John Bull, though no conjurer, was yet not quite an April-fool; and perceiving, on these occasions, the divisions among Jonathan's tenants, made his advantage of them. He took all occasions to insult him; chased his boats whenever he saw them on the mill-pond, and laid hold of his rowers, making them turn out and come aboard of his own boats, to assist in rowing and handing the sails, whether they would or not.

The *boatmen*, who principally suffered by these pranks of Squire Bull, began to grumble at being thus molested in their affairs; and, as they lounged about on the sand-beach scratching their heads for want of something else to do, talked among themselves how Jonathan was but a sneaking, milksop sort of a fellow, to suffer his boatmen, who were the best tenants he had, and paid more rents than all the rest of them together, to be treated in such an unhandsome manner. These fellows were always talking about their great rents, though everybody knew that whatever they paid Jonathan they took good care to get out of the pockets of the other tenants; and in truth paid no more rent than their neighbours.

This getting to Jonathan's ears, he wrote over once again to Bull to know what he meant by such un-neighbourly conduct; and Bull, in answer, sent him word that he did not in the least mean to hurt his good friend and loving son Jonathan, but was merely doing these things to spite his arch-enemy Beau Nap-perty. Jonathan told him, in reply, that he did not see the sense of thrashing Beau Napperty over his shoulders; and what was more, he would not submit to it from any man, not even his own father. Bull having a notion that Jonathan, notwithstanding the sound beating he had formerly given his daddy, wanted spunk to oppose him manfully on this occasion, would not budge an inch, but told Jonathan that as soon as Beau Napperty behaved himself like a gentleman, he would do so too, but not before. Jonathan replied, he did not care three farthings about Beau Napperty, who could do him no harm; and as for its being in Bull's power to make said Beau behave like a gentle-man, that was a job which the d—l might undertake, for all him. Upon this Bull snapped his fingers, and told Jonathan that he was a most unreasonable fellow, and withal a great ninny, not to see that his worthy father was affording him his protection against Beau Napperty, who, if it was not for that, would in the twinkling of an eye come and beat down Jonathan's fences, burn all his boats, and overrun all his farms with Frogmoreans. In short, Brother Jonathan ought to have sense enough to see that he was acting the part of a loving parent, who chastises his children, not out of anger, but pure affection.

" Plague take such fatherly kindness," quoth Jonathan ; " this old dad of mine, I foresee, will never be content till he gets the whole neighbourhood about his ears.   Here now is he without a sincere friend or relation in the world that can help him along except myself; and yet do I foresee that he will oblige me to turn against him with the rest.   Well, if I must, I must."   And shrugging up his shoulders, he went in search of his precious rib, to whom he communicated Bull's conduct.   Madam, as usual, began to call the squire names; after which she abused poor Jonathan ; and finally, making a sudden turn, fell upon Beau Napperty, and scored him at such a rate, that if the poor Beau had heard her he would have been mad enough, I warrant you.

When she had talked herself into an unutterable rage, and for that reason held her tongue, Jonathan undertook to sound her about taking measures to bring old Squire Bull to reason.   He told her that he had tried all peaceable means to right himself, and had even gone to law, but all in vain ; and that things had now come to that pass, that he must either give up his right to sail boats on the mill-pond, or let his rowers defend themselves when they were molested by Bull, whom, with her permission, he intended to have a bout with very soon, provided he did not mend his manners.

He mentioned that he thought, with great submission, as both he and Squire Bull were rich fellows, and had been at grammar-school, it would not be becoming in them to fight rough-and-tumble like the tenants, but with sword and pistol like gentlemen. He therefore thought that, in case he challenged Bull,

as he supposed he should be obliged to do, he ought
to be decently dressed on the occasion. Now his
regimentals, which he wore when he was in the militia,
were all moth-eaten for want of use; and he wanted
a new sword and pistol, as well as a cocked-hat like
Beau Napperty's; for, as he was going to turn out
with so respectable a man as Squire Bull, he thought
he ought to look like a gentleman, and do credit to
his breeding.

For this purpose, as he was somewhat scant of
money, he thought, if madam pleased, he would
make bold to raise the rents of the tenants a little;
for poor Jonathan, by his marriage-articles, was de-
pendent on his wife for spending-money, and in fact
could do nothing without her consent. So completely
was he tied up, that, if any one tweaked his nose
or boxed his ears, he was obliged, before he could resent the insult, to go home and ask the consent of
his wife.

Women are noted for moderation in every thing,
more especially in using that power which, by the
articles of petticoat government, is ceded to them.
Thus it fared with Jonathan, who, though a fellow of
the greatest landed estate in that part of the world,
was forced to pinch himself continually in his little
expenses, and always was worse dressed on Sundays
and holidays than any of his neighbours, by reason
of his wife's being so stingy. Though, if the truth
must be told, she was an extravagant hussy herself,
and spent more in one week than Jonathan did in
a whole year. They had many squabbles about this,
but madam had the law on her side, and was always
backed by the tenants, because she had managed to

make them believe she was the best friend they had
in the world.

When Jonathan talked about raising the rents of
his tenants a little, that he might be in a condition to
fight John Bull, my lady, after a mighty deal of chattering and talking all round the compass as usual,
refused her consent, under pretence that the poor
tenants were already pressed down with such high
rents that they could hardly keep soul and body together in their skins. Then she pretended to be so
affected that she took out her handkerchief, and wiped
her eyes till they looked as red as if she had been
crying. All this she did to impose upon the tenants,
for she was afraid they would exercise their privilege
of divorcing her from Jonathan and choosing him
another wife, if she consented to raise their rents.

She however told Jonathan, that if he could borrow
the money from the tenants, she would join in security with him, and take care that the interest should
be paid. Jonathan liked this method of getting the
money well enough; for he knew that it came nearly
to the same thing as raising the rents, and that either
way it must come out of the tenants' pockets at last.

—◆—

CHAPTER XXI.

How Jonathan's rich tenants showed him the whites of their eyes when he
sent to borrow money, because he did not offer interest enough.

WHEN Jonathan sent round to his rich tenants to
see if he could borrow a few thousands, offering to

pledge his farms for the payment, it was curious to hear the excuses they made. One had just before used all his ready money in the purchase of stock for his farm, and another had just lent it out on mortgage. A third had the day before parted with all the cash he could scrape together, to help a friend in great distress: but the truth was, he had put it in the hands of a shaver, as they call such chaps, down at one of the great landings, who had placed it out at two per cent. a month. All, however, lamented that Jonathan had not sent a little sooner, as they would rather trust him than any other man in the world.

But the most curious thing of all was the ungrateful conduct of the *boatmen*, for whose sake in a great measure Jonathan was about to quarrel with his old father. They, forsooth, had for a long while back disliked Jonathan's manners; they saw he was no friend of theirs, but always was doing them an ill turn whenever it lay in his power; they knew well enough this quarrel was all Beau Napperty's doing, and as for John Bull, though he did to be sure meddle with their boats, and tweak their noses as often as he caught them squinting towards Frogmore, yet for all that he was an honest fellow; and therefore they could not think of lending money to enable Jonathan to trouble him now in his old age. People, however, saw through these pretences, and were well enough convinced, that although a great many of them did really hate Jonathan and love John, yet that this was not the real cause of their refusing to lend their money. The truth was, Jonathan offered too low an interest: if he had given them two or three per cent. more, he might have got all they had in the world.

After all these excuses, Jonathan somehow or other got money enough to put himself in some sort of decent trim, and being now thoroughly angry at Bull, who continued to wrong and insult him wherever he went, he determined immediately to send him a challenge, provided his wife would consent.

In order to bring the good lady round, knowing all women are naturally fond of a soldier, he forthwith brushed up an old suit of regimentals which had lain at the bottom of a trunk for several years, and purchased an amazing long, rusty sword, with a hilt as large as a bushel-basket; item, a worm-eaten cartridge-box, which had been carried in time immemorial by a Hessian corporal, and used for the stowage of his pipe, his tobacco-pouch, and his Sunday whiskers. Finally, he bought one of those cocked-hats usually called seventy-sixers, from having been in fashion about the time of the Declaration of Independence. It was shaped somewhat like the iron part of a pickaxe, and from some appearances which it exhibited in the inside, where the lining was a little torn, you could tell, with a tolerable degree of certainty, that in its primitive institution it had been black.

Then did he clap on with a little paste a huge pair of black whiskers that nearly covered his whole muzzle, and, drawing on his military boots that sat as tight as his skin because he had outgrown them as he did every thing else, strutted towards the apartment where his lady usually spent her mornings. Almost the first step he made, he tumbled on his nose, by reason of his great sword getting betwixt his legs, as is usual with raw recruits. Upon this, he thought it best to lay aside his sword for the present; so he hung it up carefully, and proceeded without it toward his wife's *scolding-room*, as it was called, from its being the place she usually retired to in order to vent her eloquence.

When she saw Jonathan thus equipped, she began to laugh as if she had the hysterics, and wondered what had got into the man. Jonathan was a little nettled at this, for he expected to be hugely admired for his warlike appearance. He forthwith, without any roundabout, asked her once for all whether she would consent to his sending Bull a challenge?

Madam answered as follows:

" *You* challenge Squire Bull, you miserable milk-and-water, lath-and-plaster manikin! You, that have never handled a pistol in your whole life, and whose sword is so rusty that you can't draw it out of the scabbard for the soul of you! Only look at the fellow," continued she, turning him round and round, in a jeering way — " only look at him! Look at that gallant cocked-hat, with a little feather in it that looks for all the world like a paint-brush — and those whiskers! Heaven preserve us! why thou lookest like a very fiend in the flesh."

Then, changing her tone, she began to rate him after this fashion: —

" Tell me, thou heart of cork, soul of a half-starved tailor, and brain of potcheese, what will you do when Bull sends his boats over to plunder your farms, burn your barns and houses, and drive your boats high and dry ashore? I warrant you'll cut a great dash with that clumsy figure of yours, that huge mass of meat without any bone or sinew. Get about thy business,

I say, Jonathan — put on your every-day suit of home-spun, and don't let me hear any thing more about your challenging Squire Bull."

Any man but Jonathan would have gone near to turn her out of the house for this; but Jonathan had a better way of managing matters, and knew, by long experience, how to deal with his precious rib. He knew there were certain arguments which, when properly urged, no wife can resist. So he went and cautiously *locked the doors,** and closed the shutters in the most careful manner. What method he pursued afterward I, being a bachelor and ignorant of these matters, cannot tell. All I know is, that the effect was truly wonderful. The tender pair came forth perfectly reconciled; the lady, hanging on Jonathan's arm in the most loving manner, and chucking him under the chin, declared he was a right valiant swordsman, and might fight with Bull when he pleased.

CHAPTER XXII.

How Jonathan sent John Bull a great challenge; and how some of Jonathan's overseers put up their sneakers, and wouldn't toe the mark.

JONATHAN, having at last persuaded his wife to let him have a bout with John Bull, gathered himself together, and wrote the squire a mortal defiance; in which, though he did not call him a rascal outright,

* The declaration of war by Congress was passed with closed doors. 1885.

he pretty plainly let him see he thought him one. He told how Bull had for a long time been trespassing on his property; how he had often thrown stones at his boats, and kidnapped his boatmen; how he had taken away his boats over to Bullock manor, where he sold them as his own property, and put the money in his pockets, which was being no better than a pirate; how he, Jonathan, had tried first to reason with him, and finding that would not do, had gone to law for damages — but he might as well have gone to the d—l for justice, seeing that scurvy fellow, Justice Scout, would do any thing John told him, and say black was white any time. He broke off by saying, that since all Christian means had failed him, and things had now come to such a pass that he must either give up his right to the use of the mill-pond or defend it with might and main, he gave Bull fair notice that he and his tenants meant, thenceforward, to try what the great statute of club-law would do for them. Let Squire Bull then come out like a man, and fight him in fair battle if he dared. Then giving notice to his tenants, and especially his boatmen and rowers, to keep a sharp look-out, and not let John's tenants insult them any more without having a bout with them, he forthwith equipped him for his encounter with Bull, who he expected would be at him in a hurry.

I ought to have told you, but it slipped my memory, that Bull and Brother Jonathan being both independent freeholders, and among the quality of the neighbourhood, did hold themselves pretty high fellows abroad, though at home they were both most villanously hen-pecked. They therefore took great state upon themselves; and whenever they went out to fight, used to have their overseers and a great many of their tenants to keep them in countenance and see fair play; or, in plain English, though they had no quarrel, to break each other's heads in imitation of their betters.

Jonathan, expecting that Bull as soon as he got his letter would be down upon him like a house afire, forthwith put on his *red breeches*, buckled on his great rusty sword which was more like a scythe than any thing else, stuck a pair of mighty horse-pistols into his waistband, and took the field with a bloody intention of either sending the squire to kingdom-come, or of drubbing him into a glimpse of his senses at least. Those who remember Jonathan in his fighting trim, say that such another queer boy was not to be seen every day. He swaggered along with his toes in instead of out — was forced to chalk his feet to tell right from left — put his pickaxe hat on hind-part before, and tumbled plump on his nose ten times a day, by reason of his great toasting-iron getting between his legs in spite of his teeth. Yet, for all this, when he drew his sword, which he did with a good deal of tugging because it was so rusty, and began to flourish it over his head, there was something in his manner and a fire in his eye, that made everybody that saw him say he would be a tough morsel for old Squire Bull.

Jonathan, that he might appear in the field as became one of his estate, sent round to his *overseers* in the different farms, to put on their training-suits and come to him. A great many of these sordid fellows, who had before pretended a great friendship for him, instead of setting forth at once, went to work very busily rummaging old parchments, to see whether by the tenure of their farms they were obliged to attend on Jonathan. Others were so frightened at the very thought of looking the sturdy John Bull, who was a sort of scarecrow, in the face, that they shook like quicksilver, and began to say their prayers as loud as they could halloo. Others had the impudence to send him word, that though in truth they must say he had reason enough to fight Bull, yet being such a young lad, as it were, they thought he was a great fool; and as when one man is not a full match for another, the weaker he is the better for his bones, they would leave him to himself, in hopes he would come to his senses the sooner. They also told him they were the best friends he had in the world, and would prove it whenever he did just as they pleased and did not want their assistance.* Others, who were fellows after my own heart, turned out at once with a full intention to stand or fall with honest Jonathan, right or wrong. They were not such shilly-shally rogues as to stop to inquire who had the best of the dispute, but, like honest blades, decided at once to fight first, and inquire into the right and the wrong of the matter when they were at leisure.

* The course taken by the governors of the New England States, and the complexion of their public documents, during the war of 1812, were standing subjects of attack and ridicule on the part of the patriotic wits of the day.

CHAPTER XXIII.

Of the behaviour of the tenants when they heard what Jonathan had done;
and how the boatmen grumbled at him for doing what they had wanted
him to do a long time before, as they put forth.

WHEN the tenants got news of Jonathan's having
defied Squire Bull, though they had for a long time
been calling him a sneak for putting up with John's
insults, yet did they now fall into notable disputes,
and many of them sing to another tune.   They
stopped from their labour to argue in the fields, and
left their farms at sixes and sevens to go to the taverns
and beer-houses, and get at the why and wherefore of
the matter.   It was a rare sight to see these fellows
with a sling or a glass of grog before them, one looking wiser than the other, and giving it as his opinion
that Jonathan ought to have quarrelled with Beau
Napperty as well as Squire Bull, because that would
have shown, as clear as preaching, that he had no im-
proper liking to the Beau.   Another would make bold
to say, he ought to have had a tiff with Beau Napperty, and let Squire Bull alone; because as how the
squire was, as a body might say, as innocent as sweet
milk.   A third was morally certain that Jonathan
ought to have stood with his hands in his pockets
like a wise man, and not minded what such low
fellows said or did to him.

There was no end to the talk about this affair, and
everywhere at the taverns, blacksmiths' shops, and on
Sundays at the church-doors, you might see fellows
who would point out two ways, directly opposite to
each other, either of which Jonathan might have trav-

elled with perfect safety. Nay, such was the singular improvement which suddenly came upon people's minds, that miserable varlets might be seen, who, though they did not know that potatoes ought to be planted in the waxing of the moon, nor when it was harvest-time except by the almanac, did all at once grow so knowing, that they got to know Jonathan's affairs better than he did himself.

But the *boatmen* beat all the other tenants hollow in their talk about Jonathan. As they sat sunning themselves along the shores of the mill-pond, and beheld their boats lying useless on the beach, with their seams wide open so that you could put your fingers in them, they used to get so angry that they hardly knew what to do with themselves, or whom to lay the blame upon. At length, with one voice, they cried out that it was all Jonathan's fault; and some of the most enlightened boatmen, who could take lunar observations, and tell which way the wind blew by only looking at the compass, proved it after this manner: —

In the first place, Jonathan had no business to get so great with Beau Napperty; for that he was very great with him was so plain, that nobody ever thought of giving a single good reason for believing it. A man, to be sure, has a right to choose his friends; that is, all men except your landlords, who have no business to like anybody that Squire Bull dislikes. Then Jonathan was to blame — because, in the first place, he did not resent Bull's insults, and take better care of their boats; and he was still more to blame for refusing to be on good terms with Bull, who was one of the best boatmen in the world. Lastly, it was all Jonathan's fault — because, in the first place, he did not challenge Bull long before; and, in the second place, he challenged him at last.

This strange talk they got from some knowing school-masters, who had learned their logic out of Dilworth's spelling-book; or, mayhap, out of Noah Webster's, which we all have heard of. These fellows neglected their schools, left the doors wide open, and went about among the tenants, trying to convince them that all their troubles and difficulties arose from Jonathan's great liking for Beau Napperty, and his unnatural dislike to being tweaked by the nose, even by his own father. The tenants of these parts, as I said before, are a *'cute* set, who know how to read and write, raise onions, and *swap* horses. They therefore believed all this to be gospel, especially when the parson of the parish of *Oniono* set to work and preached a long sermon, in which, instead of telling them of the excellence of the Christian religion, the beauty of holiness, and the necessity of doing good, he blazed forth, and told them that Jonathan and all his friends were such a herd of wicked rogues, that so far from having any chance of getting to heaven, they were not fit to live upon earth; advising them, at the same time, to keep the ten commandments, and hate neighbour Jonathan like good Christians.* This sermon had great effect on the tenants; though there were not a few people that liked Jonathan as little as the parson did, who thought that a man whose *oath of consecration* obliged him to be the advocate of

* The general allusion is to the acrid political sermons of the preachers of New England — the particular one perhaps a play upon the name of the Rev. Elijah Parish, D.D., of Byfield in Massachusetts, who was extremely bitter in his discourses.

charity and brotherly love, did little credit to his sacred function when he made use of that influence which his station gave him, for the purpose of sowing ill-will and dissensions among his flock.

But the tenants who, as was generally the case, made the most rout when they heard of Brother Jonathan's having challenged John Bull, were those of a little island * the name of which I don't choose to remember; a trifling barren place, that Jonathan had bought of an old Indian for fifty fathom of white beads. One would have thought, to hear them talk, that they were to fight Jonathan's battle, and pay the piper, all alone by themselves. They threatened to take the farm away from Jonathan, though in fact it was such a mean spot of ground, and paid so little rent, that he would hardly have missed it.

I have for the most part found, that the more diminutive the man, the more fractious and irritable he will be. A dwarf of four feet high will fly into a fury at what a well-grown person, conscious of the dignity and strength of manhood, would pass by without notice. Moreover, to reduce the comparison to some sort of level with the subject, you will always find that a little shaggy lap-dog, a pug, or a half-blind puppy, will grin and yelp, and tear about this way and that, in a great passion, if you point your finger at him; whereas an honest mastiff will be pleased at this mark of your attention. This irritability in small animals arises, I think, from their being weak, and knowing that they are so; they make a great show and noise to disguise their fears and their weakness,

* Rhode Island was factious during the war, and one of the three states that sent delegates to the Hartford Convention, in December, 1814.

and it is doubtless owing to this cause that the little farm of the nameless island was so fractious and noisy.

The people in the great farms of the Middlelands mostly agreed to stand by Jonathan. Some of them, indeed, shrugged up their shoulders and looked wise; but they thought it would be a mean trick to leave their landlord in the lurch. I must do the tenants of Middlelands the justice to say, that they were among the best tenants Jonathan had, being a set of honest, sober, hard-working fellows, who were well-to-do in the world, and did not fly into a passion, as your poor knaves do, when Jonathan happened to pass them without pulling off his hat and asking after the health of their brats, and how times went with them.

A good many of these tenants of Middlelands thought Jonathan had been a little too hasty; but what of that? Under his mild protection they had been a hundred times better off than Bull's or Beau Napperty's people, and they held it a slippery trick to desert him, now he was going to loggerheads with such a mortal stout fellow as John Bull.

CHAPTER XXIV.

How John Bull was a little stumped when he saw Jonathan's challenge, and how the old fellow got the blue devils outright when his boats were beat by Jonathan's.

WHEN Squire Bull got Brother Jonathan's challenge, he was more astonished than he had been in a great while. He was so used to put upon Jonathan, that he had come at last to think he might insult him whenever he pleased. His hangers-on, too, had all along told him he might do just as he liked, for Jonathan was so horribly afraid of him he would never bring himself to resent it, because he was the greatest skulker in all the neighbourhood. John sent word to his wife, who had gone to the CHAPEL* not to pray but to talk, letting her know what had turned up. Mrs. Bull, who had a mighty dislike to poor Jonathan, was exceedingly tickled at the news, and forthwith drew hard upon the tenants for money to furnish sails and oars for John's boats. The tenants, who because they had chosen this wife of Bull's to take care of their interests at the manor house took it for granted she did so, launched out their money, though with many wry faces, for Bull had half a dozen quarrels on his hands already, and they thought a reasonable man might be satisfied with them.

The squire having by far the most boats, resolved, in the first place, before he went over to meet Jonathan, whom he swore he would make daylight shine through, to scour the mill-pond, and get a sweep at Jonathan's boats. Jonathan, who was a pretty keen lad, suspected this would be the way, and sent out some of his best boats with orders that the hardest should fend off, as the rowers say. The first thing Bull heard was, that several of his boats, on trying to seize Jonathan's, had got most bitterly bethumped. This he swore was all a lie; but some of his rowers, coming home with black eyes and broken heads, put the story out of doubt, whereupon John fell into a fit of the blue-devils, to which he was very subject. At

* St. Stephen's Chapel, where the English parliaments sit. 1835.

first he moped and moped about the house, with his hands in his breeches-pockets, and would stop for a whole hour and look at the fire, as if he didn't know where he was; so that it was feared he would tuck himself up some rainy day, that being a sort of family complaint. Well, this lasted some days, and then he grew as sour as vinegar, growled like a bear, and threatened to kick all his overseers into the mill-pond. He swore he would look into this matter himself, to see what was the reason of it all.

" If I can only find out the reason, and all that sort of thing," quoth John, " I shall be easy. But I must be pacified with a good reason, or dam'me I'll know the reason why." The overseers and hangers-on began to shake in their shoes at this, and saw that they would be turned out of doors neck and heels if they did not lay the maggot in the squire's head with a good reason. So they sent an old carpenter to tell John, that Jonathan's boats were at least six inches longer, and three inches broader than his, therefore they might well get the better of them.

Finding this made a great impression on John, they followed it up, and swore that Jonathan's boats were not only larger, but had more rowers, and, what was worse, most of these rowers were his own tenants, who, though the most faithful fellows in the world, and very much attached to him, were always running away when they could get a chance. It was no wonder, then, that he should be beat with his own cudgel. This exposition put the squire to a nonplus, and bothered his brain more than any thing he had ever heard. He took his ivory-headed cane, to which he always applied in cases of great puzzle, and, putting it to his nose, pondered in this way. "If my boats are handled in this manner by my own rowers, and all that sort of thing, how comes it to pass they fight so much better for Jonathan than for me?" This was getting between two stone walls, out of which John could not budge for the soul of him. So the squire placed himself in his arm-chair, called for a pot of strong beer, and pursued his subject till he fell fast asleep. When he woke up, they palavered him with a story of a great rising of Beau Napperty's tenants, stuck up a parcel of candles in his windows, gave the boys crackers to set off to please him, and thus tickled the old fellow into the best humour in the world. The rogues then laughed in their sleeves as usual, and one of them told the others in a whisper, "Only throw Johnny a tub, and, like a whale, he'll play with it till the boat is out of sight."

CHAPTER XXV.

How Squire Bull, finding Jonathan rather a hard character to deal with, offered to make up with him, and let matters remain just as they were.

I HAVE generally observed that people get nothing by fighting, but black eyes, bloody noses, and the reputation of having more pluck than brains. So it happened with Squire Bull, who, after putting himself to great expense to have a bout with Jonathan, and keep up the reputation of being the best boatman on the great mill-pond, got nothing for his pains, and ended about where he began, only that his

pockets were more empty, and he carried a few additional scars on his pate. Jonathan, on the contrary,
if he gained nothing else, got the respect of the neighbours, who used to call him a snivelling poltroon;
and even Squire Bull, who, being a brave old codger
himself, could not help admiring courage in others,
although he contrived to prate against him in other
matters, could not help now and then grumbling out,
" Plague take the rebellious dog; he has got some of
my stuff in him, and I have a great mind to own him
for my son again."   Many people said the old squire
would have made friends with him in good earnest, if
Jonathan, (who, like his father, was somewhat given
to bragging), had not every now and then thrown it
into his teeth that he had given him some good sound
drubbings.   This made John as mad as a hornet, for
he was as proud as Lucifer, and always called himself lord of the mill-pond.

Nevertheless, the squire would sometimes take it
into his head to say a good word or two about Jonathan, especially when it was his cue to tickle him a
little; and Master Canynge, who had quizzed him
about his fir-built boats and striped-bunting flags, on
one occasion actually drank a toast, in which he
called Mrs. Bull and Mrs. Jonathan the " Mother and
daughter."   Brother Jonathan was mightily taken
with this, and thought, now that Bull was in such a
good humour he would get him to sign a paper giving up the claim to the mill-pond, and to the right of
taking away his boatmen.   When Bull received this
application, he tipped Master Canynge the wink, as
much as to say — " What a greenhorn is my son Jonathan, not to know the difference between a civil speech

and a civil action!" He ordered Master Canynge to write a long letter to Jonathan, saying that though he had the highest respect for him he would see him hanged before he would give him any proof of it. Jonathan replied in a letter twice as long; and so they continued writing mighty civil notes, all beginning with denying each other's claims, and ending, like a challenge, with "your most obedient servant." It was enough to make you die of laughing to see how they tried to get to windward of each other. But it was diamond cut diamond; the squire was as sharp as one of his own razors, and as for Jonathan, he never made a bad bargain in his life, not even when he married.

Thus they continued to keep up the show, without much of the substance, of friendship; for the truth is, that Jonathan was so like his daddy that the old squire could never forgive him.

———◆———

CHAPTER XXVI.

How Squire Bull, with all his pretensions to good fellowship, has a fling at Brother Jonathan now and then.

HAVING no partialities for, or prejudices against, either Bull or Brother Jonathan, I have, through the whole course of this history, endeavoured to do justice to both father and son, without excusing the faults or puffing up the merits of either. But I must say that Jonathan had all along too good cause of complaint against the old man, and that after their

last set-to, the squire did not altogether behave himself like a good neighbour. The truth is, he was, like
most gouty old fellows who have held up their heads
a long while and taken great airs on themselves, not a
little jealous when he saw Jonathan treading close on
his heels, and outdoing him in many things he most
valued himself upon. In particular, Jonathan's skill
in building and sailing boats was a great eyesore to
Bull, for that was his weak side, and if you only
pointed your finger at it the old man felt it right in
the short ribs.

The squire was somewhat tired and disgusted, as
he said, with open and above-board fighting of Jonathan, who, he swore, did not understand the art of
boxing like a gentleman ; and, instead of standing off
and milling in a scientific style, would run in upon
him, and trip up his heels contrary to all rules. Now
when a man cherishes a certain degree of ill-will for
another, and does not choose to fight it out, it will
generally be found that he makes himself amends by
talking against him on all occasions, raising evil
reports, and making him out no better than he should
be.

So it was with the squire, who — when certain evil-
disposed people, who knew John's weak side, would
come over and smoke a pipe and drink beer with him,
and tell the old man how Jonathan's farms were
growing every day bigger and bigger and increasing
in number so that they amounted to almost double of
what they once were; and how he carried on a great
trade with the neighbours; and how his tenants were
the happiest and most prosperous fellows in the world
— who, I say, when he had taken these and other

doses of wormwood and tansy, would puff out huge volumes of smoke, fidget about in his big chair, and cry out in a great passion, " S'blood and fury, neighbours, what do I care for all this? Did I not beget him? Did he not learn all he knows, and more besides, from me; and is he not a slack-breeched, saucy, guessing, bragging, lying, cheating rascal, though he is my son, and they say looks as much like me as two peas? "

When Jonathan, as he was pretty sure to do, heard all this, he would get into a pretty considerable of a passion himself, and scold back again as hard as he could pelt. This was carried to the squire's ears in good time, and set his tongue going faster than ever, to the tune of the bitterest swearing you ever heard. It was an unseemly thing to hear father and son abusing and calling one another names in this way; but I must say it was in a great measure the squire's fault. He began first, and continued longest; so that if ever a son had reason to complain of his father, it was poor Jonathan, who, while he was doing all he could to establish a good name in the neighbourhood, found that John's backbitings and ill-natured remarks were continually setting people against him, and getting him into hot water. I have heard say the poison of calumny cannot be cured, even by the balsam of good actions, and Jonathan found it so to his cost.

CHAPTER XXVII.

How Squire Bull's tenants began to give up their leases, and go over to settle on Jonathan's farms.

THOUGH the tenants of Squire Bull were a set of hard-working, industrious fellows, yet Bull, who had the reputation of screwing them rather tight, from time to time raised their rents, and under pretence of building churches, paying the parson, asserting the rights of the manor, and keeping up his own dignity, kept them as poor as Job's turkey, that I have heard could not eat for bones. People in general, though ever so reasonable and judicious, don't like to part with their lawful earnings, and it is no easy matter to reconcile them to having their pockets picked by bailiffs and tax-gatherers, even though it may be according to law.

This was the case with John's tenants, who cast many a sheep's-eye over the great mill-pond toward Jonathan's farms, of which they heard such things as fairly made their mouths water. They longed to go over there; and, whenever they could get a good chance, packed up bag and baggage, wife and children, and took French leave of their crusty old landlord, without asking his permission, or bidding him so much as good-by. By this means some of his best farms lost their best tenants; and instead of having a set of jolly fellows as he once had, who could afford a little fun to themselves sometimes, he found himself troubled with whole swarms of them, who, instead of paying their rents, were obliged to come upon the parish, or labour in his workshops, which everybody said was worse than being a negro.

Though this was the natural consequence of land's being so cheap and rents' being so low in Jonathan's farms, and of a certain free and easy disposition on the part of that honest fellow, yet did Squire Bull somehow or other get it into his wise pate, that as Jonathan had seduced his boatmen away in the last squabble they had, he was now seducing his tenants in the same unneighbourly manner. He did not, or would not, see, what was as plain as the nose on his face, that this seduction arose from nothing but those good things which men run after whenever they can get a chance. Be this as it may, he called Jonathan such a grist of hard names as would make your hair stand on end to hear.

Then he went among his tenants, and, after telling them that they were the happiest tenants and he the very best landlord in the whole neighbourhood, began to cut at Brother Jonathan at a fine rate.

"My honest lads," quoth he, putting on a mighty big look, "did not your fathers, your grandfathers, your great-grandfathers, and your great-great-grand-fathers, live and flourish under me and my fathers from time immemorial, and eat roast-beef and plum-pudding" — here the mouths of the poor fellows began to weep actual tears — "I say roast-beef and plum-pudding, boys, besides stout ale and porter?"

"But, alas!" said the tenants, "we can't get any now, and are fain to live on bread and cheese."

"And suppose you are," answered the squire, waxing wroth — "suppose you are, you stupid block-heads; did not your ancestors live and flourish under

my family time out of mind, and will you be so ungrateful as to refuse to put up with a little moderate
hunger for the honour of your forefathers and mine?
Body o' me! but I see you have been seduced by that
sapskull son Jonathan, and his confounded Yankee
notions. So you won't starve at home upon scientific
principles, you ungrateful villains, hey?"

To which the tenants replied, "It is true, our forefathers have been comfortable as the tenants of your
family; but, as their children cannot be comfortable
any longer, we think we had better try somewhere
else.   We can't live on the roast-beef and plum-pudding of our ancestors."

" No!" cried the squire, his eyes almost starting
out of his head — " Not live on the roast-beef and
plum-pudding of your ancestors, you grovelling, low-
lived scum of democracy — poor fellows without
souls, that think only of your bodies! Yes, yes, I see
how it is — I see how it is, that rebellious rascal Jonathan has been seducing you. Why, you great oafs,
don't you know that the poorest d—l on Jonathan's
farms can vote at town-meetings and elections; and
that high and low, rich and poor, are all equal on Jonathan's farms? Would you live among such a mean,
plebeian set of fellows, not one of whom can carry
his head higher than his neighbour? Answer me
that, you great blockheads."

" That is exactly what we should like," replied these
honest fellows: " we are quite tired of seeing people
hold their heads so much higher than ourselves; and,
above all things, desire to have a voice at town-
meetings and elections."

Squire Bull found he had got on a snag, as they

say in the Far West farms, and tacked about as fast as he could.

" But, my honest fellows," said he, coaxingly, " don't you know that the very poorest of you, if he is wise enough, can, if he has good luck, come to be a justice of the peace, or even high-constable, in that scurvy fellow my son Brother Jonathan's farms? Would you live in a place where such low fellows get into office ? "

" We should like it of all things," said the poor tenants; " we are tired of magistrates that have no fellow-feeling with ourselves."

The squire this time ran against a sawyer, and once more changed his tune.

" But, my dear friends, don't you know that liquor and every thing else is so plenty and cheap on Jonathan's farms, that a man can get a dinner and get fuddled besides for a shilling? Would you leave your old landlord, who only keeps you on short commons for your own good, to indulge in doing as you please, and drinking as much as you like ? "

" What a glorious place ! " cried the tenants, one and all. " Let us be off as soon as possible ! "

So away they went to buy boats to carry them over to Jonathan's farms, leaving the squire to wonder with all his might, that what was so extremely disagreeable to the landlord should be so very agreeable to the tenants. He found this to be so outrageously unreasonable, that he called the poor fellows a set of ungrateful rascals, and Jonathan a rebellious son of a tinker. He cudgelled his brains for a whole week, and at length hit on a most capital way of being even with Jonathan for seducing his tenants, giving them plenty of land at a small rent, and allowing them to vote at elections.

———•———

CHAPTER XXVIII.

Of the way Squire Bull took to be even with Brother Jonathan.

JOHN BULL had a long time ago set up a good number of schools on Bullock Island, for the teaching of Greek, Latin, and other light matters, to the sons of the better sort of tenants, insomuch that some of them, it is said, came at last to tell the difference between a B and a bull's foot in Greek and Latin: whereat the squire grew as vain as a turkey-cock, and swore he had scholars among his tenants that could twist any man of their inches in all the neighbourhood.

There were besides, among them, fellows that wrote books, such as almanacs, cock-and-bull stories, and the like; and, to give every one his due, here and there a wiseacre, who knew about every thing. Some of these could explain the cause of earthquakes and burning mountains; others could tell, within a foot, the size of a star, that could not be seen without spectacles; others could prove that black was the white of your eye, provided nobody contradicted them; others could demonstrate that the moon was made of green cheese, and others tell what was inside of your head by only feeling the outside. In short, there was no end to the scholarship of Squire Bull's tenants, one out of ten of whom could almost read and write.

Now John, after having convinced his stupid tenants aforesaid of the propriety of running away to Jonathan's farms, thought to himself he would be even with him for seducing them. He determined, like the devout Quaker, not to smite him, but to give him a bad name. So, not content with abusing him by word of mouth, which he failed not to do ten times a day, John went to work, and got his great scholars to write libels against the worthy fellow, which he had posted up against the doors of churches and taverns, and repeated by the crier at all public places. " Body o' me!" quoth he, " but I'll pepper him till he is black in the face, that's what I will. I begat him, and have a right to abuse the rascal as much as I please."

These poor rogues of scribblers that John hired were glad enough to earn a liberal penny in this way, seeing they were sometimes pretty hard run for a dinner; and it was a saying among them, that, " a man must eat though he lies for it." Accordingly, they set to work to earn an honest livelihood by belabouring unlucky Jonathan pretty handsomely, as we shall see.

CHAPTER XXIX.

How one Farmer Parkinson undertook to prove that Brother Jonathan was no great farmer.

THE first fellow, I believe, that undertook to score Jonathan, was one Farmer Parkinson, who, having ruined himself by farming on Bullock Island, went over to the West farms, to show them how to manage their affairs in that quarter. But Jonathan's people had a way of their own, which they did not choose to unlearn all at once, especially as Master Parkinson did not prosper in *his* way, as they had heard. Friend Parkinson went all about among Jonathan's farms, finding fault with every thing; running down their fences; abusing their ploughs, oxen, horses, and what not; and predicting their utter ruin if they did not turn over a new leaf and learn a lesson of him. But they only tipped each other the wink, as much as to say, " the proof of the pudding is in the eating." A broken-down farmer is not the best hand in the world to teach his grandmother how to suck eggs, I guess.

So Farmer Parkinson went back to Bullock Island, and wrote an advertisement which was put up everywhere, saying that Brother Jonathan was no farmer, and as ignorant as one of his horses. The squire was tickled to death at this, and went about telling· his tenants what Farmer Parkinson had written. But they only scratched their heads, and wondered that Jonathan's tenants should grow so rich, seeing they knew nothing about farming.

CHAPTER XXX.

How Lawyer Janson * tried his hand at a fling at Brother Jonathan.

THE next fellow John hired to come over to Jonathan's farms to pick holes in his jacket, was one Lawyer Janson, who, I have heard say, never took fees from both clients, because he could not get any clients to take them from. He was, however, reckoned rather an eminent practitioner, and belonged, I believe, to that class called pettifoggers, which, reversing the order of precedence, is the highest of all.

Lawyer Janson, not getting much practice in Bullock Island, one reason of which was that the law was so dear few people could afford to buy it, offered his services to go over the mill-pond, and find out a few more of Jonathan's peccadilloes. The squire accordingly put his hand in his breeches-pocket, where great people always carry their money, and gave him enough to pay his ferriage across the mill-pond, telling him he must wait for the rest till he came back again.

The lawyer settled himself in one of the farms Down East, as I have heard; where he soon reversed the order of nature, for, having no clients and getting into debt, he was taken the law of instead of taking the law of others. Whereupon he put in a new species of common-bail, that is to say, he gave leg-bail, and ran away like a brave fellow. I heard he was in such a hurry, and was so terribly scared, that he

---

* Charles William Janson, "late of the State of Rhode Island" resided in America from 1793 to 1806. He published in London, in 1807, the Stranger in America. 4to. — *Allibone's Dictionary of Authors.*

never looked behind him till he got somewhere away
off in the Southlands, where he stopped to take breath
and make memorandums of what he had seen. Being heartily disgusted with the farms and the tenants,
he went over again to Bullock Island, where he
posted up a great handbill, charging Brother Jonathan with knowing no more of law than some great
lawyers.

"Body o' me!" said Squire Bull to his tenants,
"what do you think of that, you great blockheads,
and be hanged to you?"

" Marry, there is no great harm in that," was their
reply; "a man may have too much of a good thing
—too much of law, and too much of lawyers."

Upon this John let fly his wig at them, and swore
no poor fellow ever had such a set of blockheads for
tenants as himself.

CHAPTER XXXI.

How there next came over a smart young sprig, who was reckoned a great
beau among Squire Bull's boatmen.

THERE was, among John's boatmen, a smart, pert,
idle, good-for-nothing young fellow. His parents not
knowing what to do with him, put him aboard of one
of the squire's boats to learn good manners, and, maybe, some day or other, get to be captain of one of
them. His name was De Roos* or De Goose, I forget which; and he boasted of coming of a good

* Probably F. F. De Roos, who published in London, Travels in the
United States and Canada in 1826. 8vo.

family, because he had a name beginning with a De, though, for my part, I can't tell why. This chap having been a long while sculling about in the mill-pond without getting to be any thing but a cabin-boy, thought he might perhaps get a little into Squire Bull's good graces, by taking a trip over to Jonathan's farms, and picking a few more holes in the poor lad's jacket.

De Goose, as I am pretty sure he was called, was, as I said, a mighty fine sort of a spark, a very old boy among the girls, so that when he came over they almost tittered their little eyes out at seeing such a pretty, nice fellow. He staid a whole night and almost a day in Brother Jonathan's farms, after which he went back to Bullock Island, and posted up a paper, in which he pledged his honour that Jonathan was no gentleman, for he kept company with his tenants, and admitted mechanics into his parlour.

" There, my boys! there!" cried John to his tenants; "what do you think of that, you stupid ninny-hammers ? "

" Not quite so bad, after all," said they; " there is no harm in landlords keeping company sometimes with their tenants, if it is only to get acquainted with their characters. And as for letting poor people come into his parlour, we should like that above all things."

Upon this they gave a great huzza for Brother Jonathan, and paddled over to his farms as fast as they could.

" What stupid dolts!" cried the squire, shaking his head; " they will never know what's good for them. But I must not forget my little De Goose."

Accordingly, in pure gratitude for taking so much pains to enlighten his tenants, he made him captain of one of his old ferry-boats.

—◆—

CHAPTER XXXII.

How Squire Bull sent over one Peter Porcupine to pry into Jonathan's private affairs.

JOHN had about him an old corporal, who went by the nickname of Peter Porcupine,* one of the most abusive fellows ever known. He was always back-biting the squire, who once or twice got out of patience and clapped him up in jail for his pains. But though the squire did not like to be clapperclawed himself by Peter, he knew by experience what a bitter boy he was at getting up a pack of lies, and for that reason he got him dressed up like a gentleman, and, putting some money in his pockets, sent him over to print handbills and paste them up under Jonathan's very nose.

Peter accordingly came over the mill-pond, and played away at a fine rate, saying just what he liked, and telling as many great lies as he could invent, for Jonathan was a good-natured fellow, and made it a point of conscience to let his own tenants say what they pleased of him. To be sure they sometimes scored him pretty handsomely, but there is a great difference between the freedoms of old acquaintances

---

* William Cobbett, among his multifarious works, published "A Year's Residence in America." The above was his *nom de plume.*

and strangers. Peter was a vulgar kind of a chap, and the greatest master of bad language that ever was known. He wrote a grammar on purpose to teach people how to abuse one another in good English. Mercy upon us! how he did belabour honest Jonathan, even before he knew the poor lad by sight. He called him all sorts of names, such as rogue, fool, hypocrite, blackguard, ignoramus, negro-driver, and what not. Taking advantage of Jonathan's easy temper, he went so far as to swear he had no right to his own property, and tried to persuade the tenants to go over in a body to Squire Bull, who he said would make them as happy as the day was long, and happier too.

This was urging the joke rather too far, and at last Jonathan got his back up. He brought his action of slander against the old corporal, and cast him in swingeing damages,* which he found rather hard to pay, though he had made a good deal of money out of Jonathan's tenants, who always pay well for seeing themselves handsomely abused in black and white. Upon this the corporal had his house painted black all over, and, after throwing " a bone " for the democrats " to gnaw," he packed himself off home again, to tell John all about it.

The old squire hereupon called a good many of his tenants around him, and addressed them as follows : —

" My honest fellows ! you hear what the old cor-

---

* William Cobbett. 1762-1835. In 1796 he settled in Philadelphia, and, establishing Peter Porcupine's Gazette, took a lively interest in the political questions of the day. His intemperance in controversy provoked suits for slander by Dr. Rush and others, and the satirist was fined the sum of five thousand dollars. — *Allibone's Dictionary of Authors.*

poral says about Jonathan, and all that sort of thing. How happy you are, you great blockheads, if you did but know it. Yet you are always hankering after that snivelling fellow's farms, though he lets his tenants do almost just what they please, so that they are pretty much their own masters, and get so rich in a few years that they are able to buy Jonathan out of some of his best lands. A fine place, truly, for a gentleman to live in, hey!, you stupid rascals!"

"Not so fine for a gentleman," quoth the tenants, "but very fine for us." So they shouted huzza for Brother Jonathan, and bundled themselves off to the farms as fast as they could.

John scratched his pate, and whistled his old tune of "God save the king," which he always did when out of sorts; and turning to Peter, began calling him a great fool for abusing Jonathan for the very things that made all his tenants fall in love with the young rascal, and run after him as if they were mad. He refused to do any thing for the old corporal, who, out of pure spite to John, began to praise Jonathan with all his might, and abuse his old daddy. He swore the squire's tenants were a set of "flogged" rogues, for which John had him clapped up in jail; for, being lord of the manor of Bullock, his will was pretty much law in these cases.

"Stay there," quoth the squire, "till you learn good manners, and leave off telling lies." But he might have staid there till doomsday before that happened.

CHAPTER XXXIII.

How Squire Bull sent over one Captain All,* who, it was said, could write better tban fight, to find out some more of Brother Jonathan's faults, and how the captain, being troubled with squinting, saw every thing crooked.

JOHN BULL, being somewhat out of patience at the unaccountable effect produced among his tenants by the great pains he had taken to enlighten them concerning Brother Jonathan and his bad habits, determined to pick out one of his cleverest fellows this time, to send over on a voyage of discovery. He accordingly found out an old tarpaulin of a fellow among his boatmen, who had sailed all round the mill-pond ever so many times, and made several great discoveries that nobody else had ever seen before or ever saw afterwards. By reason of having long been in the habit of keeping a regular log-book, the captain, as he was called on account of having once commanded a bumboat, was considered to write a very good hand, and, what was more, could spell like a school-master by the help of the dictionary.

There was no end to the tough stories he told about what he had seen and done in distant parts. He had bought ever so many fair winds of an old witch Down East; had caught one of the lights that sometimes are seen in a storm sticking to the ropes of a vessel, and used it to light his binnacle with; had been among the people that live right under us on the other side of the world, and walk with their heads down-

* Probably Captain Basil Hall. He published, in 1829, Travels in North America in 1827–28. 3 vols. post 8vo. — *Allibone's Dictionary of Authors.*

ward like flies against the ceiling; had seen a sea-serpent sixteen times as long as the one at Jonathan's farms Down East, and discovered a great island in an out-of-the-way part of the mill-pond called Loo-choo, where all the people were born without heads, and yet had the longest ears he ever saw, longer even than his own.   In fact, he was supposed by some to shoot with a long bow, and went among John's tenants by the name of old Quid the tough-yarn-spinner, he being a great chewer of tobacco.

But Squire Bull liked him the better for drawing a long bow, because, he thought to himself, the captain would not stick at trifles in a good cause.   According-ly he caused the captain to be dressed up like a gentleman, that he might the better impose on Jonathan and his tenants; put a great cocked-hat bediz-ened with copper-lace on his head; stuck a pair of tarnished epaulets on his shoulders with a couple of pins; and fastened a rusty sword at least two yards long to the waistband of his breeches.   He then gave him a hearty kick of the breech, in token of his ap-probation, and sent him away with plenty of letters of recommendation, setting forth in the most pomp-ous manner his great valour as an officer, and his great accomplishments as a gentleman.

Jonathan received this doughty fellow with all the respect due to his cocked-hat, his epaulets, his long sword, and his letters of recommendation; for he was one of the most hospitable lads in the world, and kept open house to all persons, especially strangers, high and low, rich and poor.   He feasted the captain to such a degree, and plied him so lustily with good liquor, that half the time the captain did not know whether he was not walking with his head downward, like the queer creatures he had seen on the other side of the earth. With this lusty fare he grew fat, and, like all low fellows, saucy, and began to believe himself a great officer, only because Jonathan treated him better than he deserved. Jonathan, moreover, gave him letters to all parts of his estate, recommending it to his tenants to make much of the distinguished stranger, as he called him, like a young gosling as he was.

The captain went all over Jonathan's farms, asking questions of everybody, and getting into a passion if anybody asked questions of him; poking his nose everywhere, prying into every one's business, and making memorandums in his log-book. Jonathan's tenants, who are in the main a cute set of fellows, often bantered him with all sorts of tough stories, which he would write down in his log-book; but little they thought that he was going to put them out as all gospel when he got home. The captain went grumbling his way from one end of Jonathan's farms to the other, collecting everything and nothing that fell in his path, and, after eating his way manfully through and through, at last sailed over the great mill-pond with his log-book.

There never was a man half so well pleased in this world, according to the best of my belief, as John Bull was when he put on his spectacles and read the captain's log-book, which certainly was the cleverest thing ever written since the travels of Baron Munchausen, who, I ought to have mentioned before, was the captain's grandfather by the mother's side, as I have heard. For a man that squinted so mortally, it was astonishing what correct views he had taken; and nothing was wanting to a proper understanding of the whole, but to make allowance for the captain's infirmity, and take things directly contrary to what he saw them. His pictures were, in fact, all turned up-sidedown, like the odd fellows he saw walking on their heads the other side of the world. Then the log-book was published at John's expense, as was pretty generally supposed, and everybody swore it was the most philosophical work that had ever been seen, only that the captain's conclusions were always at loggerheads with his premises, and his individual examples for ever opposed to his general inferences. But this I have always thought was owing to the captain's unlucky habit of squinting, which originated, as I have heard, in his always going out in the sun without a hat when he was a little boy and used to go wading along the edge of the mill-pond to catch tadpoles.

Be this as it may, John Bull was so tickled with the captain's log-book that he gave him a new uniform, and was casting about how he might further reward his eminent services, when he was taken all aback by some one coming in to tell him that another great parcel of his tenants had packed off, bag and baggage, to Jonathan's farms, being thereto sorely impelled by the captain's philosophical conclusions.

The squire was so bothered at this, that he sat down in his arm-chair and fell into a great brown-study: never was a poor gentleman so puzzled to account for a thing as plain as the nose on his face. If he had only put himself in the place of his tenants, he would have found out, soon enough, that the very things with which he twitted Brother Jonathan, were exactly what tickled them, and made them so anxious to hold lands under his son. All he had to do was to make them believe that Jonathan was just such a bitter old landlord as himself, and there would be no danger of his practicing any more seductions upon them.

But this never occurred to the squire, and he determined to try his hand at getting up another log-book, like a headstrong, obstinate old fellow, as he was.

———◆———

CHAPTER XXXIV.

How Squire Bull dressed up an ugly old trollop* as a lady, and sent her over to try her hand at opening the eyes of his stupid tenants.

THERE was an old woman, that, as I have been credibly informed, sold fish and mussels about the manor of Bullock. Owing to her carrying a d—l of a tongue in her head, and abusing everybody that tried to beat down her prices, she had gradually got rather low in the world. Whenever she came round with her alewives and gar-fish, the people would all shut their doors for fear of a lecture; so that the short and the long of the story is, she failed in business, and, it is said, paid her creditors only one ounce of fish in the pound. She was, however, a pert, smart sort of a body, had learned to read and write at a parish-school, and might have kept a school or some such thing if she had only been able to hold her

* Frances Trollope. Domestic Manners of the Americans. 2 vols. 12mo. London. 1832.

tongue a little.   They say she was once ducked for a
common scold, but I cannot pledge myself as to that
matter.

The squire, happening to have some recollection of
the old woman, having once been pretty well lectured.
by her in a bargain for a John Dory, thought to himself, as all his male missionaries had done him only
harm, he would try what a female could do. So he
sent for her to come to him, which she did in not one
of her best humours.   John who, as I said, knew her
of old, felt a little skittish when she came, with a
great old black calash on her head, a faded silk gown,
and divers other remnants of her ancient glories, which
she always wore on great occasions.

John undertook to let her into his plan in the most
delicate way he could think of; but, though there was
something in the thing that pleased the spiteful old
creature well enough, she began to rate him soundly,
on account of some old grudges not worth speaking
of in this place.

" Marry, come up, my doughty squire," cried she,
" you can be civil enough now you want me.   You
forget, I 'spose, when you rated me about that John
Dory, which, as I am a living sinner, was as fresh as
a spring morning, though you said its gills were as
blue as indigo.   Yes, yes; but I'll let you know I'm
not to be made a fool of: I'm not to be bamboozled,
befooled, and befiddled in this way, I can tell you.   I
am an honest woman, and I don't care who knows it.
You mustn't think to poke fun into me in this way,
that I can tell you." And she gradually raised her
voice till it squeaked like a fiddle, so that the squire
was fain to stuff his thumbs into his ears.

But they say hard squalls never last long, and this one blew over in a few minutes. The squire, albeit he would like to have had the old creature ducked, having a point to gain, held in his anger like a whole team, and locked the wheels of his tongue for fear it should run down hill and dash his project all to pieces. He coaxed her at last into a better humour, and, by promising her a new hat, a new poplin gown, and a whole bladder of snuff, at last brought her to consent to go over the mill-pond to Jonathan's farms, and look into the manners and customs of the good women there, and see wherein they were wanting in civility and refinement. At the same time, the sly rogue could not, for the soul of him, help laughing in his sleeve, to think what a fine judge of such matters was this old sinner, who, he had good reason to know, had never eaten out of any thing better than a wooden trencher in all her born days.

The old creature, after bargaining for a looking-glass that she might see herself in her new dress on the passage over the mill-pond, at length set sail, and in good time arrived at the mouth of a great creek that ran a good way up into Jonathan's farms in the Far West. There chanced to be in the boat that carried over Madame Trollope, as she was nicknamed, a young single lady, who, though she had several husbands, was never married, so far as I can learn. This young single-married-woman was going over to Jonathan's farms to civilize the people, and teach the women a proper regard to morals. Now, as Madame Trollope was going to set them an example in good manners, nothing was more natural than that these two should grow very intimate, and, as it were, join stocks together.

Accordingly, they patched up a great friendship, and agreed to prosecute their benevolent intentions toward the wives and daughters of Brother Jonathan's tenants in partnership. But the old creature's tongue was such an unruly member that she could not for the life of her keep it in order; so that, by the time they began to know one another tolerably well, a separation took place. The young unmarried woman with several husbands went her way to preach up her new system of morals, and the old creature to exercise her skill in polishing the manners of the rude women of Jonathan's farms, who knew nothing of the delights of flirtation, and were so ineffably vulgar that, it is currently said, they looked upon the marriage-vow as little less than a sacred obligation.

What became of the young woman I never heard, but the old one found her way up the long creek to one of Jonathan's new settlements, where she was received and treated with the greatest kindness, and for a time passed among the simple tenants for a lady. This settlement was what they call a new clearing, inhabited by people of plain homely habits, but withal of great industry and enterprise, and gifted with a tolerable portion of good sense as well as sagacity. They had a new country to clear and cultivate, and possessed all the good qualities so generally found among an industrious population of farmers. They did not understand the frisky airs Madame Trollope gave herself, nor could they be brought to giving up reading the Bible and going to church, which the old creature said was what made them so mighty stupid about understanding the true intent and meaning of the marriage-vow.

But this was not the worst: the men actually spit against the wind; ate their dinners in a great hurry, I suppose because they had something to do afterward; and sometimes, instead of drinking wine at the dinner-table, drank a glass of bitters at the bar. But what capped the climax, they one and all resolutely declined making love to the old creature, who, now that she was dressed out so fine, had a notion that she was a beauty. She fell into a roaring fury, and all but swore the tenants of Jonathan had no more sensibility to female charms or female society than so many raccoons; and all this because they would not go about philandering with an old woman, whose voice squeaked like a fiddle, and whose face was, they say, not much unlike that of the fish called a sole.

The old creature, being disgusted with the insensibility of these stupid blockheads, got into a tearing passion, and went into the woods some way off, where she set up a school of painting and other accomplishments. But she got no scholars, because there were none to be had; and then she was taken with another tantrum, and declared the people had no more taste for the polite arts than the wild Indians. After this, she set up a shop in the settlement I mentioned before, furnished with wooden horses, humming-tops, tin swords, and all sorts of children's playthings and the like, which the tenants had no more use for than they had for the old creature's accomplishments, which I suspect were, after all, but make-believe; for I don't see how an old fish-woman could come honestly by them, for my part.

At last she got out of all patience with these stubborn people, and pronounced them, as well as I can recollect hard words, incorrigible, and utterly incapable of development. She scolded and fidgeted about for some time, and played the fine lady at a great rate; but all in vain. Nobody came to flirt with her; the women persisted in going to church instead of making love to other peoples' husbands, and the men continued to spit against the wind, and eat by sleight of hand, in spite of all she could say or do.

Finding they were of such rough materials that it was impossible to make them bear a polish, the old creature one day at a tea-party fell foul of them tooth and nail; she called them devotees, church-goers, stupid domestic drudges that did not know the delights of flirtation; finikin, minikin, mincing, mock-modest, squeamish, hard-working, domestic tabby-cats; and as for the men, she denounced them for a tobacco-chewing, spitting, gouging, fast-eating, sling-drinking set, with heads like a beetle, and consciences so soft that they were afraid to make love against law and gospel. After this, she turned her back on the company, and curling up her nose in an agony of supercilious and thorough-bred disgust, strutted majestically out of the room, and made tracks, as the saying is, for the ancient manor of Bullock, where she arrived in due season.

Squire Bull was hugely delighted to see her come back again, and all but kissed the old creature when he found what a precious mess of scandal she had manufactured for the edification of his tenants. He got it all printed, hired Captain All to swear it was every bit true, and, calling his tenants before him, thus addressed them:—

" You see, my honest fellows, and be hanged to you,

what a poor d—l is my son Jonathan, and what miserable, unpolished, vulgar dogs are his tenants. They don't give themselves time to eat, and—"

" But then they have plenty to eat," said John's tenants.

" Hold your tongues, you impudent varlets," said the squire, in a rage, "and hear what I am going to say; I was saying," — (here he took out Madame Trollope's book, which it is said Captain All wrote for her, and, putting on his spectacles, refreshed his memory by looking over some parts of it) — " Ah !, yes, here we have it all in black and white. Now listen, you intolerable blockheads. If you go over to my son Jonathan's farms, you will have no flirtations; you will know nothing of painting, sculpture, and the fine arts ; you will not be able to get a living by selling wooden horses, tin trumpets, and the like ; and, as for music, they play on the banjo, and sing nothing but the ' Old Hundred ' there.   Now I, you know, boys, am one of the most musical fellows in the world, and will teach you all to sing like nightingales — listen, you intolerable blockheads."

And then he began to roar " God save the king," so that some of Jonathan's tenants thought they heard him quite across the mill-pond, and took it for thunder.   Upon this the tenants, who are very loyal fellows, began to join chorus, and they had a bout of it among them.

" Now, my hearties," quoth the old squire, "listen to me : — if you go over to Jonathan's farms, you'll get no music except that of the ' Old Hundred.' "

" But we can't live on music," said the tenants.

" Hem ! but, you egregious ninnies, you don't see

the thing in a right point of view — as I was saying,
you'll be able to sell no wooden horses or tin trumpets."

"But you know, squire, we don't make wooden
horses or tin trumpets, and don't want to sell them."

"But, you infernal knaves — you egregious dodi-
poles — you gnat-snappers you — don't I tell you
there are no churches in Jonathan's farms, and that
his tenants only pay the parson just what they please,
the unbelieving villains!"

"The very thing," cried they all, with one voice.

"But I tell you the fellow has no more religion
than the Pope of Rome."

"Just what we want — we have paid enough to
the church and the parson," cried they all again.

"But I tell you, you ninnyhammer gnat-snappers,
that — "

Here he again had recourse to the old creature's
book, and after turning over a good number of leaves,
looked up to go on with his speech, when lo! and
behold! his tenants had marched off one and all, and
he saw them half way across the mill-pond, paddling
away for life toward Jonathan's farms.

"Body o' me!" exclaimed the squire, "I believe
the old boy is in them all, for they won't listen to
reason."

CHAPTER XXXV.

How one Parson Fibber comes over to convert Jonathan's tenants to the true church, and teach them some outlandish language, the name of which I have forgot.

THERE was a prosing old parson about Bullock Island, who sometimes eked out his living by keeping a night-school, to teach some outlandish tongue that was of no more use to the tenants than two tongues would have been. He was very much liked by people that go to church to take a comfortable nap, but among the greater part of the tenants he was reckoned a dull sort of a fellow enough. He was, moreover, a sad hand at telling fibs, by which he got the nickname of Fibber, though I believe his real name was Fiddler,* a droll name for a parson. Some said he ought to have been called Bagpipes, for he always preached with a mortal drone.

Be this as it may, Parson Fibber, finding it rather difficult to make both ends meet, and that the tenants of Bullock Island had lost all confidence in his word, so that they would hardly believe the Scriptures when he preached them, thought to himself he would go over to Jonathan's farms, where he was not so well known, and where he had heard people were mighty fond of taking a comfortable nap in church. He expected to get all at once into a good fat living, it being one of the thirty-nine articles of belief I spoke of in the beginning of this history, that there

* Revd. Isaac Fiddler. Observations on Professions, Literature, Manners, and Emigration, in the United States and Canada, made during a residence there in 1832. London. 1833. 12mo.—*Allibone's Dictionary of Authors.*

were neither churches nor preachers in Jonathan's farms. The honest tenants of Bullock Island did not know that there were plenty of churches, and more sects than churches by a great deal.

Parson Fibber played his bagpipes all through the farms, and called aloud and spared not; but he got no call for all that, and, what was worse, Jonathan's tenants demurred to learning the outlandish tongue which was of no use to them, being very busy cultivating their lands, making fences, and working like brave fellows, that they might keep themselves and their children from coming upon the parish like Squire Bull's tenants. They moreover, one and all, refused to fall asleep at his sermons, upon which he was so mortified that he turned his back upon them, and went over to Bullock Island, where he wrote a book duller than one of his own sermons, in which he indulged himself wonderfully in drawing the long bow, and many people thought outdid all his former exploits in this species of archery.

The squire, as usual, was hugely delighted with the new batch of stories against Jonathan, and, as I read in one of the newspapers of Bullock Island, promoted the parson to a *stall*, where I suppose he was allowed to eat oats with John's horses. He then sent for some of his tenants that he heard were thinking of going over to Jonathan's farms, and holding the parson's book upsidedown in his hand, began to tell them as follows:—

" My jolly fellows, I hear you talk of going over to that snivelling, hop-o'-my-thumb jockey, my son Jonathan. Now I tell you that you are a parcel of blockheads. Look here—" and then he read out of the parson's book, how Jonathan's tenants, though they all had more or less books in their houses, had no great libraries full of great folios that not one in a hundred could read, and that they had no more relig- ion than horses, for they would not give Parson Fib- ber a good fat living in reward for putting them to sleep every Sunday.

He then took down an old rusty key, which looked as if it had not been used since the invention of locks, and, after worrying and swearing not a little because it was so rusty it would not turn round, at last, with much ado opened a door, and showed them a great number of big books all covered with dust and spider- webs and looking as sleepy as if they had not been disturbed for a hundred years. He took down one, and, brushing off the dust with his coat-sleeve which turned the colour of a miller's frock, opened it and tried to read; but, being rather out of practice, he only mumbled a little to himself and shut it again.

" There, my boys," cried he, snapping his fingers, " what do you think of that, hey? aint I a scholar, you great blockheads? and yet you want to sneak over to my son Jonathan, who, considering I begat him, does little credit to his daddy, and whose ten- ants, though they can all read, write, and cipher, have no great libraries like this, and, Parson Fibber says, don't understand Greek at all. You may judge of the value they put upon learning, when it is so cheap they can get it for nothing! What think you of that, boys, hey?"

" Get learning for nothing!" cried they all, with one voice, — " Huzza for Brother Jonathan! let's be off, boys, and leave the squire to his big books, which nobody, not even himself, can understand."

So away they went, leaving John with his book in his hand, and his spectacles on his nose, swearing like a trooper. He had a great mind to take Parson Fibber from the stall, and put one of his horses in his place again, only he had somehow or other got the reputation of being the great bulwark of the church, and did not like to lose it.

———◆———

CHAPTER XXXVI.

How Squire Bull's new wife was suspected of being too great with Brother Jonathan, who it was thought had put strange notions in her head.

MUCH about this time John Bull's wife began to talk to a new tune, and take considerable liberties with the old squire's household, which, she insisted upon it, wanted reforming. She told him his house was overrun with a parcel of lazy, good-for-nothing servants, who set themselves up for gentlemen,— " Marry, come up! gentlemen indeed!", would she say:—" a parcel of idle, extravagant, good-for-nothing varlets, that don't earn so much as salt to their porridge, and eat you out of house and home! I tell you, John, if you don't send one half of them packing, and make the other half do their duty, you are a ruined man. The tenants are getting so poor that they can't pay their rents, and are going over to Jonathan's farms by dozens, while you keep on spending away and boasting of your riches, as if you had a mine of gold in your breeches-pocket instead of a parcel of good-for-nothing paper-rags, and did not owe more

than all your estate would sell for to-morrow. I tell
you, John Bull, you must reform — reform, John, I
say, or you'll be a bankrupt before you know where
you are."

" Reform ! " quoth the squire — " Reform ! I'll be
switched if I do. Who ever heard of a man of my
age reforming, except when he was on his last legs,
hey ? Now I am a hale, hearty fellow; it will be
time enough for me to reform, a dozen years hence."

Mrs. Bull began to quiz John about his legs, which
she said looked like a pair of drumsticks and shook
under him every step he walked.

" You, a hale, hearty fellow ! Why, you look like
an old, battered, worn-out glutton, who has rolled into.
a lump of bloated flesh, and cannot go, until, like a.
clock, you have been wound up every Sunday morning. Your dancing days are over, John."

" Are they, by jingo ? " cried the squire. " I'll show
you, my dear."

And he tried to cut a great caper, but was seized
with such a twinge that he roared out lustily, while
Mrs. Bull laughed ready to split her sides.

" Well, my dear," quoth the squire,. whom the
twinge had brought to reason, " I believe I am growing a little old."

" Indeed are you, John ; and, as I said before,. it is
high time for you to think about reforming. You
have been a sad fellow in your day, and don't know
how soon you may die, leaving me a disconsolate
widow, a lone woman with nobody to care for her."

" Well, well, I'll think of it, my dear," answered
John, whom the idea of being near his end had made

very penitent for the time being, as is the case with most people.

They parted for the present; and John went to consult some of his overseers and stewards, of whom he had six times as many as he needed. One of these cunning varlets, who hated the very ghost of re-form much more than he did the old boy himself, thought, if he could only make John a little jealous of his wife, he might escape for this time. So he began to insinuate that Jonathan had been putting some of his Yankee notions into her head; and, as he had be-gun by seducing his tenants, had ended by undermin-ing the virtue of his wife.

" You're right!—you're right! I see it all as plain as daylight," cried the squire, throwing up his right hand, and slapping his fat thigh with the other. " The unnatural, infamous, underhand, sneaking son of a — hem!—not quite so bad as that, either. But, if I don't be even with the young rascal, my name is not John Bull. And madam, too! I must reform! I'm an old fellow, forsooth — she's found that out, has she? I'm over head and ears in debt, am I? ' I can't walk without my legs shaking under me,' says buxom Mrs. Bull. She's found out the difference betwixt an old fellow and a young one, has she? No honest woman could have made the discovery, and be hanged to her. But I'll be even with them both. I'll chal-lenge the young rascal, and turn my wife out of doors."

He was going to set about it, when the cunning varlet of a steward reminded the squire, in the gen-teelest manner possible, of the duel they had together a few years before; and that, while the squire, (with great submission), had grown old since, and was obliged to walk with a stick, Jonathan had been waxing bigger and bigger, and stronger and stronger every day. He concluded by advising him, as the best mode of putting a stop to the further seductions of the young villain, to hold him up to the world, his tenants, and his wife, as one of the greatest rogues and blackguards in the whole world. By this course Jonathan would get such a bad character that no decent woman would dare to keep company with him.

" Why, body o' me!" quoth the squire, " haven't I tried that already a dozen times? It won't do — I tell you it won't do, for all I can say about that young rascal only makes everybody fall in love with him the more. The men all pull off their hats to him, and the women run after him like a flock of sheep. Body o' me! I begin to suspect he is a pretty decent sort of a fellow, and in time will come to do credit to the father who begat him — hey?"

" Yes," replied the varlet, with a sneer, " you'd better invite him over to the manor, and give him a fair chance with the old lady."

This stung John to the quick, and, after scratching his head, chattering at random, and stamping about like a man in a quandary, he suddenly stopped and asked the varlet what he should do. He told the squire, that, as to challenging Jonathan, that would be rather an expensive concern, and the issue very doubtful. It might end in a broken head and an empty pocket. On the whole, there was no other way than to persuade Mrs. Bull that Jonathan was beneath her notice, being a low-lived simpleton of a country bumpkin, whose sentiments, character, and person, would disgrace any lady that kept company with him.

"But what shall I do to keep my tenants from hankering so after Jonathan's farms, and adopting all his Yankee notions, hey?"

"Tell them that Jonathan don't eat with silver forks," quoth the other.

"Body o' me! so I will; if that don't do his business, I'm mistaken."

———◆———

CHAPTER XXXVII.

How Squire Bull sent over one Corporal Smelfungus* to smell out Jonathan's enormities, and who this corporal was.

JOHN was determined this time to be particular in his selection of a person to do Jonathan's business, and leave him no more character than some people that shall be nameless. Accordingly, after considerable search, he found out a fellow called Smelfungus, which I have heard was a nickname, given him on account of his always curling up his nose as if he smelt something disagreeable. He was one of the greatest grumblers in the whole manor of Bullock, which is full of them, and never was known to be pleased with anybody or any thing but himself. They say he was born grumbling, and it was foretold that he would die grumbling, as his father and mother did

———

* Captain Thomas Hamilton, R.A., author of "Men and Manners in America," published in 1833, is supposed to have been in view here. But Mr. Paulding often refers to one fictitious personage the characteristics of, or scandal connected with, several travellers.

before him. Such, indeed, was his propensity to this amusement, that, not being able to grumble sufficiently by word of mouth, he learned to write, on purpose that he might grumble on paper at the same time, and thus, as it were, kill two birds with one stone. Smelfungus was moreover a scandalous dog, and did not always stick to the truth, though he pretended to be a pious man, and very much of a gentleman withal. For my part, from what I have heard, I believe he was about as much of one as the other.

He professed to be a great stickler for good manners, though he did not practice them much himself — a nice judge of dress, though he was seldom seen in a clean shirt — and a great critic in silver forks, as most people admire what they seldom see. But what he most valued himself upon was a certain air of gentility, which he had acquired by shaving himself once a week before a piece of a looking-glass. Altogether, he was a poor creature enough, and only fit for the dirty job he was about being employed in. There are people made for every thing, and Smelfungus was predestined to write libels on his fellow-creatures.

The squire opened his project to Corporal Smelfungus, who snapped at it with a sort of instinctive eagerness. It was the very thing he preferred above all others. Then the squire told him his suspicions that Jonathan had been tampering with Mrs. Bull, and that this was the true secret of her talking so much confounded nonsense about reforming his household, letting his tenants vote at town-meetings, and twitting him continually about Jonathan's having more money than he knew how to dispose of, making

his tenants so comfortable that they hardly knew what
a tight boot felt like, and doing more about his
house with a few smart hands, than he, Squire Bull,
did with a houseful of lazy, lubberly servants. He
said he had caught her several times casting a sheep's
eye toward Jonathan's farms, and quoting him as an
example to his old father.

Smelfungus hereupon advised the squire to get a
divorce, as he had a right to do by the laws of the
manor; but John shook his head, and said that ten
to one he would only get a worse termagant, for it
seemed to him that the whole neighbourhood was
infected with Jonathan's example, and running stark
mad with reform. The corporal, who, like all the
little varmints who sneak about rich old codgers such
as Squire Bull and live by picking their pockets,
hated the word reform worse than poison, for fear it
should begin with him — the corporal, I say, was as
angry as a puddle in a storm, and grumbled out that
he would soon do Jonathan's business.

" I'll leave him no — no more character — than —
than — "

" Than you have yourself — hey, corporal ? " quoth
the squire, and fell into an honest, jolly laugh, such as
he used to enjoy in old times, before he set himself up
for a great bully, and got over head and ears in debt,
for the sake of maintaining his character as a fine
gentleman, to which he had little or no pretensions.
He was, in truth, a sturdy, off-hand, frank old fellow
enough, except toward his son Jonathan, whom, because he had begotten him, he thought he might
abuse as much as he pleased; but as to being a fine
gentleman, it was all in my eye and Betty Martin.

Though he aped the fine folks among his neighbours, he did it so awkwardly, that everybody said he might better stick to the respectable character of a country squire, hunt foxes, live among his tenants instead of travelling about to learn how to become a fine gentleman forsooth, and spend his money among those that earned it, instead of throwing it away on fiddlers, dancers, and such like caterpillars of the commonwealth.

But John did not mind all this. The greatest fool in the world is an old fool, for there is no hope of his living to grow wiser.

CHAPTER XXXVIII.

How Corporal Smelfungus gloriously succeeded in his mission, and what miraculous effects his relation had on Mrs. Bull and the Squire's tenants.

WHEN Corporal Smelfungus got over to Jonathan's farms, that hospitable young fellow feasted him heartily, and showed him every attention, as was his custom toward strangers, of whose good word he was apt to think more than it deserved.

But the corporal was determined beforehand to be pleased with nothing, being, as I said before, set upon undeceiving Mrs. Bull and the squire's tenantry, and rescuing them from Brother Jonathan's seductions. He maintained that the former was no better than she should be, and the latter a parcel of drivellers, to think the squire could learn any thing worth knowing from such a snivelling, mint-sling rum-jockey, who had no more manners than a bear, and no more morals than a pickpocket.

He went about raking up all the old stories that had been hatched against Brother Jonathan for a hundred years past, and invented as many more as he could; but it was not a great many, being rather a dull fellow, with more ill-nature than wit, and more malignity than invention.   The truth is, he was not a little put to it to find matter for running down Jonathan.   His tenants were so well off, their rents so low, and they had such a plenty to eat and drink, that the corporal did not know exactly where to take hold of him, and was obliged to turn up his nose at the merest trifles, for want of something better.

One day, being at breakfast at a tavern, he luckily saw a mustard-pot upset on the table, upon which he noted it down carefully, that Jonathan could never eat his meals without upsetting all the mustard, and did not know how to behave like a gentleman.

The next thing he did was to find fault with the great size of Jonathan's beefsteaks, which he swore were as big as newspapers, and enough to take away a man's stomach to look at.   But what was worse than all this, he had no silver forks at his table, and none but barbarians could eat without silver forks.

Happening to see a young fellow who was an officer in the militia, in his everyday clothes, wearing a dirk to show he was a soldier, the corporal put it down in his memorandum-book that all Jonathan's tenants wore dirks, and did not mind killing a neigh-bour any more than they did murdering the squire's English, as he called it.   Every man he saw that had but one eye, he concluded had been gouged to a certainty; and if any one happened to ask him the hour, instead of pulling out his turnip and answering him in a civil manner, he set him down as an impertinent, guessing, inquisitive Yankee, as Jonathan's tenants were commonly called. But he did not tell them so to their faces, for fear of being gouged.

There was an old joke, got up in a good-humoured way, about some of Jonathan's tenants away Down East selling wooden nutmegs, and playing other such pranks upon the people of Southlands; this the corporal got hold of, for he was very industrious in picking up such things, and thereupon set down the people Down East as a parcel of rogues.

Sometimes he employed himself whole days counting how many times the people spit; and again he would stand with his watch in his hand, calculating how many minutes they were in swallowing their dinner, and how many times they drank at their meals; or would listen to the free, off-hand talking of the tenants, to find out whether they spoke good grammar; and, whenever he got a chance, he would peep into the bedchambers, to see if they had any clean towels, combs, wash-hand basins, and proper conveniences under the bed. Happening to find a dirty napkin one day in a miserable tavern, in a room without a comb, he snapped his fingers in triumph, and swore Jonathan's tenants did not know what clean napkins were, and combed their hair with curry-combs. When he could find nothing to set him going, he scratched his pate, and passed his time grumbling about democratic licentiousness, and universal suffrage. All this he called speculating, generalizing, and philosophizing.

Having a great taste, like most of Squire Bull's tenants, for seeing people hanged, he went all through Jonathan's farms to find out a gallows, and being disappointed in his search, relieved his mortification by putting down in his memorandums that there was no such thing as punishing a criminal, and that it required great interest to get hanged there. All this time he was feasting and carousing it lustily among the tenants, who little thought they had an ill-natured, grumbling, tattling curmudgeon among them, spying out their little oddities, and inventing scandals when he could not find any ready made to his hands. Once or twice, indeed, he got taken down pretty handsomely. The first time was when he attempted to walk over a dinner-table, to show his breeding; and the next when he undertook to sprawl himself at full length on a sofa, among some of Jonathan's ladies. These little rubs only made him ten times the more spiteful, and he paid poor Jonathan off in his memorandums.

When he had collected together all the scandal and tittle-tattle, and pumped out of the old women all the private anecdotes they had stored up for fifty years past, he went back to Bullock Island, chuckling at his great success, and thinking to himself how he should stump Mrs. Bull, and the drivellers who had been seduced by Brother Jonathan into an admiration of his parts and an imitation of his Yankee notions.

" Well, corporal," cried the squire, as soon as he laid eyes on him — " well, my fine fellow, have you dished that rebellious rogue, my son Jonathan — hey, baby? Come, let's see what you have got; out with it, my hearty!"—and he rubbed his hands, in expectation of a high treat from the corporal's muster-roll.

Corporal Smelfungus thereupon pulled out a whole bundle of smutty paper, (for he was rather a dirty little fellow, and always carried his snuff in his breeches-pocket), and began to read off what he had set down, in a pompous manner, as though it had been well worth hearing, the squire all the time rubbing his hands, snapping his fingers, and drinking the corporal's health every two minutes.

"Body o' me!" he would cry out every now and then, "body o' me! what will Madam Bull say to that, and what will those great blockheads, my tenants, think of this. By George, corporal, but I think this will do the business, and put an end to Master Jonathan's seductions." Then would he strut about the room, the corporal following, and ever and anon having a fling at honest Jonathan out of his memorandums. After this, nothing would do but he must go to his wife and tell her all about it.

The good lady was a little stumped at Jonathan's having no silver forks, though, for the matter of that, it was but a little while since the squire had begun to use them at great doings and holidays. All the rest of the time he kept them locked up, for fear his servants would steal them, I suppose. Women, I have observed, think a great deal of such matters; and the very hardest thing they can say of a man is, that he is not genteel. Men don't mind these trifles so much, except in so far as they approach to the feelings and habits of women. Mrs. Bull thought to herself it was better to have silver forks and nothing to eat with them, than to have plenty of victuals and no silver forks. Jonathan, therefore, began rapidly to fall from her good graces.

As the corporal proceeded to read how Jonathan swallowed his meat without chewing it, piled up his bones by the side of his plate instead of picking them like a gentleman, and combed his hair with a curry-comb, Mrs. Bull began to make wry faces; but when, by way of a top-off, the corporal read out in an audible voice how Jonathan cracked his eggs at the wrong end, she gave a loud shriek, and fell into the squire's arms in a fit. When she came to again, she gave the squire a hearty smack, and promised faithfully to have no more to say to a fellow that had no silver forks, and broke his eggs at the wrong end.

"By the glory of my ancestors," cried John, "but you're the man for my money, after all, corporal. What shall I do for you, my brave fellow, hey? Hum — ha — I have it. I'll make you superintendent of the Bridewell, and you shall teach the bad women to be genteel." The corporal kissed his hand as in duty bound.

"But, body o' me!" said the squire, after a little while, "now we've done the old woman's business, let us go and get my rascally tenants out of Jonathan's seductions."

Accordingly, they went round among them, the corporal all the while reading out of his muster-roll of dirty paper, until they got a great crowd about them.

"There, there!" said the squire, when they came to the silver forks; "what think you of that, you discontented blockheads, hey?"

"Silver forks!" said the tenants; "we never saw any in the whole course of our lives; and, for the matter of that, we don't care what sort of forks we have if you will only allow us enough to eat."

"Body o' me!" said the squire, "what a set of blockheads!"

Then the corporal came to cracking the eggs; the squire again rubbed his hands, and cried out—

"There, boys, there! What think you of that, hey?"

"We avent heaten hany heggs these ten years. They hall go to the parson and the landlord," replied they.

"Hum!" said the squire.

But when the corporal came to the beefsteaks, they all cried out in astonishment—

"Beefsteaks as big as newspapers! Come, boys, let's be off." And away they scampered, shouting—

"Huzza for Brother Jonathan and his big beefsteaks!"

The squire looked askance at the corporal, and the corporal at the squire.

"Corporal," quoth John, "either I'm a numskull or my tenants are the greatest blockheads in existence."

"That's as clear as preaching," quoth the corporal; and away he went to take possession of his office.

CHAPTER XXXIX.

How Brother Jonathan got out of patience sometimes with the Squire, and scolded back again pretty handsomely.

WHEN Jonathan, who never failed to buy all the books put forth by these rogues, for he had a great curiosity to hear what other folks said of him—when

Jonathan, I say, saw how John Bull had clapper-clawed his character, he got out of all patience, and would often exclaim —

" I'll be darned if this old father of mine isn't a little too bad by half. Here he is palavering me every day of his life, and telling me he wants to be friends; and yet he does nothing but get his plaguy school-masters and old women to abuse me like a pick-pocket. I'll be switched if I don't be even with him, or my name isn't Jonathan."

And then he fell to work, putting it into the squire pretty handsomely, swearing he was the biggest liar that ever broke bread, and contradicting all John said of him, with such zeal that he sometimes denied what, to my mind, was very much to his credit.

The truth is, that Jonathan, who had now grown to be pretty much of a man, and carried his head something high in the neighbourhood, though a fine, vigorous, well-looking young dog as ever was seen, and withal a shrewd, sensible, high-spirited fellow, had a bad habit of imitating Squire Bull in almost every thing he did, whether good, bad, or indifferent. It was enough for him that John Bull did this, and said that — that he dressed after such and such a fashion, and held such and such opinions — he was pretty sure to talk, and think, and dress, and do every thing, just like the squire, without once reflecting that what might be well enough for an old superannuated fellow like Bull, was the last thing becoming in a sprightly, vigorous, springall, who never took a dose of physic in his life, and could jump over a six-rail fence without touching. All this never once came into his head; and indeed it was natural enough that he should take after his old dad, though, to say truth, he never received much kindness at his hands, and owed him more for kicks than coppers.

But, I must say, I should have liked Jonathan much better had he made use of his own gumption in these matters, and not aped the old squire in all his follies, at the same time he was bragging that he didn't care a brass farthing for him or his opinions. I always thought it showed a want of spirit in Jonathan, for whose good name I would at any time lay down my life, seeing I owe all I have in the world to his liberality and kindness as a landlord. If he could only get over this disgraceful foible, and have an opinion of his own, he would be thought much better of by all his neighbours. But he was always setting himself up for a fine gentleman, forsooth, and tacking Squire or Honourable to his name, instead of passing for an honest and independent farmer, as in reality he was.

Be this as it may, Jonathan paid the squire back as good as he sent, and called him as many hard names as John called him, which indeed was somewhat excusable, as the squire always began first, and, if he had held his tongue, everybody might have thought all Bull said of him was gospel. It was almost a pity to see such near relations, each of whom had a great many good points about him, cutting at one another at such a cruel rate; and yet one could not help laughing to see John Bull, who ten times a day called Jonathan a lying, cheating, spitting, gouging, guessing, drinking, republican sinner, complaining of him for an ungrateful rascal, because he did not love his daddy. " Did I not beget the villain with my own hand?" would he say; "and did I not physic him with a dose of patent medicine, made up of thirty-nine excellent articles, each one enough to cure a saint? and did I not pay special attention to his safety when he got to be big enough to take care of himself? and didn't I, out of pure fatherly affection, keep him short of pocket-money, that he might not run into mischief? and didn't I allow him to set up for himself when I couldn't help it? and don't I every day of my life act the part of a kind parent, by telling the upstart young puppy of his faults, as in duty bound? and didn't I beget him? Let him answer me that, the good-for-nothing, drinking, cheating, spitting, gouging, guessing, fighting, talking, bragging, disobedient, ungrateful young varlet!"

The squire forgot that Jonathan had too much of the Bull blood in him to play the spaniel, and crouch the more, the more you kicked him. He might be coaxed by kindness to lick your hand, but it would have taken even a stouter fellow than the squire, who was no chicken, to frighten or beat him into it.

In this situation were the affairs of Squire Bull and Brother Jonathan, the last I heard of them. Now and then they were mighty civil, and sometimes, when the old squire was in a rare good-humour, he would boast that never man had such a lusty, swaggering boy as Jonathan; and occasionally Jonathan would almost believe the old man had forgiven him. But before the civil words were well out of John's mouth, his old habit would come over him, as it were in spite of his teeth, of which, to be sure, he hadn't any to spare; and then, phew!, Jonathan got the old grist about his ears, and became again a spitting, guessing, gouging, cheating, bragging, cowardly, ill-bred, ill-begotten, ill-favoured, ungrateful, rebellious Yankee Doodle rascal.

All the while the neighbours stood looking on, laughing to see them pulling one another to pieces in this way, while the more sensible sort shook their heads, and observed THAT SQUIRE BULL AND BROTHER JONATHAN WERE TOO MUCH ALIKE EVER TO BE RIGHT-DOWN GOOD FRIENDS.

10

JOHN BULL IN AMERICA;

OR,

THE NEW MUNCHAUSEN.

INTRODUCTION

JOHN BULL IN AMERICA.

In 1825, thirteen years after the first publication of " John
Bull and Brother Jonathan", Mr. Paulding brought out
" John Bull in America; or, The New Munchausen". This
is an example of his rapidity of composition, it having been
written (as he states in a letter to Irving) in three weeks'
time, and in the midst of serious distraction. It is a burlesque of the rabble of English travellers in this country;
but, high as is the coloring, no person who has not waded
through a certain amount of the trash in question can esti-
mate how little of a caricature it is, nor how richly the good-
humored castigation was deserved.

It is perhaps worth while to give an idea of the sort of
matter that Mr. Paulding exaggerates. But there is such a
wealth of absurdity in the English Travels and Periodicals
of the early part of this century when treating of these
United States, that I scarcely know where to begin my quotations. However, I will strike at random, and open with one
Thomas Ashe, Esquire, or Captain Ashe, as he is sometimes
styled, who " performed " or pretended to have " performed "
some " Travels in America ", in 1806. Mr. Paulding, in his
" Sketch of Old England, by a New England man ", intimates

that Ashe cooked up his tour at home, without having visited this country; while Mr. Henry T. Tuckerman, (who, in his "America and her Commentators", has made a specialty of this branch of inquiry), seems to accept it as in good faith. In a review in The North American, Vol. XIX., attributed to Edward Everett, he is styled "the swindler, Ashe". Whether he was ever here or not, there appeared in London, in 1808, a book of travels by Captain Thomas Ashe. There were, says Mr. Tuckerman, three volumes of the English edition. A Newburyport reprint of the same year, in one volume, in which the work is credited to "Thomas Ashe, Esq.", is now before me. It is in the shape of letters. The italics in the extracts I make are the author's, and the punctuation is as printed.

In the first two pages he effectually does the business of the whole American people and their country : —

"The American States through which I have passed, are unworthy of your observation. Those to the north-east are indebted to nature for but few gifts : they are better adapted for the business of grazing than for corn. The climate is equally subject to the two extremes of burning heat and excessive cold; and bigotry, pride, and a malignant hatred to the mother country, characterize the inhabitants. The middle States are less contemptible; they produce grain for exportation; but wheat requires much labour, and is liable to blast on the sea-shore. The national features here are not strong, and those of different emigrants have not yet composed a face of local deformity : we still see the liberal English, the ostentatious Scotch, the warm-hearted Irish, the penurious Dutch, the proud German, the solemn Spaniard, the gaudy Italian, and the profligate French. What kind of character is hereafter to arise from an amalgamation of such discordant materials, I am at a loss to conjecture.

"For the southern States, nature has done much, but man little. Society is here in a shameful degeneracy; an additional proof of the pernicious tendency of those detestable principles of political licentiousness, which are not only adverse to the enjoyment of practical liberty, and to the existence of regular authority, but destructive also of comfort and security in every class of society; doctrines here, found by experience, to make men turbulent citizens, abandoned Christians, inconstant husbands, unnatural fathers, and treacherous friends. I shun the humiliating delineation, and turn my thoughts to happier regions which afford contemplation without disgust;" &c. — LETTER I. pp. 11–12.

At Pittsburg he meets with some little relief to his harassed feelings : —

"The principal inhabitants of Pittsburg are Irish, or of Irish origin; this accounts for the commercial spirit of the place, and the good-breeding and hospitality which in general prevail throughout it. . . . . The influence of these and many other gentlemen of similar sentiments, is very favourable to the town; and has hindered the vicious propensities of the genuine American character, from establishing here the horrid dominion which they have assumed over the Atlantic States." — LETTER III. p. 26.

He discusses American statesmen : —

"There are in America no real politicians; the speeches you see in papers are made by Irish and Scotch journalists, who attend the Congress and Senate merely to take the spirit of their proceedings and clothe it with a language interesting to read." — LETTER VII. p. 65.

At Wheeling he sups full of horrors, and is "stuffed" considerably by various parties. He gives a graphic account of a rough-and-tumble fight between a "Kentuckyan" and a "Virginian", in which all forms of mayhem play a conspicuous part; and, on applying to a "quaker friend" with whom he dines, receives this cold comfort : —

"As to the savage practice of fighting in the manner of wild beasts, my host entertained no hopes whatever of ever seeing it put down. It might be called a national taste, which the laws appeared afraid to violate; and therefore it reared its head above authority. Few nights elapsed without the exhibition of this new gymnastic; few mornings appeared that did not bring to day a friend or acquaintance with the loss of an eye, or the mutilation of half his features. Alarmed at this account, I asked whether this kind of conduct spread down the river."

The quaker friend gives him rather a blue look ahead:—

"I again demanded how a stranger was to distinguish a good from a vicious house of entertainment? I was answered, by previous inquiry, or, if that was impracticable, a tolerable judgment could be formed, from observing in the landlord, *a possession, or an absence of ears:* many of the proprietors of small inns being men who had left those members nailed to certain penitential market crosses in Maryland, Pennsylvania, and the Carolinas, in lieu of certain horses and cattle of which they had from time to time become the illegal owners. Furnished with these useful instructions, I left my kind entertainer, and retired to my inn with a view of passing a peaceable night. It was not so ordained."— LETTER XI. pp. 96–100.

For why? Because there is a ball that night in the tavern, and, of course, a row. He gets up to see what the difficulty is. It is soon composed, the fight being transferred to out of doors.

"Though it was by this time far advanced in the night, and I felt no disposition to retire to rest; my mind was too much agitated and full, to benefit by a too sudden, or forced repose; and I preferred the conversation of mine host one half-hour longer. It turned on the events of the day, and

the evening amusement. He very candidly admitted all I
said in favour of more civilized recreations; and even went
so far as to tell me a variety of anecdotes, which from a respect for human nature, I suppress."

He however narrates a story told and described by the
landlord as "*out of the common*, and *rather* of a melancholy
kind." The landlord is pathetic.

"I could hear no more, the Virginian himself was moved.
I ordered a light, and gaining my chamber cast myself on a
bed to rest: yet not before I cursed the ferocity of manners
which reigns in this place, and which caused the eternal
wretchedness and misery of an object so amiable and instruct-
ing as my landlord's Maria. It is intolerable. It is infamous.
Farewell, you can account for my abrupt conclusion."—
LETTER XI. pp. 101–102.

Of course. As Yellowplush expresses it, his "feelinx"
were too much for him.

In LETTER XX., p. 186., and elsewhere, he is much disgusted with "great barrens, swamps, wildernesses, and cane-
breaks," (so he spells the word), "pregnant with putridity
and disease." They must have been bold fellows who ventured to this "land of promise" after reading that.

At Paris, Kentucky, he is much affronted by a landlady
who gives him a much better breakfast than he wants, for
which and the morning feed of his horse she charges him, as
far as can be made out from his account, twenty-five cents.

"I asked her what was to pay, and cast a dollar upon the
table, enraged at the low state of some minds, their attachment to wrong, and determination to persist in evil and dull
habits, which they know to be adverse to their prosperity and
improvement." — LETTER XX. p. 190.

He compliments the ladies of Lexington, Kentucky, —
after a fashion.

"The women are fair and florid — many of them might be considered as rude beauties, but none of them have any pretensions to that chaste and elegant form of person and countenance which distinguish our countrywomen and other ladies of Europe. The absence of that irresistible grace and expression may be attributed to their distance from improved society, and to the savage taste and vulgarity of the men." — LETTER XXI. p. 192.

Thomas Ashe, Esquire, now descends the Ohio and Mississippi rivers, meeting on the way with some astounding adventures not to the present purpose, and closes his account of the country in LETTER XLII., from New Orleans, in rather an unexpected way, not favouring us with a résumé of his observations and deductions. Perhaps it may fairly be assumed that he considers that he has settled us in the beginning.

Richard Parkinson, author of the " Experienced Farmer ", and "late of Orange Hill, near Baltimore ", published two volumes in London, in 1805, under the title of " A Tour in America in 1798, 1799, and 1800, exhibiting sketches of Society and Manners, and a particular account of the American system of Agriculture, with its recent improvements."

In his " Introduction " he states that he came over the sea with the intention of renting a portion of General Washington's land, and "speculated ", i.e. expected, " to make a rapid fortune"; but — finding that the General's soil produced only " two to three bushels of wheat per acre ", and discovering (Tour, p. 52.) "no stem [of oats] with more than four grains, and these of a very light and bad quality, such as I had never seen before: the longest straw was of about twelve inches " — he very naturally, " as money was my object", was rather disappointed, and "found myself compelled to treat him [the General] ·with a great deal of frankness." Perhaps he talked to him, as the farce has it, " like a father ".

" The General . . . . seemed at first not to be pleased

with my conversation"; but, when he had left the room, Colonel Lear who had been present "did me the honour to say I was the only man he ever knew to treat General Washington with frankness." I presume if for *frankness* we read *impertinence* we shall get something like the truth.

On page 15. of Tour he says, " I take up my pen, therefore, to write the following pages, free from all unfounded prejudices against America"; but on page 16. he makes the broad assertion — "notwithstanding the low price at which the American lands are sold, the poverty of the soil is such, as to make it not to pay for labour"; — and, on page 26: — "The produce is so small and the expense so great, that I never saw any land worth having in America".

On his way up the Potomac he is invited to dinner by a Mr. Grimes, who treats him very civilly and returns him safely to his vessel. " After Mr. Grimes was gone, the pilot on board the ship said, 'Sir, you have come off very well with your friend Grimes; you have got back alive : he sometimes shoots his friends when they do not please him.' I found this to be true," &c. TOUR. pp. 46–52. One would think it had been Hop-o'-my-thumb visiting an ogre.

On arriving at Mount Vernon, Washington being absent, Mr. Parkinson becomes forthwith very thick with the steward, who " even told me many unpleasant tales of the General", &c. — TOUR. p. 53.

This will do for Parkinson. His work, besides being amusing reading in itself, is the more so in the copy which I have examined from its having been perused, (probably on the first appearance of the book), by some outraged patriot, and by him plentifully annotated in the margin with " False " — " A lie " — " Not probable " — " fool ! " — &c.

It may be observed here that the main purpose of most of these writers at that time, as is sometimes distinctly stated, is to deter emigrants from coming to this country. With the intention of furthering this object a volume was published in London, in 1823., styled "Memorable Days in America: being a Journal of a Tour to the United States, principally undertaken to ascertain, by positive evidence, the condition and probable prospects of British Emigrants; including accounts of Mr. Birkbeck's Settlement in the Illinois: and intended to show men and things as they are in America. By W. Faux, an English Farmer."

The title, dedication, and preface, are all designed to convey the assurance that he has dealt entirely in "plain delineations . . . — Pictures from life — Things as they are." As before, in the quotations I make, the italics, &c., are taken from the writer.

Having made up his mind that in all probability he never will return home, vainly endeavored to insure his life, and purchased from a physician a double-barrelled prescription "fit for both land and sea", something like the balsam of Fierabras (but much dearer), he sets sail; and, before he gets off the coast of England, picks up an item of information which he forthwith stows away for the benefit of the British public. "Navigators up the Mississippi river, frequently steal from 10 to 20 sheep at once from the farmers, and think it no crime; it being more convenient to steal than to buy." — p. 8. This, be it remembered, in 1819.

His style is enough to provoke a burlesque.

"We are off those beautiful Western isles, the Azores, abounding with herbs, grapes, wine, oil, and earthquakes." — p. 12. "I now sleep in high style every night," [aboard ship], "having under my pillow a bottle of Madeira and a basket of China sweetmeats; at my side nine muskets and a huge broad-sword; and underneath me a magazine of gunpowder and balls." — p. 20.

On Sunday, April 19th, 1819, he encounters — poor man! — "blue forked lightning", and "loud-sounding, crackling, rattling, crashing thunder, presenting a scene more sublimely horrific than any I had ever seen; the lightning might almost be handled, being what our captain calls 'double-twisted ropy.'" — p. 39.

In April, 1819, when nearing the American coast, he sees "several fat Yankee ducks and geese", p. 25; and finds Boston "highly interesting, especially when associated with the recollection of its having fought so bravely for liberty, and preferred it to English tea, sweetened with taxation, and the milk of maternal monarchy." — p. 28.

In the matter of our colored fellow-citizens he hits right and left, North and South.

"It is no unusual thing for some of the people of this country," [Boston, and New England in general], "on going to Charleston, to take their free negroes with them and sell them for slaves, by way of turning a penny, or as they say, of making a good *spec* of it. Two white gentlemen, I was told, determined on a plan to benefit themselves, and cheat the planter, or slave buyer; one blackened his face and body and became a negro; the other was his owner and salesman, and sold his friend to the planter for 800 dollars, but in less than three days he returned, a white free-man again, to divide the spoil, nor was the imposition ever discovered to prosecution." —p. 37. Wooden nutmegs must have hid their diminished heads. In Virginia "three or four slaves are wantonly shot and buried at once, when not useful nor marketable. But all this seldom excites any notice". — p. 127. "A gentleman of Washington, too kind-hearted to whip his house-negroes himself, leaves it to his wife, a fashionable, beautiful female, holding, and going to levees, yet able to cow-hide her negroes, whose screams, under the lash, scare Mrs. Little and family. A cow-hide is no uncommon appendage of ladies here!" — p. 387.

He has some experiences at Charleston, South Carolina.

"May 1st. This morning presented a poor fellow lying all

night until nine, A.M. in the street, in a hot, broiling sun, 110°
by the thermometer. He was found nearly murdered, having his legs both broken, and otherwise terribly bruised about
his head and breast, and robbed of all he had, 15 dollars.
To the disgrace of the nightly watch and city centinels, and
to the open day humanity of the citizens, here was he suffered to lie, saturated with pestilential dew, and, in the day,
left to roast and be devoured by flies, until an old Prussian
colonel offered a dollar to have him removed as a nuisance,
too disgusting to delicate nerves and sensibilities." — p. 45.

At his hotel he makes acquaintance with a certain colonel,
(native, this time), who describes himself as "a blasted lily
and a blighted heath ".

"This young gentleman, naturally witty and highly gifted,
has married and abandoned three wives, and yet is only 22
years of age." — p. 48.

Now for his dicta on the subject of American integrity, or,
rather, the lack of it.

"It is the pride and pleasure of Americans to get into
debt, and then by avoiding payment, show how adroitly they
can cheat and wrong each other. Few look upon knavery
with disgust, but rather with a smile of approbation."— p. 106.
Quoting a Mr. Lidiard, an English friend, he says : " Liberty
here means to do each as he pleases ; to care for nothing and
nobody, and cheat everybody." — p. 194. " Two selfish gods,
Pleasure and Gain, enslave the Americans. The scum of all
the earth is drifted here." — p. 417.

His social prejudices are offended.

" Certain approaches to something like equality, and consequent familiarity of the rich with the poor, both of which
classes profess to be no respecters of persons, generate a manner highly repelling to the aristocratical feelings of the well-
bred English." — p. 116. " The traveller, who must necessarily

often mix with the very dregs of society in this country, should be prepared with plain clothes, or the dress of a mechanic; a gentlemanly appearance only exciting unfriendly or curious feelings, which defeat his object, and make his superiority painful." — p. 202.

November 17, 1819, he is shocked: —

"A young lady cleaning knives! How horrid!!" — p. 261.

Every thing is going backward in the country.

"This is impossible," [i.e. to preserve civilized habits], "all barbarize here." — p. 246. "Men, systematically unprincipled, and in whom the moral sense seems to have no existence: this is the lot of all coming here." — p. 331. "The soil here is unfit for man, and for an Englishman particularly. Both mind and body barbarize and degenerate." — p. 389. He quotes a Mr. Perry: — "It was by mere accident that they ever had a constitution; it came not from wise choice or preference. In England only, exists such a preference and real love of liberty. . . . America, you see, is retrograding and quite unable of herself to achieve any thing grand. . . . . Almost all Americans are boys in every thing but vice and folly." — p. 126. He speaks in his own person: — "They know nothing of the nature of liberty, nor want to know. Law, justice, equity, liberty, are things unknown amongst them. In England, there is a good sound core, and seed that must always vegetate; here, all is rottenness." — p. 432.

In one instance, he forgets himself. Having encountered an English family known to him at home, he says: —

"The greatly needed hospitality and kindness which they met with, in passing down the river, in a pennyless condition, are highly honourable to this good poor man's country." — p. 308.

He is hard on the judiciary.

"Judge Waggoner, who is a notorious hog-stealer," &c. — p. 318. "I called to warm at Judge Russell's, who makes his own shoes, in a one-room log-hole. . . . I met and spoke, ten miles off, with two hog-jobbing judges" — &c. — p. 332.

Here is a pleasing specification of national customs. Near Zainsville, [? Ohio], he fraternizes with Mr. Chichester, a polished, gay, and interesting American gentleman," p. 177., who gives him the benefit of his experience.

"I knew a party of whites who last year in Kentucky roasted to death, before a large log fire, one of their friends because he refused to drink. They did it thus: — Three or four of them shoved and held him up to the fire until they themselves could stand it no longer; and he died in 20 hours after. No legal inquiry took place, nor, indeed, ever takes place among *Rowdies*, as the Back-woodsmen are called." — p. 179. Mr. Lidiard has sensible views. "And again, I tell the gentlemen, that if I wished to be social and get drunk with them, I dare not; for they would take the *liberty* to scratch me like a tiger, and gouge, and dirk me. I cannot part with my nose and eyes." — p. 194.

He picks up a variety of odd items in the national capital.

"Gouging still flourishes. His excellency, Mr. Monroe, while a young man, constantly kept his hair closely shorn, in order that his head might be less exposed to this brutal practice." — p. 108. He asserts that, in Georgetown, D. C., — "Almost every private family chariot in this city is found daily on the stand as a hackney coach for hire, to either whites or blacks; to all who can pay." — p. 112. "The Hon. T. Law brought, it is said, half a million sterling with him to this country, but has lost two-thirds of it. He married the niece of General Washington, the most beautiful lady in Virginia; and, at her uncle's request, Mr. Law settled on her, in case they parted, 15,000 dollars a year. The event,

which seemed thus to be anticipated, soon after occurred;"
&c.—p. 390.

Here is the summary of his observations.

"August—16th. *Picture of the condition of the American people, agricultural and otherwise.* Low ease; a little avoidable want, but no dread of any want; little or no industry; little or no real capital, nor any effort to create any; no struggling, no luxury, and, perhaps, nothing like satisfaction or happiness; no real relish of life; living like store pigs in a wood, or fattening pigs in a stye. All their knowledge is confined to a newspaper, which they all love, and consists in knowing their natural, and some political rights, which rights in themselves they respect individually, but often violate towards others, being cold, selfish, gloomy, inert, and with but little or no feeling."—p. 125.

And now for a quotation from "the celebrated Francis Guy", whoever he may have been.

"There is, indeed, a something in a real upright and downright honest John Bull, that cannot be found in the sly, say-nothing, smiling, deep speculating, money-hunting Jonathans of this all-men-are-born-equally-free-and-independent, negro-driving, cow-skin republic."

Again, F. G. makes a fine enumeration of American misdeeds and horrors:—

"Man stealing, mail robberies, piracy, murders, thefts, swindling, forgeries, lying, cheating, slavery, whips, gags, chains, and all the black catalogue of monstrous ills", &c.—p. 427.

Coming to the close of his book, after all his denunciations Faux assumes a fraternal tone;—"Let both countries wisely learn to think correctly of their several governments, and kindly of each other", p. 486.: and winds up, p. 487., by giving some hygienic instructions through observance of which it may be possible to retain one's health even in the terrible climate of America at large.

I have quoted from the scribbler last named, I fear to a wearisome extent. But I had reasons for doing so. Mr. Faux I take to have been as fine a specimen as could readily be found of the unadulterated commonplace middle-class Englishman of his day. He is, even for an English traveller, remarkably incoherent and preposterous. There is a richness and variety of misunderstanding and misrepresentation in him that is surprising. In fact he is quite a mine, and as such the author of "John Bull in America" has worked him; for he is noticeable as having supplied much of the crude ore of the burlesque. He also gave rise to the review in No. 58. of "The Quarterly", which excited Mr. Paulding's spleen, and which is so ludicrously referred to as he goes along. In addition, Mr. Faux had in his book alluded to our author in the following terms: — "A sinecure, or something in the nature of one, is held by Joseph Paulding, Esq. of Washington. The holder of this situation is enjoined to write in defence of the American character and government, and at the same time to vilify the British." — p. 397. There may then have been some little personal feeling in the roasting of the offender.

Faux also had something impertinent to say of Mr. Edward Everett, who, subsequently, among articles overhauling various works of the kind, devoted one to this book and the English reviewer thereof. Mr. Everett appears to have been somewhat annoyed; for, in "The North American", he characterizes Faux as an "itinerant miscreant", [Vol. XIX. p. 116.], and says further: — "If, again, it should seem incredible, that a person so low as Mr. Faux, should have found admission, on any occasion, in this country, to the houses and tables of respectable individuals, we beg to suggest, that, as his doing so often depends on his own word, no credit whatever is to be given to it. We have personal knowledge, that he can speak as if familiarly acquainted with an individual, who never heard of his name, till it appeared on the title page of his book." — [p. 124.]

But Mr. Everett does not waste himself on Faux. He charges the objectionable article in The Quarterly on Mr. Gifford, personally, and not simply as responsible editor [p. 94.]; and not only effectually dissects the absurdities and unveils the absolute and palpable falsehoods of the travelled varlet, but also exposes the disingenuousness, culpable carelessness, and falsification of the reviewer. He holds Gifford responsible for nothing less than national defamation; and with much reason : for it would seem impossible that an educated Englishman could have believed in the truth of those statements of Faux which he quotes as authority.

The article in The Quarterly — No. 58. July, 1823. — as appears from the statement in a note by Mr. Paulding to "The Preface of the Editor to the first edition" of "John Bull in America", was thrown out of the American republication. It is conceived and executed in the common swashbuckler spirit and style of the British reviews of that day, when discoursing anent America. The author swallows everything Faux says or intimates on his own authority or that of others, and then makes the strangest deductions. Sometimes indeed he construes strong innuendo into absolute assertion.

He puts one in mind on the whole, (considering his industry, his evident relish of morsels, and his implied superiority), of the verse of Mother Goose : —

> "Little Jack Horner, he sat in a corner,
>   Eating his Christmas pie;
>   He put in his thumb, and he pulled out a plum —
>   O, what a smart boy am I!"

Tremendous epithets and nouns substantive, — such as "prostitute rhapsody",. "radical trash", "flippant farrago of impiety, malevolence and folly", "insane drivelling", "filthy and ragged licentiousness", "squatters, rowdies, dirkers, gougers, and riflers "—fly about in an alarming way. And yet they would seem to be inadequate to the need. According to The Quarterly, the plagues of Egypt were as nothing compared to those which had befallen America; and the reviewer can see no good thing in the country, the people, or their institutions.

It were idle at the present day to analyze the article. I shall only, by way of sample, quote a dictum, prophecy, and warning appeal, with which it winds up, and which read oddly enough now.

"The want of an established national religion has made the bulk of the people either infidels or fanatics." —p. 369. " Long ages must pass away before the population, now thinly spread over the immense vale of the Mississippi, will become sufficiently dense to render any part of it a desirable habitation for civilized beings; before markets are established; places of religious worship built; schools for the education of youth instituted; slavery abolished; laws and justice duly administered; the forests and cane-brakes cleared away; the dismal cypress-swamps drained; the rotten bottoms and rank prairies reclaimed from their stagnant and putrid water; — then, and not till then, (and much will still remain to do), can the present race of emigrants, however sanguine, contemplate even the future happy condition of their descendants. In their days, or in their sons' sons' days, little amelioration is to be looked for." — p. 368. "We therefore most earnestly entreat . . . . them" [intending emigrants] "to pause, and carefully to peruse the journal of Farmer Faux, who not only gives his own opinion, but also the opinions of many who, from long experience, are better qualified to judge correctly on the subject." — p. 370.

And further The Quarterly sayeth not — at that time. But it, and the other noted English periodicals, piped pretty continuously to much the same tune.

With such material to work with, our author found it easy to place the wandering and reviewing Bull in a ridiculous light. The embarrassment really besetting him is adverted to in a notice of his book to be found in The Atlantic Magazine, of March, 1825 — Vol. II. p. 393. "After the sanction given by the Quarterly to Faux's Mirabilia, it is obvious that no burlesque could be too extravagant. On the contrary, the difficulty is, that the marvels related by that 'liar of the first magnitude' are so much in the 'Ercles' vein, that it is difficult to mount into a higher region of hyperbole." This is the truth. Rank caricature as the book now seems, whoever looks into the matter can yet clearly perceive its justification. This once admitted, one can not help being amused at the felicitous style in which the fellows of the long-bow are shown up. Even the abrupt and inconsequent manner in which the production ends is characteristic of these spoilers of paper.

I have not attempted to trace the various allusions to travels and travellers which Mr. Paulding has embroidered upon the groundwork of "No. 58". It is well, however, for the reader to remember that these people and their publications were important in their day; for there existed among us at the period a sensitiveness as to English opinion, which, happily, no longer prevails to anything like the same extent.

This sensitiveness was certainly not allowed to sleep. Mr. Tuckerman briefly sums up the whole business. "There was, indeed, from the close of the war of 1812, for a series of years, an inundation of English books of travel, wherein the United States, their people and prospects, were discussed with a monotonous recapitulation of objections, a superficial knowledge, and a predetermined depreciation, which render the task of analyzing their contents and estimating their comparative merit in the highest degree wearisome. Redeemed, in some instances, by piquant anecdote, interesting adventure, or some grace of style or originality of view, they are, for the most part, shallow, egotistical, and more or less repetitions of each other. So systematic and continuous, however, are the tone of abuse and the purpose of disparagement, that the subject claims separate consideration." — AMERICA AND HER COMMENTATORS, pp. 219–220.

It remains then to inquire into the causes of this persistent slander. There was a national jealousy, for one thing; and a desire to prevent emigration for another. These for the solid falsification: as for the rest, after all said and done, I believe that our own countrymen may thank themselves mainly for the many strange stories told of us by the genuine British traveller. There are, and always have been, many of them to whom "it is meat and drink . . . to see a clown " of this sort. They early began to stimulate that appetite for being disgusted or shocked which is so odd a concomitant of the Bull on his peregrinations. Finding his maw so capacious, they have supplied him with ample and varied sustenance, so that he has come at last, in this regard, to make good the eulogy of Polonius on the players, in Hamlet: — " Seneca cannot be too heavy, nor Plautus too light " for him — that is to say, when the matter happens to chime in with his prejudices.

I desire to express my obligation to Mr. Charles H. Hart of Philadelphia, for note-material furnished; and to Mr. Gulian C. Verplanck, for bringing to bear the memory of a contemporary of our author upon one or two questions which must otherwise have baffled me.

" THE TALKING POTATO " of the " Preface of the Editor to the first edition " is understood to have been J. Wilson Croker, one of the early regular contributors to The Quarterly, and an acrimonious and persevering disparager of this country. Of English descent, he was born in Galway, Ireland, and from 1807 to 1832 was a member of the House of Commons.

Captain Thomas Hamilton, 29th Regiment R.A., was the author of "Men and Manners in America", referred to in the "Postscript to the third edition", and there misentitled "Men and Manners in the United States". This book of travels was published in two volumes crown octavo in 1833, and in two volumes duodecimo, at Boston, in 1834. I quote a few remarks made on each side of the water about it at the time, as given in Allibone's Dictionary of Authors.

"We cannot but congratulate our countryman on the appearance of his valuable work at the present crisis, when all the ancient institutions of our country are successively melting away under the powerful solvent of democratic fervor. . . . He neither views America with the jaundiced eye of a bigoted Tory, nor the frantic partiality of an enthusiastic Democrat. He appreciates things as they really are — nothing extenuating, setting down nought in malice." — *Blackwood's Magazine.*

" The more Captain Hamilton's book is studied, the stronger will be the reader's conviction of its merits as a clear and impartial description of the American people." — *Dublin University Magazine.*

" It is undoubtedly as we have said, in point of literary execution, one of the best that have yet appeared upon the United States. The style is not deficient in strength or spirit, and evinces at times a remarkable power of description, as in the passages on the Falls of Niagara and the river Mississippi. On the other hand, it is far from being uniformly so pure and correct as might be wished — is often unpardonably coarse, and is pervaded throughout by an affected pertness and a silly air of pretension, which are offensive from the beginning, and finally become by repetition completely nauseous. . . . That a spirit of unjust depreciation is the one that predominates in his work, is — as we shall have occasion abundantly to show — very certain." — *A. H. Everett. North American Review.*

Some notes were made to " John Bull in America " by the author. Those to the edition of 1837 are distinguished by that date ; those now added, by being included in brackets.

In conclusion, I have only to observe that Mr. Paulding at the time undoubtedly did a service to his country ; and to England — for his book was appreciated there. A hearty laugh is a capital antidote to bad blood : and there was a good deal of that between the two nations about those years. He adopted the best mode of dealing with this sort of maligner. Indeed, take them by and large, were it worth while, every generation of English travellers in this country might be fairly quizzed in pretty much the same style. With a few respectable exceptions, about the same calibre of mind and the same ludicrous conceit have been brought to bear upon us up to the present hour. It is an unhandsome word to say, belike, but " pity 'tis 'tis true " ; and only the hope remains, that the time may come, when it shall be the cue of these little men to use what little influence they may hereafter have, rather in the interests of good feeling than of detraction.

W. I. P.

PREFACE OF THE EDITOR

TO

THE FIRST EDITION.

On the fifth day of August, 1824, a rather genteel-looking stranger arrived at the Mansion Hotel in the city of Washington, where he inquired for a retired room, and expressed his intention of staying some time. He was dressed in a blue frock, striped vest, and gray pantaloons; was about five feet ten, as is supposed, and had a nose like a potato. The evening of the following day there arrived in the stage from Baltimore a little mahogany-faced foreigner, a French-man as it would seem, with gold rings in his ears, and a pair of dimity breeches. The little man in dimity breeches expressed great pleasure at meeting the stran-ger, with whom he seemed to be well acquainted; but the stranger appeared much agitated at the rencounter, and displayed nothing like satisfaction on the occasion. With the evident intention of avoiding the little dark-complexioned man, he, in a few minutes, desired the waiter to show him his room, to which he retired without bidding the other good night.

[169]

It appears from the testimony of the waiter, that on going into his chamber, and observing a portmanteau which had been placed there in his absence, the stranger inquired to whom it belonged. The waiter replied: " To the French gentleman. As you seemed to be old acquaintance, I thought you would like to be together, sir." This information seemed to cause great agitation in the mind of the stranger, who exclaimed, as if unconscious of the presence of the waiter, " I am a lost man!"—which the waiter thought rather particular. The stranger, after a few moments of apparent perplexity, ordered the waiter to bring him pen, ink, paper, and sealing-wax, and then desired to be left alone. It is recollected that the dark-complexioned foreigner retired about ten, requesting to be called up at four o'clock, as he was going on in the stage to the South. This is the last that was seen, of either the stranger or the dark-complexioned foreigner. On knocking at the door precisely at four o'clock the next morning, and no answer being given, the waiter made bold to enter the room, which to his surprise he found entirely empty. Neither baggage, nor stranger, nor dark-complexioned foreigner, was to be found. Had the stranger and his friend previously run up a long score at the Mansion Hotel, their disappearance would not have excited any extraordinary degree of surprise. But the stranger was indebted for only two days' board and lodging, and the dark-complexioned foreigner had paid his bill over night. A person who slept in the next room, recollected hearing a stir in that of the stranger, as he thinks, about three o'clock, but, supposing it to be some one going off in the mail, it excited no particular observation.

This is all that could be gathered in relation to the mysterious disappearance of these two travellers. But on searching about the room a packet was found, carefully sealed, and directed " To the Editor of the ——; " the rest was wanting, and the omission was probably occasioned by some circumstance occurring at the instant, which led to the singular affair above detailed. Some days having elapsed without any thing occuring to throw light on the transaction, it was thought proper to open the packet, the direction of which afforded no clew by which to transmit it to the editor intended, in the hope that something might be learned from it that would lead to a discovery of the names, or the friends, of these mysterious persons. On inspection it proved to be a manuscript of travels in the United States, of which the following is a faithful transcript. Though, as the reader will perceive, it explains very satisfactorily the principal portion of the preceding details, there was nothing in it which could lead directly to a discovery of the name and residence of the unfortunate gentleman, whose fate, although still enveloped in doubt, is but too easily anticipated. All that appears certain from the manuscript is, that the stranger was an Englishman, travelling to New Orleans on business, and that he probably was in some way mysteriously made away with by the little dark-complexioned foreigner, of whom a description has been given, and for whom a reward has been offered, in the public papers, without effect. His name, as given by himself in the examination before the magistrate in New York, is probably fictitious.

After mature reflection, it was decided to publish

the manuscript, as the best and cheapest mode of extending the inquiry concerning the identity of this unfortunate stranger to all parts of the reading world, and thereby acquiring further information. In addition to this motive, it was thought that a work of such extraordinary merit as to style, sentiment, and accuracy of detail, deserved to be made known. Much discussion took place in respect to the selection of a title for the work, which had been omitted in the manuscript. To announce it simply as a book of travels in America, would have been to place it on a footing with the various romances which have been published under that title within the last thirty years. Of these we have lately had such a profusion that the public is rather tired, as we are informed by the booksellers. Some familiar and striking title-page, no matter whether applicable or not to the character of the work, was therefore necessary to excite public attention, and it was finally decided to adopt that which appears, and which we will now proceed to explain.

The character of these travels being that of severe and inflexible truth, a title was chosen in direct antithesis, partly in a sportive imitation of the facetious philosopher Lucian, who gave the name of " A True Story " to one of the most improbable fictions of antiquity; and partly in allusion to Dr. Jonathan Swift, who in like manner disguised one of the gravest of satires under the mask of " A Tale of a Tub," than which nothing can be more opposite to its real character. Thus have we availed ourselves of the catachresis on this occasion, not only for the purpose of agreeably surprising the reader into the perusal of a work of incomparable veracity under the garb of a work of fiction, but also to administer to the public taste, which, owing to the witcheries of that mischievous person called the " Great Unknown," hath an unseemly propensity towards romances and the like.

In this we are justified, not only by the foregoing high authorities, but in an especial manner by the example of certain great critics, who place at the head of their articles, by way of title-page, the name of a book about which they say not one word in the whole course of their lucubrations. So may we see certain well-meaning and orthodox writers, publishing what they call " candid examinations," and " cool considerations," of and concerning certain disputed points, which, to say the truth, are neither candid nor cool, but marvellously the contrary. We mention not these things in a spirit of hostility, but to justify by their examples our adoption of the figure of the catachresis. The reader will therefore err most egregiously if he supposes for a moment that the following work, whatever be its title, bears the most remote resemblance to, or is in any wise tainted with, the egregious fictions of the genuine Munchausen.

Touching the real author of this work, whom we may safely pronounce a second and still greater " Great Unknown," we have our suspicions on the subject, suspicions almost amounting to a certainty, which we shall proceed to lay before the reader. At first, for divers good reasons, we were inclined to suppose the author was no less a person than the " Great Unknown" himself, who, as is asserted, resided in America some time. But however rich, redundant, and inexhaustible, may be the invention of this extraordinary incognito, no one, we think, will deny to our author, notwithstanding his general character of severe veracity, a vigour of fancy and a vein of inventive sportiveness, vastly superior even to the " Great Unknown." We must therefore discard this suggestion, and proceed to put the reader in possession of our settled conviction on this matter, which, as will be seen, amounts to next to a demonstration.

To come to the point without further circumlocution, we have the best reasons as well as the highest circumstantial testimony to warrant us in the assertion, that the author of this work, was, and if living, is still, one of the principal writers of the Quarterly Review — the very person who wrote the masterly review of Faux's Travels in the fifty-eighth number.* To arrive at this conclusion it is only necessary to compare the two works, in the articles of style, temper, feeling, and in short everything which goes to the indication of a personal identity. The style of this work displays the closest resemblance to that of the article on Mr. Faux's Travels, and indeed all the articles relating to the United States, in the Quarterly Review. The same classical severity and mildness of rebuke, where rebuke is necessary — the same happy aptitude in the selection of choice flowers of rhetoric — the same amiable zeal for religion — the same charity to all men — the same principles of universal benevolence — the same gentlemanly observance of the slightest minutiæ of dainty, I might say exquisite, breeding — run through each and all of these

---

* The reader must consult the English copy for this article, which was so extravagantly complimentary, that even the American bookseller modestly omitted it in his re-publication of the number.

productions. Nay, the same expressions and peculiar phrases which characterize the reviewer, occur in almost every page of our author. We have the " turbulent spirit of democracy " — the " wanton violations of the Sabbath " — the " total disregard of religion " — the " spitting, gouging, drinking, duelling, dirking, swearing, strutting republicans " — the " white-robed, levee-going, cow-hiding fine lady " — the " hog-stealing judges " — " the illusions of transatlantic speculation " — " the flippant farragoes of impiety, malevolence, folly, and radical trash " — together with an infinite variety of the favourite phrases of the Quarterly, repeated over and over again with a facility which, we think, can only be accounted for on the supposition that the author and reviewer are one and the same person.

Again, a perfect similarity of temper as well as style reigns throughout both productions. The same display of candour, good nature, urbanity, morality, piety, orthodoxy, and loyalty — the same inflexible impartiality and love of truth — the same chivalrous gallantry to the ladies — the same high-toned courtesy to the gentlemen of this republic — and the same intense horror of the turbulent spirit of democracy — live, breathe, and move, in each. It were an extreme stretch of credulity, to suppose that one kingdom, one quarter of the world, or even the whole universe, could possibly contain two persons so highly and so equally gifted with such extraordinary qualifications. It would be too much for one age. We read indeed of a young Mede, who assured Cyrus that he had two souls; but the idea of two separate persons having one and the same soul is altogether preposterous.

The author of this work, and the superintendent of American affairs in the Quarterly Review, are therefore manifestly identical. This decision acquires additional support from the continual reference to, and quotations from, the latter work, interspersed throughout the former. It is scarcely possible to believe that any person but the reviewer himself could so accurately remember and refer to the most admired passages. Our author, indeed, seems never to have had the Quarterly out of mind, and this circumstance, together with the fact of his always carrying it about with him, and reading it on all occasions, is another decisive proof; since we have occasion to know from our own experience, that an author ever prefers his own works to all others, as certainly as a parent does his own children.

Other symptoms of identity occur in almost every page. Both these productions are equally remarkable for that friendly disposition to the people, the government, and institutions of the United States, which has caused the Quarterly to be so extensively circulated in this country, and patronized by its most distinguished citizens. It would be absurd to suppose that two persons, and those persons foreigners, should simultaneously be animated by such disinterested feelings of good will towards the people of this, or any other, country. We notice, likewise, several other striking similarities; especially an equally accurate knowledge of the geography and history of the United States. The amiable credulity of our author, in occasionally suffering himself to be imposed upon by the relations of others, is also a characteristic of the reviewer, who it must be confessed sometimes stretches his belief into the regions of the marvellous. This credulity is joined with a certain engaging simplicity, which appears, in his occasionally exhibiting himself in a ridiculous light without appearing to be aware of it, and relating things which a more artful and wary person would pass over without notice. This we look upon as the strongest proof of his veracity, and a guaranty for the truth of every thing he advances upon his own authority. In regard to what is told him by others, we would advise the reader to receive it with some grains of allowance.

Having thus, as we presume to imagine, pretty clearly established our position, that the author of the following pages is also the writer of American criticisms in the Quarterly, we shall proceed to indulge in a few speculations as to the precise individual to whom the people of the United States have so frequently been indebted for such friendly notices.

It cannot be the laureate, Mr. Southey, because we are assured he has lately taken rather a dislike to republicans, on account of their blamable indifference to his epic poems. Having in one of these taken the trouble to confer upon them a respectable degree of dignity and antiquity, by peopling the country with a colony of Welsh, commanded by a real prince with an enormous long pedigree, it is another proof of the ingratitude of republics, that the Americans should be so indifferent on the occasion. The laureate's dislike is, therefore, however much it may be lamented, not to be wondered at. But besides this, we have occasion to know that the laureate finds it such a difficult matter to do justice to the glories of his present gracious sovereign, that he has been high and dry aground upon a birthday ode for the last nine months, and there is no telling when he will be delivered. It is whispered in literary circles, that he has called for another butt of sack, to float him off. Others say that, in addition to this, he is engaged upon a second " Vision of Judgment," in which his old antagonist, the late Lord Byron, is condemned to a most unheard-of punishment, to wit, that of reading over all the laureate's epics, sapphics, &c., not forgetting Wat Tyler, twice a year, till he becomes orthodox, and believes in the divine right of kings.

Neither do we think it can possibly be Mr. D'Israeli, it being pretty generally understood that he is entirely devoted to the ladies, and that his specified duty is to keep an eye upon Lady Morgan, to whose " flippant impieties," &c., his *acknowledged orthodoxy* is held to be a most sovereign antidote.

We had at one time settled it in our minds, that these productions came from the pen of the good-natured creature who has so long presided over the Quarterly, and made it renowned throughout all Christendom, for that refined and high-wrought courtesy which is only to be acquired in the cabin of a Newcastle collier. These suspicions were strengthened by our being credibly informed of a little good-tempered old gentleman, who was in this country some time last Spring, and was so delighted with every thing he saw that he fell seriously ill of an ecstatic transport, from which he was finally recovered by smelling a bottle of the pure essence of democracy. These facts staggered us a little; but positive information has since been received that the good man was at that time confined to his house, No. 68 Grub street, with a dyspepsy accompanied by lowness of spirits, occasioned, as is conjectured, by the late act of Parliament abolishing lotteries, whereby his office of comptroller of lottery-offices naturally falls to the ground. It is surmised that the orthodox old gentleman hath it in serious contemplation to abandon the Quarterly, become very wicked, and devote himself to democracy and impiety, unless they bolster up his principles with another sinecure.*

The reader will doubtless give us due credit, when we assure him we have reduced it to a probability, approaching very near to certainty, that the real author of the productions which have been the subject of this inquiry is a gentleman of great orthodoxy, generally known in England by the appellation of " THE TALKING POTATO." We have been at some pains to come at the origin of this whimsical distinction, but upon the whole have not succeeded exactly to our wishes. By some, it is said, that it arose from his talking as if he had a hot potato in his mouth; by others, that it came from his having a nose wonderfully resembling the *Solanum Tuberosum*, or red potato. But the most general opinion is, that it originated in his once having had the misfortune to require trepanning, when Sir Astley Cooper, the great surgeon, was astonished to find the entire cavity of the brain occupied by a thumping Irish potato. This fact was communicated to the college of physicians, but without mentioning

* Previous to this act, abolishing lotteries, Mr. G., it is understood, held two sinecures; to wit, that of paymaster to the "Honourable band of Gentlemen Pensioners," and that to which we have just alluded. The former was given him to support his loyalty, and the latter to maintain his orthodoxy. It is supposed that either his loyalty or his religion will be buried under the ruins of the lottery-offices.

the name, and may be found in one of the volumes of their transactions.

This gentleman, besides his holding "something in the nature of a sinecure", is a member of Parliament, and, as we are informed, one of the genteelest writers of the Quarterly. Besides all this, he is considered the best joker in the House, with the exception of Mr. Canning. He has not the wit of Mr. Canning, but then, as the country members are wont to say in a debate on the causes of agricultural distress, while they are splitting their sides with laughter, "he talks so like a potato." It is a state secret of which we have chanced to become possessed, that "The Talking Potato" did actually come over here, some time in the late recess of Parliament, for the sole purpose of ascertaining the real causes of various naval phenomena which occurred during the late war between England and the United States — a subject which had excited great curiosity among my lords of the Admiralty. We understand that he ascertained, pretty clearly, that the whole secret lay in the trifling circumstances, of a superiority of ships, officers, seamen, and gunnery. This discovery put him in such good humour, that he was wrought upon to compliment the people and country in the polite manner exemplified in the following pages. It is surmised that the result of his mission, in relation to naval matters, will appear in the next edition of Mr. Robert James's * Apology for

[* There is a confusion of names here. *Robert* James (1703–1776) was the inventor of the celebrated fever powder known by his name. The person intended is, no doubt, *William* James, who published in 1822 a "Naval History of Great Britain, from 1793 to 1820", in 5 volumes octavo. The Edinburgh Review and Blackwood, as quoted in Allibone's Dictionary of Authors, thus speak of it: — "This book is one of which it is not too high praise the English Navy. With respect to his object in going to New Orleans, we have some suspicion that it might have been a part of his mission to account for the wonderful disparity of loss in the great battle between the British and the stout hero who defended the city.

The foregoing contains all the particulars we have been able to obtain in elucidation of the following work. We cannot, however, refrain from expressing our earnest hopes, that the doubts of his friends, and the fears of his country, in regard to the fate of this unfortunate gentleman, may be speedily removed by his reappearing and claiming this work, to the credit and profits of which he is entirely welcome. Should the contrary be the case, we beg permission to offer our sincere condolences — to my lords of the Admiralty and to the country members, on the loss of their favourite jester; to the Quarterly Review, on the loss of its most classical writer; and to the nation at large, on the loss of so useful a person as " The Talking Potato."

WASHINGTON, 10th October, 1824.

to assert, that it approaches as nearly to perfection, in its own line, as any historical work perhaps ever did; and we must acknowledge that we cannot contemplate without admiration the impartial and unwearied zeal for historical truth which alone could have supported the author through his tedious and thankless labours." — *Edinburgh Rev.*

" His work is an inestimable one." —*Blackwood's Mag.* 1827.]

JOHN BULL IN AMERICA;

OR THE

NEW MUNCHAUSEN.

CHAPTER I.

Impressions of the author previous to his arrival in America — Embarks from Liverpool — Voyage — Sea-Serpent — Arrives at Boston, the capital of the state of Kennebunk — Account of the city — Manners of the people — Mansion-House Hotel, kept by William Renshaw, an Englishman — Turbulent spirit of democracy — Negroes — Earthquakes — Inundations — Intemperance — Ignorance — Impudence — Barbarity — Athenæum — Literature — Naval officer — Turbulent spirit of democracy — Quarterly Review, &c. — Leave Boston.

PREVIOUS to my departure for the Western paradise of liberty, my impressions with regard to the country were, upon the whole, rather of a favourable character. It is true, I did not believe a word of the inflated accounts given by certain French revolutionary travellers, such as Brissot, Chastellux, and others; much less of those of Birkbeck, Miss Wright, Captain Hall,* and the rest of the radical fry. I was too conversant with the Quarterly Review to be led astray by these Utopian romancers, and felt pretty well

---

* Not Captain Basil Hall, but Captain Francis Hall of the Light Dragoons. 1837.

satisfied that the institutions of the country were altogether barbarous. I also fully believed that the people were a bundling, gouging, drinking, spitting, impious race, without either morals, literature, religion, or refinement; and that the turbulent spirit of democracy was altogether incompatible with any state of society becoming a civilized nation. Being thus convinced that their situation was, for the present deplorable, and in the future entirely hopeless unless they presently relieved themselves from the cumbrous load of liberty under which they groaned, I fell into a sort of compassion for them, such as we feel for condemned criminals having no hope of respite and no claim to benefit of clergy.

Under this impression, and with a determination to look to the favourable side of the subject on all occasions, to be pleased with every thing I saw, and to make a reasonable allowance for the faults originating in their unhappy situation, I left England. I can safely lay my hand on my heart, and declare to the world that I was, and still am, as free from prejudice against any nation whatever, as any English traveller who has ever visited this country.

Being fully aware of the superiority of British ships and British sailors, I declined the advice of certain merchants at Liverpool to embark in one of the line of American packets, and took passage on board the British brig Wellington, for Boston, as my business was principally in New Orleans, and I wished to arrive at the nearest port. I did not like to go directly for New Orleans, being apprehensive of the yellow-fever, which rages there all the year round, with such virulence that the people all die off regularly once in two years. Our passage was long and tedious, so much so that the packet in which I was advised to sail from Liverpool arrived at Boston four weeks before the Wellington. But this I am assured was owing more to good fortune than to any superiority either in the ship or sailors, over those of the mistress of the seas. I passed my time both pleasantly and profitably in reading the Quarterly.

On the seventieth day from losing sight of Old England, we made land at Cape Hatteras, the eastern point of Boston Bay, which we entered just before sunset; and, being favoured with a fine fair wind from the North, came up to the wharf in about two hours from entering the Capes. Coming up, we saw the famous sea-serpent, but he was nothing to those I had frequently seen in the Serpentine, so called from its abounding in these articles. Being very anxious to go on shore, I desired one of the sailors to call a hack, which very soon arriving, I ordered the fellow to drive me to the best hotel in the place: accordingly he put me down at the Mansion-House Hotel, kept by William Renshaw, a place of great reputation throughout the United States. The fellow charged me a quarter of a dollar, which is twice as much as I should have paid in London! Being determined not to be imposed upon, I appealed to the landlord, who assured me it was all right; so I paid him, after giving himself and his horses a hearty malediction.

The landlord, civilly enough, considering the country I was in, desired to know if I wished to have a room for the night. I answered him in the affirmative, and begged, as a particular favour, that he would put me into one with not more than six beds in it. He seemed a little surprised, but assured me my wishes should be gratified. I was accordingly shown into a neat room enough, with a single bed. Ay, ay, thought I, this landlord knows how to distinguish his guests — but my wonder subsided when the waiter, who I was surprised to find was a white man, told me his master was an Englishman.

Soon after, I was called down to supper, where I found twenty or thirty persons, all perfect strangers to me, and who, seeing I was a stranger I suppose, paid me those little civilities, which, to one who knows the world, are always sufficient to put him on his guard. Accordingly I declined them all, and answered the questions put to me rather short, insomuch that a person, whom I took to be a naval officer, seemed inclined to quarrel with me. Nothing, indeed, can be more disgusting to a stranger than these civilities from people one does not know; and nothing gave me a more unfavourable impression of the rude manners of these republicans, than the freedom with which they chatted about their private affairs, and joked each other before me, a perfect stranger. It displayed a want of — tact — a familiarity so different from the conduct of people in similar circumstances in London, that I retired to my room in disgust. I afterwards learned that the naval officer threatened to " lick " me, as he called it, for my surly ill manners, as he was pleased to denominate my gentlemanly reserve.

I retired to rest, and found my bed tolerable enough; but the American goose-feathers are by no means so soft as those of London. In the morning

I went down to breakfast, determined to keep these forward gentry at a distance. But it did not appear to be necessary, as none of these rude boors took the least notice of me, and if I wanted any thing, I was obliged to call the waiter to bring it to me, for no one offered to hand it about the table. I was exceedingly disgusted at this Gothic want of politeness, which, however, was nothing strange, considering the vulgar habits of equality which prevail in this republic; so I called for a coach, with an air of importance, and rode round the city, with a view of seeing into the character and habits of the people.

The first thing that struck me, was the vast disproportion of negroes, in the streets and everywhere else. I may affirm, with perfect veracity, that nearly one half the inhabitants of Boston are black. Each of these poor creatures has a white man always standing over him, with a large club about the thickness of a man's arm, with which he beats the poor slave for his amusement. I assure you I have seen, I may say, a thousand instances of this kind of a morning. There is hardly a slave here that has not his head covered with scars, and bound up with a handkerchief; and almost every step you take, you perceive upon the pavement the stains of blood, which, I am assured by Governor Hancock himself, is that of the negroes. I have seen a lady of the first distinction here, walking the Mall, as it is called, with a stout black fellow behind her, and occasionally amusing herself with turning round and scratching his face till it was covered with blood. This *Mall* is a place of about half an acre, covered with dust, with a few rotten elms, and a puddle in the centre.

Even the little children here are initiated into human blood almost as soon as they are able to walk; and the common amusement of young persons is to stick pins in their black attendants, while every boy has a little negro, of about his own age, to torture for his pastime.

The blacks here, as I was assured by his excellency the Governor, whose name is Hancock, have but one meal a day, which is principally potatoes, and fare little better than the miserable Irish or English peasantry at home. The Governor told me a story of a man, who tied his black servant naked to a stake, in one of the canebrakes near the city, which abound with a race of musketoes that bite through a boot. Here he was left one night, in the month of December, which is a spring month in this climate, and the next morning was found stone dead, without a drop of blood in his body. I asked if this brutal tyrant was not brought to justice. The Governor shrugged up his shoulders, and replied, that he was now a member of Congress!

To an Englishman, who is accustomed to see white men only in a state of slavery and want, it is shocking to see black ones in a similar situation. My heart bled with sympathy for the wrongs of this injured race, and I could not sufficiently admire the philanthropy of the members of the Holy Alliance who have lately displayed such a laudable compassion for the blacks.

Next to the continual recurrence of these disgusting exhibitions of cruelty, the most common objects seen in the streets of Boston, are drunken men women and children. I was assured by the Mayor, Mr.

Phillips, one of the most charitable and philanthropic men in the State of Maine, that, on an average, every third person was drunk every day, by nine o'clock in the morning. The women however, don't get fuddled, he tells me, till after they have cleared the breakfast table and put the room to rights, when they set to and make merry with the young children, not one in a hundred of whom ever sees the inside of a school or a church. The consequences of this mode of life are, that the whole of the people exhibit a ruddy complexion, and what appears at first sight to be a strong muscular figure; but on a closer examination the roses will be found to be nothing more than what is called grog-blossoms, and the muscular appearance only bloated intemperance.

Ignorance is the natural result of a want of knowledge, as the Quarterly says. Consequently, where children never go to school, it is not probable that learning will flourish. Accordingly, nothing can equal the barbarous ignorance of both the children and grown-up persons in this republican city. I happened to be at the house of a judge of one of the courts, and was astonished to find, on my giving his son, a boy of about twelve years old, a book to read, that he could not comprehend a single word! The poor mother, who was, I suppose, a little mortified on account of my being a stranger, (they don't mind these things among themselves), patted the booby on the back, and assured me the poor boy was *so* bashful! Most of the justices of the peace here, make their mark, instead of signing their names to warrants, &c.; and, what is difficult to believe, many of the clerks in the banks can't write their names. I never saw a school while in Boston. There is a college, to be sure, but I was assured the professors did not quite understand English. The Rev. Cotton Mather, one of the most enlightened and popular preachers here, has written a book called the Magnalia, in which he gives a variety of witch stories, such as would be laughed at even among the Indians, but which they all believe here, as firmly as Holy Writ. The work is just come out,* and affords apt illustration of the state of the human intellect on this side of the Atlantic.

Religion is, if possible, in a worse state than literature, manners, or morals. There is not a single church in Boston, nor any religious exercises on Sunday, except in a few *school-rooms*, by the Methodists and other fanatics. I am assured it is the custom all over New England, as well as in the states of Newburyport and Pasquotank, to spend the Sabbath like every other day in the week, except that they put on clean clothes, a thing never thought of, even among the most fashionable ladies, except on that occasion.

Boston is a terrible place for fevers and agues. Every one of the inhabitants, except the slaves, is afflicted with them in the spring and autumn, as sure as the leaves appear in the former, and fall in the latter. The consequence is, that they look like so many peakish and miserable ghosts, and, if you go into the shops, you may hear the money jingling in the pockets of the shop-keepers by the mere force of habit,

[* The *Magnalia* was printed in London, in folio, in 1702 . . . It was not till 1820 that it was reprinted in America, at Hartford. — *Duyckinck's Cyc. of Am. Lit.*]

even if the poor man should happen, at that moment, to be free from the ague, or " shake," as they call it.

Besides this, they have earthquakes and inundations, three times a week if not more. After the earthquake generally comes an inundation, which destroys all the crops for hundreds of miles round, and covers the country so that the tops of trees and chimneys just appear above the water. This is succeeded by a fog so thick, that many persons are lost in the streets of Boston, and wander about several days, without being able to find any of the houses. This is the origin of the phrase " I guess," so universal in New England; for these fogs are so common, that one half the time people are obliged to " guess" at what they are about. Hence, too, the half pint of whiskey which every man takes in the morning the first thing he does after getting up, is called an anti-fogmatic.

These are the principal things I observed in my morning's ride. At dinner the naval officer took occasion to make himself most indecently merry with certain sarcasms on the stupid, surly, self-importance, which *some* people attempted to pass off for real dignity and high breeding. The rudeness of republicanism, indeed, is obvious to the most superficial observer, from the first moment a man sets foot in this country of beastly equality. After dinner, a person who had been troubling me with his attentions since my arrival, offered to carry me to the Athenæum, a great literary institution, where they talk politics and read newspapers, which they mistake for literature. I must not forget to observe, that nothing can be worse than the taste of these people, which is perfectly barbarous, except their genius, which is perfectly barren. Nothing is read here but newspapers, almanacs, dying-speeches, ghost stories, and the like. Their greatest scholar is Noah Webster, who compiled a spelling-book, and their greatest poet the author of Yankee Doodle. The utmost effort of republican genius is to write an additional stanza to this famous song, which, in consequence of these perpetual contributions, is, by this time, almost as long as a certain Persian poem, which, if I recollect right, consisted of one hundred and twenty thousand verses.

I brought letters to some of the principal magnificoes here, but did not deliver them. I like the dinners and old wine of these vulgarians, but really it is paying too much for them to be obliged to listen to their vulgar hemp, cotton, tobacco, and nankeen speculations, without being allowed the privilege of laughing, or even yawning in their stupid faces. Then one is obliged to drink wine with madam, be civil to her dowdy daughters who " guess they have no occasion for dancing," and — what is the climax of horrors — retire from the dinner-table to the drawing-room, to hear miss break the sixth commandment in the matter of half a dozen sonatas, and two dozen of Moore's Melodies.

By the time I had sojourned a single day in the land of promise, I began to be mortally *ennuyé*. I inquired of the waiter if there was any thing in the *fancy* way going on. He replied, there were plenty of fancy stores in Court street! I asked if there was likely to be a mob soon, as I had heard these republicans amused themselves in that way. He replied, that mobs never happened in Boston. Any executions? No. " My G—d," exclaimed I in despair, " what a dull place!" I devoted the evening to packing up, and, after supper, being desirous to make an impression on these bumpkin demos, called out loudly to the waiter, in my best Corinthian tone—" Waiter! — you infernal waiter!" " Here, sir." " Waiter, bring a boot-jack and pair of slippers." " Waiter—you infernal waiter," replied a voice which I took for an echo. " Here, sir," said the waiter. " Waiter, bring me two boot-jacks, and two pair of slippers." On looking round, I perceived the echo was my old enemy, the naval officer. Being determined, however, to take no notice of such a low fellow, I again called out —" Waiter, bring a candle into my chamber, and a warmingpan to warm my bed." " Waiter, bring two candles, and two warmingpans, into my chamber: I shall sleep in two beds to night", cried echo. I gave him a look of withering contempt and walked out of the room, leaving behind me a horse-laugh, which, as I judged, proceeded from these illiterate cyclops. Before I went to bed I looked over the fifty-eighth number of the Quarterly, to refresh my memory.

CHAPTER II.

Turbulent spirit of democracy — Leave Boston for Charleston, N.C. — Great ship — Captain Hull — Eating negroes — Cruelty — Judge D. — Yankee dinner — Mode of eating — Terrapins, cant word for young negroes — System of farming — Yale college — Ignorance of the professor — Hoax — Turbulent spirit of democracy — Turkey Buzzards, called eagles here — Fogs — Drunken driver — Mail robbers — Wild beasts — Little Frenchman — Turbulent spirit of democracy — Yankee breakfast — Judge, colonel, deacon, driver — Spirit of democracy — Shooting at a mark — Unlucky mistake — Spirit of democracy — Catastrophe of Ramsbottom, &c.

BEING determined to hold as little communication as possible with the turbulent spirit of democracy, the next day, without asking any questions, I took the stage, crossed a bridge to the north of Boston which bestrides the Potomac river, and in less than half an hour arrived in Charleston, the capital of the state of North Carolina, a city famous for eating negroes. It is about three miles from Boston. There is a navy-yard at this place, which I visited, and saw a ship building there which is four hundred and twenty yards long, and, as Capt. Hull, the commandant, assured me, would carry three hundred long forty-two pounders. She is called a seventy-four! The captain, who is a tall rough-looking man, with black eyes and immense whiskers, told me in confidence, that the only way he could persuade the Yankee sailors to stand to their guns in his engagement with the gallant Dacres, was by promising them, in case of victory, to roast the fat black cook of the Constellation, as his ship was called, for supper. Nothing will make these cannibal republicans fight like a temptation of this sort.

Charleston is about the size of Boston, but has

neither pavements nor sidewalks, and alternates between mud and dust, and dust and mud. In summer
it is all dust, in winter all mud. Indeed I began
to perceive, the moment I arrived here, that I had got
amongst a different sort of people from those of Boston. There was no one to be seen in the streets but
negroes stark naked as they were born, with their
backs striped like a leopard in consequence of the
frequent application of the lash. In fact, the principal
article for sale here at the retail shops, is the cow-hide,
as it is called, that is, a hard ox-skin, twisted in
the shape of a whip. Almost every man you see has
one of these in his hand, and a spur at his heel, to
make people believe he carries the whip for his horse.
But I was assured by the head waiter at the City
Hotel, kept by Mr. Chester Jennings,* in Charleston,
that it was for the purpose of beating the slaves.
Nothing indeed will tempt the whites to exert themselves in this enervating climate, but the luxury of
" licking a fellow," as they call it; and almost the first
thing I noticed, in coming into the city, was a tall,
lank, cadaverous figure, strutting up and down, cutting and hacking with his cow-hide at every negro
man, woman, and child, that came in his way. I inquired of the driver what these blacks had been guilty
of. " Guilty," replied he, " guilty — eh! O, lord bless
you sir, it's only Judge D—— amusing himself with
the niggers." It made my heart bleed to see the
blood running down their backs. It was almost as
bad as shooting the Irish peasants for being out after
nine o'clock.

[* Well known in New York, forty years ago, as the landlord of the City
Hotel.]

I had scarcely been at my hotel an hour when this same Judge D—— called upon me, as a stranger, and invited me to dinner the next day. My blood rose up against the brute, but as I wished to see whether some of the stories told about these people, and which they deny, were true, I accepted his invitation. The party consisted of Judge D——'s wife, two daughters, and about a dozen of the principal men of the place, among whom was the governor of South Carolina, Mr. Heister.* Behind each of the seats, as well the judge's as those of his lady and daughters, stood a black boy or girl, as it happened, perfectly naked, and each of the guests was provided with a cow-hide, with which to chastise any neglect of duty on the part of the slaves. There was cut and come again. The judge and his guests cut their meat and cut the negroes, alternately, and I particularly noticed the dexterity of the young ladies in touching the tender places with the cow-hide, as well as their infinite delight in seeing the victims wince under the application. One of these poor wretches having the misfortune to break a plate during dinner, was taken out, put under the window by the overseer, and beat so cruelly that her moans were heard over half the city. When she came in again, the tears were rolling down her cheeks, and the blood trickling down her naked back. The indifference with which every one of the company but myself beheld all this, convinced me that it was the custom of the country.

The dinner was, in the main, good enough. That is to say, there was a plenty of things naturally good,

[* Joseph Heister was governor of Pennsylvania, from December 1820 to December 1823.]

but, what was very remarkable, it was brought up in wooden dishes, out of which they all helped themselves with their fingers, knives and forks not being in use in America, except among a few English people. There was a very suspicious dish on the table, which they called terrapin soup, in which I observed what had exactly the appearance of the fingers and toes of little negroes. I afterwards learned that this was actually the case, and that terrapin is the cant name for black children, as papoose is for those of the Indians. During the dessert, an unlucky slave happened to let fall a knife to which he was helping his mistress, who snatched it up in a great passion and gave him a deep gash in the face. I dropt my knife and fork in astonishment, but nobody else seemed to notice this horrible incident.

The next morning I strolled out into the fields, with a view of seeing the system of rural economy practised in the South. One of the best-managed plantations, I was told, was that of his excellency Governor Hancock, whose name is signed to the declaration of independence, said to be written by one Jefferson,* a player belonging to the Philadelphia theatre. The governor is a brisk, troublesome little man, about forty. His plantation is at a place called Ompompoonoosuck — a name redolent of barbarism. I saw plenty of slaves, and a scarcity of every thing else. The principal products are rice, cotton, and tobacco. The rice grows generally upon the high grounds; but the cotton requires to be covered with

[* Joseph Jefferson, represented by the critics of his time as an excellent actor — grandfather of his namesake, whom we of the present day know to be admirably gifted in the same art.]

water occasionally. The best is called Sea Island, because it grows upon little islands in the mill-ponds, which the people here, according to their universal practice of hyperbole, call seas. As for the tobacco, this filthy and unwholesome weed is found to flourish best in the negro grave-yards, where it is commonly raised, and where you may every day during the month of January, when it is ripe, see the children of the slaves gathering it from the very graves of their parents. This tobacco is used as food by men, women, and children, who eat it as we do salad. Here I saw the poor negroes working bare-headed, and I might say bare-backed, in the broiling sun, which sometimes actually sets fire to their woolly heads, of which I saw several examples in the course of my travels. Two or three heads were already beginning to smoke, and I was told, if I staid half an hour longer I might see them in a blaze. However, having seen enough to convince me that the system of farming here was execrable, and finding it getting rather cold, I returned home by another route, which gave me an opportunity of seeing Yale college.

In reconnoitring about, I fell in with one of the professors, to whom, willing to see whether the poor man understood Latin, I paid my compliments *in forma pauperis*. The professor, after staring at me with a most ludicrous expression of ignorant wonder, asked me whence I came, and upon my answering "last from Charleston, South Carolina," shrugged up his shoulders, and replied, "it was really so far off, that he could not undertake to direct me," although the steeples were full in sight! From this we may judge of the state of learning and information on this

side the Pacific. Being determined to hoax these
poor souls, I filled a box with pebbles, old mortar, and
crumbling brick-bats, which I sent to the faculty as a
valuable set of American minerals; whereupon they
unanimously bestowed upon me the degree of doctor
of laws. There were some vitrified masses I picked
up near an old glass-house which caused great speculation, being considered unquestionable volcanic productions. When questioned as to their locality, I
sent them on a wild-goose-chase in search of a burning mountain.

Becoming tired of Charleston, its negroes and turkey-buzzards, (which the turbulent spirit of democracy has dubbed eagles), and desirous of getting to
New Orleans as early as possible, I took a seat in the
stage for Portsmouth, Georgia, and departed before
daylight the next morning. When it should have
been daylight, the fog was so thick it was impossible
to see the leaders, and I'expressed some apprehension.
One of the passengers assured me however, that, as
the driver was drunk as a matter of course, daylight
was of no consequence — it was trusting to Providence at all events. Indeed, I am assured by persons
of veracity, that travellers in this country place their
chief dependence on the horses, who, being left pretty
much to themselves in consequence of the intoxica-
tion of the drivers, acquire a singular discretion, and
seldom run away except when the driver is sober.
Thus we travelled under the guidance of instinct, till
near ten o'clock, when objects gradually became visible along the road. The driver about this time waked
up, and I was congratulating myself on his appearing sober; but the same communicative passenger

assured me it was of no consequence, for he would be drunk again by the time breakfast was over.

I had heard a great deal about the populousness of the country in the neighbourhood of Boston; but I can safely affirm that, during the whole of this morning's ride, I saw neither house nor human being along the road. We heard indeed a deal of barking and howling at no great distance, which the communicative passenger assured me was that of various kinds of wild beasts, that abound in these parts. He told me they frequently surrounded the stage, devoured the horses, and, if their hunger was not then satisfied, topped off with the driver and passengers. Indeed, what with mail robberies, which happened almost every night, and attacks of wild beasts, there was little hope of getting to the end of a journey of a dozen miles alive. "*Boutez en avant!*," roared out a little Frenchman in a corner, taking a great pinch of snuff at the same time. All this, thought I, comes of the turbulent spirit of democracy.

Breakfasting at a little town, which, like all other towns in this country, is called the *city* of Hartford, I saw a young lady devour thirty-six cucumbers moistened with a quart of vinegar. After which, she sat down, played Lodoiska on the piano, and then went into the field to pull onions. Such horrible incongruities are generated in the rankness of democracy! There was a child of about eight years old in the room, who called for an antifogmatic, which he drank off at one swallow, after which he lighted a cigar and amused himself with singeing the woolly pate of a little black boy, or *terrapin* as they call them when made into soup. According to the prediction of the communicative passenger, the driver was nodding again on his seat in less than half an hour after starting. I was so provoked that I threatened to *lick* him, as the naval officer said at Boston. But the communicative passenger cautioned me against this, assuring me the driver was a man of great consequence — a member of congress — judge of the court — colonel of militia — justice of the peace — deacon of the church — constable, and keeper of the county jail withal. "So," continued the communicative passenger, "he can issue a warrant — take you into custody — try you for an assault — clap you in jail — keep watch over you when there — and finally, have you prayed against by the whole congregation." "Diable!" exclaimed the little Frenchman, in broken English; "these democrat Yankees have as many offices as their citizen-hogs have hind legs." "Why, how many legs have our citizen-hogs, as you call them, monsieur?", said the communicative passenger. "Why, eight at least," replied the other, "or they could never furnish the millions of hams which I see every where. Diable! I have breakfasted upon ham — dined upon ham — and supped upon ham, every day since I arrived in this country. Yes sir, it is certain your pigs must have at least eight hams a piece;" upon which he politely offered me a pinch of snuff, which I refused with cold dignity. If I know myself, I have no national prejudices; but I do hate Frenchmen.

Though anxious to gain information, I cannot condescend to mix with these rank republicans, ask questions, and take the usual means of gaining it. I wanted to know the reason of such a multiplicity of offices being united in one person; but it was enough for me to permit these low-lived scum of democracy to give me information, without demeaning myself to ask for it. Luckily the little Frenchman, like all his detestable countrymen, was fond of talking. " Pray," said he, " how comes it that his honour the colonel, deacon, stage-driver, has so many offices; or, as you Yankees say, so many irons in the fire ? One would think that men were as scarce in this country, as hams are plenty." " Why, the truth is," replied the communicative traveller, " that being one of three persons out of the whole county that can read, it is necessary he should labour in a variety of vocations, for the good of his country. Besides, as every democrat is by nature and habit a drunkard, a sober man among them is like a good singer at a feast; the one is knocked down for all the songs, and the other is under the necessity of playing the jack-of-all-trades." " Diable!" exclaimed the little Frenchman, " do you call this colonel stage-driver a sober man ? " " Why, not exactly," replied the other; " but this valuable person has been drinking so long and so constantly, that habit has become second nature, and he is never so wise, valiant, discreet, and pious, as when he is full charged with apple-brandy." So much for the spirit of democracy, thought I.

The country through which we passed, everywhere exhibits traces of the lazy, ragged, and dirty genius of democracy, who prides himself on his beggary, and riots in the want of all those elegancies which civilized nations consider essential to existence. A few miserable negro huts without roof or windows, and a few half-starved, half-naked negroes, dot the sterile landscape here and there. The only white people we saw, were a knot of half-drunken savages, assembled about a log-hut, shooting at a mark. Here we stopped to water the horses, and I looked about to see the mark at which they were trying their skill. " You are curious," said the communicative traveller, " to know what they are shooting at. Look at that little negro. They will tie him to yonder post anon, and shoot at him till he is torn to atoms, as they do at turkeys, for sixpence a shot." Another proof of the horrible spirit of democracy. The person who gave me this information added, that when they had finished this trial of skill, they would, in all probability, turn to and take a few shots at each other for mere amusement.

We arrived at Portsmouth, an inland town, capital of Georgia, where, being heartily sick of this bundling, guessing, tippling den of democracy, I thought I would, for once, depart from my ordinary rule, and inquire when I might calculate on getting to New Orleans. I accordingly put the question to the landlord; but the little impatient Frenchman, who was close at my heels, took the word — " New Orleans! Diable! are you going to New Orleans, monsieur?" Thinking his surprise might have some connexion with the yellow-fever, I was thrown off my guard, and, before I knew it, condescended to answer, " Yes, I am " — but with cold dignity. The little villain took a huge pinch of snuff, blew his nose like a trumpet, and exclaimed — " To New Orleans! You are going to New Orleans, and I am going away from it as fast as I possibly can! One of us must be going the wrong way, that's certain. Pray," said he, turning to the communicative traveller, " will monsieur be good enough to tell me whether I am travelling north or south, to New Orleans or Passamaquoddy?" "Due north — in the very eye of the North star — to Passamaquoddy, and not to New Orleans, monsieur," answered the other. "Monsieur," said the little villain, turning to me, and offering a pinch of snuff with a low bow — "Monsieur, when you get into a stage coach, do you ever condescend to inquire where it is going? I am an old traveller, and, as we are going to part, never perhaps to meet again, let me conjure you, by the memory of your ancestors and the victory of Waterloo, never to set out on a journey without inquiring whither you are going. However, monsieur, it is an ill wind that blows nobody good. I am going no farther North than this place, shall finish my business here this afternoon, and to-morrow, if monsieur pleases, we will set out for the South, which I assure you is the very best way to New Orleans." "And I," said the communicative traveller, "shall also return in the morning, and mean to go South as far as the city of Charleston, so that we shall have the pleasure of each other's company for a thousand miles at least." "A thousand miles!" repeated I, for here again surprise overcame my dignified reserve — "Why, I thought"———. But I stopped short, being unwilling to give the little rascal of a Frenchman another laugh, by letting him into the secret of a certain blunder which shall be nameless. "On the whole," observed the communicative traveller, "you have not lost much by this little ride out of your way. You have had an opportunity of seeing one of the finest and best-cultivated parts of the country; and a portion of the most moral, as well as enlightened, of the people. And you have lost no time by the little excursion, for, I am credibly informed, such has been the mortality at New Orleans, that there is not a single human being left alive there. Nay, the very dogs, cats, and parrots are extinct. You may as well wait, therefore, till it is peopled again, which will be very soon, for the folks in this country, particularly the democrats, don't mind dying in the summer, if they can only have a merry winter beforehand." Here our conversation was interrupted by a loud cry of " Help — murder — help!" proceeding from an adjoining room. On running in to see what was the matter, we found that a son of the landlord, (who, by the way, was a general), about eight years of age, had thrown his mother down on the floor, and was beating, biting, scratching, and mauling her in a dreadful manner, while the general stood by, laughing and clapping his hands in ecstacy, every moment crying out, " That's it — that's my fine fellow — O! he'll make a brave republican!" Such are the first lessons of children in this chosen land of bundling, gouging, drunkenness, impertinence, impiety — and, to sum up all in one word, *democracy*.

Heaven be praised, thought I, the force of democracy can go no further; but I was mistaken with a vengeance. Just at this moment we had a terrible explosion, which I at first thought was the little Frenchman sneezing: but it turned out, on inquiry, to be something of a far different nature. Though my heart sickens at the bare recital, I shall give the story, for the benefit of all the admirers of democracy.

It seems a fellow of the name of Ramsbottom, a man-milliner by trade, and a roaring patriot, had taken offence at a neighbour whose name was Higginbottom, because his wife had attempted to cheapen a crimped tucker, and afterwards reported that he sold his articles much dearer than his rival man-milliner over the way, whose name was Winterbottom, and whose next-door neighbour, one Oddy, was Winterbottom's particular friend. In the pure spirit of democracy, Ramsbottom determined to dirk, not only Higginbottom and his wife, and Winterbottom, and Oddy, and their wives; but all the young Higginbottoms, Winterbottoms, Oddys, and little Oddities. It was some years before Ramsbottom could get them all together, so as to make one job of it. At last he collected the whole party at his own house, to spend their Christmas eve, and determined to execute his diabolical purpose. It appears, however, from what followed, that he had previously changed his mind as to the dirking, probably because it was too much trouble: (for these democrats hate trouble above all things). Just as they were up to the eyes in a Christmas-pie, the explosion which I had just heard took place, and the whole party, Ramsbottom, Higginbottom, Winterbottom, and Oddy, together with their wives, and all the little Ramsbottoms, Winterbottoms, Higginbottoms, Oddys, and Oddities, were blown into such small atoms that not a vestige of them was to be found. I saw their bodies afterwards, all terribly mangled and torn to pieces. Such is the intense and never-dying spirit of vengeance generated by the turbulent spirit of democracy, that the desperado, Ramsbottom, it appears, did not scruple, like the republican Samson of old, to pull down destruction on himself, that he might be revenged on his enemies.

CHAPTER III.

Little Frenchman — Treatment of Slaves — Mode of baking sawdust cakes — Kitchen-furniture — Spirit of Democracy — Apostrophe — Mode of paying bills by the Yankees and French — Little Frenchman again — Solitary inn — Attempt to rob and murder the author — Bandit disguised as a stage-driver — Arrival at Boston — Gives the little Frenchman the slip.

In order to get rid of the little Frenchman, with his confounded mahogany face, gold ear-rings, and dimity breeches, who seemed inclined to be impertinently jocular with my mistaking the way to New Orleans, I determined to say nothing, but defer my journey a day longer.

Accordingly I apprized the landlord of my intention, and suffered the stage to depart without me. With a view to keep up my dignity, as well as to acquire all the information possible, in relation to the country, its people, and manners, I determined to remain in my room all day, take my meals in dignified retirement, and seize every opportunity of questioning the waiter. From him I gathered many precious items concerning the blessed effects of the turbulent spirit of democracy.

He solemnly assured me, that all the servants eat off the kitchen floor, which, in these parts, instead of boards, is usually of mud, well trodden by the pigs. In this land of equality, these animals are admitted to all the privileges of citizenship, vote at elections, and, I believe, are eligible to the highest offices, provided they are natural-born pigs. On my inquiring how they understood the votes of these freeholders, he replied, that a grunt was always considered as a suff-rage in favour of the democratic ticket, and a squeak for the federal or aristocratic party. Hence abundance of pains is taken to teach the pigs either to grunt or to squeal, according as their owners belong to one party or the other; and many a vote is changed by certain sly pinches of the pigs' ears, as they are brought up to give their suffrages.

The waiter further informed me, in the course of my investigations into kitchen affairs, that the poor servants, who are all blacks and slaves in this part of the country, had neither beds nor covering at night, but pigged together in the ashes, where they often squabbled and fought all night, either to get near a little live coal, or to keep each other warm by exercise. As to food, one may *guess*, as these vulgar democrats say—one may guess what that is, when I state, on the information of the waiter, that the week before I came to Portsmouth, in this very kitchen, a murder was committed by one gentleman of colour on another, in consequence of a dispute about the property of a bone which had been picked six days in succession. The murderer at last seized the bone, hit his adversary on the temple, and killed him instantly; after which he buried him in the mud of the kitchen, and sat himself quietly down to gnaw his prize. The waiter further stated, that they were allowed no cooking utensils, and that the way they generally baked their bread, which is altogether of sawdust, was to lie down at night, with the soles of their feet, on which they had plastered the dough, extended towards the fire. They then go to sleep, and by the time the cake begins to burn their feet so as to wake them, it is done. This sawdust bread is their chief food; but candour obliges me to state, that once in a great while they are treated to a bit of spoiled codfish or tainted pork, which makes them almost run mad with ecstacy. Determined to make the most of this meeting with such an intelligent fellow, I continued to question him concerning the number of pots, kettles, stew-pans, &c., in the kitchen — their state, quality, and condition — whether they had any knives and forks allowed them, and if the latter had three prongs? — whether the little negroes were taught their prayers? — and whether the pigs were permitted to eat out of the same dish with them? Touching the pots and kettles, he assured me, upon his honour, that there was but one pot, with one ear, in the whole establishment; that the kettle was still worse off than the pot, having had no handle within the memory of man; that the only knife they had was half the stump of a blade, without edge or point, which, however, was rather a lucky circumstance, since, as they were always fighting at meals on account of the scarcity prevailing, they would do mischief if they had knives; that, as to forks, it was the landlady's maxim that fingers were made before knives and forks; that the little people of colour were taught nothing but swearing; and that the pigs always breakfasted before them, on account of being considered freeholders and entitled to vote.

In this way I gained more insight into the nature of the turbulent spirit of democracy, than if I had mixed with half the people of the town, and asked as many questions as a Yankee democrat. Indeed I had read in all our books of travels, that these bundling, gouging republicans, although they asked a dozen questions in a minute, were principled against answering any.　This, I was told by the waiter, arises, in a great degree, from the fact that almost every white man is generally in court a dozen or twenty times a year, for some offence or other, (principally that of murder,) in consequence of which they get a habit of being shy in answering interrogatories. " But," said I, at the conclusion of my examination, " how does it happen that you are so plump and well clad, if your fellows are thus naked and starved ? " " Why," replied the fellow, showing his white teeth from ear to ear—" Why, if master must know, I make a point of helping myself out of the dishes, as I go in and out; and my master keeps me well dressed, for the honour of the house."　Alas! thought I to myself, here is another proof of the demoralizing effects of slavery!　This honest man is obliged to descend to the degradation of rifling apple-tarts, and embezzling mouthfuls of mutton, to keep himself from starving!— O, Wilberforce!, well mayest thou endanger the lives of all the white people of the West Indies, in thy attempts to benefit the blacks!— O, Buxton !,* well mayest thou be permitted to poison half the people of London with thine execrable small beer, in consideration of thy godlike philanthropy!— And, O, Betty *Martin!*, well mayest thou be allowed to hunt, shoot, and hang up the wild Irish, in consideration of thine eloquent speeches in Parliament, in

[* Sir Thomas Fowell Buxton, for seven years, beginning with 1811, was partner in a brewery.　Returned member of Parliament from Weymouth in 1818, upon the retirement of Wilberforce, in 1825, he became leader of the anti-slavery party in England.]

behalf of brawned pigs, crammed turkeys, and plugged lobsters!

In the evening I paid my bill, which seemed rather to astonish the landlord, and in truth it was a most swingeing one. At first I demurred; but upon the poor fellow's assuring me he was obliged to charge strangers, particularly Englishmen, treble, and sometimes quadruple, to make up for the losses sustained by his own countrymen and the Frenchmen, who generally went away without paying at all, I paid him with the air of an English nobleman, expecting he would dub me My Lord; but he received the money with perfect indifference, and did not even condescend to bow or thank me. Such is the influence of the turbulent spirit of democracy!

In the morning, as usual in all parts of this country, we set forth before daylight, so that I could not see my fellow-passengers. Two reasons combine to produce this republican custom of travelling before day, and after dark. In the first place, it gives opportunity for robbing the stages, the drivers and owners of which, as I am assured, are, generally, in league with the bands of robbers which infest all parts of this country, to the number, sometimes, of two or three thousand in a band. In the second place, as there are generally two or three pick-pockets in every stage-coach, and forty or fifty in every steam-boat, the darkness gives a capital scope for the exercise of this fashionable republican vocation. Aware of this, I always rode with my hands in my pockets, and was now indulging in this salutary precaution, when a sudden jolt of the jarvie brought my head in full contact with the back of a passenger on the seat before me. "Diable!" exclaimed a voice which seemed to be familiar to me, and then all was silent again. Not long after, there exploded a sneeze which shook the whole vehicle. "Good Heavens!" ejaculated I, "I'm sure I've heard that sneeze before; it must be my little Frenchman!"—But there was no help for it now, and I determined to keep him at an awful distance.

Daylight showed the mahogany face, gold ear-rings, and dimity breeches, of the little Frenchman, and by his side the communicative traveller. All at once it occurred to my mind that these two men were accomplices in some scheme for robbing me. I was confirmed in the suspicion by the confounded civilities of the little Frenchman, who expressed infinite pleasure on the occasion, and offered me a pinch of snuff every two minutes. "We thought we had lost you," said he, "and were regretting the absence of such an agreeable companion." I made no reply but by a stiff inclination of the head, and continued with my hands in my pockets, my pocket-book in one, and my watch in the other. "Pray, monsieur, what a clock is it?", said the Frenchman. Aha! thought I, are you thereabouts? So I told him my watch had run down, and held it faster than ever.

This mode of disposing of my hands was very inconvenient on these rough democratic roads, and occasioned me to bounce about to the no small annoyance of these Jonathans, who threw out divers unmannerly hints, which I treated with perfect contempt. "He must have his pockets full of guineas," said the little Frenchman in a whisper, winking at the same time at the communicative traveller. I understood all this perfectly, and, when we stopped to dine, managed to exhibit a neat pair of hair-triggers to these two worthies, who exchanged very significant looks thereupon. " It won't do," observed one to the other, in a desponding tone.

The house we put up at for the night was in a lonely wood, at a distance of several miles from any human habitation. The owls whooped, the wolves howled, the whippoorwills whistled, the frogs croaked, the katydids katydidded it, the crickets chirped, and every sound seemed fraught with melancholy thoughts and mournful anticipations. During supper, and afterwards, I perceived an exchange of mysterious looks between the Frenchman, his companion, the landlord, and the landlord's wife, and detected them in various secret conferences. In one of these I overheard the landlady say, in reply to some question of the communicative traveller, who seemed to be an old acquaintance, " we killed him last night, poor old creature; I was almost sorry for him." My blood ran cold — some venerable traveller, doubtless, thought I.

Now thoroughly convinced that there was a plan to rob and murder me in this lonely place, I determined to defeat it by sitting up all night with a pistol cocked in each hand, ready to defend myself. In spite of the hints, questions, and entreaties, of the landlord and his wife, I persevered in my plan, although I was obliged to take to the kitchen fire, which I did under pretence that they were going to make up a bed for themselves in the room where I was. In this situation I continued, a pistol ready cocked in each hand, until, as I judge, about two or three o'clock, when a door suddenly opened and a bandit cautiously entered

with a dark lantern in his hand.   Thinking there was
no time to be lost, I let fly at him, and he fell flat on
his face, bellowing murder with all his might.   Immediately there was a great stir; the landlord, his wife,
children, servants, the stage-passengers, and lastly the
little Frenchman and the communicative traveller,
bounced in, helter-skelter, crying out " what's the matter — what's the matter!"   I stood with the other
pistol ready to fire, and bade them approach at their
peril.   " Diable!" exclaimed the little Frenchman,
stooping down to examine the body, " he has killed
our driver."   " Not exactly," cried the fellow, jumping
on his two legs as brisk as a grasshopper — " but if I
don't have him up before the justice for shooting at a
fellow for only coming in to light his lantern, to see
to put together his horses, darn my soul."   I insisted
upon it he was a genuine bandit, and that he had
come into the kitchen on purpose to rob and murder
me, or at least keep me in custody till my friends
paid my ransom.   But I found they were all in league
against me, and was finally glad to compound with the
pretended stage-driver, by treating him to a pint of
whiskey.   It is thus that strangers are always served
in this democratic paradise.   They must either sit
still and be murdered by inches, or pay a composition
for defending themselves.   To carry on the deception,
the fellow with a dark lantern was actually mounted
on the coach-box, with a view, I suppose, of making
a more successful attempt the next night.   But in this
he was disappointed, for, the moment we got to Boston, I took my portmanteau under my arm, darted
round a corner, and hid myself in a remote part of
the city.   In my retreat I heard the little Frenchman

exclaim, " Diable! this is what you call taking French leave, I think."

———◆———

CHAPTER IV.

The author congratulates himself on having got rid of the little Frenchman — Is in danger of being twice robbed and murdered — Neglect of common decency in taverns and steam-boats — No knives and forks — Dirty hands and faces — Astonishing number of people with one eye, or two black eyes — Explanation of Governor Hancock — Gouging — Spirit of Democracy — Leaves Boston - Passes through Ohio, Alabama, and Connecticut — Attempt to rob the mail on Sunday, by a footpad who turns out to be a deacon of the church — Amusements of the people — Holy Alliance — Bellows Falls — Steam-boats invented by Dr. Isaac Watts, who wrote the Book of Psalms — The Yankees ignorant of the points of the compass — Their mode of navigation — Little Frenchman again — Mode of deciding elections — Rudeness of boatmen and captain — Attempt of the little Frenchman to rob the author.

" THANK heaven," said I, " I've got rid of the little Frenchman, the bandit, and his whole crew," as I seated myself snugly in the quiet retreat of a hotel in which I had sought refuge. I slept pretty soundly that night, with the exception of two attempts to rob and murder me; one, by a person who opened my door, but who, seeing the barking-iron, shrunk back and pretended to have mistaken the room; the other by the chamber-maid, who came in, after I had gone to bed, with an excuse that she had forgot to put water in my pitcher. By the way, nothing can equal the neglect of these turbulent democrats in all the common decencies of life, particularly washing their hands and faces. On board the steam-boats, where there are perhaps a hundred people, one does not see above two or three washing themselves of a morning. As for combs, I asked for one at a first-rate hotel in Boston, and the waiter replied, " Comb, sir? — oh, I suppose you mean curry-comb." He then went his way, mumbling to himself " I wonder what the man wants of a comb, for he keeps no horses." As they have no knives and forks, either for want of knowing their uses, or for fear the passengers would steal them, it is easy to conceive the disgust an Englishman must feel at seeing them diving in the dishes with their filthy fingers. Another characteristic feature of these people is, that more than one half of them want an eye, and those that happen to have two, generally exhibit a black ring round one or both. On inquiring into the cause of this peculiarity, I was told by his excellency, Governor Hancock, that men, women, and children, were so given to fighting and gouging, that it was next to a miracle to see one of them without one eye gone, or at least without a pair of black eyes, which is reckoned a great beauty in these parts. So much for the turbulent spirit of democracy, thought I to myself.

Having staid three days, to give the little Frenchman, the great bandit, and the rest of them, a fair start, I thought I might safely proceed on to the South. Accordingly I took passage in a stage, and departed on the fourth morning, as usual, before daylight, for the convenience of being robbed and murdered on the way. This happens generally about three times a week; but it is in the true spirit of democracy to sport with property and life. Our road carried us through the states of Ohio, Alabama, and Connecticut, among the people of steady habits, as they are denominated. All I can say is, that the sooner they change these steady habits the better, for it will hardly be believed, that we had scarcely entered the confines of Connecticut, the very centre of steady habits, when, although it was Sunday, (a sufficient reason for deterring any christian highwayman), we were stopped by a footpad, who demanded money with as little compunction as a he-wolf. Upon my showing my pistols however, he sheered off, and the driver whipping up his horses at the moment, we luckily escaped that time. The incident of a single footpad's attempting thus to rob a whole stage-load of people, furnishes another proof that stage-drivers and stage-owners, not to say a majority of stage-passengers, are accomplices of these bands of robbers. Had it not been for my pistols, we should all have been robbed to a certainty, and most probably the rest of the passengers would have shared my spoils. What exhibits the turbulent and impious spirit of democracy in all its turpitude is the fact, that the driver, after getting fairly out of sight, turned round to the passengers with a grin, and exclaimed, " I guess I've distanced the deacon." So that this footpad was one of the pillars of the church!

I have nothing to add in addition to these disgusting details, except that, as far as my sight could reach on either side of the road, I could see nobody at work but the poor gentlemen of colour, half clothed, as usual. The white people were for the most part employed—the men, haunting the taverns, running horses, fighting cocks, or gouging one another's eyes out— the women, sitting along the road, chewing tobacco, and spitting in the faces of passers by — and the little boys and girls, beating and otherwise maltreating, their parents. To vary these amusements, they sometimes made a party to hunt a little naked negro with their dogs, which I observed were all blood-hounds. My heart bled to see these cruel mastiffs, less cruel indeed than the turbulent spirit of democracy, tugging at their naked haunches, and I could not help invoking the philanthropic genius of the Holy Alliance to interfere in behalf of these oppressed beings.

About five in the afternoon we arrived at Bellows Falls, at the mouth of the Ohio, where I embarked in the steam-boat for New York. These steam-boats, all the world knows, were invented by Isaac Watts, who wrote the book of psalms. Yet the spirit of democracy, as usual, has claimed the honour for one Moulton, or Fulton, I forget which; although it is a notorious fact, that Isaac Watts died before this Fulton was born. This settles the question. But there is no stopping the mouth of a genuine democrat. Our course lay upon a river which the Yankees call the East river, although, to my certain knowledge, it runs directly West. But it would be tasking the ignorant spirit of democracy too much, to suppose its votaries could possibly tell the points of the compass. Indeed I was credibly informed, that their most experienced navigators universally judge of their course within soundings by the colour of the mud or sand which adheres to the lead, and when this indication fails them, trust to Providence.

While sitting in a state of indolent and contemptuous abstraction, with my back to as many of the company as possible, I was roused by a sneeze that I could have sworn to in any part of the world. " It is

the c——d little Frenchman! Here's Monsieur Ton-
son come again!" I would as soon have heard the
last trumpet as this infernal explosion. In a few minutes he espied me, and coming up with the most pro-
voking expression of old acquaintanceship, offered me
a pinch of snuff. "Ah! monsieur, I am so happy!
Diable!—my friend and I thought we had lost our
agreeable companion;" and, thereupon, he made me
a delectable low French bow, that brought his long
nose within an inch of the deck. He then left me for
a moment, and returned with his friend the veritable
communicative traveller, who had the insolence to
claim acquaintance, from having travelled a few days
in the same stage with me. A good sample of the
forward, impudent spirit of democracy! I expected
every moment to see the great bandit with his dark
lantern, to complete the trio, but for some reason or
other he didn't make his appearance. "Ah! monsieur," cried the little Frenchman, "you don't know
how we have missed your agreeable society. Diable!
I have not had a good laugh since we parted." Then
he offered me a pinch of snuff, a civility which he repeated at least a hundred times in the course of the
day, though I always declined it in the most dignified
and contemptuous manner.

Disgusted with every thing I saw, and most especially with this rencounter, I determined to mortify
these free and easy gentry by taking not the least
notice of any person whatever, and going without
my dinner on purpose to spite them. Many of the
women looked hard at me, with an evident desire to
be taken notice of; but I always turned my head
away, resolved to have nothing to say to them. Sev-

eral persons also came round, and made attempts to engage me in conversation, but I answered them in monosyllables, and they went away, whistling to hide their mortification. My contempt for the little Frenchman increased every moment, by observing the pains he took to be agreeable. He talked, laughed, bowed, offered his box to every one that came in his way, and complimented the women, till all were delighted with him, and he seemed as much at home as if he had been born and brought up among them. Despicable subserviency! contemptible hypocrisy!, to pretend to be pleased with these scum of democracy.

When the dinner-bell rang I remained on deck, until one of the waiters came up to tell me dinner was ready. I took no notice of him. In a few minutes the little Frenchman assailed me. "Is monsieur ill?" "No!" said I. "No? Eh bien — what is the matter? Ah! I guess, as these Yankees say. If monsieur has no money, never mind, I will pay for his dinner. Come, come." I replied, in great wrath at his infernal mistake, upon which he went down, and, as I afterwards learned, proposed a subscription for a poor passenger, who was obliged to go without his dinner for want of money to pay for it. One may judge of the humanity of these people, from the fact that not one of them contributed a cent. One woman turned up her nose, and exclaimed, "Marry come up — I thought as much; pride and poverty generally go together." Another declared she would not give a pin to save such a rude humgruffian from starving; and a third pronounced me a strolling player out of employ. The communicative traveller, on coming up after dinner, endeavoured to comfort me for the loss of my meal, by observing I had not missed much by it. " There is nothing but snatching and quarrelling for the favourite bits, and the ladies did nothing but scold and pull caps. Then, it is just as likely as not, you would have been seated between two greasy enginemen in red flannel shirts, one a negro perhaps, (for they all dine together), who would have made no scruple of gouging one of your eyes out, if you had happened to get possession of one of their tidbits. You were well out of the scrape." Glorious spirit of democracy, thought I to myself.

Towards evening the boat stopped at a place called the city of Annapolis. Every thing is a city here. A blacksmith's shop, with a church, and a pig-sty, is a city, and must have its corporation, if it be only that that the spirit of democracy may revel in a little brief authority. An office of any kind is their darling, and a whole state will be convulsed about the election of a constable. These elections are generally carried in the last resort by the cudgel and gouging; and I am assured that the number of one-eyed people, and people with black rings round their eyes, is generally doubled by one of these struggles of principle. As we approached the wharf, I was standing among a coil of ropes, with my back toward the great city, when one of these sticklers for equality, in a red flannel shirt, came up and desired me to move out of the way. The fellow was civil enough for that matter, but I only answered his impertinent intrusion with a look of withering contempt. Upon this, he gathered a part of the rope in coils, in his right hand, and when we were ten or a dozen yards from the wharf, threw it with all his force, with a design to knock down a person who stood there. But the chap was too dexterous for him, and caught the end of the rope in his hands, and immediately fastened it to a post. The whole brunt of this Yankee joke fell upon me, for my feet being entangled in the end of the rope thus thrown, it tripped up my heels and laid me sprawling on the deck. The little Frenchman officiously helped me up, and offered me a pinch of snuff by way of comfort; but as for the democratic gentry, they seemed rather to enjoy the thing, and if the truth was known, I dare say were at the bottom of the joke. I cursed the fellow heartily; but he coolly answered—"'Twas your own fault; I asked you to get out of the way." So much for the turbulent spirit of democracy.

I stepped ashore, to escape the giggling of these polite republicans, and rambled to the distance of a couple of hundred yards. While here, I heard a bell toll, and then a hallooing, and saw them making signals for me to come on board; but I was determined to treat them all with silent contempt, and continued my walk. The shouting continued, and I don't know how far I might have strolled, if I had not been suddenly roused by the noise of the boat's wheels. Turning round, I found the vessel was fairly under way; whereupon I condescended to run, and halloo as hard as I could bawl. After some little delay the wheels were stopped, and a boat was sent to take me on board, where, instead of making an apology, the brute of a captain told me I deserved to have been left behind. "If it had not been for the persuasions of your friend," pointing to the little Frenchman, "you might have staid ashore till next trip, and welcome." "*My* friend," exclaimed I, and turned to the

officious little mahogany man with a look of withering contempt: whereupon he offered his box, and
assured me he would not have lost my charming
society for the world. These persevering civilities on
his part, and especially this last impertinent interference, confirmed me in my suspicions that there was a
deep-laid plan to rob and murder me the first convenient opportunity. What added weight to these apprehensions was the fact of my continually detecting
him and his companion, the communicative traveller,
conferring together, with divers shrugs on the part of
the Frenchman, and significant smiles on that of his
friend.

When we came to draw lots for our berths, it was
so managed by the captain, (who was no doubt an
accomplice), that I drew one in a remote part of the
vessel, forward. But, owing to some failure in the
plot, the little Frenchman and his companion both
drew berths in the cabin abaft, which I perceived dis-
concerted them not a little. But they soon rectified
the mistake; for upon the complaints of two feeble
old gentlemen, that they should find it fatiguing to go
into the forward-cabin, the Frenchman seized the pretext, and, with one of his confounded low bows,
offered his berth to one of the cripples, while his companion did the same to the other. I saw through all
this, and determined to play them a trick, by lying
awake all night to watch them, with my pistols ready.

Late in the night, and when all the lights were out,
I heard somebody get out of a berth on the opposite
side, where the little Frenchman slept. — The person
went upon deck, and, after staying a minute or two,
groped his way down again, and cautiously ap-

proached the place where I lay with my pistol cocked. Presently he laid his hand upon my throat, doubtless with an intent to choke me first, and rob me afterwards at leisure. At this instant I fired my pistol, just as the little Frenchman ejaculated in a whisper, "Diable! I am lost!" Confusion reigned, lights were brought, and the whole affair was disclosed. I solemnly charged the little Frenchman, who had escaped my shot, with an attempt to rob and murder me; while he as solemnly asseverated, that he had got up upon a necessary occasion, and, on his return, took the right hand instead of the left, by which means he had encountered my berth, instead of his own which was directly opposite. The passengers, captain, and all, being, without doubt, accomplices in this attempt, sided with the Frenchman; believed every word he said, and gravely advised me to take care how I fired pistols in the cabin of a steam-boat. This was all the satisfaction I got for this nefarious attempt. The little Frenchman even had the assurance to play the injured party, and actually offered to forget and forgive. "It was all a mistake," said he, "and let us think no more of it." So he offered me a pinch of snuff, which I rejected with dignified contempt.

CHAPTER V.

Frog's Neck — Bull - Frogs — Hell - Gate — Impious spirit of democracy — Mode of passing Hell-Gate — Fondness of the Yankees for dying accounted for — Dutch courage — Mr. Robert James — Country seats — Sandy Hook — Navy-Yard, &c. — Little Frenchman — Author takes lodgings with a gentleman of colour at the *Hotel des Huitres* — Bill of Exchange — Unprincipled behaviour of the Yankee merchant — Quarterly Review — Description of New York — Basis of republicanism — Agrarian law — Quarterly — Classification of the citizens of New York — Extensive circulation of the Quarterly Review — Gratitude of the people of colour — Beggarly pride of republicanism — Propensity to thieving among the higher classes — Picture of the manners and morals of the people, drawn by the landlord — Quantity of flies and musketoes — Law against killing spiders — Little Frenchman, &c.

ABOUT daylight I was roused by a most horrible noise, which resembled nothing I had ever heard before. On going upon deck, I perceived the whole surface of the water, as far as the eye could reach, covered with immense bull - frogs, who leaped and croaked, to the infinite delight of these tasteful democrats, who were all gathered together to hear this charming concert, which they would prefer to the Commemoration of Handel. Some of the largest of these frogs actually jumped upon deck, and a canoe alongside was nearly upset by three or four of them clambering up its sides, at one and the same time. The place is called *Frog's Neck*,* and never was there a spot more aptly named. There is a little settlement near this, called New Rochelle, peopled by Frenchmen, who were doubtless attracted by the frogs. But such is the ardour of these refined republicans for this species of music, that the legislature has

[* Throg's Neck.]

15

enacted a law, making it death to kill one of these delightful musicians.   To kill a man here, is a trifle — but to kill a frog, is capital!

Shortly after leaving Frog's Neck we came to the famous pass of Hell-Gate, as it is impiously called by the profane spirit of democracy.   It is the *Scilly* and *Charybdis* of the New World, and nothing but the special protection of Providence can account for the .occasional deliverances that happen to these reckless republicans in passing it, which they do every hour of the day and night.   As soon as they begin to distinguish its roaring, which can be heard at a distance of thirty miles except when the frog concert intervenes, all hands, captain, pilot, and the rest, set to and drink apple-brandy, or whiskey, so that, by the time they come to the Hog's Back, they are as drunk as swine. They then lie down flat on their faces and let the vessel take her course.   This preparatory tippling is what they impiously call receiving " extreme unction," and preparing for death, which the communicative traveller assured me not more than one out of three on an average escaped.   I could not help expressing my wonder that these people should thus recklessly sport with their lives. " O, as to that," replied he, " what with the curse of democracy, the grinding oppressions of unrestrained liberty, together with the total insecurity of property under mob law; and the total insecurity of person, in consequence of the universal practice of robbery and murder, of which you have had ample experience, — I say, what with all this, ninety-nine in a hundred of these, my wretched countrymen, would as soon die as not, and some of them a great deal rather, only to escape the blessings of democracy." "But," said I, "why don't these miserable creatures say their prayers, and make some little preparation to die like Christians, instead of thus beastifying themselves?" "O," answered he, with a coolness that made me shudder, "this is what we call *Dutch courage;* and I assure you, upon my credit, that I never knew a genuine Brother Jonathan who could be brought to face an enemy, or die with decency, unless he had his skin full of whiskey, and was well '*corned,*' as we say. This was the way in which we gained all our victories last war, both by sea and land." Good, thought I, here is the testimony of one of their own countrymen. Mr. James shall add this to his apologies for Blue and Buff, in his next edition.

This conversation happened after safely passing this tremendous strait, which we did as it were by miracle. Between this and New York, the communicative traveller pointed out to me some two or three of what he called magnificent country-seats, which seemed to me about the size of pigeon-houses. I took no notice of him or them, but affected to be in a fit of abstraction, with my eyes fixed on vacancy. Turning the point of Sandy Hook, we came in full sight of the city, its bay, and islands. I saw that several of these people were watching to detect in me some symptoms of surprise or admiration, so I resolved to disappoint them, and turned my back to the city, keeping my eyes fixed on the opposite shore. The communicative traveller, supposing I was looking at the Navy-Yard, where several large ships were lying, observed: "That is the Cyane, near the red store; or perhaps you mean the other — that is the Macedonian; or perhaps you mean the one next her — that is ——." I could stand it no longer, but was fain to turn round and look at their detestable city.

When we came near the wharf, the little Frenchman came up to me with a low bow and the offer of his box as usual. " I hope monsieur, my friend, and myself, shall take lodgings together. As we are strangers in a strange place, 'tis pity we should part. I assure you I shall not rob monsieur," said he, with an impertinent, significant, smile. I told him at last I should lodge that night on board, and depart the next day by the boat in which I came. " What!" replied he, " is monsieur going to New Orleans again? But in truth we are sorry to lose your very agreeable company, monsieur, and hope that we shall meet again when you come back from New Orleans." So saying, he bowed profoundly low, and departed, accompanied by his friend, and by my most devout wishes never to set eyes upon either of them again.

Desirous to avoid any public attentions, and most especially to escape the honour of being made a citizen of New York, which the corporation insist upon bestowing upon every stranger of distinction in order to add some little respectability to their sty of democracy, I took a private lodging with a respectable man of colour who kept the Hotel des Huitres in Water street. According to the fashionable London mode, I intended to direct all those who asked my address to the City Hotel, where there is generally such a concourse of people that the bar-keeper never knows the names of half the boarders. My first business, after taking possession of my lodging, was to present a bill of exchange, drawn on one of the most respectable merchants here, (if such a term can be applied to a Yankee pedler), by one of our first London bankers.

I found him in his counting-room, with a jug, (as I presume, of whiskey), at his side, and pretty well "corned," as the communicative traveller says, though it was hardly nine o'clock. He received me with a sort of bear-like republican civility, which I ascribed to the awe in which they stand of Englishmen, to whom they are one and all indebted more than they ever mean to pay. He read my letter, looked very deliberately at the bill of exchange, and then, folding them both up carefully, offered them to me. "Is it convenient for you," said I, "to cash the bill at once?" "No sir, not very convenient." "I suppose, then, I must be content with your acceptance at the usual sight." "My good friend, I don't mean to accept it, I assure you." "No, sir?" said I, bristling up, for I began to suspect some Yankee trick — "and pray may I take the liberty of asking the reason of this extraordinary conduct?" "Certainly. The banker who drew this bill, by my last advices is a bankrupt and a swindler. He has no effects in my hands, nor is he ever likely to have. I am sorry for your disappointment, but I cannot accept your bill of exchange." I snatched the letter out of his hand and hurried from the room, and my disappointment was almost balanced by the pleasure I felt at this early confirmation of my impressions with regard to the character of these republican merchants, who, I was satisfied from reading the Quarterly Review, never paid a debt of any kind, there being no law in this country to oblige them. I had no doubt that the story of the drawer of my bill, (no less a man than Mr. Henry Fauntleroy,* who keeps two mistresses, and three splendid establishments), being a bankrupt and swindler, was a fabrication, invented to evade the payment. Such is the universal practice here, and thus is the reputation of half the merchants of Britain ruined in this country. The genuine republican merchant never stops payment and compounds with his creditors, (which they generally do twice or thrice a year), without putting it all upon his correspondents in England, who are, in fact, always the greatest sufferers. This story they all make a point of believing, because they all are, or expect soon to be, in the same predicament. It is a proof of the generous credulity of honest John Bull that he still continues to trust, and be cheated by, the turbulent spirit of democracy, as the editors of the Quarterly Review justly style it, in their usual strain of genteel irony.

Relating the story of my disappointment to my worthy landlord, I thought he looked rather shy, as if he expected it to be the prelude to a long score. But I at once satisfied his doubts by showing him a few guineas, and telling him I always paid my bill every Saturday night. He then resumed his confidence, and proceeded to let me into the secrets of this unprincipled and profligate city, which, being the general rendezvous of people from all parts of this puissant and polished republic (as the Quarterly calls it), presents at one view a picture of the bless-

[* The famous case of Henry Fauntleroy, who forged powers of attorney through which he disposed of three hundred and sixty thousand pounde' worth of Bank of England stock. Arrested Sept. 10th, 1824, tried in October of the same year and found guilty, he was hanged at Smithfield in the following November.]

ings of pure and undefiled democracy. That my readers may have the clearer idea of a genuine republican city, I shall be more particular in my description, especially as this is considered as the very pink of all the cities of the New World.

New York, the capital of the state of New Jersey, so called from being originally settled by Yorkshire horse jockeys, is situated on the main land, between two rivers about the size of the Thames, though not quite so large, that being unquestionably the greatest river in the world. That on the east they call the North, and that on the west, the East river, by a very pardonable blunder, as it would be taxing the spirit of democracy too severely to preserve the least acquaintance with such aristocratic trumpery as the points of the compass. The blessings of ignorance constitute the basis of republicanism, as the Quarterly says with its characteristic wit and humour.

Most of the houses are built of pine boards and generally about half-finished, the owners for the most part stopping payment before the work is completed. There is a great appearance of bustle, but very little business in fact, as the spirit of democracy impels these people to make a great noise about nothing. To see one of their peddling merchants staring about in Wall street, one would suppose he was overwhelmed with the most momentous affairs, when, if the truth was known, his whole morning's business consists in purchasing a dozen birch-brooms, or a pound of wafers. There is also a great appearance of building here, but this is partly owing to the necessity of new houses to replace the old ones, which generally tumble to pieces at the end of three or four

years, and partly to the inveterate habit of emigration characteristic of the restless spirit of democracy,
which deters people from remaining long in one
place. Hence they are perpetually on the move from
one part of the city to another. Sometimes whole
streets are deserted in this way, and then, as new
buildings become necessary, the cry of these republican braggarts, as the Quarterly calls them, is about
the number of houses building and the vast increase
of the city. Sometimes they pull down a street and
build it up again, merely to impose upon strangers an
idea of its prosperity, and attract emigrants from
England, although those who have been weak enough
to come hither for the last six or eight years are, with
the exception of a few sent home by the British Con-
sul, every soul of them on the parish.

The people of New York may be divided into three
classes, those that beg, those that borrow, and those
that steal. Not unfrequently, however, all these professions are united in one person, as they are a very
ingenious people, and almost every man is a sort of
Jack-of-all-trades. The beggars constitute about one
third of the population, and are supported with great
liberality by the other two classes, who, remembering
that charity covers a multitude of sins, make use of its
broad mantle in this way, and, upon the strength of
their alms, claim the privilege of borrowing without
ever intending to pay, and robbing Peter to give away
to Paul. One of the most popular preachers here is a
notorious gambler, but, at the same time, is considered
little less than a saint, because he professes to give
all his winnings to the poor. Another person, an
alderman, generally breaks into a neighbour's house

every night, but, as he gives away all his plunder in alms, he is one of the most popular men in the city. Another, who is a judge of the court, generally manages to pick the pockets of both the parties in a suit, and the jury think themselves lucky to escape; yet he is adored for his liberality, and the beggars, who, like the pigs, all vote, talk of running him for the next governor.

The borrowers consist of the most fashionable portion of the community, the people who give parties, ride in their coaches, and hold their heads considerably higher than the beggars. The most approved mode of practising this thriving business is this: — A gentleman gives a grand entertainment to a select number of friends, each of whom he manages to intercept as he goes out, and makes him pay pretty handsomely for dinner in the shape of a loan. When one set gets tired, he invites another, and so on till his debts amount to sufficient to make it worth while, when he affects to stop payment, as he calls it, though he never began yet; takes the benefit of the laws for encouraging debt and extravagance; and, on the score of his numerous charities, is generally recommended for some public office. This is the last resort of rogues in this pure republican system, as the Quarterly affirms. My landlord, the gentleman of colour, who was in the habit of waiting at many of these great dinners, assured me he recollected but a single instance in which the guests escaped paying the piper in this way, when the entertainer let them off, in consequence of having picked their pockets at table. I asked him how it happened that the guests did not resent or complain of this treatment. " O," replied he, "it is diamond cut diamond — every one has his turn, and it amounts to an equal division of property in the end — a republican Agrarian law, as the Quarterly says." "What, do you read the Quarterly?" said I. "O yes; we all read Massa Quarterly — he love us people of colour so much." He further assured me the people of colour had it one time in contemplation to send out half a dozen of their prettiest ebony lasses to England, that the gentlemen of the Quarterly might have their choice of them for wives. But the ladies of colour, having been persuaded by some of the white belles of fashion, who envied their high destinies, that all these gentlemen lived in *Grub street*, one of the most ungenteel places in all London, turned up their pretty pug noses, and demurred to the proposition.

I was delighted at this information, which not only proved the extensive circulation of this valuable Review, but likewise the gratitude of the people of colour for the exertions of its conductors in their behalf. It is enough to make the eye of philanthropy water, to hear, as I have done, that such is the pride of these beggarly republicans, that they will not admit a gentleman or lady of colour to any intimacy of association, it being even considered a disgrace to enter into a matrimonial connexion with them! This is another beautiful illustration of the beggarly pride of these upstart republicans, as the Quarterly says.

The class of pick-pockets, shop-lifters, and thieves of all sorts, is probably the most numerous of the whole community. Nobody ventures to carry money in his pocket, and when the ladies go out shopping they always hold their purses in their hands. Even this is no security, for it generally happens that they are snatched away before they have gone a hundred yards. One of the shopkeepers here assured me it seldom happened that a lady came into his shop without pocketing a piece of lace, a pair of gloves, or something of the kind, provided she could not get at the till. It is the universal practice to search them before they depart; and, from being used to this, they submit as quietly as lambs. Plenty of company to keep them in countenance, and long habit, render them indifferent to discovery, as the shopman assured me. Two or three ladies came in meanwhile, and were suffered to go away without being searched by the shopman, who, as I found to my cost afterwards, was all this while busily employed in emptying my pockets. Yet, for all this, these bragging republicans boast that it is unnecessary for the country people to lock their doors at night. My landlord assured me that this was the fact, but that it arose from the conviction that locking them would be of no service, every man, both from education and habit, being exceedingly expert in picking locks.

" The consequence of all this," continued the worthy gentleman of colour, " is a general, I may say irremediable, relaxation of manners, and a total want of prudence and principle in all classes. Drunkenness, impiety, insolence, extravagance, ignorance, brutality, gluttony, and every vice that can disgrace human nature, are the ordinary characteristics of these spawn of filthy democracy, as the Quarterly says; and if there be any thing in which these people are not utterly detestable, it is their fondness for oysters, which enables me to get a tolerable livelihood. This fondness is sharpened by the exquisite relish of breaking the laws at the same time that they gratify their appetites — the corporation of the city, for the purpose of monopolizing, having enacted that no oysters shall be brought to market, but what they eat themselves." Nothing, indeed, can equal the tyranny of the laws in this country; nor would it be possible to live under them, did not the turbulent spirit of democracy compound for itself, by breaking them all without ceremony.

It is another consequence of the relaxation of morals among these virtuous republicans, that the relaxation of the laws is in proportion to the relaxation of morals. To such an extent has this been carried, that these people may be said to have no laws at all. All sorts of crimes are here committed with perfect impunity; and it is a common saying, that it requires more interest to be hanged, than to attain to the highest dignity of the republic. Drunkenness is here the usual and infallible apology for crime; and as the mass of the people are usually *corned*, as my friend the communicative traveller says, this excuse is seldom out of place. But what puzzled me, after seeing all this, was, that the jails, bridewells, and penitentiaries, which abound in almost every street, were full of people. My worthy landlord, however, explained this to my satisfaction, by assuring me that such was the abject poverty and consequent misery of a large portion of these patent republicans, (as the Quarterly says), that they actually broke into these receptacles by force, being certain of getting board and lodging for nothing.

I was struck with the quantity of flies and musketoes, (the latter of which sing most melodiously), that infest the streets and houses all the year round, and fly into one's nose and ears at every convenient opportunity. To remedy this intolerable grievance, there is luckily a species of spider, which spins across the opening of the ear a web in which these insects are caught. It is no uncommon thing to see half a dozen or more flies and musketoes dangling in the ear of a fine lady. There is a law to prevent the destruction of these spiders, as there is against killing the turkey-buzzards, which abound here, and are the only street-scavengers, if we except the citizen-pig freeholders, as the Quarterly calls them.

CHAPTER VI.

Total absence of religion — Indivisibility of a king and a divinity, and of democracy and impiety — Examples of the Puritans and Charles the Second — Necessity of wealth, honours, and exclusive privileges, to the very existence of religion — Quarterly — Barbarous love of finery — Mode of procuring it — Ignorance — Story of a blue-stocking — Lord Bacon — Ill manners — Total neglect of education — American Chancellor of the.Exchequer can't write his name — House of Representatives obliged to have a clerk to read for them! — Attempt of an English lady to establish a boarding-school, and its result — French dancing-masters, how treated, &c.

ONE of the first things that disgusts a pious man, as all Englishmen, particularly English travellers, are, is the horrible profanation of the Sabbath in New York. This contempt of religion and its observances arises partly out of the turbulent spirit of democracy, and partly from the want of a privileged church establishment, such as has made Great Britain the bulwark of religion in all ages. There is in the first place such a natural and indivisible association between a king reigning over his people by divine right and Divinity itself, that it is next to impossible a true subject should not be a true believer. On the contrary, the pure spirit of democracy, which rejects the divine right of kings, will naturally resist every other divine right, and thus it has happened that impiety and rebellion have ever gone hand in hand. Every person versed in the history of England must be familiar with innumerable examples of this truth. Waiving a reference to all others, it is sufficient to recollect the total relaxation of religion and morals which prevailed among the Puritans who rebelled against Charles the Martyr, and the brilliant revival of piety and the Church on the accession of his son. In fact, it is a maxim with all orthodox writers, that a pious people will always be obedient to their sovereign, not so much because he governs well, as because he governs by divine right.

A few obvious positions will in like manner demonstrate the absolute necessity of a liberally endowed, exclusively privileged, church establishment, like that of England. Money is universally held to be the sinews of war; and inasmuch as money is essentially necessary to enable the sovereign to defend and maintain the rights and interests of the government, so is it equally necessary to enable the bishops and dignitaries of the Church to defend the consciences of the people against the dissenters, and all other enemies of the Church. It is a pure democratic absurdity to suppose that men will fight for their country from mere patriotic feelings, or that they will preach for nothing. Hence it is essentially necessary that both should be equally well paid; for, as the promise of the plunder of a city stimulates the soldier to acts of heroism, so in like manner will the promise of a good living of ten or fifteen thousand sterling a year stimulate the dignitary of the Established Church to fight the good fight of faith the more manfully.

In fact, as the Quarterly says, "the want of an established church has made the bulk of the people either infidels or fanatics." There will never be any pure religion here, until they have an Archbishop of Armagh with sixty thousand acres of glebe, and a Bishop of Derry with one hundred and fifty thousand. It is these and similar noble establishments in Ireland, that have made the people of that country so orthodox, and so devoted to the king.

This mode of stimulating the zeal of pious dignitaries by wealth and honours is accompanied with other special advantages. In proportion as the hierarchy is enriched by the spoils of the people, the latter, becoming comparatively poor, are precluded by necessity from indulging in vicious extravagance and corrupt enjoyments. They will practise, perforce, abstinence, economy, self denial, and the other domestic virtues so essential to the welfare of the lower orders. Hence it is sufficiently obvious that, in proportion as you curtail the superfluities of the commonalty by taxes, tithes, high rents, and poor-rates, you guaranty to them the practice of almost all the cardinal virtues. Again:— In proportion as the people become poor, they will necessarily pay less attention to the education of their children; and I fear no denial, except from radicals, democrats, and atheists, when I assert, that, considering the mischievous books now in circulation on the subject of liberty and such impieties, the greatest blessing that could possibly happen to the lower orders would be the loss of the dangerous faculty of reading. In no age of the world were this class of people so devoted to the honour of the priests and the glory of their kings, and consequently to the interests of religion and human rights, as when a large portion of them could not read, and were without any property they could call their own. I appeal to the whole history of mankind for proof of the maxim, that ignorance and poverty are the two pillars of a privileged church and the divine right of kings.

It may be urged by radicals, democrats, and unbelievers, that the rule which ordains the diminution of certain vices by the absence, equally ordains their proportionate increase by the multiplication, of the means of their gratification; and that, consequently, the rich prelates and nobility must necessarily become corrupt in proportion to the increase of their wealth. But even admitting this to be true, the people are gainers by the arrangement, since, by this means, their sins and transgressions are shifted upon their superiors, who answer the end of a sort of scape-goats, or peace-offerings, under cover of which the poor entirely escape. It is therefore plain, that the more rich and wicked the privileged few become, the more will the lower orders be exempt from the sinful consequences of wealth. Let us hear no more then of the impious slang of democracy, as the Quarterly says, which would persuade poor deluded innocence and ignorance that equal rights and a general diffusion of knowledge answer any other end than to make people thieves, murderers, gougers, bundlers, unbelievers, blasphemers, rowdies, and regulators, and, to sum up all in one word, republicans.

When it is recollected, therefore, that the essence of the turbulent spirit of democracy consists in the rejection of not only the divine right of the king, but of the equally divine right of the bishops and deans and archdeacons to their thousands a year, it will readily be conceded that a pure republican cannot possibly have any religion. Accordingly, as I before observed, the first thing that strikes a stranger who is used to the exemplary modes of keeping the Sabbath in London and all other parts of England, is the total neglect of that day in every portion of the United States. In New York, indeed, there are plenty of churches, but they were all built before the millennium of democracy, as the Quarterly says, and under the pious auspices of our Established Church. The first thing these blessed republicans did when they returned to the city, on the conclusion of the peace, was to break all the church-windows, and broken they have remained ever since. One steeple has a ring of eight copper kettles, instead of bells, which being rung by the old deaf sexton, gives singular satisfaction to the commonalty — I beg pardon — the sovereign people — who assemble on Sundays to dance to the music in front of the church. As to going to church to hear divine service, nobody pretends to such anti-republican foolery. The shops are all kept open on Sundays, so that one can see no difference between that and any other day, except that the good folks drink twice as much whiskey, and put on their newest

suits, in which they stagger about with infinite dignity, until finally they generally tumble into the gutter,
spoil their finery, and sleep themselves sober. Such
are the genuine habits of the turbulent spirit of democracy, as the Quarterly says. My worthy landlord
assured me that the African church was the only one
in which there was a chance of hearing a sermon, and
that even there the whole congregation was sometimes
taken up and carried to the watch-house, under pretence that they disturbed the neighbourhood with
their groanings, howlings, and other demonstrations
of genuine piety. The true reason was, however,
that these bundling, gouging democrats, as the Quarterly calls them, have such a bitter hostility to all sorts
of religion, that they cannot bear that even the poor
negroes should sing psalms. However, as it is the
first duty of a Christian to hide the faults, and draw
a veil over the transgressions, of his fellow-men, I
shall abstain from any further comments on the horrible depravity of republicanism in general, and Yankee
republicanism in particular. But I must not omit to
mention that, in this, as well as every other town in
the United States, there is a society for the propaga-
tion of unbelief, secretly supported by the government, most of the principal officers of which are
members. Their exertions were inveterate and un-
ceasing, and they displayed the same zeal in making
an atheist of a devout Christian that we do in the
conversion of a Jew. Of late these societies have
remitted their labours, in consequence of there being
no more Christians to work upon.

The love of dress, glitter, and parade, is one of the
characteristics of a rude and republican people; of

course we see it displayed here in all its barbarous extravagance. Every thing they can beg, borrow, hire, or steal, is put on their backs, and a fine lady somewhat resembles a vessel dressed in the colours of all nations. It is impossible to tell what flag she sails under. This finery is for the most part hired by the day, of the milliners and pawn-brokers, and there are dresses which can be had at from two shillings to a dollar a day. The first young ladies of the city, who never know their own minds, but always "guess" at it, as the Quarterly says, principally figure in these hired dresses; and it is by no means uncommon for one of them to be hauled out of the City Assembly or a fashionable party by a pawn-broker, in consequence of having kept the dress longer than the time specified. One might suppose such an accident would disturb the harmony of the company, but the other young ladies continue to dance away without taking any notice of the unfortunate Cinderella thus stripped of her finery, or perhaps content themselves with *guessing* what the matter may be. I ought to mention here, that, though the young ladies always "guess," the young gentlemen are commonly given to "reckoning" upon a thing — a phrase which becomes exceedingly familiar by a long habit of running up scores at taverns.

Notwithstanding all the cant and boasting of these turbulent democrats about the necessity of education to self-government, the general diffusion of intelligence, and all that sort of thing, it is most amazing to see the ignorance of the best-educated people here. A young lady of the first fashion who can read writing, is considered a phenomenon; while she who has read

Lord Byron is held a blue-stocking, and avoided by all the dandies for fear she should puzzle them with her learning. Such, indeed, is the natural antipathy of genuine republicanism to all sorts of literature, that the only possible way of teaching the little children their a, b, c, is by appealing to their inordinate appetites, in the shape of gingerbread letters well sweetened with molasses. The seduction is irresistible, for no genuine Yankee republican can make head against treacle. I, one night at a literary party, happened to mention some opinion from Lord Bacon * to a young lady who had the reputation of being rather *blue*. "Bacon, bacon?"—replied she briskly—"O! I *guess* we call it gammon. But we don't put '*Lord*' to it, because it's anti-republican." I took occasion to apprise her, with as little appearance of contempt as possible, that *our* Bacon was not gammon, nor ham, but no less a personage than the present Lord Chancellor of England, the sole inventor and propounder of human reason and the noble art of philosophy. "I *guess* he must have made a power of money by it," said the learned lady. "Did he get a *patten* for his invention? We always get *pattens* for any great discoveries in *Amerrykey*." Upon this she started up, ran giggling over to some of her *set*, and continued the whole evening laughing at me, thus joining ill-manners to ignorance. But what can you expect from a gang of barbarians, among whom learning is considered anti-republican, as the young lady said; where, to be able to read is an insuperable obstacle to promotion, and where the present Chancellor of the Excheq-

[* "Lord" Bacon, so generally styled, was properly Francis Bacon, Viscount St. Albans and Baron Verulam.]

uer of the United States, who is considered as one of their best scholars, signs his name with a *fac-simile* — that is, by deputy? This deputy they were obliged to send to England for, on account of the few persons who could write being all engaged in forging the signatures of bank notes. Even the House of Representatives, where all the wisdom and learning of the nation assembles, is obliged to employ a clerk to read the papers, messages, &c., for the edification of the country members, whose education has been neglected in that respect.

To sum up my remarks on the subject of literature here, I may say, with perfect truth and impartiality, that the education of youth consists in learning to drink whiskey, eat tobacco, love dirt and debauchery, despise religion, and hate kings. An English lady attempted to establish a boarding-school for young ladies a few years ago, but the genius of democracy would not submit to her salutary restrictions. The young ladies first pouted; then broke into the kitchen, where they devoured all they could find, and came very near eating up the black cook; and finally set fire to the house, and ran away by the light of it: since which nobody has been hardy enough to set up a school for young ladies, except two or three desperate Frenchmen. These confine themselves to teaching them dancing, which, being an art congenial to savages, they acquire with considerable docility. They sometimes, to be sure, pommel the poor Frenchmen black and blue with the heels of their shoes; but candour obliges me to state, that I never heard of their tearing the dancing-master in pieces, or eating him up alive.

CHAPTER VII.

Quotations from the Quarterly — Poverty of invention and want of originality of republicans — Dr. Watts — Emigrants, their situation here —
Story of one — Author advises him to go home and tell his story to the
editor of the Quarterly — Promises him a free passage to England — Reflections, &c.

ONE may truly say, with the Quarterly,* "the
scum of all the earth is drifted into New York," notwithstanding what Miss Wright and Captain Hall †
may affirm to the contrary, in their "prostitute rhap-
sodies, and flippant farragoes of impiety, malevolence,
and radical trash," as the Quarterly says. "Godless
reprobates, brutal and ferocious tyrants, thieves, swind-
lers, and murderers," as the Quarterly says, "make up
the mass of the population." "Robberies, burglaries,
and attempts at murder, disgrace the city every day;
and one cannot walk the streets in the daylight, without seeing fellows lie in the gutters, with broken legs,
arms, &c., who continue, day after day, without being
noticed by the nightly watch or the open eye of humanity, to roast in the sun, and be devoured by the
flies," as the Quarterly says. Indeed, I can safely,
and from experience, affirm that the Quarterly is perfectly justified in asserting that, "Insolence of demeanour is mistaken for high-minded independence;"
that no reputable English traveller ever saw man,
woman, or child, blush here, except, it might be,
English people not yet properly acclimated; that the
speeches of lawyers and members of Congress are all

* Vide No. 58, Eng. Ed.
† Captain Francis Hall of the Light Dragoons. 1887.

jargon and nonsense; that the preachers of the gospel bellow out their sermons in their shirt sleeves;
that the judges are, for the most part, worse criminals
than those they try; that dogs are trained to hunt
young negroes, instead of to point game; that men,
women, children, negroes, strangers, congregate together at night, in one room; that not one in ten of
the slaves dies a natural death, they being, for the
most part, whipped till they mortify and the flies eat
them; that the moral air is putrid; that the land is all
hung up in the air to dry; that the air is one animated
region of flies, musketoes, and other noxious insects;
and that such is the influence of the turbulent spirit
of democracy, not only upon the moral and physical
qualities of the people, but upon the very elements
themselves, that the latter are not less perverted than
the former.   All this I am ready to swear to, and so
is the Quarterly Review.   Respect for the precept of
our pure English orthodoxy which inculcates charity
and good-will to all men prevents my indulging
any further upon this topic.   For the present, I shall
content myself with summing up the characters of
these patent republicans, in the words of the Quarterly.

"Fools must not come here, for the Americans are
naturally cold, jealous, suspicious, and knavish —
without any sense of honour.   They believe every
man a rogue until they see the contrary — and there
is no other way of managing them except by bully-
ing.   They have nothing original; all that is good or
new is done by foreigners, and yet they boast eternally." *   In proof of this I may add, that they claim

* Vide No. 58, Eng. Ed.

every thing, and have even attempted, as I before
observed, to rob poor Dr. Watts of the credit of having invented the steam-boat. I have little doubt but
they will lay claim to his psalm-book before long.
There is every day some invention trumped up here,
which has been exploded and forgotten in England,
and for which a patent is procured without any difficulty. It is only to swear to its originality, and that
is a ceremony which no genuine republican will hesi-
tate a moment in going through. This city is full of
foreigners; but what can possibly induce them to
come here, I cannot conceive. I have not met with
a single Englishman that was not grumbling at his
situation, and discontented with every thing around
him. The inns are filthy — the boarding-houses not
fit to live in — the waiters negligent and saucy — the
wines poison — and the cooking execrable. Yet they
remain here with an unwarrantable pertinacity, in
spite, not only of the Quarterly, but of the bitter lessons of experience they receive every hour.

One morning as I was walking up Chestnut street,
the principal promenade in New York, I saw a poor
drunken fellow wallowing in the gutter, and talking
to himself about Old England. This circumstance,
together with his dialect, which partook somewhat of
the Yorkshire purity, excited my curiosity and com-
miseration. I helped him up, conducted him to my
lodgings, and put him to bed to sleep himself sober.
After he awoke and had refreshed himself with a
dozen stewed oysters, I inquired his history. His
tale so happily illustrates the common fate of English
emigrants to this El Dorado, (as the Quarterly calls
it), that I shall give it in his own words, as nearly as

possible. The poor man could neither read nor write, and had been, as will be perceived, the dupe of those interested speculators and agents of this government, who write books to deceive the ignorant and unwary English.

"I was very comfortably situated in Old England, the land of liberty religion and roast beef, except that one fourth of my earnings went to the tax-gatherer, another to the poor-rates, and another to the parson and landlord. But still, as I said before, I was happy and contented; when I happened to read Mr. Birkbeck's ' radical trash,' as the Quarterly says, which turned my head, and put me quite out of conceit with the blessings of English roast beef and English liberty. About this time the man came round to tax my house, my land, my horses, oxen, cattle, servants, windows, and a dozen or two more small matters. A little while after, the parson sent for his tithes, the landlord for his rent, and the overseers of the poor for the poor-rates. All these, coming just upon the back of Mr. Birkbeck's mischievous book, put me quite out of patience, so I made up my mind to emigrate to America.

"I sold off all that I had, turned it into English guineas, and went down to Liverpool, where I took passage. Supposing I should have no use for money in the States, after paying my passage I spent the rest in treating my fellow-passengers at the tavern, and set sail, with empty pockets, yet full of spirits. The Captain was a full-blooded Yankee democrat, and the greatest little tyrant in the world. He held that it was much better to steal than to labour,* and,

* Vide 58th No. of the Quarterly.

by way of illustrating his theory, robbed me of twenty guineas on the passage. On my remonstrating with him, he told me that it was the universal custom of his country, and I might make it up on my arrival in New York, by robbing the first man I met with.

"Our passage was long, and, as the Captain had not laid in half enough provisions, we were obliged to cast lots at the end of a fortnight, who should be killed and eaten. The first lot fell upon me, but I bribed a poor simple Yankee, with a guinea, to take my place. Our Captain insisted upon the privilege of knocking the man on the head, it being one of his greatest delights; there was nothing he preferred to it, except hunting little people of colour with blood-hounds. Out of ten passengers in the steerage, I was the only one that got to New York alive, the rest being all killed and eaten. When I stepped ashore, I was so hungry, and had got such an inveterate habit of eating human flesh, that I immediately laid hold of a fat fellow, and bit a piece out of his cheek. Un-luckily he turned out to be an alderman, and I was forthwith taken to the Bridewell,* where I made acquaintance with several of the most fashionable peo-ple of the city, who generally spend a part of their time there. I had read of this in the Quarterly, but did not believe it till now; and, when I get home to Old England, I intend to publish it all in a book of travels. I shall make a good round sum by it, if I can only get one of the Reviewers to write it down for me, and say a good word in the way of criticism.

[* The Bridewell, in the City Hall park, was a place of detention for persons arrested on a charge of crime or misdemeanor; also, for persons sen-tenced to short terms of imprisonment.]

" The Bridewell is a pleasant place enough. Once a week they have an assembly; on Sunday they play at all-fours; and every day in the week they tipple delightfully, in company with the judges of the court, the corporation, and a select number of the clergy. For my part, I should not have minded spending the rest of my days there; but this was too great a luxury. So I was turned out at the end of a fortnight, to make room for a lady of fashion, who was caught stealing a pig in Broadway. From the Bridewell I went sauntering down the street, expecting every moment that some one would call out to me to come and do some little job, and pay me a dollar for it. But I might have saved myself the trouble, for not a soul took the least notice of me, until at last an honest fellow slapped me on the shoulder, called me coun-tryman, and asked me into a tavern to take a swipes.

" Having been somewhat corrupted by the fashion-able society in Bridewell, I suffered myself to be seduced, and went in with him. Here, while we sat drinking, I told him my situation, and the difficulty I had in getting employment. He asked me if I was a sober man, and on my assuring him I never drank any thing stronger than water, exclaimed, 'By my soul, brother, but that is the very reason. Nobody ever thinks of employing a sober man here; and if you look for work till doomsday, you will never find it unless you qualify yourself by seeing double, by which means you'll get two jobs for one.' I told him I had no money, and, if I had, nothing should tempt me to drink. 'Oho!' cried he, ' You've no money to pay your shot, eh?' So he fell upon me, and gouged out both my eyes, besides biting off a good part of my nose, under pretence that I had sponged upon him, as he called it; but the landlord afterward assured me it was only because I would not drink, it being the custom here to beat people to death, or roast them alive, if they won't get drunk.

"Finding it was the custom of the country, and that there was no getting along without it, and that drink I must or starve, I took to the bottle, and soon got employment in sweeping the streets, and in other miscellaneous matters. Agreeably to the good old maxims of English prudence, I determined, in my own mind, to drink up only three fourths of my wages, and save the rest to buy a farm in the western country, where I intended to go and set up for a member of Congress, when I had qualified myself by being able to walk a crack after swallowing half a gallon of whiskey. But my prudential resolves were of no avail, for the gentlemen-sweepers told me it was against the law to save our wages. On my demurring to this, they took me before the judge, who decreed me a beating, besides taking away the money I had saved, which he laid out in liquor, and we got merry together.

"Seeing there was no use in laying up money, I thought it best to follow the custom, and, from that time, regularly spent at night what I earned during the day. I led a jolly life of it, but it was, like the Bridewell, too good to last for ever. I fell sick, owing to the unhealthiness of the climate, which causes a large portion of the people to die off every year. They carried me to the hospital, where they would not give me a mouthful of liquor; kept me upon soup-diet, and cut off my leg with a handsaw, by way of experiment.　How I ever got well, and got my leg on again, I can not tell; but you will hardly believe it, when I assure you, that, after keeping me here in perfect idleness for six weeks, and curing me, they most inhumanly turned me out into the streets to begin the world again!　That emigrants to this land of promise should be obliged to work for a living was too bad, and I determined not to submit to such an imposition; so I snapped my fingers at them, swore I would see them hanged first, and threatened them with the vengeance of the Quarterly.　'This is a pretty free country, to be sure,' said I, 'where a poor emigrant is obliged to work for a living.'

" Walking in a melancholy mood down the street, I all at once thought of what the captain of the Yankee ship told me, about its being the universal opinion and practice here, that it was much easier to get a thing by stealing than working for it.　This sophistry of the captain corrupted me on the spot, and I took the first opportunity of putting the theory into practice by cabbaging out of a window a watch which hung so invitingly that I could not resist the temptation.　I put it into my pocket till I got to the church, where I pulled it out in order to set it by the clock.　Just at that moment a fellow, with all the characteristic insolence of democracy, (as the Quarterly says), laid hold of me and the watch, and, before I could muster presence of mind to knock the impudent rascal down, lugged me off into court, where I was examined and committed.　Instead of enjoying myself in jail for a year or two, according to the custom of Old England, before trial, I was brought up the very next day, tried, sentenced, and accommodated for

three years in the state-prison, before I could say Jack
Robinson. It was in vain I pleaded the custom of
the country, and appealed to the sacred name of liberty, and the authority of the Yankee captain. The
judge coolly told me that the custom of the country
applied only to natives, and that, not being even
naturalized, I deserved more exemplary punishment
for trespassing upon the peculiar privileges of the free-
born sons of liberty. 'By the time you get out of
prison,' said his honour, 'you will be qualified for citizenship, and may then steal as many watches as you
please.' I bowed, thanked his lordship — who, by the
way, (only think!), wore neither gown nor wig — and
withdrew to go through my initiation into citizenship.

"People may talk of the state-prison, but, for my
part, if any thing could tempt me longer to breathe
the pure air of liberty in this land of hog-stealing
judges * and shoe-making magistrates, it would be
the hope of spending three more such happy years.
I had plenty of meat every day, (which, to a hard-
working man of the land of roast beef, was enchant-
ing, if only on account of its novelty), and did not
work half so hard as at home. As for the loss of
liberty, any person who reads the Quarterly must consider that a great blessing. They were obliged to
turn me out neck and heels, at the end of my delightful seclusion. In revenge I picked the turnkey's
pocket, got gloriously fuddled, and was ruminating in
delightful recollections of Old England, when your
lordship found me, and carried me home with you.
By the way, I should like a few more of those capital
oysters. To make an end, I am now balancing

* Vide 58 No.

whether I shall take out my citizenship, and thus qualify myself for the Yankee mode of sporting; steal another watch before I become privileged, and so get into that paradise, the state-prison, again; or apply for a free passage to the land of liberty and roast beef. They tell me I shall be provided for, if I will give a certificate that it is impossible for an English emigrant to exist in this country. For my part, I am not particular, and am ready to say, or swear to, any thing, to be revenged on these bloody Yankees, who first put a man in jail, and then turn him out again, against all the rules of liberty and good government."

I advised the poor man to go home to England, and promised to get him a free passage. I also gave him a letter to the editor of the Quarterly, requesting him to take down his story, and make an article of it in his next number, for the purpose of deterring all his deluded countrymen from adventuring to this land of bundling, gouging, guessing, and democracy. The fate of this poor, deluded, honest, and industrious emigrant, ought to be a warning to all those who sigh for the blessings of pure democracy, and believe in the impious radical slang of Miss Wright, Captain Hall, Birkbeck, and the rest of the polluted, putrid, pestilent, radical fry, as the Quarterly says. The best of these English emigrants are actually obliged to work for a living, and, if they are not lucky enough to get into the Bridewell or state-prison, more than two thirds of them actually starve to death.

CHAPTER VIII.

Seeming inconsistencies and contradictions in this country — Explanation of
these — Park — Battery — Sunday amusements — Spirit of democracy —
Impiety — Specimens of republican conversation — Theatre — American
play — American Roscius — Kean — Cooke — Cooke a great favourite,
and why — Plays and actors, all English — Little Frenchman! — Author
changes his lodging — Attempt to rob and murder him by the little
Frenchman and his companion — Spirit of democracy.

THE more I see of the people of this country, the
more I am struck with the seeming inconsistencies
that I every day encounter. That they are the greatest cowards in existence is clear from the repeated
assertions of the Quarterly; yet they are continually
fighting and quarrelling. That they are utterly destitute of every feeling of personal honour * is proved
by the same authority; and yet the young men are
all duellists, and risk their lives every day upon the
point of honour. There is no country in the world,
as I have before stated, where thieving, house-break-
ing, and murder, are so common, and yet the shop-
keepers hang out their richest goods at the doors and
windows; the housewives leave their clothes out all
night to bleach or dry; the country people leave their
implements in the fields without scruple, and there is
a general carelessness in this respect, which would
seem to indicate an honest and virtuous people. But
a little study and attention soon lets one into the
secret of all this, and the explanation becomes perfectly easy.

That quarrelsome people, and those who run wan-

* Vide No. 58, Eng. Ed.

tonly into danger, are, for the most part, cowards, is demonstrable. He, for instance, that seeks to quarrel, seeks to fight — he that seeks to fight, seeks to die — he that seeks to die, seeks never to fight more — and he that seeks never to fight more, is a coward. To explain the seeming contradiction to the old maxim, that knavery is always suspicious of others, it is only necessary to refer to the fact, that people careless of their own property are generally the most apt to make free with that of others, and this constitutes the very essence of the spirit of democracy. The people don't mind being robbed, because they can easily reimburse themselves by plundering their neighbours of twice the amount. Indeed, such is the inveterate passion for pilfering, that it is no uncommon thing for a man to rob himself, that he may have an excuse for making reprisals upon his friends. On one occasion I went into a jeweller's shop, which I found deserted by every body. After staying long enough to have filled my pockets with jewels, the shopman came in, and, glancing his eyes round to see if all was safe, seemed very much mortified that I had not robbed him. I heard him mutter to himself, " one of your d——d honest Englishmen."

It is in this manner that the society of which the pure spirit of democracy forms the basis is constituted; and this is what is practically meant by equal rights. It puzzled me at first, how a society so constituted could possibly subsist for any length of time. But the wonder is easily explained. To be free, a people must be in a state of barbarity — to be in a state of barbarity, is to approach to a state of nature — to approach to a state of nature, is to come near it — to come very near it, is to be on the verge — and to be on the verge, is ten to one to fall in. Hence a free people must be in a state of nature, where we know all things are in common, and consequently all men thieves. If it be urged, that a people in a state of nature can have no system of laws, I answer that there is no essential difference between a people who have no laws, and a people who pay no regard to them. The pure spirit of democracy is nothing but a state of nature, as the Quarterly has sufficiently proved; and the people of this country are all bundling, gouging, scalping, guessing, spitting, swearing, unbelieving democrats.*

In my various walks about the city, I visited the Park, as it is called, and the Battery, the pride and boast of these modest republicans. The Park is situated at the intersection of Hudson and Duane streets, and is very nearly, or quite, large enough for bleaching a pair of sheets and a pillow-case all at once. Judging from newspaper puffs, you would suppose it was an elegant promenade, encompassed with iron railing; but I may hope to be believed when I assure my readers that no one walks there but pigs and washer-women, and that the part of the fence which still remains is nothing but pine. There is no other park in the city. But the Battery! O, you should see the Battery — for seeing is believing. I visited it on Sunday afternoon, when I was told I should see it in all its glory. I saw what we should call a wharf, jutting out into a sluggish puddle about half a quarter of a mile wide, which they call a bay. On this wharf were a few poles stuck up — they had no

* Vide No. 58. Eng. Ed.

leaves or limbs, but I was assured they would grow
in time.   Here I saw hundreds, not to say thousands,
of people, strutting, or rather staggering, about in
dirty finery — some hugging and kissing each other
with the most nauseating publicity — others singing
indecent and impious songs — but the majority of
them, in the true spirit of democracy, gouging and
dirking each other for amusement.   In one corner
might be seen a group wallowing and rolling about
in the mud like drunken swine — in another, half a
dozen poor wretches gouged or dirked, writhing in
agony amid the shouts of the people — and in a third,
a heap of miserable victims in the last stage of yellow
fever.   Nobody evinced the least sympathy for them,
and here no doubt they perished with a burning fever,
exposed to a broiling sun, with the thermometer at
110 degrees, the usual temperature of this climate,
winter and summer.   Here they remained to have
their eyes stung out by musketoes while living, and
to be devoured by flies when dead.   I shuddered at
the scene, and turned to another quarter, in hopes
of seeing a boxing match, or some polite, refined exhibition — but in vain.   Such is the celebrated promenade of the Battery at New York; such the Sunday
amusements of enlightened and virtuous democracy!
Nothing could equal the gross and vulgar impiety of
their conversation, of which the following specimens
will furnish an illustration : —

No. 1. — " Well, neighbour, how d'ye get on ? "
      " O, by degrees, *as lawyers go to heaven!*"
No. 2. — " When do you go out of town ? "
      " Why, I think of going to-morrow, *God
      willing.*"

No. 3. — "*Bless my soul*, neighbour, where have
you sprung from?"
"*Why, Lord love you*, I sprung from the
clouds, *like Methuselah!*"
No. 4. — "Well, friend, how does the good woman
to-day?"
"Why, thank you, *she complains of being
a little better!*"

Enough of this. One's blood runs cold at such
impious profanity. Indeed, the people are, one and
all, grossly indelicate and impious in conversation, as
the Quarterly says.*

To vary the scene, and to obliterate in some degree
the painful impressions occasioned by the groups I
have attempted to describe, I strolled into the play-
house, which is always open on Sundays, from ten in
the morning till any time the next day. But I only
got out of the frying-pan into the fire, for such a bear-
garden never Christian man unluckily entered. The
theatre† is nothing more than a barn, abandoned by
the owner as not worth being rebuilt, with a thatched
roof, and stalls for a good number of cattle, which
are now converted into boxes for the *beau monde.*
The hay-mow is now the gallery, and the rest is all
boxes. Shakspeare being considered anti-republican,
and the English dramatists being generally unpopular,
the exhibition consisted of a drama, the production
of a first-rate republican genius. The plot cannot be
unravelled by mortal man; but the catastrophe consisted in a drinking-bout between some three or four

* Vide No. 58, Eng. Ed.

[† The Park theatre, burnt in 1820, rebuilt in 1821, was, about this time,
in the full tide of prosperity.]

admirers, for the possession of the heroine. It is to be understood that there is no sham here. All is real drinking; the audience will endure nothing less, and the pleasure consists in the actors all getting really and substantially drunk. This is what the best republican critics call copying life and manners, of which the aggregate here consists in drunkenness, impiety, and debauchery.* The successful hero, who carried off the lady, swallowed three quarts of whiskey, the only liquor considered classical, and such was the delight of the audience, that one and all cried out, " Encore! encore! let him drink three more!" The hero, however, hiccoughed an apology, hoping the audience would excuse the repetition. He is considered the Roscius of the age, and thought far superior to Kean, or Cooke, though the latter was rather a favourite, on account of his once having paid court to the national taste, by performing the character of Cato, elegantly drunk. This they called the true conception of the part, it being utterly impossible to admit the idea of a sober patriot or republican. The notion savours of aristocracy, and one would run the risk of being tarred and feathered, by suggesting such a heterodoxy in politics.

It is one of the most unanswerable proofs of that total want of genius, invention, and originality, with which these people have been justly charged, that the plays represented at this theatre, and throughout the whole of the United States, are entirely of British manufacture. Were it not for Shakspeare, Milton, Newton, Locke, Bacon, Professor Porson, and a few more illustrious English dramatic writers, the theatres

* Vide Quarterly, No. 58, Eng. Ed.

in this country could not exist. Shakspeare's Tom and Jerry is played over and over again, night after night; and Bacon's Abridgment as often, if not oftener. Another proof is, that they import all their actors from England, it being a singular fact, that, although the people are actually drunk two thirds of the time, in their poverty of intellect they cannot play the character of a tippler with any remote resemblance to nature. They seem, indeed, destined to put all old maxims to rout, and among the rest that of "Practice makes perfect;" since none are so frequently intoxicated, and yet none play the character with so little discrimination.

While indulging in comparisons connected with the superiority of Englishmen, English horses, dogs, beer, beef, statesmen, reviewers, travellers, poets, pickpockets, philanthropists, tipplers, and tragedians, over all people, and more especially this wretched scum of democracy,* I was roused by a sneeze, which went to my very heart. A horrid presentiment came over me; I dared not look in that direction, but remained torpid and inanimate, till I saw an open snuff-box, reached over from behind, slowly approach my nose. 'Twas the little Frenchman, with his mahogany face, gold ear-rings, and dimity breeches! "Ah! monsieur — monsieur — is it you? I am so happy! Are you going to New Orleans yet? I hope monsieur has not been robbed or murdered above once or twice, since I had the pleasure to part from his agreeable company?" I received him, as usual, with a look of freezing contempt; but this had no effect upon the creature, who continued to chatter away and bore me

* Vide Quarterly, No. 58, Eng. Ed.

with his confounded snuff, till I was out of all patience. I should, most certainly, have tweaked his nose, had I not been previously warned by the communicative traveller, that he was a professed duellist, who minded dirking a man no more than a genuine republican, and that he had been long enough in the country to become very expert in gouging. I could have got him killed outright for ten dollars, that being the usual rate in this country;* and people jump at a job so congenial to their habits and feelings. Besides, those who favour the profession for a livelihood have not much employment at present, as almost every genuine democrat prefers killing for himself. But upon the whole I concluded to let the fellow off, not being as yet sufficient of a republican to relish the killing of a man, either in person or by deputy.

The little Frenchman insisted upon knowing where I put up, no doubt with a view of consummating his plan of robbing me; but I was resolved to keep that secret to myself. The more shy I was, the more curious he became, so that I had no other way of escaping his inquiries than leaving the box, under pretence of getting some refreshment. The moment I got clear of him, I bolted out of the house, and made the best of my way to my lodging. Just as I entered the door, however, I heard the well-known sneeze, and, glancing round, beheld the little Frenchman and the communicative traveller, watching me from the opposite side of the way. The thing was now quite plain; no one could mistake their object, and no time was to be lost. I determined to change my lodging that very

* Vide Quarterly, No. 58, Eng. Ed.

night. So, calling my worthy landlord out of bed, I paid his bill, took my portmanteau under my arm, and proceeded to the City Hotel. There I asked for a room with a double lock to it, which was shown me by the waiter, who, by the way, looked very much like a bandit, and eyed me with a most alarming expression of curiosity.

"Thank heaven," said I, after double-locking the door, "I think I've distanced that little diabolical French cut-throat and his accomplice, for this night, at least." Carefully loading my pistols, and placing them on a chair at the bedside, I sat down to refresh my memory with the 58th number of the Quarterly. After poring over the disgusting detail of the gougings, drinkings, roastings, and impieties of republicanism, till my blood ran cold and my hair stood on end, I retired to bed. Somehow or other I could not sleep. The moment I attempted to close my eyes, visions of horror arose, and my imagination teemed with the most appalling, vague, and indefinite dangers, that seemed to beset me, I knew not where or how. As I lay thus under the influence of this providential restlessness, I heard in the next room that appalling and never-to-be-forgotten sneeze, which never failed to announce the proximity of the little Frenchman. I started up, seized my pistols, and stood upon the defensive, determined to sell my life as dearly as possible. Presently some one tried the lock of my door, and I was just on the point of firing, when I heard a voice, saying, "This is not the room, sir — you sleep in number forty"; and they passed onward.

What rendered my situation the more critical was the circumstance of there being an additional door to

my room, communicating with that of the French
bandit, which I had not observed before. Cautiously
approaching it with a pistol cocked in either hand, I
found it locked indeed, but words cannot describe my
sensations when I discovered the key was on the
other side. However, a few moments restored me to
the courage of desperation, and I ventured to peep
through the key-hole, when I saw a sight that froze
my blood. The little Frenchman, with his dark mahogany aspect, was sitting at a table with a case,
not of pistols, but of razors, one of which he was
carefully stropping. Ever and anon, as he tried it
upon the palm of his hand, he observed to the communicative traveller: " Diable! — it will not do yet —
'tis certainly made of lead." At last, however, it
seemed to satisfy him, and he exclaimed with diabolical exultation, " Ah, ha! he will do now — here is an
edge to cut off a man's head without his feeling it."
I instinctively drew my hand across my neck to ascertain if my head was safe on my shoulders, and at
that moment heard the voice of the communicative
traveller: — " Had not you better wait till to-morrow
morning?" " Diable, no — we shall not have time —
now or never — I will not spare a single hair a minute longer." A slight movement followed this, and
the little Frenchman observed in reply to something
which escaped me in the bustle: — " One don't want
any assistance in these matters — I can do it very well
myself." The bloody-minded villain! thought I; he
wants to have all the pleasure of killing me to himself. Some one got up, moved towards the door,
tried the lock, and seemed just on the point of opening it, when, thinking no time was to be lost, I fired

my pistol bang against the door. "Diable!" exclaimed the little Frenchman, " here is our old friend, Monsieur John Bull, the agreeable gentleman, come again. Somebody must be robbing him, beyond doubt. Let us rescue him by all means." They then attempted to unlock the door, under pretence of rescue, but I cried out in a tone of deep solemnity, " Stand off, villains! I have still another loaded pistol, and the first of you that approaches is a dead man. Enter at your peril!" By this time the whole house was in an uproar; the lodgers bundled out of their rooms, half dressed; the servant maids ran about, squeaking; and several ladies fell into fits. I am safe enough for the present, thought I, but nevertheless there is nothing like being prepared; so I held fast my loaded pistol, while the crowd, which at length collected at my door, attracted by the smell of the powder, called out to know what was the matter. " There has been an attempt to rob and murder me," answered I. " By whom?", inquired the voices. " By a little mahogany-faced Frenchman and a communicative traveller," answered I. " Monsieur is under a grand mistake," cried the little Frenchman. " He was going to cut my throat," cried I. " I was going to cut off my beard," answered the little Frenchman — upon which the pure spirit of democracy burst out into a loud laugh. " He must have been dreaming," said one. " He has had the nightmare," said another. " He must be drunk," cried a third. " He must be mad," cried a fourth. " By no means," cried the little Frenchman — " Monsieur has only been reading the Quarterly Review, and is a little afraid of the spirit of democracy. He shall shoot him one day with a silver bullet." Hereupon they all burst into a hideous democratic laugh, which is ten times worse than a horse-laugh, and scampered off to bed, leaving me at the mercy of the two bandits. Such is the protection afforded a stranger, and particularly an Englishman, in this bundling, gouging, dirking, spitting, chewing, swearing, blaspheming den of democracy.*

CHAPTER IX.

Author goes to the police — Description of the magistrate — Mistake of his worship — Examination of the little Frenchman — Author quotes the Quarterly — Mr. Chichester — Dr. Thornton — Frenchman acquitted, to the great delight of the democrats, who all like the French — Why — Sympathy in favour of rogues here, and reasons for it — Philippic against democratic judges, magistrates, lawyers, and democrats in general — Moral air tainted, according to the Quarterly — Author leaves the city of abominations, for fear of becoming a rogue by the force of universal example — Turbulent spirit of democracy — Quarterly Review.

THE morning succeeding the attempt to rob and murder me, I inquired my way to the police-office, which I finally discovered at a cobbler's stall, in one of the filthiest streets of the whole city, called Patty-pan Lane. I found his worship sitting on his bench, in a leather apron, most sedulously occupied in mending an old boot. On my informing him I had business, he looked down at my feet, very earnestly — " Hum! Why, your boots don't seem to want mending — but let us see." So he seized hold of one of them, and, in attempting to pull it off, laid me sprawling on the floor. He then fell into a passion with my boots,

* Vide No. 58.

and swore the fellow that made them so tight ought
to be " dirked," the usual phrase for the punishment
of slight offences among these humane republicans.

It was with some difficulty I made him understand
my business was not with the cobbler, but the magistrate. " Well, go on with your information," replied
he, " while I finish my job; I can take a stitch while
you tell your story." So he fell to work lustily,
while I proceeded to detail the events of the last night.
When I had done, he looked at me for a moment, and
then, with the true gravity and demeanour of a genuine republican magistrate, burst into a horse-laugh,
and took into his mouth a huge quid of tobacco.
" And you are positive their intention was to rob and
murder you?", quoth the sage Minos. I offered to
swear to it, upon which he handed the book, and administered the oath. " Very well, we must send for
these bloody-minded villains, and see what they have
to say for themselves. A little Frenchman, with a
mahogany face, gold ear-rings, and dimity breeches,
say you? We must describe the villain, as you don't
know his name." On receiving satisfaction as to this
point, he procured a warrant, which he signed with a
cross, being unable to write his name; desired me to
witness his mark; and sent off one of his apprentices
to bring the offenders.

In a few minutes he returned with the little
Frenchman, his companion, and almost all the lodgers
at the City Hotel, landlord, waiters, and all. His
worship laid down his awl, and the examination
began.

" What is your name?"

" Pierre François Louis Maximilian Joseph Maria

Gourgac d'Espagnac de Gomperville," answered the little bandit.

" A whole band of robbers, in the person of one little Frenchman," observed his worship, turning to his clerk, and directing him to write it down. The clerk demurred to this, as to write it was quite impossible.

" Well, then," said his worship, " write down *Hard name*, and proceed. Whence came you, where are you going, what is your business, and how came you to put this gentleman in bodily fear last night?"

" I came," replied the bandit, " from New Orleans, which, as monsieur knows," (making me a low bow), " is not far from Portsmouth, in New Hampshire. I am going to Charleston, to which place I hope to have the pleasure of monsieur's company "—(making me another low bow); " my business, it seems, is principally to rob and murder monsieur "—(another bow); " and I came to put him in bodily fear, by reason of sharpening my razors at night, which I generally do before I shave myself"—making me another low bow, and offering his box.

" Hum!", quoth his worship, eying the little Frenchman's stiff black beard, " A man with such a brush under his nose might reasonably strop his razors over night, I should think, without being suspected of any intent but to cut up his own stubble field. But what other proofs have you of this intent to rob and murder, hey?"

" My own conviction," answered I.

" Ay, but a man's conviction is no proof of guilt, except it be a conviction by judge and jury," answered the learned justice.

" The word of a gentleman."

"Pooh! the word of a gentleman is no better than the word of any other man. Every man is a gentleman in this free country," replied the democratic Solon.

"Did they break into your room?"

"No — but they tried the lock."

"Did they actually offer you any violence, or attempt to cut your throat?"

"No — but the little Frenchman sharpened his razors at me."

"Have you any witnesses to prove the attempt?"

"The circumstances are, of themselves, sufficient; besides, they have followed me all the way from Portsmouth, and this is not the first time the little Frenchman and his accomplices have made the attempt.

"Followed you!" quoth Solon; "travelling in the same stages and steam-boats and putting up at the same houses is what generally happens to people travelling the same route — this is no proof of wicked intention."

The little Frenchman now appealed to the crowd of City Hotel people, who, beyond doubt, were all his accomplices, and who testified that he had been there two days before I made my appearance, which the stupid cobbler-justice observed was proof that he had not followed me, at the same time hinting to the Frenchman that he had good grounds for an information against me for following *him!* Finding they were all in league together, I determined to overwhelm the justice, the clerk, the witnesses, and the culprits, by one single irresistible testimony. I took from my pocket the fifty-eighth number of the Quarterly, which I always carry about me; and, turning to page three hundred and fifty-seven, read in an audible voice as follows:—*

" Mr. Chichester told him," (Mr. Faux), " that ten dollars would procure the life and blood of any man in this country." Mr. Chichester also told him, that " he knew a party of whites, who, last year, roasted to death before a large log fire one of their friends, because he refused to drink." †

" And who is Mr. Chichester?" said the ignoramus, who, it is plain, never reads the Quarterly.

" Mr. Chichester is a polished, gay, interesting gentleman, travelling in his own carriage from Kentucky to Virginia," replied I, reading from the Quarterly. ‡ Again, sir, "Judge Waggoner, who is a notorious hog-stealer, was recently accused, while sitting on the bench, by Major Hooker, the hunter, gouger, whipper, and nose-biter, of stealing many hogs, and being, although a judge, the greatest rogue in the United States." § Again, sir, we read from this same unquestionable authority, " Doctor Thornton, ‖ of the post-office, observed to him that *this* city, like that of ancient Rome, was peopled with thieves and assassins, and that during his residence in it, he had found more villains than he had seen in all the world besides."

" And pray who is Doctor Thornton—is he in court?" cried this pious minister of justice.

" Doctor Thornton," replied I, "is a gentleman of character and learning—he has invented a new alphabet."

" Diable!" interrupted the little Frenchman—" 'tis not the only thing he has invented I believe."

---

* Vide No. 58, *English copy.*   † Ditto.   ‡ Ditto.
§ Ditto.   ‖ Ditto.

I continued, without noticing the interruption, " Dr. Thornton, sir, is an Englishman, and that is a sufficient warrant for all he says. I know, moreover, from the best authority, that by his eloquence he prevented the gallant Cockburn from burning the capitol and president's house during the late war." *

" Diable !" again interrupted the little Frenchman, " am I to be convicted of murder upon the testimony of the goose whose cackling saved the capitol ? "

" But what do you intend by all this ? ", replied his worship petulantly, and casting a wishful eye at the old boot, as if he wanted to be stitching again.

" I mean, sir," replied I solemnly, " to prove by this testimony, that as ten dollars is the price of blood in this country, that as Judge Waggoner is a notorious hog-stealer, and that, as Doctor Thornton affirms, your cities are peopled by thieves and robbers — that in such a country, and among such a people, the mere sharpening of a razor at such an unreasonable hour is presumptive proof, sufficient to hang half a dozen Frenchmen and democrats."

But the little Frenchman, who had by this time sent and suborned the president of a bank and two or three directors, his accomplices no doubt, offered their testimony to prove that he was a person well known to them, of ample means and unblemished character, equally above the temptation as the suspicion of robbery or murder. Upon this, in spite of my own testimony and the authority of the Quarterly, the precious cobbling justice dismissed my complaint, and apprised the little Frenchman that he might recover damages

[* The Capitol and Presidential mansion were burned by the British, August 24th, 1814.]

of me if he chose. But the horrid bandit had other objects in view; and, after receiving the congratulations of all present, (for these people adore the French only because they take a little pains to be agreeable), turned to me with a most diabolical smile, made me a low bow, offered his box, earnestly hoped he should have the pleasure of my agreeable company to Charleston, and assured me, upon his honour, he would never attempt to cut my throat again since he was born.

From this specimen of the mode of administering republican justice, and of the character of the judges, who are, for the most part, pig-stealers, and who never read the Quarterly, one may judge of the chance an Englishman has of protection or redress. Every body is in league against him; it is sufficient for a man only to be accused of doing wrong, in order to excite the universal sympathy in his favour. The officers of the courts, the magistrates, judges, lawyers, and spectators, all have a fellow-feeling for a criminal, having all been, or expecting soon to be, in a similar predicament; and the accuser is thrice lucky, if he does not change places with the accused. The lawyers who are most expert in snatching murderers from the gallows are certain to be made magistrates, and the most dexterous pig-stealer is predestined to be a judge of pig-stealers. The sheriff, not long since, was obliged to hang his own nephew for the murder of his mother, who was the sheriff's sister, as these virtuous self-governing republicans thought it a pity to hang a man for such a trifle, and not one of them would tie the knot! The moral air is putrid, and even the most honest Englishman cannot breathe it without his principles being tainted with the plague of democ-

racy.   Feeling this to be actually the case with myself, I determined to change the air as soon as possible, and before I became a villain outright; and
not caring to go back again to the hotel to meet the
banditti and their accomplices, I desired my old landlord, the gentleman of colour, to go and pay for my
lodging, and bring my portmanteau down to the
steam-boat just then departing for the South.   I embarked in her, shaking the dust off my feet, as I left
this city of abominations, in which, though I had
staid but two days, I had seen more of the turbulent
spirit of democracy than in all the world beside.   No
wonder, seeing " it is peopled by thieves and robbers ;" and the Quarterly affirms it to be the place
where the " scum of all the earth" * is collected.

———◆———

CHAPTER X.

Miraculous escape in crossing the East River to Jersey — Author makes his
     will previously — Number of people at Communipaw on crutches — A
     fellow-traveller tells a story accounting for it — Manner of keeping the
     Sabbath — Little Frenchman identified — Inhumanity of republicans —
     Drunken driver — Philosophical reasons why republicans must naturally
     be hard drinkers — Apostrophe in praise of oriental despotism and abject
     poverty.

THE steam-boat in which I embarked, as stated in
the last chapter, conveyed us across the East River to
the Jersey shore without bursting her boiler, which
was considered little less than a miracle, as there is
scarcely a day passes without a catastrophe of this

* Vide No. 58, Eng. Ed.

kind which is fatal to a dozen or twenty persons. Yet the people go on board these vessels with as little hesitation as they would enter their own doors. Indeed, their carelessness of their own lives is equal to their disregard of the lives of others, and they encounter the risk of being scalded to death, with as little concern as they feel in dirking an intimate friend, or burning him on a pile of logs for not drinking.* For my part, I took the precaution, previous to my embarkation, to settle my affairs and make my will. It proved, however, unnecessary in this instance, as we were safely landed in the city of Communipaw, the capital of that state.

The first thing that struck me in roaming about here waiting for the stage, (which was delayed for the purpose of giving the driver time to get drunk), was the vast proportion of people upon crutches. Almost every person I met had lost his feet and a part of his legs; some at the ancles, some at the calves, and a few at the knee. On inquiring of a person who was to be my fellow-traveller the cause of this singularity, he gave me the following details, than which nothing can more brilliantly illustrate the manner in which the Sabbath is kept, or rather profaned, among " these bundling, gouging, spitting, swearing, dirking, drinking, blaspheming republicans." †

" You must know, sir," said my informant, " that the people of this city and its neighbourhood are notorious all over the country for dancing. Such is their fondness for the amusement, that they don't know when to stop; and if it happens to be Saturday night, they are pretty sure to dance till daylight on

* Vide No. 58. Eng. Ed.   † Ditto. Eng. Ed.

Sunday morning, let what will happen. About three years ago there was a grand ball given, at which the mayor, aldermen, and all the fashionable people of the town, were present. Unluckily it happened to be Saturday night, and the company continued dancing till the clock struck twelve. But not a soul heard it, they were so busy in shuffling 'hoe corn' and 'dig potatoes,' and if they had, nobody would have abated a single shuffle. Just as the clock struck, there came in a little dark gentleman, with gold ear-rings and a mahogany face, and dressed in a full suit of black, except that he wore dimity breeches."

" The little Frenchman, by Heaven!" exclaimed I.

" You shall hear anon," continued he. " The little dark gentleman cut into a Scotch reel without ceremony, and danced with such extraordinary vigour and agility, that every body seemed inspired. The young fellows threw off their coats first, then their waistcoats, and there is no knowing how much farther they might have proceeded had not good manners prevented. The buxom Dutch girls of Communipaw kicked up their heels, and gambolled with all the vivacity of young elephants; and bundling came to be very seriously contemplated. But it would have done your heart good to see the fiddler, a gentleman of colour belonging to Squire Van Bommel, who gradually got his fiddle locked fast between his breast and chin, where he wedged it up with both knees, while his mouth gradually expanded from ear to ear, as he played Yankee Doodle as if the d——l was in him. The little dark gentleman was the life and soul of the party; bowed to every body, danced with every lady, complimented every body, offered his box to every body, took snuff with every body, and sneezed—"

"O! the little Frenchman," cried I, "I'll bet a hundred pounds!"

"You shall hear," continued my companion. "All was joy, laughter, capering, singing, bundling, swearing, gouging, dirking, and hilarity, when by degrees the young damsels and lads began to find their bare feet coming to the floor, which reminded them it was time to stop dancing. But it was too late now. There was a spell upon them, and they continued to dance away by an irresistible impulse, till, by and by, first went the skin off the soles of their feet, then the feet themselves. Still they continued dancing, and the shorter their legs grew the higher they capered, and the faster the fiddler played Yankee Doodle, the dark gentleman vociferating all the while, in concert—

'Yankee doodle keep it up,
Yankee doodle dandy;
Mind the music and the step,
And with the *gals** be handy.'"

"But how did it happen," said I, "that the dark gentleman, alias the little Frenchman, did not lose his feet and legs too?"

"I have not yet said he didn't," replied my companion. "But your suggestion is correct. He kept capering away without either feet or legs diminishing, any more than if they had been of steel. But no wonder, as you will find in the sequel. The company continued to caper and jig it, till the legs of many were entirely danced away, and it has been asserted that the fiddler's chin was more than half gone. Nay, there have been those who do not scruple to affirm that several heads, without either feet, legs, or body at

---

* This shows that even the devils don't speak good English among these enlightened republicans.

all, were seen cutting pigeon-wings and taking the partridge-run with all the alacrity imaginable. But touching this there is some contrariety of opinion.

" Certain it is that the dancing continued with unabated vigour, the little dark gentleman still setting the example; and the fiddler, having entirely worn out his fiddle-strings, was sawing away tooth and nail upon the edge of his fiddle. And here I must remark a most extraordinary circumstance, which is, that the longer they danced the shorter they grew, by reason of their wear and tear of feet, legs, &c., so that, beyond all doubt, had they danced much longer there would have been nothing left of them, not even the hair of their heads. Luckily, however, an old one-eyed rooster, who sat upon one leg on a pole that lay across the crotches of two trees, and where they generally hung up their pigs by the hind legs — "

" What!," interrupted I, " do they hang pigs in this country ? "

" Yes," replied my companion, with a sigh. " But the less we say about that the better. You will hardly believe it, but they hang them up with their heads downward;" and thereupon he took out his handkerchief and wiped his eyes. Well may you blush and weep over the inhumanity of your countrymen, thought I. The Quarterly shall hear of this.

" But," resumed my companion in a hurried manner, as if anxious to direct my attention from this horrible cruelty, " let us go back to the old rooster, who, about daylight, clapped his wings, and crowed so loud that you might have heard him across the river. No sooner had the little dark gentleman heard the clapping and crowing, than he made one bound up the chimney, without making his bow to the company, or taking leave of six ladies to whom he had engaged himself to be married the next morning. He was heard to sneeze as he ascended the chimney, which thereupon burst with a terrible explosion of red-hot bricks, which flew about in the sky like great fire-flies, hissing like serpents. This was succeeded by a drizzle of flowers of brimstone, which cured all the people thereabouts of the Scotch-fiddle. The fiddler was found two days afterwards, with his head buried in a salt-marsh near Communipaw and his stumps dancing in the air, scraping Yankee Doodle like a devil incarnate. The dancers all ran home."

" What," said I, " without their legs — how could that be ? "

" I can't say," replied he, " but run they did as fast as legs could carry them, although, as you have ocular demonstration, they must have done it without legs. To conclude, the doctors, hearing of this catastrophe, came over in shoals from New York, thinking they would have some profitable jobs; but, to their great mortification, found all the stumps perfectly healed by what seemed to be the application of a red-hot iron, so that they paid their ferriage across the river and ran the risk of the bursting of the boiler for nothing. It is observed that the dancers all continue to smell of brimstone to this day. Sometimes, particularly during storms of thunder and lightning at night, the windows of the house in which the dance took place look as if the whole was on fire, and some have said they saw the little dark gentleman dancing there surrounded by old women on broomsticks. This is doubtful; but certain it is that the old one-eyed rooster was killed the following Christmas night in a battle royal between the Harsimusites and the Hobokenites, in which the former were worsted."

" I suppose," said I, "this cured them of dancing on Sunday mornings."

" Not in the least," replied he. " These very people you see upon crutches, are eternally jigging it and frisking their tails. You shall see."

So he began whistling Yankee Doodle, and, in the space of five minutes, at least thirty people, without a single leg among them, gathered round us, dancing most incontinently. I turned in disgust from this incorrigible race of impious republicans, whom the loss of legs cannot restrain from a breach of the Sabbath, and who persevere in their enormities even in despite of miracles, as the Quarterly says. But my reflections were interrupted by the arrival of the stage, the driver being at length " prime bang up," that is to say, as drunk as a lord.

In the course of my travels, I have often reflected on the causes of that universal and inveterate propensity to drunkenness which is the characteristic of this people, and the result is, that it is another of the delectable offspring of the turbulent spirit of democracy. Nothing is more certain than that a people will be restrained in proportion to the restraints under which they labour. In proportion to the freedom they enjoy will be the freedom of their indulgences. It is only by taking away the freedom of action, and the means of obtaining these indulgences, that you can make the vulgar either tolerably religious or decently moral. The right of self-government is another word for freedom from all moral and religious restraints, and it is a self-evident deduction, that a man who don't honour the king will seldom fear his Maker. Again — the consciousness of freedom generates among the vulgar, (and all free people may be called vulgar), a certain degree of impudence, a hardy confidence which carries a man above those salutary restraints which the opinion and influence of society impose upon mankind. Lastly, where a large portion of the people can earn a superfluity beyond the wants of themselves and their families, they will be almost certain to devote their substance to riot and debauchery.

It is thus with this wretched spawn of democracy. Boasting, as they do, of the right of making their own laws, they naturally claim and exercise the right of breaking them whenever they please. Being free from the salutary restraints of European and Oriental despotism, they naturally throw off all restraint; having more money than is necessary to supply the wants of life, they naturally grow wasteful; and feeling themselves equal to any and every man they meet, they inevitably become insolent and intemperate. It would be considered proof of a most mean and abject spirit, for a genuine republican to show his respect for any society whatever by behaving with decency and keeping himself sober.

Such being the case, happy, thrice happy, are those who have no voice in making the laws, for they will be the more likely to obey them. Happy, and four times happy, are they who never taste the unhallowed cup of freedom, for they will not be ruined by the absence of all restraints. Happy, and six times happy, are the people who have no taste of that fatal equality which generates a vulgar confidence that disdains all subserviency to rank, dress, and equipage — and happy above all happy people, are those who, being stinted in the means of procuring even the necessaries of life, will never be able to indulge in enervating pleasures, or the excesses of intemperance.

* * *

CHAPTER XI.

Infamous roads — Infamous stages — Infamous stage-drivers — Republican mode of mending roads — Englishmen are known here by an air of distinction — Story of the English emigrant to English Prairie — Sudden obscurity of the atmosphere — Reason of it — Indian summer, its real origin — Stage starts, and leaves the author behind — Insolence of the driver — Spirit of democracy — Miserable effects of freedom — Universal stimulus wanting in a republic — Gross and impertinent freedoms in republicans.

UNDER the protection of that providence which is said to take the special guardianship of drunken stage drivers, we proceeded on, over one of the most rocky, rutty, and infamous roads I ever travelled. The spirit of democracy disdains to pay any regard to the laws for mending roads, it being an approved maxim, that the best way to mend the roads is to let them mend themselves. Yet, notwithstanding this, there are turnpike gates every two or three miles, especially in New England and the other Southern states, where they take enormous toll of all strangers, particularly Englishmen, who, being distinguished by a certain air of nobility which causes them to be all taken for *milords* by the French and Italians, are easily detected by these cunning Yankees.

Notwithstanding the situation of the driver and the roughness of the roads, we jolted along without any accident, and rather more pleasantly than usual. One of my companions turned out to be an Englishman, which, in truth, I had not suspected before, though I might have known it by his speaking such pure English. I was rather inclined to be shy of his attentions; but the moment he informed me he was a native of Yorkshire my suspicions vanished, for an Englishman may be trusted all the world over, all the world knows. By degrees we became sociable, for I saw he was a man of education and discernment, by his always addressing me as my lord. One inquiry led to another, and at length he told me his story, which I shall set down word for word, as a warning to my simple, credulous countrymen, who are allured to this land of promise by the modern Moses of transatlantic speculation, as the Quarterly says.

" Hi was very well hoff at ome," said he, " aving a good farm, with comfortable hout-ouses, and plenty of stock, say five undred Norfolk sheep, forty or fifty Bakewell cows, and two bulls of the Tees-water breed. But someow hor hother, Hi went beindand every year. The rents Hi paid to keep hup the dignity of the nobleman, my landlord — the taxes Hi paid to support the splendours of the king, God bless him — th tithes Hi paid for supporting the established church, without which hevery body knows there can be no religion — the poor-rates which Hi paid to keep hup that state of poverty and dependence without which no people can be virtuous and appy — hall these put together, pulled me down every year by little and little. But hall these were has nothing compared to

certain hother matters. The cost of maintaining Hold
Hingland, in the igh latitude of the bulwark of religion, fell ard upon me — then hafter that, the putting
down of Bonaparte and securing the liberties hof
Heurope fleeced me pretty andsomely. But Hi might
ave got hover these, but for a plentiful arvest, which
coming on the back of hall the rest, stripped me of the
fruits of my labours, and brought me pretty deeply
hin debt.

"Habout this time, Satan, who halways his hat ha
man's helbows hin time hof distress, threw hin my
way that mischievous radical Birkbeck's book habout
the Hinglish Prairie, which seduced me hinto the
hidear of selling hoff my hall and hemigrating to
Hamerrykey."

" Did you ever read the Quarterly ? " said I.

" Nay — but Hi have hattended the Quarter-Sessions
pretty regularly for many years past," replied he.

" Ah ! what a pity — what a pity," said I — " if you
had only read the Quarterly, you'd never have come
to this land of gouging, dirking, bundling, and guessing."

" Hi guess not," quoth he, and went on with his
story.

" Hi was ha saying, that Birkbeck's book fell hin
my way, hand gave such ha seducing picture of the
prairie, that Hi sold hoff hall the stock Hi ad saved
from the landlord, the king, the church, the paupers,
the bulwark of religion, the securing hof the liberties
hof Heurope, hand the plentiful arvest. The proceeds
Hi turned into guineas, hand quilted them into the
waistband hof my breeches."

I shall give the remainder of his narrative in Yankee English, for really I have been long enough here to find the writing of pure English rather awkward.

"I embarked," continued my companion, "for Boston, which, I learned from a gentleman who told me he superintended the geography of the Quarterly Review, was close by English Prairie.* On landing there, which I did without being shipwrecked, although the vessel was a Yankee and the captain and crew drunk all the voyage, the first thing I did was to ask how far it was to English Prairie.—I was in a hurry, and wanted to get there before night. The landlord, of whom I inquired, after scratching his head some time, replied:—

"'English Prairie—are you going there?'"

"Yes—I expect to be there before dark."

"'Do you? Why then I guess you mean to travel in a balloon—don't you?'"

"Dam'me, sir," replied I, "do you mean to hoax me?"

"'Hoax—what's that?'"

"I say quiz me."

"'Quiz—what's that?'"

"I say," replied I, "can you tell me how far it is to English Prairie?"

"'Why, if you really wish to know—I can't say exactly, for I never was there—but I should guess it can't be less than twelve hundred miles, or thereabouts.'"

"Twelve hundred d——ls," cried I.

"'No, not devils,'" said Jonathan, "'but miles; and devilish long miles, I reckon.'"

[* English Prairie. A post village of McHenry County Illinois, 50 miles N.W. of Chicago.—*Am. Gazetteer.*]

" Looking about, I saw a map of the States, which, by the way, is a usual thing all over this country, the people being eternally travelling by maps. On examination, I found, to my·utter astonishment, that brother Jonathan was right. I might as well have gone to English Prairie by way of the Cape of Good Hope, as of Boston. This was one of the first blessed effects of Birkbeck's book. On referring to it, I found indeed that he had stated the distance and the route; but it had escaped my notice, confound him.

" However, since I had come so far, I thought I would not go back with a flea in my ear, and so I determined to seek the distant land of promise."

" What a pity — what a pity," interrupted I, " you never read the Quarterly."

" I am determined to read nothing else from this time forward — at least if I can procure a copy," replied he; upon which I handed him the English copy of the fifty-eighth number, telling him it was heartily at his service during the time we travelled together. He thanked me, called me my lord three times, and proceeded : —

" It would be tedious to give an account of the difficulties, mortifications, insults, dangers, and scrapes I encountered in my journey. I was four times robbed of all I had in the world. I was six times gouged, eight times dirked, and several times roasted at a log-fire, before I arrived at English Prairie. By the blessing of Providence, however, I got there at last, and much good did it do me. My first disappointment, in not meeting the back country close by the sea-shore, was nothing to those I encountered here. Instead of finding the backwoods all cleared away, comfortable houses, barns, fences, hedges, ditches, school-houses, churches, bishops, noblemen, and kings, I found a parcel of rude, hard-working men, with axes on one shoulder and guns on the other. The first thing they told me was to cut down the trees, which were generally about the size of a hogshead. I laid close siege to one for three days, and found, by a pretty clear deduction, that it would take five days more to bring it to the earth. I then counted the trees upon my plantation, and calculated that if I lived to the age of Methusaleh I might possibly clear a place big enough for a potato patch.

" My next inquiry was, as to how they procured their food. ' You must go into the woods,' said a fellow in a hunting-shirt and moccasons, ' there is plenty of deer and wild turkeys.' ' But I never fired a gun in my life,' answered I. ' Then you're a gone sucker,' cried he, at the same time gouging out one of my eyes, I suppose to qualify me to take aim with proper accuracy. Not being able to cut down trees, or shoot deer and wild turkeys, I was in a fair way of starving. I resolved, as the last resort, to take to the poor-house. But, in this barbarous place, there was no poor-house to be found. I then applied to my good neighbour who had favoured me by gouging out one eye, for a piece of venison. He gave me a saddle and a wild turkey, saying, at the same time, in the most unfeeling manner, ' Every body works here, friend, and every man provides for himself. Don't come again begging. You're chopping on the wrong log.' Whereupon he gouged out another eye. Shortly after, he came to invite me to a barbecue, as it is called, which is a sort of feast, where they generally serve up a baked Indian or two, whom they have hunted and shot in the course of the morning. I expressed my abhorrence of this cannibal feast, and declined going, upon which he gouged out another eye, and swore he'd not leave a single eye in my head if I didn't go. Thinking it better to eat Indians than be blind, I signified my con-sent, and accompanied this hospitable person.

" It would be impossible to describe this feast. Suffice it to say, that it ended in a scene of drunken-ness and bloodshed, that was enough to sicken a pirate or a republican. The conclusion was, that every soul present was either murdered or left insen-sible on the ground — after which they threw me upon a log-fire, and burnt me to a cinder, because I wouldn't drink ' Confusion to the Holy Alliance.' My misfortunes did not end here. In one night they robbed me of twenty or thirty pigs, it being their maxim that it is more convenient to steal than buy, which constitutes the quintessence of republican ethics,* as the Quarterly says. I was on my way to the judge, to complain of this theft, when I met my gouging friend, to whom I related my misfortune. He burst into a horse-laugh, which resolved itself into a yell, and tapered off with the Indian war-whoop. When he had done, he solemnly assured me that my pigs were now in the judge's pen; that his honour was the most noted pig-stealer in the place, and had been elevated to the bench solely on that account, it being shrewdly suspected that he would from a fellow feel-ing let off all the pig-stealers, who constitute the majority of the people. ' It is of no use,' said he, ' to go to the judge. Your only remedy is to try and steal

* Vide No. 58. Eng. ed.

somebody else's pigs.   If you can rob the judge, you will get his place to a certainty.'   I expressed an abhorrence of this mode of righting myself; upon which he swore I had reflected upon the native character, and gouged out one of my eyes.

" Soon after, it was buzzed about that I had been on the point of appealing to the laws for redress, and moreover demurred to the Indian law of retaliation, the only law in force at English Prairie.   For these heinous offences, I was informed privately by a worthy English settler who had been like me seduced by Mr. Birkbeck, that they had hired a man to dirk me for ten dollars, the usual price of blood in this country, as Mr. Chichester says.*   Thinking it high time to take care of myself, I sold my land at less than half price to the worthy English settler, and made off, with all the speed in my power, for a civilized Christian land.   I had almost forgot to tell you, that, just on the skirt of the Prairie, I met a party of ladies belonging to the settlement, who roasted me alive at a log-fire.   It was a mercy that I escaped."

" Pray," said I, when he had finished, " do they ever read the Quarterly at English Prairie ? "

" The Quarterly! Lord bless you — they read nothing but Tom Paine.   I never saw any other book in all the Western country."

" Not read the Quarterly!" exclaimed I—" Ah, that accounts for their barbarity."

We now entered a dense, smoky, drizzling atmosphere, which succeeded so suddenly to a bright cloudless day, that we did not know what to make of it. As we proceeded, the density and drizzling increased,

* Vide No. 58. Eng. ed.

19

so that it became impossible to distinguish the road, which, however, was of the less consequence, as our driver had been for some time nodding on his seat, fast asleep. Suddenly the horses stopped of themselves, at what (after a considerable degree of peering about) I discovered to be a house, on the long piazza of which were seated an immense number of fat fellows with broad-brimmed hats, smoking and spitting in the true republican style, that is to say, in their neighbours' faces.*   This circumstance accounted for the smoky and drizzling atmosphere, which extended upward of three miles in circumference, and obscured the entire city, which was called Communipaw. Such is the extent of this practice of smoking tobacco, that, at a certain period of the year, during the autumn, when the people of the country have finished gathering in the products of their fields, and their leisure time comes, they commence a smoking festival, in which every man, woman, and child partakes. This festival lasts five or six weeks, during which time the atmosphere throughout the whole country becomes so hazy and obscure that they are obliged to burn candles all day, and a perpetual drizzling prevails, owing to the unseemly habit of spitting, which all our English travellers have heretofore noticed among these immaculate republicans. This season is called the Indian summer, and the people pretend to ascribe it to the Indian custom of burning the long grass of the immense prairies in the West. But the above, I can assure my readers, is the true solution.

Being resolved not to sit still in the stage and be spitten to death, (for all the stages here are without

* Vide Quarterly.

covering, for the convenience of letting in the rain), I jumped out and sheltered myself under a neighbouring shed. By and by I heard the driver calling for his passengers, but I was determined not to be hurried, and took no notice of his insolence. Presently I heard the cracking of the whip and the rumbling of the wheels, when I thought to myself I had better condescend to call, and stop him. Accordingly I sallied forth in the fog and drizzle, calling out to stop as loud as I could bawl, and running every now and then against a long pipe, invisible in the obscurity. The sound of the wheels served as a sort of guide through the Cimmerian shades; but, as ill luck would have it, just as I came up with the stage, which I afterwards discovered had been stopped at the pressing instance of my companion, I unfortunately fell into a ditch by the roadside, where I was grievously annoyed by a concert of frogs, which, mistaking me, I suppose, for King Log, jumped upon me, and sung with true republican melody.

" You democratic rascal," cried I to the driver, " what business had you to go off without me ? "

" Why," replied the impudent scoundrel, " I thought you had gone off without me. I hallooed till my throat was so dry that I was obliged to call for a pint of whiskey to whet my whistle."

" But why didn't you stop, when I called ? "

" Why," replied the villain, " it was so foggy I couldn't see which way the sound came from."

Upon this I was going to thrash him soundly for his insolence, when my companion advised me not to attempt it. Said he, 'ten to one you will lose both eyes and the better part of your nose, for this fellow

has exactly the look of a first-rate gouger.'   I thereupon determined to put up with the affair, considering
it a portion of that series of imposition, impudence,
rudeness, and barbarity, which constitutes the basis
of the republican character.*

It is in truth impossible to be in this country a day,
without being thoroughly convinced of the fact, that
the possession of freedom necessarily brings with it
an overwhelming mass of ignorance, corruption, and
barbarity.†   This position is supported by the history
of the world and the example of all nations.   The
republics of Greece were little better than nests of
barbarous libertines, as is proved by the licentious
freedoms which Terence, and other comic writers,
took with persons in authority at Athens;—also, by
their banishment of Grotius, perhaps their most illustrious citizen.   Their whole claim to learning consisted in being able to talk Greek; and as to theii
excellence in the mechanical arts, such as sculpture
and painting, they are far excelled by the manufacturers of Birmingham and Sheffield, in skill, and by
the pot-bakers of Staffordshire, in the art of painting
And how *can* it be otherwise, since it is morally impossible it *should* be otherwise, in all free states.

The great and universal stimulus to excellence of
every kind is a desire to please those above us.   To
the applauses of our equals we are indifferent, and the
admiration of our inferiors only excites our contempt.
A conquering general, followed by thousands of people shouting at his heels, throwing up their caps, and
giving way to all the extravagances of vulgar enthu-
siasm, surveys the vile crowd with disdain, and sighs

* Vide Quarterly, No. 58, Eng. Ed.   † Ditto.

for the glorious privilege of being permitted to kneel
at the footstool of his most august and gracious sovereign, and to kiss his hand. What is the applause
and admiration of a whole people, compared to being
made a Knight Companion of Bath, and called *Sir?*
This noble desire to please the great, is founded on
the conviction that they alone are worth pleasing, because they only have the power of rewarding. It is
by their approbation and influence alone that merit
can hope to attain to its reward, in the possession of
titles, the only object of honourable ambition, and of
wealth, the sole means of rational enjoyment.

But where there is no distinction of rank and all
men are equal, the universal stimulus is wanting.
There is nobody to please worth pleasing, because
there are no kings, nor nobility, whose smile alone con-
fers distinction; and there is nothing worth tasking
our genius to attain, because there are neither titles,
ribbons, nor pensions. Hence arises the lamentable
lack of illustrious men in ancient as well as modern
republics, and the deplorable contrast they exhibit
when compared with the splendours of Sesostris,
Xerxes, Alaric, and Prince Esterhazy in his diamond
coat. It is unnecessary to multiply examples to prove
that the human mind can never attain to its highest
elevation in a republic, and that as the United States
never have produced, so it is probable they never will
produce, a truly great man, until their government
has titles, pensions, and ribbons to bestow.

The same causes lie at the root of that coarseness,
rudeness, and forwardness of manner, for which these
immaculate republicans (as the Quarterly says*) are

* Vide Quarterly, No. 58, Eng. ed.

so infamously distinguished. All the regulations of polite life, and all refinements of manners, are the result of imitation; and people never think of imitating their equals, much less their inferiors. Now, nothing can be clearer than that where all are equal, as in this immaculate republic, there can be nobody to be imitated, and consequently no refinement of manners, and no judicious perception of what is due to themselves or to others. People unacquainted with the divine majesty of a king, the splendours of his nobility, and the wealth of his bishops, cannot possibly have any proper idea of the dignity of human nature. Having no standard among them, it is plain they must degenerate into barbarism, merely for want of a proper example. That awe which seizes the mind in the presence of a king, runs through all the gradations of life. In the presence of a nobleman, it becomes a due respect for rank — in that of a bishop, a proper sense of religion — and finally, by degrees, it settles down into that refined sentiment of politeness, which proportions its attentions to the dress, equipage, and general appearance of wealth, which a man exhibits to the world.

Here, on the contrary, where the vulgar system of equality extends to all classes, there exists a certain low jealousy of the pretensions of every man who carries any appearance of superiority or holds himself aloof from the crowd. If he does not sit at table with tag, rag, and bobtail, and condescend to sleep three in a bed with any body the landlord pleases to select for his companions, he may reckon himself fortunate in escaping without the loss of an eye and a piece of his nose. An instance of this barbarous antipathy to broad-cloth coats, which I omitted to notice at the time, occurred in the steam-boat, coming from Boston. I was dressed in a blue frock of Shepherd's best regent's-cloth, handsomely embroidered, and every thing else in the first London style, and was leaning over the side railing, when I felt some one almost touch my elbow. On turning round, I saw a fellow in a gray suit of domestic manufacture, a half-worn hat that smacked of the last century, and shoes with soles at least an inch thick. If the truth were known, I verily believe he wore hob-nails in them. I gave him a look which would have sent a peasant, in any civilized country, about his business in a hurry. But the creature remained hanging over the railing, close at my elbow, and, on our passing a fir-built vessel with a bit of striped bunting at her mast-head, had the impudence to speak to me. " That, I believe, is Old Ironsides," said he. I looked at him with a vacant stare, and said nothing. "I was saying," resumed the homespun creature, "that ship is the United States frigate Constitution. What a fine old ship!" — and then his eyes sparkled most intolerably. I looked at him with my quizzing-glass, dropped my under lip, and turned on my heel, without taking any further notice of him or Old Ironsides, and walked to another part of the boat. In about half a minute he followed me.

" Pray, sir," said he, " have you the misfortune to be deaf?" No answer.

" Are you dumb, sir?" No answer, but a persevering glare through the quizzing-glass.

" If you can neither speak nor hear, may be you can feel," said the turbulent spawn of democracy, raising his fist, which was luckily arrested by the little Frenchman, who, I suppose, was resolved that nobody should murder me but himself. "Diable!" cried the little man, "what is the matter — what has Monsieur John Bull done, that you will knock him down, eh?" A Frenchman, somehow or other, can do any thing with barbarians. The homespun monster dropped his huge paw, and resumed a perfect good humour.

"I am wrong," said he, "because he is a stranger I perceive. Had he been one of my own countrymen, I would have *licked* him for his ill manners."

"Why, what did monsieur do?" asked the little Frenchman.

"I spoke to him twice, and he would not answer me. It is the duty of every gentleman to answer a civil question. He was a stranger and alone, and I thought I would speak to him."

"Diable!" said the little man, "don't you know this is the great Monsieur John Bull, the bulwark of religion, the grand restorer of the liberties of Europe, who gained the battle of Waterloo all by himself, and who is the most learned, polite, and refined gentleman, in the whole world? *Eh bien* — it is lucky he did not look you stone dead. Don't you see his coat cost ten times as much as yours? Diable! it was great courage to speak to him once, much more twice."

Here all the company burst into a coarse republican laugh, I could never tell at what, and the homespun monster departed with something on his tongue which sounded very much like "a dumbfounded potato." From this little anecdote the reader may form some faint idea of the gross freedom which pervades the manners of these republicans, who pay no more respect to regent's-cloth, than they would to the regent himself.

——◆——

CHAPTER XII.

Miserable country — People astonished to hear him talk English — Arrive at an inn — Six or seven dead justices lying in the court-yard — None of the Americans speak or write English — Filial piety and parental affection among genuine republicans — Mint-juleps — Barbarous indifference to life in republics — Pig-stealing — Conversation with the emigrant — Broiling a republican — Republicans great snorers — Dr. Thornton's reasons for it — Night scene — Is robbed — Landlord's ethics — Apostrophe to liberty — Phenomenon of emigration explained — Anxiety of republican damsels to attract Englishmen — Pulling caps — Meets an old acquaintance.

AFTER travelling all day over rough roads, and through a dreary, barren wilderness, which is, however, considered one of the best-peopled and best-cultivated parts of the country, and where every body was astonished to hear me speak English, we arrived late in the evening at Louisville, the capital of the state of Tennessee. In walking up from the stage-coach to the inn, I stumbled over something, and what was my horror at discovering a dead body weltering in blood! A little way further on, I stumbled over another, and in this way encountered six or seven, in less than the space of thirty yards. Inquiring the cause of their deaths, and the reason of their exposure in this manner, the landlord seemed at a loss to understand me for a few minutes, which I ascribed to my speaking pure English. After a little reflection, however, he seemed to recollect himself.

" O — ay — yes — I recollect — we had a *blow-out* here last Sunday, and half a dozen troublesome fellows, they call justices, were done for by the brave *rowdies*.* They won't interrupt sport again, I guess."

I turned sick at the barbarous indifference of this immaculate republican, and asked him why they suffered these bodies to remain thus without burial. " O, we let them lie there as a warning to our meddlesome magistrates how they disturb the amusements of gentlemen. We were just roasting a John Bull for not drinking his allowance of whiskey, when these gentry thought proper to interfere, but we soon did their business." I may as well remark here, once for all, that if I make these republicans talk good English in my journal, it is only because it is utterly impossible to reduce their jargon to writing, and, if it were, no civilized reader could possibly understand it. There is not a being living, who is a native of the States, that can talk or write English.

I designed to question mine host still further on this matter, but just at the moment there was a great uproar in an adjoining room, accompanied by cries of murder, upon which he hurried away " to see the sport," as he was pleased to term it. This sport, as I afterwards learned, consisted in an attempt by a promising young republican of about seventeen to gouge his father, who had refused to call for another mint-julep. My companion, who happened to look in, undertook to interpose, but narrowly escaped losing one of his eyes, if not both, by the hands of the old gentleman, (every body is a gentleman here), who caned him for his impertinent interference, patting the

* Vide Quarterly.

promising youth on the head, and swearing he would turn out a true republican. Not content with a single julep, he called for a whole gallon, and they both got lovingly drunk together. Such, indeed, is the rage for mint-juleps here, that nobody will buy a farm at any price unless it produces plenty of mint.

Reflecting on the barbarous indifference to life which characterizes these republicans,* I did not know but they might take it into their heads to kill me, and therefore proposed to my companion, the worthy emigrant, that we should sleep in the same room that night, for mutual comfort and protection. He seemed delighted with the proposal, and we accordingly, after supper, adjourned to a double-bedded room, the door of which we locked, my friend putting the key into his pocket for safety. He then took out the fifty-eighth number of the Quarterly, and began to read the review of Faux's celebrated tour in America, which he said he could almost swear he had written himself, so exactly did it tally with his own observation and experience.

" And do the judges actually steal pigs?", inquired I. " Pigs!", answered my friend, " ay, and every thing else they can lay their hands on. It is a common thing for them to summon a man before them, in order to insure his absence from home, that they may have an opportunity of robbing his pig-sty without interruption." †

" And they take bribes, too, I suppose?"

" You may say that," replied he. " There is not a judge in the whole country that can resist a pig or two. But it is seldom so high a bribe is offered, ex-

* Vide Quarterly.　　　　　　† Vide Quarterly.

cept when a man wants to be acquitted of two or three murders. The most common douceur is a paper of pins, and for this you may get a decision which will entitle you to a thousand or two acres of the best land in the world. You will have to kill half a dozen *squatters* in order to get possession, but this is considered a mere trifle."

" And were you not jesting, when you talked about their burning people on a log-fire when they refuse to drink ? "

" Not in the least," said he; " I solemnly assure you that nothing is more common than such a frolic. I knew several instances of fathers serving their own children, and boys their own fathers, in this manner, during my stay at English Prairie; and it is certain the custom is common in all the states."

Just at this instant a most poignant smell pervaded our room, like that which accompanies the broiling of a rasher of bacon on the coals. My friend snuffed up the savoury aroma, and exclaimed,

" There!—they are at it now, I'll bet a thousand pounds. They're broiling some poor fellow, to a certainty." *

" 'Tis bacon," said I.

" 'Tis a man," said he. " I can swear to the smell. I've had too much experience to be mistaken." And thereupon he began reading the fifty-eighth number of the Quarterly again, with tears in his eyes.

It now waxed late in the night. The smell of the broiled republican subsided, the uproar of the inn gradually died away, and nothing was heard save the owl, the whippoor-will, the bull-frog, the wolf, the

* Vide Quarterly.

watch-dog, and the sonorous tuning of many a vocal nose chaunting sweet hallelujahs to the pure spirit of democracy. The Americans are, in truth, the greatest snorers in the world, which is doubtless owing to their all sleeping with their mouths wide open. I was puzzled to account for this habit, until Dr. Thornton afterwards assured me they slept with their mouths wide open for the convenience of swallowing a mint-julep, which was always poured down their throats before they awoke in the morning, to keep them from getting the intermitting fever. Late as it was, I felt no inclination to sleep. I looked out of the window, and by the light of the moon could distinguish the bodies of the unfortunate magistrates, their pale faces turned upwards, and their white teeth shining in the silvery ray. Presently I saw a man cautiously stealing along towards the piggery, which is always in one corner of the kitchen for the sake of security. He disappeared through the kitchen window; in a few moments a musket was fired, and I heard no more of the matter. The next morning all was explained. It was a neighbouring judge, who, feeling an inclination for one of mine host's fat porkers, invaded his pig-sty that night. But, to use the landlord's choice phrase, " he got his bitters,"—that is to say, he was shot through the head by mine host who was on the watch, and I saw his body lying with the rest the next day.

Still sleep fled from my eyes, " the *innocent* sleep," for it could not exist amid these republican horrors. My companion grew more and more ardent in his persuasions for me to go to bed. " We will take turns to watch, and I will begin. Have you any arms ?— give them to me." I handed him my pistols, and at length overcome by his persuasions went to bed.   It was long ere I could compose myself to rest; but finally the fatigues of the day by degrees overpowered my apprehensions, and I fell asleep.   How long I slept I know not, but I was disturbed by something rummaging under my pillow, where I had placed my watch and pocket-book.   The lights were all out, and I could see nothing; but, thinking the little Frenchman was certainly come again, I called out " Murder!", as loud as I could, and thereupon heard the door open, and somebody run off down the passage, as fast as possible.   Presently mine host, and several other persons, came into the room with lights, and inquired what was the matter.

" There has been an attempt to rob and murder me," replied I.

" Well, what of that?" replied mine host.   " You need not have made such an infernal uproar, and disturbed the whole house about nothing."

" Nothing!— do you call robbing and murdering a man, nothing?"

" Yes," replied he, "just next to nothing.   I have known a dozen people robbed and murdered in this house, with less noise than the stirring of a mouse. But let us see if you have lost any thing."

On examination, I found my watch and pocket-book, which I had placed under my pillow, safe; but my pockets were rifled, and my pistols missing, together with the fifty-eighth number of the Quarterly.

" But where is your companion?" asked some one. " Far enough from hence by this time, I'll warrant you," said mine host.

" What d'ye mean by that?" said I.

"I mean that he has got your purse and pistols, and you won't see him again in a hurry. The moment he came into the house last night, I knew him for the English swindler who broke jail last spring."

"And why didn't you tell me he was a swindler?", said I indignantly.

"Why, to say the truth, I took you for another. Such pointers generally hunt in couples. Besides, there is so little difference, among us genuine republicans, between an honest man and a swindler, that the distinction is not worth pointing out."

"I shall go to the justice and lay an information," said I.

"You needn't give yourself the trouble," replied mine host carelessly; "there was but one justice left in all this county, and him I shot last night for making free with my pig-sty."

"O, liberty!", ejaculated I, in the bitterness of my heart, "thou art but a name — or rather thou art a name for all that degrades and disgraces human nature. Well may the Quarterly" — Here my soliloquy was cut short by the blowing of the driver's tin trumpet, the signal for departure, and what further I would have said must remain a secret to posterity for ever.

The disappointed emigrant from English Prairie did not make his appearance, and I pursued my journey, wrapt in solitary reflections. Insensibly I fell into a train of thought which led to an inquiry into the extraordinary paradox, that a country like this, destitute of every virtue, and devoid of every attraction under heaven,* should thus have imposed upon the whole world, (except the Quarterly Reviewers),

* Vide Quarterly.

and lured from all parts of Christendom crowds of emigrants, who, tired as it would seem, of the calm and happy security of legitimate governments, have sought misery and disappointment in these barbarous wilds. But mankind, thought I, have ever been the dupes of boastful pretension and arrogant assumptions of superiority. The credulity of ignorance is unbounded: and when we revert to the belief even of sages and philosophers; the errors of Galileo and Copernicus, with regard to the great system of the universe; the blunders of Newton; and the follies of Philopoemen; it were hardly just to blame the errors of the common people. It is, therefore, excusable in the peasantry of distant countries, that they should be thus seduced by thousands to leave their homes, by the impudent falsehoods every day palmed upon them by Mr. Birkbeck and other retailers of radical trash.

But there is one thing which puzzled me at first. Notwithstanding the disappointments of these poor people, their being gouged, dirked, roasted, and pillaged of their porkers by the judges; their being regulated and rowdied, and obliged to cut down trees as big round as a hogshead — notwithstanding there is neither law, gospel, decency, nor morality in the whole country, and that no honest person can possibly live in it — notwithstanding that every emigrant, without exception,* is sighing, ready to break his heart, to get home — notwithstanding all this, I say, it is a remarkable fact, that not one in a thousand ever goes home again! They actually seem to be fascinated to the spot by the charm of misery and despair, like the bird which flies into the jaws of the rattlesnake, in pure

* Vide No. 58, Eng. ed.

horror of his detestable rattles and poisonous tooth. Nay, some of them even contaminate the pure Cockney blood of Englishmen, of which the old giants were so excessively fond,* by mixing it with that of the " guessing, gouging, bundling damsels " of this abominable democracy. Not content with flirting with them, they actually marry them, that is, when they are very rich, which indeed is some extenuation. But, in justice to these unfortunate men, I must acknowledge that such are the pains taken by these republican damsels to attract and entrap our countrymen, that it is a miracle that any one escapes. I happened to go into a shop, not long since, to buy a laced cap on speculation, for which the man asked nearly twice as much as when I looked at it some time before. On my complaining of this, he replied —

" O, sir, the price of laced caps has risen a hundred per cent. lately."

" From what cause ? " said I.

" Why, sir, the truth is, that Major Tightbody, the tall, handsome Englishman, has lately arrived, and the young ladies have been pulling caps for him at such a rate, that it is computed upwards of five hundred have been more or less torn to pieces in consequence. Judging from your appearance, sir," continued he, bowing, " I should not be surprised if you had been accessory to the destruction of a few." Whereupon I bought his cap without further hesitation.

But to return to the main point : — the pertinacity with which these poor deluded emigrants persist in

* " Fee, faw, fum,
I smell the blood of Englishmen ;
Dead or alive I will have some."
Jack and his bean-stalk.

remaining in this miserable, degraded, debauched, de-istical country, convinces me that people may actually be persuaded out of their five senses. This is the only way of explaining the phenomenon; for it is im-possible, by any other hypothesis to account for their continuing to suffer in this dog's misery, when they can be sent home free of expense, provided they will only make affidavit on their arrival that there is neither food, raiment, religion, law, nor honesty, among these republicans. As an illustration of this unaccountable attachment to misery, I will relate an incident that occurred to me in Philadelphia. In strolling about one morning, whom should I meet but the unfortunate, deluded, and seduced emigrant I had picked out of the gutter in New York and procured a free passage for to England. The fellow was, as usual, pretty handsomely " corned," as my friend, the com-municative traveller, has it. On expressing my sur-prise at his being still here in this miserable country, he hiccoughed out —

" Why, please your honour, I considered better of it afterwards; for, says I, ' this is a d——d miserable country to be sure, but then Old England is rather worse, and a prudent man will always stick to the les-ser evil, my hearty.' " " Go to the ——," said I. " I'm going to the tavern," quoth he; and staggered over to the sign of some famous Yankee general — I believe they call him Washington.

CHAPTER XIII.

Author congratulates himself on being alone in the stage — Detestable sociability of republicans — Turbulent spirit of democracy — Driver a freeholder — Sunday sports among republicans — Republican mode of driving into a place in style — Republican students — Republican courage — Republican law to encourage learning — Republican impiety — Republican bargain between a republican professor of divinity and a republican old widow — Republican lies — Republican students — Republican frolic — Republican mode of paying tavern-bills — Arrival at Philadelphia — Story of Ramsbottom — Liberty the root of all evil, &c.

I FOUND myself alone in the stage this morning, greatly to my satisfaction. Nothing, indeed, is so annoying to a well-bred Englishman as being in company with half a dozen of these immaculate republicans, who think, because they pay the same fare, they have a right to talk with any of their fellow-passengers without ceremony. They have, in truth, a most detestable sociability about them, which obtrudes itself upon every body, and pays no more respect to a stranger in a fashionable coat, than to an old acquaintance in rags. They stand as erect in the presence of a great man as in that of a little one, and I verily believe if the king were to come among them, they would use no more ceremony in asking him questions, than if he were a pig-stealing judge. This insolent familiarity is another of the precious products of the turbulent spirit of democracy, which, by inculcating the absurd doctrine of equality, destroys that salutary deference to wealth and splendour, without which it is scarcely worth a man's while to be either rich or splendid. It sickens me to see a fellow in a threadbare coat and tattered wool-hat making up

to a gentleman, with his head erect and his hat on the
top of it, and asking him a question without the least
stammering or hesitation, as you will see done every
day in this bear-garden of democracy. The pleasure
I felt in being alone was, notwithstanding, somewhat
alloyed by the idea of travelling unarmed in this
region of banditti, and without any companion to
assist me in case of an attack. But, when I came to
recollect that considerably more than three fourths of
the people of this puissant republic were themselves
rogues and banditti, I comforted myself with the assurance that if I had any fellow-passengers, it would
be at least three to one in favour of their robbing me
themselves, rather than protecting me from others.

I soon found, however, that I was reckoning without my host, in supposing I should be rid of the
annoyance of talking. The driver turned out a most
sociable fellow, and seemed to think it incumbent
upon him to entertain his solitary passenger. He
took occasion to inform me that one of the houses
we passed belonged to no less a person than himself;
that he was sole proprietor of one hundred acres of
land; and that he was only driving the stage on this
occasion in consequence of an accident that happened
to the person who usually officiated. I thought it best
to humour the fellow, having been assured by an intimate friend, (one of the writers of the Quarterly), that
if the stage-drivers of this country got displeased with
their passengers, they always took the first opportunity,
in passing a bad piece of road, to upset the carriage
and break some of their bones. As to the risk they
themselves run 'on these occasions, they think nothing
of it, being at all times perfectly willing to endanger

their own necks for the pleasure of revenging an affront. For this reason all travellers in this country, who wish to escape with whole bones, make a point of being agreeable to the stage-drivers and treating them to whiskey at every tavern. This is the only way they can travel with any remote chance of safety.

Such being the case, I was resolved to humour the fellow, and be affable; so I asked what the accident was which procured me the honour of being driven by a republican landholder.

"O, a mere trifle," replied he — "he happened to get both eyes gouged out yesterday in a frolic."

"Frolic!" said I — "do they frolic here on Sundays?"

"To be sure they do; it's an idle day, and what else should they do — you wouldn't have them work, would you?"

"Why, no; but then they might go to church, you know."

"Church! — what's that? O, now I recollect. I saw a church once in Nova Scotia; but we've none in these parts, so it would be rather a long Sabbath-day's journey to find one."

"Well, but they might stay at home and read the Bible, or some other good book; or they might at least say their prayers."

"Read!" quoth Jehu — "why, d——n me if I don't believe you're of our bloody aristocrats! No, no; we love liberty too well to oblige our children to go to school, and they love it too well to go if we sent them. Nobody can read here but your emigrant foreigners, and that's the reason we don't allow them to vote or hold offices."

A precious admission, thought I; the Quarterly shall know this. "But what becomes of your children while they are growing up, and before they are put to a trade or can work in the fields?"

"O, they are left pretty much to themselves, to learn the habits of freemen. They play in the road, and amuse themselves with frightening horses as they go by. Or they worry the puppies and kittens for amusement, when there are no little *niggers* to set the dogs at. Their principal business, however, is to learn to chew tobacco, spit against the wind, drink whiskey, and beat their mothers for a frolic."

A hopeful bringing up, thought I. "But is it possible that you have neither churches, preachers, school-masters, nor Bibles, among you?"

"Not a son of a b——h of them," replied he. "We want nothing here, and, of course, there is no necessity for praying, nor for parsons and churches. For your school-masters, they only serve to break down the spirit of liberty by whipping the boys; and for the book you mention, I think I did see one once somewhere or other, I believe in Nova Scotia."

"But what do you do, then, on Sundays?"

"O, we don't want for amusement. We spend it in drinking, dirking, gouging, pig-stealing, swearing, guessing, bundling, and other pleasant recreations.* But we begin to tire of these, as you know people will after a while, and besides, there are hardly any peepers left in the whole country, and the sport of gouging begins to fail. My driver and myself were the only two left in forty miles round with a pair of eyes a piece, and he lost both his, yesterday, as I told you. I expect mine will go next."

* Vide No. 68, Eng. ed.

"This is quite melancholy," said I. "What will you do when there are no eyes to be gouged out? You will have to sit down like another Alexander, and weep that there are no more worlds to conquer."

"No danger of that," replied Jehu. "There is always plenty of variety. When the eyes are all out we fall to biting noses,* and, by the time they get scarce, the little boys will grow big enough to have their eyes put out. It is like the spring, when one flower pops up as another fades — when strawberries are succeeded by cherries, and cherries by blackberries, and blackberries by apples, pears, peaches, pumpkins, and potatoes. But yonder is Princeton, and huzza for a dashing drive up."

So saying, he cracked his whip, put his horses to their speed, routed a flock of sheep, ran over a litter of pigs, two blind men, and a professor of mineralogy with his pockets full of specimens, and finished by upsetting the stage against a pump, to the great delight of a mob of ragged little republicans at the inn-door, who, I afterwards learned, were students of the college pursuing their studies. Luckily I escaped with only a broken shin, which fortunate circumstance the rascal insisted gave him a legitimate claim to a double allowance of whiskey at my hands.

Princeton is the capital of old *Kentuck,* as these republican slang-whangers call it, by way of expressing their affection for that dirking, gouging, swearing, drinking, blaspheming state.† Its principal boast is a college, in which reading and writing by the Lancaster method has lately been introduced. There was a formidable opposition to the introduction of these

* Vide Quarterly, No. 58, Eng. ed.   † Ditto.

aristocratic branches of education, but at length the parents of the students consented, on condition that the matter should stop here. The legislature accordingly passed a law, declaring a forfeiture of the charter in case of the introduction of any more of these pestilent novelties. The only books they are permitted to read are Tom Paine's works; and such is the rigour with which this statute is enforced, that a student was expelled the very day before my arrival, only for having a Bible in his possession. It was in vain that he proved himself incapable of reading, having got only as far as " No man may put off the law." He was made a martyr, in the interest of republicanism. What became of the offending Bible cannot be certainly said, but it was whispered that the professor of divinity, (a sort of sinecure here), exchanged it with a pious old lady for a starched band which belonged to her deceased husband.

Having an hour's leisure on my hands, I visited the outside of the college, which is a log-hut of about a hundred feet in length, with a thatched roof. The windows are all broken, it being the principal recreation of the students to try their skill by throwing stones at a particular pane, and whoever hits it first is entitled to be head of his class for the day. I did not enter this classic fane, having been told that the penalty of such intrusion on the part of a stranger is a gallon of whiskey, which I did not think worth incurring. Somebody pointed out to me the field where, as these ever-lying, ever-boasting republicans say, General Washington beat the English and Hessians most terribly, and took nine hundred prisoners. Here I met an old British soldier, who assured me

that he was not only at this battle, but at every one during the American rebellion, and, that so far from this
being the fact, it was the British that beat General
Washington, and took nine hundred prisoners of the
Yankees. He further assured me that they never
gained a single victory in both their wars with England, and that their whole history was a tissue of lies
from beginning to end. I asked him why he did not
go to England, and write a history to that effect. " It
will be reviewed in the Quarterly, which will swear
to all you say; certify that you are an honest man,
and tell the truth;* and finally praise your work, so
that you will certainly make your fortune by the sale,
and perhaps get a pension to boot."

" But, to tell you the truth, master, I left his majesty's service without taking leave. They might — you
understand ? "

" By no means," said I; " hundreds of deserters
have been received and cherished, only through their
telling the truth of these bragging Yankees."

At dinner I was very much annoyed by young students, who gathered round and amused themselves
with snatching things from the table, so that in a
little time there was nothing left for me to eat. At
first I had thoughts of resenting this impertinent
outrage, but observing that each one carried a dirk
in a side-pocket, the handle of which was perfectly
visible, I thought it prudent to say nothing, and join
in the laugh which accompanied every successful
transfer of meat or vegetables. As it happened, however, I was sufficiently revenged, for in the end they
fell out about a favourite bit, drew their dirks, and in

* Vide No. 58, art. Faux.

less than five minutes every soul of them lay dead upon the floor. The uproar brought in the landlord, two or three professors, and a justice of the peace, who, instead of interfering, stood by, enjoying the frolic, as they called it, and laughing at every successful push.

The stage now drove up, greatly to my satisfaction, as I was heartily sick of this classic abode. Such indeed was my haste, that I jumped in without paying my bill, which the landlord politely reminded me of. On my making an apology, he replied carelessly, " O, never mind, sir, this happens so often with our republican travellers, that I think myself well off if one in ten pays me, and him I always charge for all the rest." By this time there was a crowd of ragged students gathered about, and, on its being whispered that I was certainly an Englishman because I paid my bill, there was a cry of " Gouge him! gouge him!", which certainly would have been done, had not the driver charitably whipped up his horses, and distanced the barbarians, who followed us for half a mile, shouting and hallooing like Indians.

That the spirit of democracy should thus penetrate into the hallowed recesses of learning and science is not to be wondered at. Liberty is the root of all evil; since nothing is more certain than that if men have not the power to do a thing the will signifies nothing. Hence it arises that rogues and ruffians are chained, to prevent the indulgence of their bad passions. Nothing is so effectual in preventing evil, as taking away the power of doing evil. The more free a people are, according to the Quarterly,* the more

* Vide No. 68, Eng. ed.

wicked they will be, because the privilege of doing every thing not forbidden by the laws will be followed, in the natural course of things, by the liberty of doing every thing contrary to the laws. These axioms are so self-evident that it is unnecessary to insist upon them any further.

After passing through Natchitoches, Passamaquoddy, Michilimackinac, and other places, whose appearance is as barbarous as their names, we arrived at Philadelphia, the capital of the state of Moyamensing. As this is considered the most orderly, polite, civilized, and literary city of the States, I comforted myself with the hope of meeting with a different reception from what I had been hitherto accustomed to, among these immaculate republicans, as the Quarterly says. But, alas!, my hopes rested on a foundation of sand. We had scarcely entered the city when the stage was stopped by a crowd of people gathered around a fresh dead body. The history of this transaction is as follows, and furnishes a happy illustration of the blessings of pure democracy.

It seems a fellow named Ramsbottom, a man-milliner by trade, and a genuine republican, had taken offence at a neighbour whose name was Higginbottom, because his wife had attempted to cheapen a crimped tucker at his shop, and afterwards reported that he sold things dearer than his rival man-milliner over the way, whose name was Winterbottom, and whose next-door neighbour was one Oddy. In the pure spirit of democracy, Ramsbottom determined to dirk, not only Higginbottom, but Winterbottom, and Oddy, together with their wives, and all the Higginbottoms, Winterbottoms, Oddys, and little Oddities.

It was a long time before he could get them all together, so as to make one job of it.* At length he
collected the party at his own house, to keep their
Christmas eve, and determined to execute his diabolical purpose.   It appears, however, from what followed, that he had changed his mind as to dirking;
for, just as they were up to their eyes in a Christmas-
pie, a sudden explosion took place, the house blew
up, and every soul perished, Ramsbottom, Higginbottom, Winterbottom, Oddy, the little Ramsbottoms,
Higginbottoms, Winterbottoms, Oddys, and Oddities.
Such is the ferocity and thirst of vengeance generated
in the hot-bed of democracy, that this desperado,
Ramsbottom, scrupled not, like the republican Samson of old, to pull down destruction on himself, only
for the pleasure of being revenged on his enemies.*

CHAPTER XIV.

Philadelphia — Origin of the phrase, "coming out at the little end of the
  horn " — Republican sour bread — Spirit of Democracy — Advances in
  civilization here — Marquis of Tweedale — Watchmen — Story of a
  republican watchman, and a republican market-woman — Literature —
  Port Folio — Franklin, Washington, and all the great men of this country, born under the King's government — Cooper, Walsh, Irving, all
  visited England — Theory on this head — State of religion — Jefferson —
  Madison — Adams — Republican gratitude — Little Frenchman — Black
  dog — Sodom and Gomorrah — Author gets into the wrong box — Brutal
  conduct of the captain of the steam-boat — Author is tempted by Satan
  in the shape of the little Frenchman — Bristol — Author goes to bed in
  dudgeon without supper — Catastrophe of the cook in consequence.

THE city of Philadelphia, (every thing is a city here),
is a little higgledy-piggledy place with hardly a decent

* It will be perceived that our author is very fond of this story. — *Am. Ed.*

house in it, whose principal trade consists in the exportation of toffy and pepperpot. It is situate between two rivers, the Delaware on the West, and the Schuylkill on the East. The former is a decent sort of a river, but nothing to be compared to the Thames, or the Avon. The streets, for the most part, are laid out in the shape of a ram's horn, at the little end of which commonly reside that class of people who have been unfortunate in business. Hence the expression, " coming out at the little end of the horn." There are no public buildings, nor indeed any thing else worthy of a stranger's notice, and so I pass them by as unworthy of notice.

I took lodgings, (for I hate your first-rate hotels), at the sign of the Goose and Gridiron, where, for the first time since my arrival in the States, I tasted sweet bread.* I was at a loss to account for this phenomenon, until I found my landlady was an English woman. It is a singular fact, noticed by all travellers in this country, that, go where you will, the bread is sure to be sour. Whether this is owing to the yeast, to the bad taste of these republicans, or to some intrinsic quality in the wheat, I cannot say. I am rather inclined to the latter opinion, because the grapes in this country, as well as the apples, peaches, and every species of fruit I tasted, are as sour as vinegar. There must be some acidity in the soil or air, or both, to produce this disagreeable singularity. Or perhaps after all it is owing to the turbulent spirit of democracy.

It is not without some reason that Philadelphia is called the Athens of America, since, among other

* Vide No. 68, Eng. ed.

advances in civilization, the people sometimes wash their hands and faces. This practice was introduced about seven years ago, by the Marquis of Tweedale and his suite. It was at first violently opposed, as an aristocratic custom, unworthy of freemen; but it gradually made its way, and there are now few, except the radicals and ultra democrats, that demur to the practice. The popular opinion is, however, rather against it, and it is seldom that a person with clean hands and face is elected to any office, unless he can demonstrate his republicanism by a red nose, a black eye, or some other unequivocal mark of his high calling.

The city has also a nightly watch, a peculiarity I did not observe either at Boston or New York. Here watchmen are obliged to call the hour through the whole night, an excellent regulation, as I supposed, since this is pretty good evidence of a man's being awake. But the spirit of democracy evades every salutary regulation it seems, and I was assured by a worthy alderman, a native of England, that these fellows, from long habit, call the hour as regularly sleeping as waking, so that this afforded no additional security to the citizens. The alderman told me that not less than three or four watchmen were robbed at their posts every night; and nothing was more common than a fellow to be bawling out " All's well," when somebody was actually picking his pockets. The alderman related a humorous instance.

It seems a sturdy watchman, (who, being considered the best of the gang at a nap, was always placed at some responsible post), was nodding in his box, when a wag of a thief took off his hat, and put in its place a night-cap, which he had stolen from an old apple-woman who lived near the ferry-stairs in High street. The hat he straightway carried to her house, and left there. The old dame, upon discovering the theft, set out bright and early, with the watchman's hat on her head for want of a better, to lay her complaint before the police, when, as luck would have it, she saw the vigilant child of the night, still nodding in his box, with *her* cap on *his* head. The Amazon seized her property, and cried out " Stop thief! " with such astonishing vigour, that she actually awoke the watchman, although people who best knew him thought it was impossible. The watchman, rubbing his eyes, and seeing the apple-woman with *his* hat on *her* head, naturally concluded that the cry of " Stop thief! " applied to her. Upon which he conducted her at once to the police-court, to which the lady followed with great alacrity, supposing she had the watchman in custody. When arrived at the court, there was the deuse to pay. The watchman charged the apple-woman with stealing his hat; the apple-woman charged the watchman with stealing her cap; the police-justice scratched his head ; and the clerk gnawed two goose-quills to the stump. But what was most to be admired, two lawyers were, literally, puzzled to death by the knotty controversy; and to puzzle a Philadelphia lawyer is proverbially difficult. In conclusion, the watchman was broken, as the safest course; but the sovereign people, looking upon him as an oppressed citizen, immediately elected him an alderman.

There is a great show, or rather affectation, of literature here, and the good people crow in their cups a good deal, on account of the oldest periodical paper in the States being published here. It is called the Port Folio,* and is really so old that it may be justly pronounced quite superannuated. But I did not find any other special indications of a flourishing state of literature. To be sure, here and there you meet with a young lady that can read large print, and a young gentleman that can tell a B from a bull's foot, by the aid of a quizzing-glass. But there never has been an original work produced here of American manufacture; and the only translation I ever met with is that of the almanac into High-Dutch. They likewise boast of one Franklin, a great hand at flying kites, and one of the first manufacturers of lightning-rods. I had heard him spoken of respectfully at home, so am willing to allow he was clever. But after all, what have these people to boast of on this head? Both Washington and Franklin, and indeed all the respectable sort of men who figure in the history of this country, were born under the king's government, and are therefore to all intents and purposes Englishmen. Franklin spent a long time in England, and though there is no account of Washington's ever having been there, his being able to read and write, of which there are pretty clear proofs, furnishes a sufficient presumption that he must have been there, or where could he have got his learning? At all events, they lived the best part of their lives under the genial and fostering influence of monarchial institutions: and that all their talents and virtues originated in that circumstance is proved, first, by their never having done any thing worthy of admira-

[* 1800—1827, under the editorship successively of Joseph Dennie, Nicholas Biddle, Charles Caldwell, and John E. Hall.]

tion, after the establishment of the republican system here; and secondly, by the singular fact, that, from that time to the present, there has not been a man of ordinary talents or acquirements produced in the country. Mr. Cooper and Mr. Irving have, it is true, gained some little reputation; but I am credibly informed that the former of these gentlemen has been once or twice in England, and that the latter never wrote English until he had been long enough there to forget the jargon of his own country. So, after all, they furnish no exception to my rule, which I have the happiness to say is sanctioned by the Quarterly. As to Mr. Walsh, who had the hardihood to tilt with the Quarterly, he I know was a good while in England, and there it was, beyond doubt, he polished his lance, and learned all the arts of literary warfare. But to put the matter at rest for ever, it is utterly impossible, as I have sufficiently proved, for any thing elegant, or good, or beautiful, or great, to take root in the polluted sink of that earthly pandemonium, a genuine republic.*

Religion, like literature, is at a low ebb here, or rather there is neither ebb nor flood, on account of there being no religion at all. This might be expected from the absence of an established church with exclusive privileges over all denominations of sectarians. The Quakers are numerous here, and it is utterly impossible there should be any pure orthodox religion where they predominate, since we all know that they preach voluntarily, as the spirit moves them, and without fee or reward. Now, I have already proved that a religion which costs nothing is good for nothing.

* Vide No. 58, Eng. ed.

It unquestionably is with religion as with every thing else, the more we pay for it the higher value we set upon the purchase, and the better we are likely to become.* On the contrary, a people who get their piety gratis, must, of necessity, in a little time become impious. In proof of this, I was told by my landlady, a very respectable widow, that there was a society in each of the wards of the city, composed of the principal Quakers and others, to put down religion altogether, by the simple and certain means of not persecuting any particular sect, or giving any one exclusive privileges. This wicked design, aided by the destruction of all the Bibles, which they have bought up and burned, is likely, my landlady assured me, to banish, at no distant period, every trace of orthodoxy from this crooked, Quakerish, and abandoned city. It is better to be a bigot without religion than religious without bigotry. Nothing, in short, leads so inevitably to an indifference to all religion, as the doctrine of toleration, which makes all equal in the participation of wealth and civil rights. The enjoyment of superior privileges and immunities on one hand, and the deprivation of them on the other, generates a salutary opposition between the two parties, exceedingly favourable to the interests of religion. The party in the enjoyment of these superior immunities will endeavour, by superior piety, to prove that it deserves them ; and the party out of possession, will strive, by the same means, to prove that though it may not possess, it at least deserves, a full share. Thus will the worst passions of the mind, envy, hatred, and fear, as it were by miracle, harmoniously conduce to the pres-

* Vide Quarterly.

ervation and increase of the true faith. But there is nothing of this in the pure system of democracy, and consequently there is no religion but unbelief, no morals but what consist in a total relaxation of morality, and no deity but Satan, the first republican on record, as the Quarterly says.

As these immaculate republicans have neither religion nor morals, so are they entirely destitute of gratitude. It will hardly be believed, but is nevertheless a fact, that Mr. Jefferson, the author of their famous Declaration of Independence, the oracle of republicans, the former president of the United States, and, after Satan, the prince of democrats — the man whom the people toast at all their public meetings, and pretend to revere next to Washington — is, at this moment, an actor on the Philadelphia boards for bread!* I saw him myself, or I would not have believed it, bad as I think these miserable republicans. Yet, with this damning fact staring them full in the face, they are every day boasting of their gratitude to their benefactors, at the gorgeous feasts given to General La Fayette. I hope the Quarterly will touch them up on this score in the next number. Of their other surviving presidents, Mr. Madison,† as I was assured, teaches a school in some remote part of Virginia, and Mr. Adams lives in great obscurity somewhere in the neighbourhood of Boston! This is a natural consequence of abolishing the excellent system of pensions and sinecures. I confess, I felt a

* The author has confounded our old favourite the comedian, with Thomas Jefferson, the late president. But this is a mistake pardonable in a stranger. — *Am. Editor.*

[† The Right Reverend James Madison, bishop of Virginia, was president of William and Mary College, at Williamsburg, Va.]

little ill-natured satisfaction at the fate of Jefferson and Madison, when I considered that the first picked a quarrel with England on pretence of maintaining the rights of his country, and the other had the wickedness to declare war against her, while she was struggling for the liberties of Europe, now so happily secured in the keeping of the Holy Alliance. Nor indeed could I find it in my heart to be sorry for Mr. Adams, who was one of the prime movers of the rebellion, and a principal pillar of the revolution.* Nothing can furnish a clearer proof of the divine right of kings than the fact, that history does not record an instance of a man who took arms against his sovereign, ou whom some signal punishment did not fall, by special interposition of Providence.†

These reflections, which crossed my mind on seeing an ex-president performing the character of Diggory, were suddenly interrupted by what seemed the sound of a trumpet, directly behiud me. On turning round, to note its source, I was struck with horror — it was the little Frenchman, blowing his nose, with his confounded flowered Madras handkerchief. The story of the diabolical dance at Communipaw — of the little dark gentleman, who could be no other than Satan himself, so like the little Frenchman — rushed upon my mind. I grew desperate — started up — tumbled over the people in the box — burst open the door, and hurried through the lobby into the street, without once looking behind me. Just as I left the box, I heard the little Frenchman say in reply to some question, " Monsieur is not mad — diable!, he is only a little afraid of robbers."

[* The traveller confounds Samuel Adams with John Adams.]
† Vide Quarterly Review — Clarendon's Hist. Rebellion, &c. &c.

As I walked hastily on toward my lodging, I heard a footstep, pat, pat, close behind me. 'Tis the little Frenchman, thought I — and mended my pace. Still the footsteps continued — pat, pat, pat. I began to run — still the pat, pat, pat, continued, until I arrived at my temporary habitation, where, necessarily stopping for a moment till the door was opened, I felt two great paws pressing heavily upon my shoulders. The door opened, and I rushed in, almost oversetting my good landlady, who eagerly inquired what was the matter. "Satan is at my heels," replied I. "Lack-adaisy! is that all? Nobody minds him here. Indeed, he is so popular that the people would send him to Congress, I dare say, if he liked." "O Sodom and Gomorrah!" said I, "is there no brimstone left for these impious, rebellious, republican cities!" The worthy lady paid no attention to this apostrophe, but began to pat a great Newfoundland dog, a mighty favourite, exclaiming, "Why, poor old Neptune, where have you been all this while?" — then, turning to me, "he must have followed you to the play-house; I noticed he took a great liking to you from the first."

The night was spent in almost sleepless anxiety. My thoughts continually reverted to the little French-man, the dancing gentleman at Communipaw, and the great black Newfoundland dog, until they got so jumbled up that for my life I could not separate them. I became feverish with indescribable terrors; and, if I chanced to fall into a doze, was ever and anon disturbed by attempts to break open my door, accompanied by strange and unaccountable moanings and whinings, for which I could not account. The spirit of democracy seemed to be letting slip all his legions of malignant fiends to torture me, and I resolved to quit for ever this city of horrors. Accordingly, I rose early, hastened my breakfast, and inquired of the good landlady if there was any conveyance to the South that day.

" There is a steam-boat which starts about this hour; but you're not going away in such a hurry ? "

" This moment", I replied, seizing my portmanteau.

" But you had better send for a porter to carry your baggage."

" Send for the d——l, in the shape of a little Frenchman or a great black dog," said I, impatiently, removing my portmanteau.

" Better call a hack, then," replied she; " it's a long way."

" I'll not wait a minute for all the carriages in this diabolical city."

" Why then, sir, you had better settle your bill before you go — if you are not in too great a hurry."

This being done, I sallied out with hasty steps toward the river, where I jumped into the first steam-boat I met with, and was felicitating myself on my escape, when I actually ran my nose right into the mahogany face of the little Frenchman. Starting back, I fell over a basket of onions belonging to an old woman, who let fly at me in the republican style. I was now satisfied in my own mind — " He must be either the evil one, or he deals with the evil one and is therefore a witch." To ease myself of these distracting doubts, after we had left the wharf I called the captain of the steam-boat aside, related my story, and proposed tying the Frenchman neck and heels

and throwing him overboard, to see if he would sink
or swim.   The brute, who I have no doubt was also
in league with Satan, laughed in my face, and replied,

"I would oblige you with pleasure, but we are not
allowed to try witches nowadays, in this manner."

"Not try witches!" cried I in astonishment; "what
d'y'e do with them, then?"   (Another proof, thought
I, of the absence of all law as well as gospel here).

"Why, we generally let them run — the Old Boy
will get them at last, you know, and pay them for all
their pranks.   But, to tell you truth, we don't believe
much in witches nowadays."

"Nor in fairies?"

"No."

"Nor in the Prince of Hohenlohe's miracles?" *

"No; I never heard of him."

"Nor Joanna Southcott's?" †

"No; I never heard of her either?"

"Nor vampires?"

"No."

"Nor ghosts?"

"Not a single mother's son of them."

"And what do you suppose has become of them
all?"

[* Alexander Leopold Francis Emmerich, prince of Hohenlohe-Walden-
burg-Schillingsfurst, born in 1793, died in 1849. He studied theology,
and was ordained priest in 1815. He made a great noise in the United
States by his pretended miracles, especially the relief of Mrs. Ann Mattingly,
of Washington, D.C., from a tumor, in response to his prayers, March 10,
1824.]

[† A female fanatic, who flourished in England at the close of the last,
and beginning of the present, century. She made the most shocking pretensions, which nevertheless were believed in by many persons. She was,
doubtless, insane.]

" They went away about the time the race of giants and mammoths disappeared, I suppose."

" In the name of Heaven," cried I to this unbelieving reprobate, " what do you believe, then ? "   .

" Why, I believe the moon is not made of green cheese, and that the little Frenchman is no witch," quoth he, and went coolly about his business.

He had just gone from me when the little Frenchman came up and offered his box.

" Ah, monsieur, you ran away from me last night, but I have caught you again this morning.   Diable ! I believe the fates ordain we shall never part again." Heaven forbid !, thought I ; but remained silent, hardly knowing what to say.

" Is monsieur going to New Orleans yet ? ", continued he, after a short pause.

" I am on my way," replied I, with as much the air of distant hauteur as I could muster up on the occasion.

" Then monsieur has somehow or other turned his nose the wrong way again.   Diable !, you are going back to Portsmouth, as sure as a pistol."

Thou father of lies and deceit, thought I, you shall not impose upon me again, either in the shape of a little Frenchman, or in that of a great black dog.   So I said nothing, but eyed him with a look of most mortifying incredulity.   He shrugged up his shoulders, took a pinch of snuff, and walked away, to frisk among the ladies, with whom the Old Harry has always been somewhat a favourite.   The captain, who had just been ashore to steal a score or two of pigs for the supply of his passengers, soon after came up, and asked me, with a smile, if I had found out whether the little man was a witch or not? I evaded his question, in the true republican style, by asking which way we were going, South or North.

" Why North, to be sure, sir."

" Toward New Orleans?"

" No — right from it as straight as an arrow."

" And why didn't you tell me so?" replied I in a rage, for I could not stand this imposition.

" I did, as soon as you inquired. It's not my business to tell every passenger the way to New Orleans. Every steam-boat is not going there, and the best thing a stranger can do is to ask before he goes on board."

I now positively insisted that he should turn the vessel right about, and land me where he took me up.

" What, go back twenty miles, with a hundred people, to rectify the blunder of one! No, no, sir; you must go on to Bristol. I shall return in the morning, and take you back, so you will only lose one day after all. But here comes the witch; perhaps he will take you back on a broomstick." So saying, he went away without paying any attention to my remonstrances. Presently the little Frenchman came up, and inquired what was the matter. I stated my case, and asked his advice, for at this moment I felt that to trust to Satan himself was better than to rely on a republican.

" What shall I do?" said I.

" Appeal to posterity and the immortal gods!" said he, with an air of diabolical sublimity, at the same time taking a mortal pinch of snuff that smelt like brimstone.

" There are no gods in this impious country," answered I in despair; "and, as for posterity, I am a bachelor and never mean to be married—so I can have no posterity!"

"There is a way, monsieur," quoth the little Frenchman, with an insinuating and fiendish smile.

"What!" cried I, with an ungovernable burst of indignation—"would you tempt me, Satan! But thy arts are vain. No, diabolical instigator. Know I am a true-born Englishman, a defender of the faith, and a bulwark of religion. No! Be thou Asmodeus, Ashtaroth, Belshazzar, or the Devil on two Sticks—be all mankind extinct for want of posterity, and be there no posterity to appeal to—let me be going North or South, or East or West, to New Orleans or New Guinea—all this shall happen before Satan shall tempt me to the sin of—"

"Of what?" said the little d——l of a man. "Of what shall never defile my tongue in the utterance," said I, with the air of a hero.

"Well, if monsieur will neither appeal to posterity, nor to the immortal gods, there is no more to be said. And now I think of it, no more is necessary. See!, we are just at Bristol, where they land passengers. You can stop here to-night, and return to Philadelphia to-morrow morning. I am sorry to lose your agreeable company, but I am going on a little way farther to the North."

This last information was of itself sufficient to determine me to take his advice, though I could not help suspecting in my own mind that he had some devil-born design in his head. Accordingly, here I landed, the little Frenchman taking leave of me in the most friendly manner. "I am sorry to lose monsieur's agreeable company — but, as I am going North, and monsieur South, who knows but we may meet again." Heaven forbid, thought I, as they loosed the rope, and the boat ploughed her way down the stream.

I found out a lodging, where I ordered supper, and, while it was getting ready, could not help reflecting on the brutal inhospitality, the unfeeling rudeness and ferocity generated in the polluted hot-bed of republicanism. The conduct of the Captain of the steamboat, in first receiving me on board — his refusal to turn back only twenty or thirty miles to land me again — and the stolid indifference with which the passengers listened to my just complaints — all these rushed together on my mind, and put me into such a passion that I determined to be revenged on the whole race of republicans by going to bed without my supper. This I did, to the utter discomfiture of the landlord, the chamber-maid, the hostler, and particularly the cook, who killed himself with a spit, in a fit of despair, at my refusing to taste his terrapin soup.

CHAPTER XV.

LUCKILY, though alone and unarmed, having lost
my pistols as before stated, I escaped being murdered
that night, which good fortune I attribute to the attention of the people having been called off by an
affair which took place during the evening. I shall
relate it, for the purpose of illustrating the true spirit
of democracy.

It seems a fellow by the name of Ramsbottom,
a man-milliner by trade, and a great stickler for the
rights of man, had taken offence at a neighbour whose
name was Higginbottom, because his wife had attempted to cheapen a crimped tucker at his shop, and
afterwards reported all over town that he, Ramsbottom, sold his things much dearer than his rival man-
milliner over the way, whose name was Winterbottom, and whose next door neighbour was one Oddy.
In the pure spirit of democracy, Ramsbottom determined to dirk, not only Higginbottom, Winterbottom,
and Oddy, together with their wives, but likewise all
the little Higginbottoms, Winterbottoms, Oddys, and
little Oddities. It was several years before Ramsbottom could get the whole party together, so as to

make one job of it. At last, after an interval of about ten years, he collected them all at his house, to keep their Christmas-eve, and determined then and there to execute his diabolical purpose. It would appear, however, that he had previously changed his mind as to the dirking, probably on account of the trouble of killing so many, one after the other; for, just as they were all up to the eyes in a Christmas-pie made of four-and-twenty blackbirds, an explosion took place — the house blew up, and every soul, Ramsbottom, Higginbottom, Winterbottom, Oddy, and their wives, together with all the young Ramsbottoms, Higginbottoms, Winterbottoms, Oddys, and Oddities, were scattered in such invisible atoms, that not a vestige of them was ever afterwards discovered. Such is the deadly spirit of revengeful ferocity generated in the polluted sink of democracy. The desperado, Ramsbottom, who was considered rather a peaceable person among these barbarians, scrupled not, like the old republican Samson, to pull down destruction on his own head, that he might be revenged on a poor woman for cheapening a crimped tucker.

This affair set the people talking and tippling all night, and to this circumstance I ascribe my good fortune in escaping being robbed and murdered, the usual fate of strangers whose ill-fortune detains them at this place after dark. In the morning the steamboat stopped, as the little Frenchman told me she would; and, taking the precaution to inquire whether she was going North or South, I went on board. The Yankee Captain saluted me with a good-humoured smile enough, and observed, " You are going the right way now;" but I took no notice of his

insolent familiarity. At breakfast I was seated opposite a dish of terrapin soup, and next to a fat lady of
colour, who desired me to help her to some, which she
devoured with infinite satisfaction, although you could
distinguish the fingers and toes of the poor little terrapins, as plain as day. I could not stand this exhibition of cannibalism, but rushed on deck to relieve
my oppressed feelings. That these white republicans,
destitute as they are of all traces of human feeling,
should indulge in this detestable dish, was not to be
wondered at; but that the people of colour should
thus commit the unnatural crime of feeding upon
their own flesh and blood, was enough to deprive
them of all sympathy. But this only shows the force
of a bad example. Looking up as they do to the
whites, as their superiors in every respect, they naturally imitate them even in their crimes, and eat terrapin soup because they see their betters do it.

During the passage up the river to Philadelphia, I
was, as usual, annoyed by the obtrusive impertinence
of the spirit of democracy. Having fought seven
years for the freedom of speech, these people seem
determined to enjoy the full benefit of their struggles.
Morning, noon, and night, in stage-coaches and steam-
boats, they will talk, whether there is any body willing to listen or not; and one reason why they never
go to church is that they would there be under the
necessity of remaining quiet for at least one whole
hour. Strangers in particular are sure to be specially
annoyed with their forward loquacity; and it is sufficient that a man appears to be a foreigner, and to
prefer solitude, to ensure his being intruded upon by
some one of these talking republicans. If you won't

tell them who you yourself are, what is your business, where you came from, and whither you are going, it is all one to them; they will turn the tables upon you, and tell you their own story. Nay, rather than not talk, they would enter into a voluntary confession of murder, and plead guilty to a breach of the whole decalogue.*

One of the most inveterate of these talkers beleaguered me on this occasion. "I reckon you're a stranger," said he, coming up to where I was, apart from the rest, leaning over the railing as usual, pondering on the barbarity and wickedness of these immaculate republicans. I made him no answer. "You don't seem to be one of our people?", continued he, inquiringly. No answer. "I guess you're an Englishman." This fellow, thought I, has some little cleverness; he has observed the superiority of my dress and air. "What makes you think so?", replied I, in a tone of distant condescension. "Why, somehow or other you English always seem to be out of sorts, as if something were on your conscience like. You go moping and moping about by yourselves, and if any body speaks to you, you look as if you would eat them up. Now we Yankees think there is no great harm in speaking to any man, in a civil way, and that a civil question is worth a civil answer any time."

I debated a moment whether I should turn my back upon him, pull out my fifty-eighth number of the Quarterly, (which I had procured in Philadelphia), and take no further notice of this fellow. But, somehow or other, I did not like his looks. He was

* Vide Quarterly.

a tall, muscular figure, straight as an arrow, with a keen, large eye, and an air of insolent independence, that seemed to challenge equality with any man, in spite of the plain simplicity of his garments. Besides, he had much the look of an expert gouger, and I thought it better to listen to his impertinence than lose my eyes.

"And so," said I at last, "you don't like us Englishmen?"

"Why, I can't say that exactly; but if you would not take such pains to make yourselves disagreeable, we should like you a great deal better. We have had some pretty hard brushes with you to be sure, but we Yankees are a people that soon forget injuries, so long as you don't insult us. Now, for my part, I'd rather a man would cut off my head at once than spit in my face. We don't like to be insulted."

"But who insults you?"

"Why, I don't know — but somehow or other it strikes me that, when a man comes into a strange country, the people have a right to talk to him civilly, and it is rather bad manners in him not to answer. It looks as if he thought himself better than other people. Now we Yankees fought seven years to make ourselves equal to any people on earth, and what's more we are determined to be so, let what will happen."

"I'm sure nobody prevents you."

"Prevents us! No, I reckon that would be rather a difficult matter. But we Yankees can tell an Englishman half a mile off, by his being so shy. He seems as if he was too good to be spoken to. Now we think a man was made to be spoken to, or else there is no use in being able to speak at all."

" Nobody hinders you from talking."

" True.   But there is such a thing as not being answered, and this, as I said, is what we don't like. If we ask you questions about yourselves or your country, it is a proof we feel some curiosity about you — and if we tell you about ourselves and our affairs, it is that we don't suspect you of being rogues who would take advantage of us, by knowing our business."

" But can't a man, especially in this free country, take his choice whether he shall talk or be silent ? "

" To be sure he can.   But then, when he takes his choice whether to answer a civil question or not, he must also take his choice sometimes whether he will be knocked down or not.   To refuse to answer a question — I mean a question put in a civil way, and without meaning to give offence, is to insult the man that asks it. Now what can be done with a man who will neither answer a civil question, nor resent an uncivil one by word of mouth ?   There is but one way, and that is to knock him down.   If that don't make him speak, I don't know what will."

An excellent method.   Here's your true republican ethics, thought I — but there was no use in quarrelling with the fellow, so I thought it best to humour him.

" And so you don't like us Englishmen because we don't talk ? "

" That is one reason.   We think a man that can't open his mouth in a strange country, except to find fault with every thing, had better stay at home, and keep himself in a good humour."

" Very well.   Is that your only reason ? "

" Not altogether.   You go home and tell lies about

us, after staying at our houses, and being treated to the best that we have. There was, last spring a year ago, a fellow that fell sick at my house of an ague and fever, and staid with me two months without paying a cent, for I scorn to take board of any man. Would you believe it! He wrote a book when he went back to England, wherein he said my home was as dirty as a pig-pen — my wife a slut — my children savages — myself a pig-stealer — and my country a den of drunkards, gougers, thieves, and men-killers. Ay, and the worst of it was, that he made as if I had told him so myself, and so belied my countrymen. I am neither gouger, dirker, thief, nor man-killer, but " — and here his eye lightened with terrible ferocity — " if I ever meet that man again in this country, there'll be daylight shining through somebody."

" And so then, you dislike us Englishmen because we won't talk to you, nor praise you ? "

" We don't want you to praise us — only speak of us as we are — tell the truth, the whole truth, and nothing but the truth. It's a dirty business to come here, and eat and drink at our tables, and sleep under our roofs, (perhaps, sometimes, in the same room with our wives and children), and then go home and publish to the world that we have neither manners nor decency, because we did not send you to lie in the woods rather than receive you as it were into the very bosoms of our families. For my part I should be ashamed to look my dear country in the face, did I turn a stranger from my door because I had no where to put him but in the same room with myself, my wife, and my children."

" Well, but," said I in a soothing tone, " you should

not mind what these people say. They are a set of
low, contemptible fellows, who want to get a little
money, and have no other way of doing it but by telling a parcel of lies to please the vulgar."

"I know it. But still it's no way to abuse us, and
then find fault with us for not liking you. Every
man in the United States is a part of his country as
much as a sailor is of a ship, and if you want his
friendship you must not run her down."

"But to return to the subject of answering questions. You Yankees are thought to be rather too
much given to the practice of asking them."

"Well," replied he, smiling, and showing a set of
teeth white as snow, "I believe there may be something in that. But the truth is, we take an interest
in every thing going on in the world, and we like
to hear the news. Then we frequently, in the course
of our lives, change our professions three or four
times, and like to collect all we can from strangers
as well as others, in the way of information. What
is of no use to the farmer or tradesman, may come in
play when one gets to be a member of Congress or a
judge, and for this reason a man wishes to learn as
much as possible from every-body he meets. Most
people like to show their knowledge, so there is no
offence in asking questions to bring it out."

I began to be tired of this tall fellow's prating,
and to get rid of the trouble of answering his questions, rather than from any curiosity, asked him concerning a few particulars, which led to the following
relation. There is no way of gaining a genuine
Yankee's heart so effectually as to ask him for the
history of his life and adventures. They are all Rob-

inson Crusoes in their own opinion, and never lose an opportunity of playing the hero of a story, even if they have to invent it themselves.*

"I was born in New Hampshire; raised in the western part of the state of New York; married in Ohio; and am now settled, for the present, in the state of Missouri." Jupiter!, thought I; the man has travelled over half the globe in three lines. "I have been a man of various enterprise, and miscellaneous occupation. At seventeen years I commenced land-surveyor in the Genesee country, which was then something of a wilderness, and hardly afforded me employment, so that I had sufficient leisure to visit my native town and get married. I forgot that neither my wife nor myself were worth ten dollars. However, we don't forget such things long, that's one comfort. We returned to Genesee with one dollar in my pocket, and none in that of my wife. For some time I did not make much money; but then we had plenty of children, which, in a new country, are better than money. However, I managed to save a little every year, with the intention of buying a few hundred acres of land. But the land rose in price faster than I made money. So that by the time I had got together five hundred dollars, land was a dollar and a half an acre. This won't do for me, thought I; but just then the people began to talk of Ohio, where land was selling at that time for two and sixpence an acre. 'Betsey,' said I, 'shall we go to Ohio?' 'To the end of the world, John,' replied she; and away we scampered the next day. Here I bought a good stout farm, cut down some trees for a place for my

* Vide Quarterly.

house, girdled others for a place for my wheat, and built a log-house twenty feet long at least. People soon flocked round, and in a little time there was some occasion for law: so they made me a justice of the peace. Not long after, it was thought but proper to introduce a little religion: so I took to reading a sermon, every Sunday, at the request of my neighbours. By and by, it was thought prudent to embody a company of militia for protection against the Indians: so they made me a captain of militia. In a year or two, there was a town laid out and a court-house built. This introduced two new wants — that of a judge and a town-treasurer: so they made me a judge, and a town-treasurer. Then followed, as a matter of course, the urgent need of a newspaper: so a newspaper was set up, and I volunteered as editor.

" These honours were very gratifying, to be sure, but all this time my family was increasing both in size and number. I had six girls and five boys, some of them six feet high. I began to be uneasy about providing for all these. I had only sixteen hundred acres of land, and that was not enough for them all. The thought struck me that I could sell it for enough to buy six or eight thousand in Missouri Territory. ' Betsey,' said I, ' will you go to Missouri?' ' To the end of the world, John,' said the brave girl. So, the next day but one, we hied away to Missouri, where I bought a few thousand acres. We were almost alone at first; but in a year or two people came faster and faster, so that from a Territory we became a State, and wanted members of Congress. So they made me a member of Congress. But the country is getting too thickly settled for me — and I think next year of moving up

the river five or six hundred miles, to get out of the
crowd.   I am now on my way to Washington, where
I mean to make speeches like a brave fellow.   But
see, we are just arrived, and I must look to my baggage." He then shook me by the hand, and gave me a
hearty invitation to come and see him next summer,
when I should probably find him somewhere about
the mouth of the Yellowstone.   I thanked him, as
in duty bound, and so we parted.

This wandering Gentile may stand for the whole
progeny of democracy.   Such is their utter indifference to home and all its delightful associations, that,
rather than stay there and get upon the parish, they
will leave their kindred, friends, and household gods,
to herd with Indians and buffaloes in the pathless
wilderness.   If they cannot live in one place, they try
another; if they cannot thrive by one trade, they turn
to another; and so ring the changes until they succeed at last.   Hence, as a natural consequence, they
turn drunkards, swearers, dirkers, spitters, bundlers,
gougers, and blasphemers, caring neither for God nor
man, and finally sink into the polluted pool of diabolical democracy, a prey to bitter remorse and con-
suming recollections.*

I am reminded, by the familiarity of this back-
woodsman, of the filthy republican practice of shaking hands, which prevails in this country.   Such is
their insolent familiarity, originating doubtless in the
turbulent spirit of democracy, that the most ragged
genius that labours in the streets or fields will thrust
forth his brawny paw to shake hands with the President himself, who would be considered unworthy of

* Vide Quarterly.

his station if he declined this insolent familiarity. If two strangers happen to travel together two or three days in a stage, they cannot part without shaking hands; and this insufferable assurance extends so far, that I have been actually more than once insulted by being offered the hand of a landlord at whose house I happened to sojourn for a few days. On being introduced to a person, no matter how inferior, he would feel himself terribly affronted, and ten to one gouge you, if you declined his offered hand. Such is the vulgar hail-fellow-well-met familiarity engendered by the possession of equal rights and the absence of a king and nobility to teach the people their proper distance.*

When I came to pay my fare, the captain, with a smile of unpardonable insolence, declined to receive it, observing, that as I had gone up the river with him by mistake, he could not in conscience charge any thing for bringing me back again. I had no doubt that he did this merely to escape the consequences of having put me to the expense and inconvenience of twice travelling thirty or forty miles. But I was resolved not to let him off so easily; and accordingly, the moment I landed, inquired the way to a magistrate. I found this worthy seated in his office, which, judging from appearances, must have been at no distant date, a stable or a pig-sty. His worship, before I could open my business, desired me to wait a little, " and be d——d to you," till he was at leisure. It seems he was receiving the report of Master Constable, who had been out on a scouting party. The following dialogue passed between them : —

* Vide Quarterly Review.

" Well, Simon, where are your prisoners ? "

" I caught them."   It would have been too much for the spirit of equality to have added, " your worship."

" Well, what did you do with them ? "

" I gave the defendant fifteen lashes."

" And what did you do with the plaintiff ? "

" I gave him fifteen lashes too."

" And what did you do with the person who laid the information ? "

" Why, I gave him twenty-five lashes for giving us so much trouble."

" You did right," said his worship; " these rascals ought to be discouraged."

I began to commune with myself, that if this was the republican mode of administering justice, the less I had of it the better.   After hesitating a moment, whether it was worth while to receive twenty-five lashes for the pleasure of seeing the captain get fifteen, and finding the balance rather against me, I made his worship a low bow, and departed without further ceremony.   In going out I heard his worship say to Simon — " Curse that fellow; if I was not just now engaged on a pig-stealing party with the mayor and aldermen, I'd lay him by the heels."*

* Vide Quarterly.

CHAPTER XVI.

Author's malediction on Philadelphia — Quarterly — Is again beleaguered by a modest republican — Their conversation — Various accidents and lucky escapes at Natchitoches, Vincennes, Utica, Vandalia, Tombigbee — Big and Little Sandy, Big and Little Muddy, and Big-Dry, Rivers — Arrival at Baltimore — Insolence of the Baltimoreans — Buys a horse and sulky, to escape the intrusion of the spirit of democracy — Terrible picture of slavery — Pine woods — Stops at a lone house, which turns out to be the rendezvous of banditti — Providential escape — Leaves his watch behind — Despatches Pompey — Pompey's account of his mission to Old Hobby — Arrival at Washington.

LEAVING my malediction upon the city, the people, the magistracy, and every living thing else within it, I departed from Philadelphia, as usual out of humour with the world, and disgusted with the whole clan of immaculate republicans. As we were rapidly passing up the river towards the South, I retired as far from every-body as I could, and sat down to look over the fifty-eighth number of the Quarterly, in order to refresh my memory with some of the most striking beauties of the turbulent spirit of democracy. But, go where you will, it is impossible to keep clear of the intrusion of these free and easy republicans. While thus occupied, one of the most decently dressed and respectable republicans I had hitherto seen, came walking back and forth, passing and repassing before me. I laid down my book and went into the cabin for a moment, to get my handkerchief which I had left there, and which I found exactly in the same place. This I mention as one of the wonders of this new world.

Returning to my post, I found this modest gentleman had taken up my book and was turning over the leaves; but he condescended to return it to me, with an apology for the liberty he had taken.

"I felt some anxiety to see it," said he, "as I perceive it contains the article on Mr. Faux's Travels, which was omitted in the republication here."

"Indeed!" replied I, with cool indifference; "pray what was the cause of the omission?"

"I understand it contained certain libellous passages concerning a respectable gentleman in this country, and his connexions. For my part, I think it ought to have been preserved. A criticism degenerating into a string of libels is a curiosity peculiar to the present refined age of literature."

"The greater the truth, the greater the libel," said I. "Your countrymen I hope are not afraid or ashamed of the truth."

"No, not when we can get it pure and unmixed. But sketches, at best degenerating into caricature, and, for the most part, drawn from the very worst specimens of manners, and by persons animated by the worst feelings of hostility, who have not even the discretion to hide their malignity, are not subjects of very pleasing contemplation, certainly."

I took up the book, and, opening it at the review of Faux, began questioning the man as follows, making it my text.

"Can you deny, sir, that it is the very nature of a democracy to make men turbulent, ill-mannered, ferocious, drunken, beastly, and rude to the last degree?"*

"I have in some measure brought this discussion

* Vide No. 58, Eng. ed.

on my head," replied he with a smile, "and will answer you as I should not under other circumstances. — Cast your eyes around the deck; there are probably seventy, perhaps a hundred, persons, in sight. They come in all likelihood from almost every section of the United States, and are of different grades, stations, occupations, and education. Do you see any one drunk?"

I looked around, and, though the deck was covered with men, women, and children, wallowing like swine in the filth of debauchery, replied, "why — no — I can't say I do exactly;" being resolved to hear what the gentleman had to say for himself.

' "Do you observe any appearance of turbulence, rudeness, ferocity, or indecency?"

Just then a couple of deacons set to, and gouged out each other's eyes; but I was resolved to see nothing, and replied —

"None in the least."

"Do you suppose, sir, that if this drunkenness, rudeness, turbulence, ferocity, this dirking, gouging, swearing, and impiety, were so universal a characteristic as the Quarterly is pleased to affirm, there would not be some examples exhibited here among so many persons, of such various occupations and characters coming from all parts of the United States?"

"Of course, of course," said I, with a glance directing his attention to a fellow who had just dirked his second cousin and thrown him overboard. But my gentleman kept his countenance in a manner worthy a true disciple of brazen democracy.

"I will not pretend to deny," continued this intolerable proser, "that our people have something of the wild flavour about them, or that they partake in some degree of the imperfections incident to their history and situation. Let your travellers tell us of these in the spirit of friendly admonition, and note our good qualities as liberally as they reprobate our faults. Accustomed as Europeans are to a world a little on the wane, they are too apt to mistake the manly frankness of freemen for a forward impudence, and to confound the virtues of independence of spirit with the opposite vices of a freedom from all salutary restraints. Exemption from that sense of inferiority which makes the subjects of a monarch pay such abject deference to rank and wealth is too often mistaken for rudeness; and thus the very feeling of personal independence, which is essential to the preservation of freedom, is laid to our charge as a proof of barbarism and ferocity. But," continued he, smiling, " if perchance you are a traveller of the literary class, I may some time hence figure in your book as an example of that inveterate love of talking which has been ascribed to our people. I shall therefore conclude by observing that the difference is, that our world is not quite ripe, and yours is somewhat decayed. We think our world is the better for blooming in all the freshness of youth; while you appear to be of opinion that your world, like a cheese, is the better for being a little rotten." He then slightly bowed and left me, before I had time to make a cutting reply. But I was determined to pay him off at a proper time.

After passing through the towns of Natchitoches, Vincennes, Utica, Vandalia, and Tombigbee, and crossing the Big-Sandy and Little-Sandy, not forgetting the Big-Muddy and Little-Muddy, rivers — (did ever Christian man hear such names!) — we arrived at the great city of Baltimore. I should not omit to mention that I was robbed at Natchitoches, gouged at Utica, roasted at a log-fire in Vandalia, and dirked at Tombigbee. Besides these accidents, I was all but drowned in Big-Dry River, but luckily escaped by its having no water in it. This was a pretty tolerable chapter of accidents for one day, and may serve as an antidote to the delusions of transatlantic speculation, the seductions of Mr. Birkbeck, and the democratic slang of Miss Wright, Capt. Hall, and the rest of the radical fry of democracy, as the Quarterly says.*

It was my intention to spend two or three days at Baltimore, but, happening to take a walk on the morning of my arrival, I encountered a monument purporting to have been erected to the memory of certain persons who fell in an action with the British in the late war, in which the latter were defeated, and their commander, Gen. Ross, was killed. There was no standing this insolent exhibition of republican vanity, and I determined to stay no longer in a place where such studied attempts are made to mortify the feelings of Englishmen, and perpetuate hostility between the two nations. There is also another monument going up here to the memory of the rebel Washington, an additional proof of the justice with which this place has been denounced as the very sink of democracy. Accordingly I bought a horse and sulky, being resolved for the future to travel by myself, in order to get rid of the impertinent intrusions of these free and easy republicans and enjoy my own

* Vide No. 68, Eng. ed.

company unmolested. For this purpose I crossed over to the Eastern shore of Maryland, and travelled on a by-road to the city of Washington.

I thought the negroes were ill-enough-off in New-England, but it was nothing to what I saw here. The road was lined on each side with naked negroes begging for charity, this being their only refuge from absolute starvation, as their masters allow them nothing. Instead of scarecrows to frighten the birds from the corn, you generally see negroes hung up in the fields for that purpose. I cut one poor fellow down just in time to save his life, and on inquiring the cause of his being thus inhumanly punished, he told me his only offence was eating a piece of mouldy bread which he found one day in the cupboard! Yet such is the force of habit, that this miserable wretch, instead of thanking me for saving his life, skipped over a six-rail fence, joined a party of blacks at work in the field, and struck in with might and main in the songs they were singing! I thought of the fable of the swan singing in the agonies of death, and drove on.

Towards evening, the road led through a country of thick melancholy pines, which deepened the approaching gloom; and the houses became farther and farther separated. I had now proceeded several miles without seeing a habitation, or meeting a single human being. The night was fast approaching, and I began to anticipate a lodging in the woods, when, to my great joy, I saw a light gleaming, or flickering, at fitful intervals, through the branches of the trees. As I approached, I could distinguish by the help of the moon, which now rose in cloudless majesty, a desolate, dilapidated mansion, the windows of which were for the most part broken, and the walls half in ruins. Two or three dogs saluted me as I rode up, with a republican growl. They were silenced by a shrill voice, crying, "Be quiet Nap—get out Cæsar, you villain." The dogs obeyed the command, and sneaked away.

"Who's there?", continued the voice.

"A traveller," replied I, "who is benighted, and in want of food as well as rest. Can you accommodate me for the night?"

Here was a pause of a minute, during which the female went into the house to consult the master, as I supposed, for at the expiration of that time a man came forth, and in a hoarse voice said to me,

"We can give you a bed and supper, such as they are. Alight sir, and my boys will see to your horse."

I accordingly entered the house through a door which opened directly into a large room, at one end of which there was a brisk fire which served instead of candles. "Sit down," said the old man, handing me a straw-bottomed chair, "and we will see what we can get you for supper." Then, raising his voice, he cried—"Clementina!"

"I'm coming, daddy," answered somebody, and forthwith in came Clementina, a damsel of at least six feet in her stockings. She looked like a sibyl, with eyes black as a coal and wild as those of an antelope, and long lank hair, glossy and straight, hanging about her neck and shoulders. I confess I felt rather odd at seeing her, but my feelings were nothing to those which rushed over me on entrance of the two *boys,* as the old man called them. They were at least seven feet high, raw-boned, and savage in their aspect; with nothing on them but a linen shirt and trowsers. Though I came in a fashionable gig, and was dressed in the most fashionable travelling-costume, they seemed not to feel the least embarrassment in my presence, but took chairs and sat down at my side with the genuine air of republican insolence. I tried all I could to look dignified, but in spite of myself could not repress certain apprehensions, which gradually came over me, and undermined my sense of superiority. The old man and his wife, who, by the way, though apparently advanced in years, were as tall and as straight as the children, asked me a great many questions in the way of guessing and reckoning, while Clementina bestirred herself in preparing and bringing in the supper.

When it was ready they all sat down without ceremony, and with as little ado invited me to follow their example. Here was a practical illustration of the blessings of equality; but I was determined to put up with their insolence for one night. The supper consisted of loads of meat, ham, venison, and game of various kinds, in quantities sufficient to feast an army. I began to sum up the probable amount of my bill, as I concluded I should have to pay for the feasting of the whole family, and for what was left besides. "Help yourself," said the old man, "and don't be a stranger — I'm sorry we have nothing better — but you're heartily welcome." Most people are welcome, thought I, for their money; but I said nothing.

"We cannot afford tea and coffee," continued the old man, "but here is some old whiskey that I hope you will like.   Come, help yourself, and here's to Old Hickory."

My stomach turned at the very smell of this execrable beverage; but, recollecting the republican custom of roasting their particular friends by a log-fire for refusing to drink, I thought fit to help myself and make as if I drank.   In this way supper passed off smoothly enough, and the old man then directed Clementina to make arrangements for the night. " You boys will be obliged to give up your room to the stranger, and Clementina will make you up a shake-down in the corner here."   While this was doing, I amused, or rather perplexed, myself in looking about the room, and wondering where these people could procure such luxuries as venison and wild game. But, as the light flashed in a remote and obscure corner on one side of the fireplace, I was struck with horror at seeing three rifles hanging one below the other upon hooks fixed in the wall.   The whole truth flashed upon me at once.   I am in a den of banditti, thought I, and my moments are numbered.   They will murder me to-night, and none will know my wretched fate.   The old man will lay out all my money to-morrow in whiskey — the boys will go a courting in my new gig, dressed in my dandy coats, and Clementina will figure in my patent corsets.   I burst into tears at the awful anticipation.

" What ails you ? ", said the old man.

" Maybe he has got the stomach-ache," quoth the old hag, who now began to look just like one of the Great Unknown's remarkable old women.

" Take a little more whiskey," said Clementina, with a look of diabolical tenderness.

At first I was going to reject it with infinite contempt; but, on second thoughts, and considering what I had to go through that night, I determined to fortify myself with Dutch courage after the manner of the Yankees; and, if I must die, die like immortal Cæsar, with decorum.

"Your bed is got ready," said Clementina; but I determined to sit up and defer my fate as long as possible. They now began to yawn, and one after the other retired, wishing me good night, until decency obliged me to follow their example. My room opened directly from that in which we were sitting, and where the two boys were to sleep, no doubt, as I felt assured, to be handy for murdering me. I retired to my room, the door of which I attempted to fasten; but there was nothing but a latch. I looked at the sheets, but they were white as snow, Clementina having, as I concluded, taken the precaution to pick out a pair not stained with blood, so as not to alarm me. I looked under the bed, and discovered something that greatly resembled a trap-door, with leathern hinges.

This discovery overset me entirely. I paced my room to and fro, and listened in breathless anxiety to every sound. If a mouse stirred, my heart leaped into my throat. I heard the owl and the whippoorwill, those ill-omened birds, screeching and flapping their wings at my window, and mingling their warnings with the distant howlings of half-famished wolves. I was determined not to lie down, for fear of going to sleep; and at length, to while away the time, took up the fifty-eighth number of the Quarterly. But this only added to my boding apprehensions. As I read of the gougings, bundlings, dirkings, and guessings;

of roasting alive on red-hot log-fires — of ten dollars being the price of a man's life in this country — and of all the diabolical horrors of turbulent democracy — my spirit failed me, and I sunk insensible on the floor.

How long I remained in this unconscious state I cannot say; but I was roused at length by a noise of mingled howlings, barkings, cacklings, and crowings, that entered my very soul. Presently after I heard a stirring in the next room, and a light shone through my keyhole. It is all over with me now, thought I — my time is come. " Now I lay me down to sleep," said I to myself, and waited in silent resignation. At length I ventured to look through the key-hole, and saw a sight that froze me into horror. The two young bandits had taken down their rifles, and while loading them the following dialogue passed in whispers : —

" D——n him but I'll do his business; I'll give him his bitters."

" Hush!" replied the other; " you'll wake the gentleman."

Again there was a confused noise of howling, barking, and cackling, without. " Now is our time," said one; and both of them made, not for my door, but out of that which led into the yard. I breathed again for a moment, until I heard two guns fired at a little distance. They are murdering some poor unfortunate travellers, thought I, and my time will come next. In about half an hour they returned, and threw something, that fell like a dead heavy weight, on the floor.

" By G——d we've done for him at last," said one; " the rascal fought like a tiger. Let's strip the gentleman of his hide."

"No, no," replied the other, "wait till—" here his voice sunk, and I could only guess at what was meant. I grew desperate, and tried to push up the window, but it was fastened down with nails, to make all sure, and prevent my escaping that way. I tried the trap-door, but it turned out to be no trap-door at all. I listened again, but by this time all was silent in the next room. A moment after I heard the voice of the old man calling his "boys," and perceived, to my astonishment, that the sun was just peeping above the eastern horizon. Daylight, which emboldens the innocent, appals the guilty, and I now felt myself safe. I came out of my room, with an air as unconcerned as possible, and was received as if nothing had happened.

"Good morning, good morning," said the impudent old republican; "I am afraid you was disturbed last night. The boys were out after a bear that has beat up our quarters several times. But he'll never come again, I reckon. Isn't he a *whopper?*", continued he, pointing to the carcass in a corner. A happy turn, thought I, but I'm not to be humbugged by a cock-and-bull story. They pressed me to stay to breakfast, but I was resolved not to trust myself a moment longer with these banditti, and requested them to get my gig ready as soon as possible. In the mean time I asked the old man for his bill.

"We don't keep a tavern," said he.

"I know that," replied I significantly; "but you will take something for your trouble?"

"Not a cent—every stranger that comes here is welcome to what I can offer. I have little money, but a plenty of every thing else; and it is not often we have the pleasure of a stranger's company in this out-of-the-way place. You are heartily welcome to your bed and supper, and will be still more so if you will stay to breakfast."

His refusal to take pay was another proof, if any had been wanting, of the profession followed by this awful family. Banditti are always above taking money that is honestly their due, and require the zest of a little murder and bloodshed to make it worth having. I bade them good-morrow with very little ceremony, and set off in a brisk trot; but before I had got a quarter of a mile I heard some one hallooing, and, looking back, perceived one of the young giants coming after me in a pair of seven-league boots, as it appeared by his speed. I concluded they had repented having spared my life, and had sent this fine boy to despatch me after all. Under this impression I put my horse on his mettle, and soon distanced the fellow, notwithstanding his seven-league boots. I rode ten miles without stopping, being determined to get out of the very atmosphere of this nest of banditti, if possible.

By this time I was hungry, and conceiving myself pretty safe from any immediate pursuit, stopped at an inn of tolerable appearance. The landlord, according to the custom of the country, took the first opportunity to ask a few dozen questions, ending with, " Pray what o'clock is it ? " I told him I didn't know, for I was resolved not to satisfy his impertinent curiosity. " O, ay," said he, " I see you haven't any watch." On examination I found this was but too true, and it at once occurred to my recollection that I had left it at the den of the banditti in the forest. I asked mine host if he knew these people, describing them and their establishment.

" What, old Hobby, that lives in the Pines, about ten miles off? Know him? Lord bless your heart, every-body knows *him*."

I then condescended to tell him of my misfortune, and desired to know how I could get my watch again. He answered, very shrewdly, that I had only to go back for it. But I would not have trusted myself there again for twenty watches. I told him I did not like the trouble of going back so far, but would pay any person reasonably that would ride over and get it for me. A bargain was struck with Pompey, the black boy, in which it was covenanted that the said Pompey, on returning with my watch in the space of three hours, should receive from me a silver dollar for his pains. Pompey accordingly mounted a raw-boned courser — fastened a rusty spur to his bare heel — departed at full gallop — and returned with my watch in less than two hours and a half.

" Did they refuse the watch, Pompey?" said I.

" No!" replied Pompey with a grin.

" What did they say?"

" They said," replied Pompey, wonderfully enlarging his grin, "that Massa was the drollest man they ever see in all their born days."

I felt no curiosity to inquire their reasons for this complimentary opinion, but paid Pompey his dollar, and said no more on the subject. After breakfast I set out for Washington, where I arrived in safety, thanks to my good stars.

CHAPTER XVII.

Washington — Dr. Thornton — Story of the roaring reprobate republican,
Ramsbottom — Story of an English emigrant farmer — His project —
Disappointment. * * * * * * * * * * * * * * *

" EVERY thing is morally and physically mean at
Washington," as the Quarterly says.* The breezes
are perfumed by nuisances of all sorts — the flies die
and mortify in the oily butter, and are eaten by the
people as a great luxury † — drinking, dirking, and
gouging, are the ordinary amusements — profanity
and cheating the order of the day — the fire-flies and
frogs furnish the lights and the music — the men are
boisterous and rude — the children intolerable — the
women all as ugly as sin — and, to sum up all in one
word, I was assured by Dr. Thornton who saved the
capitol from being burnt last war, that " the whole
country, like ancient Rome, is peopled by thieves and
robbers." ‡ The doctor told me in confidence that
although, like many other deluded Englishmen, he
had been induced to leave his country, yet he was determined not one of his posterity should take root
after him in this detestable district.§ The doctor pre-

---

* Vide No. 58, Eng. ed.   † Ibid.   ‡ Ibid.

§ There is reason to suspect that the person here quoted was not the Dr.
Thornton he professed himself to be, but an impostor; or at any rate that
the doctor was bantering our traveller on these occasions. It is quite impossible he should have been serious. There is the same unwarrantable freedom
taken with the name of this gentleman in Faux's Travels, as will be seen in
the 58th number of the Quarterly, (English ed.), to which our author so frequently refers. By the way, people should be careful how they attempt to
hoax English travellers with these stories, for they will certainly record them
as actual facts. — *Editor.*

sides over a department where models of machinery are deposited, and it furnishes another proof of the total ignorance of these immaculate republicans, that they were obliged to select an Englishman for this station, because there was not a single native in the whole country, that was qualified for the place. The doctor did not exactly say this, but he intimated as much. He also further assured me that there was not a single invention patented here that he himself had not previously anticipated. Yet these people pretend to original genius.

To exemplify the state of manners and morals, as well as the ferocious, intemperate passions engendered and fostered by the turbulent spirit of democracy, the doctor related to me the following anecdote. The affair took place a few days before my arrival.

It seems a fellow by the name of Ramsbottom,* a man-milliner by trade, and a roaring republican, had taken offence at a neighbour whose name was Higginbottom, because his wife had attempted to cheapen a crimped tucker at his shop, and afterwards reported that he sold his things much dearer than his rival man-milliner who lived over the way, whose name was Winterbottom, and whose next-door neighbour on the right hand was named Leatherbottom, and on the left Oddy. In the pure spirit of democracy, Ramsbottom, who was reckoned rather a good-natured fellow for a republican, determined to dirk, not only Higginbottom, Winterbottom, Leatherbottom, and Oddy, but likewise their wives, together with all the little Higginbottoms, Winterbottoms, Leatherbottoms,

---

* Our author forgets that he has told this story before, two or three times. But this is excusable in a stranger. — *Printer's Devil.*

Oddys, and Oddities. It was several years before Ramsbottom could get them all together, so as to make one job of it. At last, however, he collected the whole party at his own house, which was next door to the doctor's, to keep their Christmas-eve, and determined to execute his diabolical purpose. It appears, however, that he had previously changed his purpose of dirking — on account of the trouble probably, as he was a lazy dog. Be this as it may, just as the whole party were up to their eyes in a Christmas-pie, a horrible explosion took place — the house blew up, and every soul, Ramsbottom, Higginbottom, Winterbottom, Leatherbottom, their wives, and all the little innocent Ramsbottoms, Higginbottoms, Winterbottoms, Leatherbottoms, Oddys, and Oddities, were scattered in such minute and indivisible atoms, that not a vestige of them could be found the next day, except a little bit of Mrs. Higginbottom's forefinger, that was known by the length of the nail; it being the custom of the ladies of Washington to let that particular nail grow, for the purpose of protecting themselves against gouging at tea-parties and elsewhere. Such is the ferocity and deadly spirit of vengeance generated in the hotbed of polluted democracy, that the desperado, Ramsbottom, it appears, like another republican Samson of old, hesitated not to involve himself and all his family in destruction, only to be revenged upon a poor woman for cheapening a crimped tucker.

The first thing in Washington that excites the notice of a stranger who has been used to living under a monarchical, or, what is the same thing, a Christian, dispensation, is, that there is not a single church in the whole city. This however is the case with every town and city in this country founded since the revolution, when, the turbulent spirit of democracy getting the upper hand, as might be expected the building of churches was dispensed with as highly aristocratic. So much, indeed, did the British troops feel the want of some place of religious worship when they entered the city during the late war, that, as I was assured by Dr. T——, the gallant Cockburn actually delayed setting fire to the President's house a whole hour, to afford them a decent place to say their prayers in. The doctor solemnly declared to me it was the most edifying sight he ever witnessed, and that he looked upon the gallant Cockburn as one of the genuine representatives of the pious crusaders of yore, for he never went on a burning or plundering expedition without saying his prayers beforehand.

On Sunday morning, (as it was, for the reason before stated, impossible for me to attend church), it being excessively hot, I took my umbrella, and strolled out into the solitudes of this immense city. I had not proceeded far, when I was assailed by a mob of some two or three hundred negroes and boys, who began pelting me with various unseemly missiles. Not knowing what offence I had committed, I was in considerable perplexity, when a sober respectable person came up and explained the whole matter. " It is the custom here," said he, " where but few persons enjoy the luxury of hats, to put them on the top of their umbrellas instead of their heads, in order to make them the more conspicuous. Your omitting to do this has caused a suspicion of your being an Englishman, and that you have not already lost both eyes and part of your nose, and been roasted at a log-fire, is a great piece of good luck." By his advice, I immediately did homage to the genius of democracy, by placing my hat on the top of my umbrella, and hoisting both over my head. This appeased the mob, who gave three cheers, under cover of which I retreated, accompanied by the stranger, who I at first took it for granted had a design to rob me, if not something worse.

Upon further intercourse and examination, however, I had a shrewd suspicion of his being one of my own countrymen. He was a stout, square-built man, with a broad ruddy face, redolént of small-beer; all which appearances were in perfect contrast with the rawboned, cadaverous figures of the natives. Instead of the light loose pantaloons, short gingham coats, and detestable straw hats, which constitute the summer dress of the Yankee gentlemen, he wore a frock of genuine British broadcloth, a pair of corduroy breeches, and woollen stockings, all which gave him a respectable and responsible appearance, although rather warm for the season. These peculiarities, together with a certain politeness of manner and purity of language, almost persuaded me that he was a true Englishman, and presently afterward, seeing him wipe his nose on the sleeve of his coat, I became satisfied my conjecture was well founded. We soon became sociable, and continued our walk together some time. I found him, like all the Englishmen I have met with here, out of humour and discontented with every thing — the people, the country, the government, the air, the water, and most especially the system of farming and the obstinate ignorance of the American farmers.

" I brought with me to this country," said he, " rising of two thousand guineas, with part of which I bought a farm in Pennsylvania. Being determined to show them something in the way of farming which they never saw before, for the honour of Old England, I sent home for iron ploughs, iron harrows, and iron rakes ; in short I had every thing of iron, even to my hog-trough. I also imported an English bull, English cows, English sheep, English hogs, an English dairy-woman, an English ploughman, English ploughs, and all sorts of English farming implements. All this cost me a great deal of money — but I was determined to show the Yankee farmers something, for the honour of Old England.

" As I expected huge crops, owing to my improved system of English farming, I built large barns for my wheat and hay, large stables for my horses, oxen, cows, sheep, and other stock, for I was determined they should be well lodged. I spent a vast deal in hedging, ditching, and other improvements, the labour of which was rather expensive, and made another great hole in my guineas. However, I was resolved to show these bumpkins something in the way of farming, for the honour of Old England.

" I was so much taken up with these preparatory arrangements that the season passed away before I had time to put in my crops, so that I was under the necessity of purchasing food and fodder for myself and my English stock, which made another hole in my guineas. However, the spring came on, and I set to work to show the Yankees something in the way of farming, for the honour of Old England. My bull had been stuffed and curry-combed till he had grown a perfect monster, so that, when I turned him into the field, the neighbours came from ten miles round to see him. An old Quaker, whose farm joined mine, said to me, 'Friend, I fear our earth is not strong enough for thy bull;' but I paid no attention to his slang.

"Being perfectly satisfied, from the analysis of Sir Humphrey Davy, that wheat, rye, corn, and the other grains cultivated in this country, contained little or no nourishment as compared with other products, I determined to put my whole force upon a field of four acres, which I devoted to the cultivation of *ruta-baga*. With my iron plough, my iron harrow, and my English ploughman assisted by two Yankee labourers, in the course of two months I put my four acres into such order as never had been seen before. It was a perfect garden. The rows were as straight as arrows, and there was not a clod of earth above ground as large as an egg to be seen. Every-body came to admire, but as yet nobody imitated me, — such is the ignorant and insolent obstinacy of the Yankee farmers.

"'Friend,' said my neighbour, the old Quaker — 'friend Shortridge, what art thou going to put into thy field here?'

"'Ruta-baga.'

"'*Ruta-baga!* — what is that, friend John?'

"'Turnips,' replied I.

"'Well, why didn't thee call them so at first? If thou talkest Latin here, nobody will understand thee, friend John. But what art thou going to do with thy turnips?'

"'I shall feed my cattle, sheep, and hogs with some, and sell the rest to my neighbours.'

" ' But thy neighbours will raise their own turnips, and will not buy.'

" ' Then I will send them to market.'

" ' What, sixty miles, over a turnpike ?   That will be a bad speculation, friend John.   Thee had best put in a few acres of wheat and corn.   They will pay the expense of taking to market.   Thy turnips will cost more than they will come to.'

" ' Not I, indeed, friend Underhill,' said I. ' Sir Humphrey Davy says there is little or no nourishment in wheat and corn.'

" ' No ? ', quoth the old Quaker, with a sly glance at his round portly figure ; — ' I have lived upon them all my life, and never made the discovery, friend John.'

" My ruta-bagas flourished to the admiration of the whole neighbourhood; and when I came to gather my crop in the fall, there was a heap as high as a hay-stack.   Some of them measured eighteen inches in diameter.   I was as proud as a peacock, for I had now done something for the honour of Old England. I determined to give my cattle, sheep, and hogs, a great feast, and invited my good neighbour, the Quaker, to see how they would eat *ruta-baga.*   A quantity was nicely cut up and thrown to them one morning, but, to my astonishment and mortification, not one would touch a morsel.   Whether it was that they had become spoiled by a fine season of grass I cannot tell; but the bull turned up his nose — the cows turned their backs, and so did the sheep — while the pigs ran away, screaming mightily. ' Thee should set them to reading Sir Humphrey Davy, friend John,' quoth my neighbour — ' they haven't learning enough to relish thy Latin turnips.'

" The autumn was now come, and there was a long winter before me, for which, I confess, I was but ill-provided. Relying on my specific, I had neglected my grass, or rather had pastured it the whole season; depending on my turnips, as I said before, for winter food for my stock. I sent a load of them to market, but the tolls and other expenses swallowed up the price of the venture, and brought me a little in debt. I then offered to exchange ruta-bagas with my neighbours for hay and other products, but they shook their heads and declined, to a man.

" On the back of this came the loss of my famous bull, who one night got into a piece of low-ground, where he sunk in, and perished before morning. ' I am sorry for thy loss, friend John,' said the old Quaker; ' but I told thee our earth was not strong enough for a beast with such little short legs and such a huge body.' To mend the matter, my plump, rosy-faced, English dairy-maid got married to a young fellow of the neighbourhood, whose father was a rich farmer, and my imported ploughman, being told that a dram in the morning was good for keeping off the ague and fever, seemed to think he couldn't have too much of a good thing, and was fuddled from morning till night.

" Winter came on, and a terrible long hard winter it was. For some time I purchased of the neighbours what I wanted for my family and stock, but the spring turning out very backward, and the frost continuing till late in April, all kinds of food for cattle and stock became so scarce that there was none to be had for love or money. As a last resort, I resolved again to try the ruta-bagas. Accordingly, after preparing my cattle and pigs by a long fast, I offered some to their acceptance. It was Hobson's choice, and they nibbled a little, making divers wry faces withal. By degrees they took to it more kindly, and ate freely. But somehow or other, so far from thriving or growing fat upon this fare, they dwindled away, so that many of them gave up the ghost, and those that were turned to pasture in the spring looked like skeletons. The old Quaker came to inspect them one day. 'Thy cattle are rather lean, friend John,' said he, 'but there is one comfort, they will not sink into the marshes and perish, like thy fat Teeswater bull.'

" 'Thus ended my first season of farming. It had not realized my expectations to be sure, but I had now grown somewhat wiser by experience, and was resolved this year to do something handsome for the honour of Old England. About this time my brother, a capital Norfolk farmer, wrote me word Sir Humphrey Davy had just announced to the world an analysis of carrots, by which it appeared that they contain a greater quantity of saccharine matter than any other common vegetable, and consequently more nourishment. Seizing this hint, I turned my attention immediately to the cultivation of carrots, being resolved to reap the benefit at once, before anybody should enter into competition. I selected a field of sixteen acres, which I employed six labourers to prepare and cultivate under my direction. 'John,' said the old Quaker, 'what art thou about this season? Art thou in love with thy Latin turnips still?'

" ' Pshaw!' replied I, ' carrots have twice as much saccharine matter. I am going to cultivate carrots.'

" ' Friend John, thou wilt never prosper till thou

callest things by their honest Christian names. But what dost thou expect to do with thy sixteen acres of saccharine matter?'

" ' I shall feed my cattle with part, and send the rest to market.'

" ' Ah! John, John,' exclaimed the old Quaker, ' remember thy turnips with the hard name.'

" My crop of carrots was amazing. I had such a quantity I did not know what to do with them, for my neighbours had enough of their own, and they were not worth taking to market. My cattle, to be sure, having little else, sometimes tried to eat them, but they some how or other didn't thrive, and besides this, I and my family could not live upon carrots. This winter, therefore, I was again obliged to buy almost every thing I wanted, and the remainder of my guineas vanished. Not only this, but I was compelled to take up money from the old Quaker to a considerable amount, to buy stock to replace several of my horses, cows, and sheep, that died during the winter; for, some how or other, the saccharine matter of the carrots did not seem to agree with them. Every time I went to the Quaker to borrow money, he would say, after letting me have it, ' Friend John, thee had better plant corn and sow wheat and rye, as we do, though they don't contain quite so much of the saccharine matter.' My reply usually was, ' Friend Underhill, thy money is better than thy advice. I didn't come all the way from Old England to learn farming of you Yankees.'

" But, although I put in practice regularly the most approved methods recommended by Arthur Young and other great English farmers, and adopted every improvement I saw published by the English agricultural societies, I as regularly went behindhand every year, and was obliged to borrow money, every now and then, of the old Quaker, who never failed to repeat his advice, which I always treated in the same manner. Whoever heard of a thorough-bred English farmer demeaning himself by imitating these ignorant Yankees?

"I had forgot to mention, among other instances of the obstinacy with which these republicans adhere to their barbarous notions, that they resisted all my persuasions to adopt the wholesome English custom of wearing woollen garments during the summer. They stuck to their straw hats and linen shirts and trowsers, and laughed at my corduroy breeches and worsted stockings, though I proved to them they were much the more healthy and comfortable. To be sure, I used to perspire a little in the dog-days — but what of that? I was resolved not to sacrifice the honour of Old England to the ignorance of these raw republicans. The old Quaker came to me one day, when the thermometer was at ninety, and said in his sly way, 'Friend John, if thee is cold, I will lend thee my great coat, for verily it is a bitter day, for the season.' I took no notice of what he said, for, though I really did feel a little uncomfortable, it would have been too great a triumph for these people, to see me adopting any of their notions.

"At the end of three years I went one day to the old Quaker, to take up some more money. 'Friend John,' said he, 'hast thou ever read in Sir Humphrey Davy, or any of thine oracles, that borrowing-day is always sooner or later followed by pay-day? Thou hast been borrowing for the last three years, without paying either principal or interest. I cannot advance thee any more, for thy farm will scarcely sell for what will pay the debt thou already owest me.' This was a thing that had not struck me before, as I had never read of it either in Arthur Young or any other approved agriculturist. As it was known all over the neighbourhood that my farm was mortgaged for its full value to the Quaker, my credit was now gone; and, in order to raise money for the supply of my increasing wants, I began to cut down the trees, and sell the timber to the wheelwrights and others.

" Hearing of this, the old Quaker came to me, and said, ' Friend John, if thou goest on in this way, thy farm will, by and by, be without wood, and will not sell for wherewithal to pay my mortgages. For thy sake, as well as mine, I shall foreclose.' He did so. My farm was sold at public sale by the sheriff, and bought in by the old Quaker to save himself from loss. When I was on the point of quitting the neighbourhood, he came to me and said, ' Friend John, thou art going away among strangers, without money. Here is fifty dollars to begin the world again, which thou wilt pay me when thou art able, and I will give thee a little advice that will, if thou takest it, be worth ten times as much. It is, to remember whenever thou comest into a strange country, there is always something to learn, as well as to teach. The same shoe will not fit every body's foot, neither will the same mode of farming suit every country. The best farmer is not he that raises the greatest crops, but he that raises them at the least expense. In thy country, land is dear and labour cheap — in ours, labour is dear and land cheap. This must needs make a difference in the quantity of labour which it is profitable to put on thy land, so that the product will pay for thy labour. Moreover, thy big bull with the little short legs, and thy big fat sheep and cows that can scarcely waddle along, will do for the smooth lawns, close-shaven hills, and cool skies of thy country, but they will not stand our hot summers, our swampy low-grounds and our rough rocky mountains. Moreover, I do most especially recommend thee to eschew turnips with Latin names; to plant corn and potatoes; sow wheat and rye, like thy neighbours; and, above all, abjure Sir Humphrey Davy and his saccharine matter. Farewell, friend John; I wish thee better success another time.' "

I have given this story as nearly as possible, for the purpose of exhibiting at full length a warning example to our English farmers at home, who may be about to emigrate to this country. In order to succeed, they must, in the first place, accommodate themselves to situation and circumstances, which is contrary to the independent nature and feelings of a true-born English-man. Instead of the soil, climate, products, and seasons, accommodating themselves to their mode of farming, as they ought to do considering its immense superiority, our farmers, forsooth, must pay homage to the genius of democracy, and degrade themselves by stooping to learn where they came to teach. They must consent to grow articles that will pay for carry-ing to market, although they don't contain half the quantity of saccharine matter which others do — they must plant corn and wheat, instead of carrots and ruta-baga — they must unlearn their own knowledge, and adopt the ignorance of others — they must even consult the wayward appetites of their imported cattle and pigs, who seem actually to become sophisticated, by breathing the air of democracy, and occasionally smelling to the Yankee cattle over a stone wall.

After spending the whole morning together, strolling along the shady river, we returned to dinner. The day was so excessively hot that I almost caught myself envying the Yankees their short gingham coats, straw hats, and linen pantaloons. My poor friend in the woollen stockings panted like a tired mastiff, and perspired like an ox; but still there was something very respectable in his blue broad-cloth frock, striped swans-down waistcoat, corduroy breeches, and gray worsted hose. I forgot to mention that this deluded, though worthy, man had come to Washington for the purpose of petitioning the congress to establish a farm at the public expense, and under his special direction, with the view of giving a practical illustration of the benefits of a system of farming adapted to an old country, when applied to a new one. But his proposal was treated with the most stupid indifference by the arrogant, self-sufficient, bundling, gouging, guessing, drinking, dirking, spitting, chewing, pig-stealing, impious genius of democracy, as the Quarterly says. * * * * * * * *

POSTSCRIPT

THE THIRD EDITION.

———

IT is with singular satisfaction the publisher of this work announces to the public that, notwithstanding the very suspicious circumstances under which the writer disappeared from Washington, as related in the preface, it hath been ascertained to a moral certainty that he not only escaped with life but is still living. It is supposed that he took the opportunity of his room-mate's being asleep to make good his escape; so that we rejoice to have it in our power to vindicate the little Frenchman, (who, we confess, is a great favourite of ours), from the atrocious suspicions which, to our shame be it spoken, we assisted so materially in giving currency to.

What became of the amateur of the Quarterly after his miraculous disappearance is not certainly known; but, from what we shall relate, it will appear that he continued his researches into the nature and depravity of a republican government, finished the tour of the United States, and returned safely to England, where he published an account of his travels, so perfectly similar in style, character, and sentiment, to the present production, as to prove his identity with our author beyond all contradiction. Anybody who reads the late work called " Men and Manners in the United States ", and compares it with this, will require no further proof.

But, if any further proof should be wanted, the following fact will silence the most resolute doubter. It so happened, that, when this distinguished navigator visited the city of Washington on his second tour to this country, (which it is presumed he undertook for the purpose of supplying the loss of his invaluable manuscript, as related in our preface), he put up at the Mansion Hotel, the very house from whence he so strangely disappeared. The same waiter still retained his post in the hotel, and immediately recognized the companion of the inscrutable little Frenchman, who, it was afterwards ascertained, had departed in an early stage for the South, without exciting any notice, so that the incident was forgotten at the time.

The distinguished navigator was at first inclined to deny his identity, and demurred to the payment of the small score he had run up previous to his abrupt secession some years before. But the proofs were so strong, that, though he had disguised himself in a clean dicky to pay a visit to the President, he was finally compelled to plead guilty and settle his bill.

Thus is this mysterious affair at length cleared up, to the satisfaction of the world, and the exonerating of the little Frenchman from all suspicion of murder or abduction. It was a singular coincidence, which many people thought rather remarkable, that, on the very day the distinguished navigator arrived at Washington from the North, on his second visit, the little Frenchman came in from the South, with the same mahogany face, and the same ear-rings; but we regret to say he had changed his dimity breeches for a pair of cloth ones, the weather being rather cool. The little man recognized his old travelling companion with evident gratification, and at once put an end to all doubts as to his being the same person.

The behaviour of the distinguished navigator, on occasion of this rencounter with the little Frenchman, was rather ludicrous, as we have heard. He received his cordial shake of the hand with trembling dignity, and tried to look big, as the vulgar say; but it would not do. The deportment of the little man was so irresistibly frank and good-humoured that he could have no pretext for rudeness, and suffered him to shake his hand, while he cried out, " What!, hasn't monsieur got to New Orleans yet?" But the distinguished navigator, it seems, had not got over his fears of robbery and murder, and made a precipitate retreat from Washington within an hour after this meeting, although he was engaged to dine with all the heads of department in succession, and invited to thirteen evening entertainments. He crossed the bridge over the Potomac towards the South; but immediately returned by the Georgetown ferry, and shaped his course North as fast as he could drive. It is supposed this manœuvre was to deceive the little Frenchman.

It gives us great pleasure to state that the author of " Men and Manners " arrived safely in New York, and on being offered by the publisher his due share of the profits of this work generously refused to receive a farthing. It only remains for us to retract the assertion in our prefatory notice in regard to the gentleman known as THE TALKING POTATO, which we do, at the same time expressing our regret at the misconception. The present work undoubtedly belongs to the author of " Men and Manners ", and we are sorry that he should have been so long deprived of his honours by any mistake of ours.

New York, 1834.

THE END.

Cambridge: Press of John Wilson & Son.